The Angel's Shadow
a novel of 'The Phantom of the Opera'

Louise Anne Bateman

Copyright © 2014 Louise Anne Bateman

All rights reserved.

ISBN: 1500574600
ISBN-13: 978-1500574604

DEDICATION

*To my family
who love me for myself.*

ACKNOWLEDGMENTS

This novel, a variation of '*The Phantom of the Opera*' owes its inspiration to the original novel by Gaston Leroux, and the musical adaptations *The Phantom of the* Opera and *Love Never* Dies, by Andrew Lloyd Webber and the creative teams that have kept it alive since 1986.

I would also like to thank the 'Phans' who gave *The Angel's Shadow* their enthusiasm and encouragement from its earliest beginnings.

CHAPTER ONE

It is easier than you might think to get out of an opera house. After a performance the audience leaves, the set is struck, the auditorium cleaned, the stage swept, and then everyone goes home. I had slipped out of the dormitories as quietly as I could, out of the window and over the flat roof of the stables to where the ivy was thick enough to climb down. It had seemed like such an adventure; the risk, the anticipation, choosing the night when my mother was away from the Opera Populairé and sneaking unaccompanied into the streets of Paris.

And now, in the dark, the romance had fled from the situation. The arm around my waist was strong and supportive, but I had lost my sense of direction and the city had become a labyrinth in which beasts roamed. There were eyes on me in the darkness.

Jacques' hand lifted the bottle to my lips again.

"Drink, little Meg, or you'll freeze."

The liquid burned in my throat as I swallowed.

"Where are we going?"

"Don't be afraid, child." Jacques' voice was quiet, gentle. "It'll be all right. You said you were going to be a prima donna, one day. I'm just taking you to somewhere you can perform for me."

My head was swimming, my footsteps erratic, and only Jacques' arm around me prevented me from sinking down onto the cobbles. He had been so attentive to me in the public house, talked to me as if I were already the shining star of my future, rather than a single chorus girl among dozens. He had brought me food, drink, and then offered to walk me home. Now, I had no idea which way the Opera House was; the meagre light seemed to be moving like floating insects in front of my eyes. Good Lord, my head...

"That's it, Meg..." Jacques whispered, his breath hot against my cheek. How long had we been walking? When had we stopped? When had my back been pressed against a stone wall? I could feel its roughness through my cloak. Jacques pressed his lips against my cheek, a soft kiss, on the corner of my mouth, and then his mouth was on mine, hard and insistent. His body was against mine, his fingers working at the clasp of my cloak.

"What are you doing?" I gasped.

"Shh…" He kissed me again, and yet, could it be called a kiss? It was a forceful, demanding pressure, his body pinning me to the wall, and something hard was pressing against my abdomen. God, did he have a weapon? No… no, it wasn't a weapon… my fuzzy brain was darting to the conversations I had overheard the older dances having in the dormitories, of their encounters with men. God, he wasn't going to…

I heard the material of my bodice ripping as he grasped it between his hands and tore it open. His fingers were against my chest, nails digging in; in my rush to dress myself without disturbing my roommate I had not bothered trying to lace myself into my corset. His teeth bit me just above the top lip. I could hear myself whimpering, protesting, I tried to move, but Jacques was pushing me downwards onto the cobbles and all my strength was gone.

"Don't…" I managed "Please, don't…" but he paid no heed. One hand went over my mouth, the other lifting my skirts over my knees. *"Please!"*

There was a movement in the shadows behind my assailant as he pressed himself against me with a moan of pleasure, a darker patch against the darkness. His hands ripped away my underwear. Another second, and I knew I would lose my purity, all because of my own stupidity. Jacques' head snapped back and then around to the side and I heard a dreadful crack. There were black gloves against his skull before his weight left me and he fell to the side. I was half lying on the cobblestones, my back against the wall, my skirts pushed around my waist and one breast exposed by my ruined bodice. The man before me was crouched over Jacques' body like a spider. He was entirely in black, one half of his face in shadow, but the other, his right side, glowing as white as bone. He slowly lifted his head and looked around at me, and I felt unable to move.

You're him…

I would have spoken the words aloud, but all that came past my lips were gasping sobs. It was his voice that flowed through the darkness.

"Mademoiselle Giry." He sounded… so calm, that he might have been greeting me at a garden party. Goosebumps were pricking my skin, from the cold, the terror, and that *voice*…

There was a swishing sound as he swept the black cloak off his shoulders, a gloved hand lifted my back from the wall and the fabric was around my own shoulders, his fingers arranging it to conceal my nudity. In my mind, he seemed to move like a dancer; I could hear the music in my head, his actions matching it. His arms were around me, one snaking around my back, the other under my knees, and he was lifting me. My own arms went around his neck and I clutched him like a father. He smelled of

THE ANGEL'S SHADOW

sweat and candle wax and *safety*... and I pressed my face into his jacket and sobbed.

"Shh..." He whispered into my hair. "You're safe now... but you must be silent, Meg... hush..."

I tried to obey him, but I don't know how much noise I was making. All I remember of that journey was shivering in his arms, hearing his heartbeat in his chest, feeling the wind through my hair, but the cloak protecting me from its fierceness.

"Mademoiselle Giry?" A hand tapped my cheek. Another tap, harder. "Meg."

I opened my eyes. He was leaning over me, one hand still against my cheek, his gaze on mine. I blinked up at him; were his eyes different colours? He was lit by candlelight, soft against his skin, his jaw lightly stubbled.

"I know you," I said, feeling my words slightly slurred as they passed my teeth.

His lips twitched. A smile? It was difficult to tell, with one side of his mouth covered by the white mask.

"And I know you, Mademoiselle Giry."

"Meg," I corrected.

"Meg." His eyes were searching my face, and I wondered what he was looking for. "What did you think you were doing tonight?"

"I..." I shook my head. Excuses, reasons, lies filled my head, but I simply couldn't speak, and I felt myself flood red with shame.

"Hmm." He stood up. "Stay here."

He walked away from me, and I found myself gazing around. The walls were made of stone, rough and yet seemingly carved into deliberate shapes and separate rooms. Nature had not created this...

I sat slowly, the black cloak still wrapped tight around my body. I was lying in a bed shaped like a bird, and I realised after a moment that I recognised it. It was a set piece from the opera *Del Marinaio Canzone*, with a blanket that seemed to have been sewn together from various fabrics in every shade of red. As my eyes travelled around, I saw opera in every place. There were props and costumes everywhere, make-up, wigs and masks... I could hear water somewhere close by. Against one wall there was a curtain, as if a window was there, and against another, an organ, its pipes reaching up to the uneven ceiling. By the side of the bed was a toy monkey holding a pair of cymbals, but I didn't recognise it.

My rescuer returned, carrying a tray with a bowl, a cloth and a small bottle, with something long and white draped over his arm. He had removed his jacket and wore a black waistcoat underneath, black trousers,

5

black boots, and a white shirt. The white somehow looked dull in comparison with the mask, which still appeared to glow as the candlelight flickered. He sat down, the draped garment revealed to be a dressing gown as he set it on the bed.

"Take off the cloak." He commanded and I flinched away from him. His eyes caught mine. "If I had wanted you, little dancer, I would have taken you already. A man who has the strength to snap a neck would have no trouble subduing a child like you, as I think you already know." His words stung, bringing tears to my eyes, and I wondered if he was being deliberately cruel. "Take off the cloak."

I did as he said, fear rippling through me as my ruined dress left my skin on display. He open the bottle, tipped it over the cloth and reached out to me, and I moved one hand across my body to the opposite shoulder in an attempt to shield my modesty.

"Meg Giry." His tone was impatient and I lowered my hand into my lap. He dabbed at a scratch on my chest, just above my left breast, where Jacques' nails had caught me as he ripped my bodice. I could feel the embarrassment heating my face.

"How do you know who I am?" I asked, in an attempt to diffuse my own tension.

"This is my Opera House, girl, and I know everyone in it." He replied, matter-of-factly. "I know who everyone is and what everyone is doing. Even in the dead of night when they are climbing out of windows." His eyes flickered to my face. "I hope that is shame I see, girl."

"It is." I whispered, and winced again. "How do you know what you're doing?"

"I read books."

I nodded and his gaze focused on my lip and the tooth mark just above it.

"I have heard you singing in the darkness." I don't know what made me say it, but it just tumbled out. "I've heard your voice. I've heard what you say to her. She calls you her angel. An Angel of Music."

"Christine." The way he said her name was a sigh, almost a song on two notes. He took my chin in his hand and began to tend to the cut above my lip with a clean corner of the cloth. "And what do you call me, Meg?"

"My mother says you are the Opera Ghost."

"A name as good as any other. Ghosts and phantoms can move wherever they like, girl. I am watching everyone and if I see you behaving so foolishly again then you will have more to face than just the possibility of rape in the streets of Paris. Your Opera Ghost may not be there to save you next time."

I shivered, and the shame flooded me again. He rose to his feet and picked up the tray.

THE ANGEL'S SHADOW

"For now, you will heal. Put on the dressing gown, and then I will return you to your dormitory."

He left me again as I pulled the dressing gown on over my clothes, feeling calmer as I covered myself. Until I saw the strip of fabric that had been underneath it. It was a piece of thick cloth, long but slim, and my heart thumped as I picked it up.

"Put that on too." He had returned on silent footsteps, wearing the jacket once more. I swallowed hard.

"What is it?"

"It is a blindfold, Meg, you can see that perfectly well."

"And why am I to wear it?" My voice sounded strangled. He stepped closer to me, his voice low.

"Because I do not want visitors, Meg. This is my home and it would be inconvenient for me if you were to find your way back here uninvited, or if you were to tell anyone else where to find me."

"I won't tell anyone." I gasped. "I swear it."

"I know." He took my chin in his hand again and looked directly into my eyes. "I saved your virtue tonight, and possibly your life. The least you can do in return is obey me and let me keep my privacy. I am not blindfolding you in order to cause you harm. I am not going to molest you or hurt you in any way. You must trust me." He took the blindfold from my numbed fingers. "Trust me." He moved around me, placed it over my eyes, the world turning dark, my breath catching in my throat as he tightened the knot behind my head. "Trust me." Both hands were on my shoulders. "Now walk forward. Stop. There are five steps ahead of you. Take them carefully."

And this way he guided me through the darkness, over stone, over water in a boat that creaked, up stairs, around corners, and all the while he spoke to me, his voice smooth as silk and soft as a whisper, his hands a constant presence on my shoulders, until at last we stopped.

"You have returned." He whispered, his breath cool against my ear. "Goodnight, Meg Giry."

With a tug, the blindfold was gone. I saw a flicker of white as my eyes adjusted to the gloom of the corridor outside my dormitory, and nothing more. I was alone.

"Goodnight, Opera Ghost," I whispered to the darkness. "Goodnight, Angel."

CHAPTER TWO

It was two days before my sins found me out. Christine had seen the cut above my lip when we had risen the morning following my escapade into Paris, but I had managed to convince her that I had inflicted the injury myself by tripping on the stairs and cutting myself on the banister as I fell. None of the other girls noticed the scab, or if they did, didn't comment upon it. A teenager's skin is often blemished, and the exhausting daily routine of a dancer takes its own toll on a young woman's beauty.

I put Jacques out of my mind as much as I could, allowing the rehearsals for the next opera to blot out everything else. Music has a power that cannot be equalled by anything else, an energy to it that burns in the soul, and that words alone cannot express. I gave myself to it as I danced in rehearsals, hummed the tunes to myself during the brief rest hours, listened to the orchestra's various instruments separate and together. There is a magic in music that is surpassed by little else.

Only Christine knew that something was wrong. When we were alone and a tune was on my lips, she harmonised with me, and even though the pureness of her voice made me feel inferior, I would never tell her. It was in the darkness of my dreams that music was blotted out by terror. Over and over again I found myself in the dark streets of Paris, pinned down by a man with more strength and cunning than myself. Sometimes the Ghost bore down on Jacques and snapped his neck, and I felt gratitude for a few seconds before his hands reached for my throat as well. Once, I ripped off the white mask that concealed the right side of his face, only to find that it was Jacques underneath, and the nightmare began all over again.

I was in the Ghost's lair, on his bed, and he was ripping at my clothing, his hand over my mouth as his hardness pressed against me in an attempt to deflower me, and I shrieked at the mask above me.

"Meg!" A hand was shaking me "Meg, wake up!"

Christine was leaning over me, her eyes concerned, her hand on my shoulder.

THE ANGEL'S SHADOW

"You were screaming," she said softly.

"Oh, Christine!" I flung myself at her and buried my face in the dark curls that spilled over her shoulder, letting terror flood from me through my tears. Christine rocked me in her arms, rubbing my back, whispering "Shh…" over and over.

Christine Daaé and I had been inseparable since we had first met when we were six years old. She had been brought to the Opera House as an orphan, her speech layered with a Swedish accent that had faded during the ten years of our friendship. There were three months between us, age-wise, and although Christine was dark and I was fair, many newcomers to the Opera House had assumed we were sisters, Christine the older with the additional inch or so in height she had over me. We had *become* sisters to each other for all intents and purposes.

"Tell me what's wrong," she said now as my sobs turned into hiccups.

"It was just a nightmare." I pulled back from her and wiped my eyes with the back of my hand.

"It was more than that," Christine insisted. "You've not been yourself all day."

I looked at her and *wanted* to tell her the truth about the previous night, about how frightened I'd been, about how I'd witnessed a man being killed. About how the Opera Ghost had saved me… and then I saw that she was dressed. She had been rehearsing in secret, singing with her Angel of Music in the dark. I had a secret from her and she had a secret from me. I couldn't tell her that my Opera Ghost and her Angel of Music were one and the same.

"A nightmare," I repeated.

"You must have been working too hard." She said softly as I lay down again. "Try and get some more sleep."

She stroked my hair as I closed my eyes, and began singing under her breath. I couldn't understand the lyrics as they swept over me in her mother tongue, but I knew they were a comfort.

"*Sömn, kära en, sömn. Det kommer att bli bättre komma soluppgång.*"

She had sung it to me before in times of distress, and told me it was a lullaby her father had sung to her when she was small. I let the intent behind the foreign words lull me, as if she were my angel, guarding me against more nightmares, and slept.

"Meg Giry!" The shout made all the girls in the ballet room jump. I looked up from the barre to see my mother standing in the doorway, dressed in her customary black. She had returned to the Opera House late last night and I had not yet seen her; and she looked furious.

"Madame Giry?" I queried. It was our custom that I would address her such when we were rehearsing, as at such times we were mistress and pupil, rather than the mother and daughter we were in private.

"My office, now!"

Christine gave my hand a gentle squeeze and then let go. I walked across the room towards Mother, aware of all the eyes following me with curiosity. Even the girls who had their backs to me were watching in the mirror as I passed. Mother stepped to one side to let me out through the door, then looked back at the room of dancers.

"Giselle, you are in charge for this lesson. Take the girls through the steps of *Ophelia* that we did last week, and I expect to see some improvement when I return."

We walked through the Opera House to the small office that Mother used in the role of concierge, where she worked on papers and helped with the wages of the staff. She opened the door and gestured.

"Inside."

I entered, and heard her close the door quietly behind me. A shiver ran up my spine; the softness proved how angry she was.

"What is it, Mother?" I asked timidly, not daring to turn around.

"What happened the night before last, Meg?"

"I don't know what you—"

"Don't lie to me!" She shouted, slamming one hand down onto the desk. There was a newspaper open under her palm, and I saw the headline: Man Found Dead. The article told that a local merchant, Jacques Lassiter, had been found in a backstreet alleyway with a broken neck, apparently the victim of a mugger, since his money and other personal possessions were missing.

Surely he hadn't stopped to rifle the pockets of a corpse?

My mind reeled back over that night, trying to remember how long it had been before the Ghost had left his grisly spider-stance and wrapped his cloak around me. I didn't know.

"I... I crept out into the city." I managed after a moment of staring at the newspaper. "I went into a public house and met this man and then..."

She stepped in front of me, her eyes on mine, and then the back of her hand struck me so hard across the face that I went stumbling backwards.

"I have told you and told you never to go into Paris after dark by yourself!" She shouted. "And the moment I leave the Opera House you go straight off and disobey me, and look what happens!"

"I'm sorry," I stammered, hand to my stinging cheek as the tears began to fall. "I'm so sorry... please..."

"Don't you dare plead with me, Meg!" She marched around me and shoved me towards the desk "Stupid child!"

I didn't have to be told what to do, I simply closed my eyes and pressed my palms against the desk. Madame Giry was hardly ever seen without a

THE ANGEL'S SHADOW

cane, which she used to tap out the beats of the music against the floor. Now it was to be used for another beating, and it was one like I had never endured before. Her second blow brought me to my knees, and it was followed by more across my back. I had been holding onto the newspaper as I fell and it was still clutched in my hands as I cowered on the floor, trying to take my punishment with as much dignity as I could, the words of the news report floating before my eyes.

It can't have lasted long; a dancer's body is her greatest asset and my mother knew that beyond anyone. I knew she would never do anything that would permanently prevent me from pursuing my career, and yet she was so angry that I wondered if she might forget, and inflict more damage than she meant to.

When it was over at last, she knelt with me and took me into her arms, a sobbing mess as I was, and she was crying too.

"You could have been so badly hurt, Meg." She cried as she rocked me. "You could have been *killed!* You might have been if it hadn't been for *him.* My God, Meg, I love you so much, I couldn't bare it if anything happened to you. The thought of what almost happened…"

"I'm so sorry," I whimpered, and my tears were not for myself and the bruises that were already starting to colour my skin, but for her, and how frightened she must have been when she found out what had happened to me.

She kissed my forehead and wiped my eyes. "All is forgiven now. Go to your room, Meg. Go and rest. And say a prayer thanking God that *he* was there to protect you."

"But the rehearsals," I protested weakly.

"Shh. You are well-versed in the upcoming performance, Meg. A few days' leave will do you no harm. Now go."

I went, moving slowly as my aching body tested itself with every step. My back throbbed and I wondered if I was bleeding. Cumbered by my slow and ginger pace, it seemed as if there were people everywhere. A stagehand who must have overheard what was happening leered at me.

"Has little Giry been a naughty girl?" He asked, sticking his tongue out in a grotesque way.

"Shut your mouth, Buquet!" I snapped "Go hang yourself on a backdrop rope!"

He laughed and as I passed I saw with disgust the arousal in his trousers. I had seen more than enough lust for one week. Desperate to be alone, I decided to take the longer but probably quieter route of going through the auditorium, knowing it would be empty at this time of day. A few of the lamps were lit, but the stage was in darkness and I had to feel my way carefully along the rows of seats. The material of my rehearsal dress brushed against the velvet, and I thought of the fabrics these chairs were more accustomed to; silks and laces and satins. I had heard someone tell me once that a seat in one of the Boxes cost more per performance than some of the staff got paid.

There was someone in one of the Boxes. I froze, turning my gaze upwards to follow the flash of white in the darkness. It was like a shadow, silent and almost not there at all, and yet I felt so sure...

"I see you!" I shouted into the darkness.

"Perhaps you see too much, Mademoiselle Giry." *His* voice came from out of the darkness, but it was to my left, not where I thought I had seen the white of a half-mask.

"Are you following me?" I demanded. The beating was taking its toll on me and I could feel myself trembling. "Are you following me *again?*"

"Again, little dancer?" The voice was in front of me now, deep and musical. "Weren't you glad of my intervention last time?"

"How are you *doing that?*! Where *are you?!*" I spun and the movement sent pain rippling through my body. I bent forward against the row of chairs in front, gasping, squeezing my eyes tight shut to stop more tears escaping. His voice came again, close, off to my right now.

"Ghosts are *felt*, girl, rarely seen. Phantoms can move where they will."

"You told her!" I accused through gritted teeth.

"I told her." He confirmed. "Any responsible person would tell a parent that her child had been in such danger."

"Only if it concerned that person, and you are not my father!" My eyes sprung open. "Are you?"

His laugh was genuine and sounded so human in the darkness that for a moment my Opera Ghost melted into a man.

"No, Mademoiselle, I am not your father. But yes, I told your mother what happened to you."

"And she beat me!"

"She punished you, and it was no more than you deserved. Your attitude this moment suggests that a further beating would not go amiss." I felt myself shiver at the threat in his tone. "Some lessons are hard-learned, Meg, and I trust that this punishment will mark your soul for far longer than it marks your back."

"Were you watching us?"

Silence. Had he been? And if so, from where? My eyes scanned the dark auditorium, the small scratching noise of my nails against the velvet sounding loud in my ears.

"Are you still there?"

I felt the air moving at my back and was suddenly too afraid to turn.

"Go and rest, Mademoiselle Giry." His breath was soft against my neck and goose bumps rose there. I could almost feel his lips close to my skin. "Rest, my disobedient child."

THE ANGEL'S SHADOW

I walked along the row of seats to the other side of the auditorium, my own footfalls the only sound in the silence, the heated pain of my body the only feeling I could sense. It wasn't until I opened the exit door that I looked round. The auditorium was silent. Empty.

CHAPTER THREE

Healing properly took a little over a week, and thanks to a herbal concoction Mother bathed my sore back with, her cane left no scars. Towards the end of my third day of rest, Christine brought a fish pie to our room for me, trailed by the inquisitive nose, whiskers and tail of the Opera House's cat, Figaro. Christine was deeply disturbed by what had happened, and although I tried to explain that my punishment was warranted and wiped the slate clean between Mother and I, she just stared at me with worried eyes.

"But what can you possibly have done to deserve such a beating?"

Christine was so gentle and innocent that no one had ever laid a hand on her, and she seemed to lack the impulse that made me want to push the rules as far as they could bend. As long as music was part of her daily life, she seemed happy. I told her as much of the truth as I could, leaving out the intervention of the Opera Ghost, making it seem like I had managed to fight off a suitor's unwanted advances. Figaro jumped up onto my bed and I had to catch him quickly around the middle before he buried his face in my pie.

"And so she punished me, for putting myself in danger and for disobeying her when she specifically told me not to go into Paris alone."

Christine sighed and reached out to pet the ginger tabby cat that still had his eyes fixed on my plate.

"I still don't like it."

I smiled. "You just don't like seeing people hurting. You're like a princess in one of your Swedish folk tales. I'm like the wicked witch."

She laughed at last. "You could never be a wicked witch."

"Ugly stepsister?" I picked out a bit of fish from the pie with my fork and lifted it up with my fingertips to offer to Figaro.

"Oh, Meg, don't be so ridiculous." Her eyes showed worry again. "But… the nightmares…"

"Are past," I insisted. "I haven't woken you by having a nightmare, have

I?"

"No," she admitted.

Of course, it wasn't true; I *had* woken almost every night because of the dreams that tore through my sleep, plagued by masked men. Christine hadn't known because she wasn't in the room. Every time I woke, I saw that her bed was empty, and knew she was having singing lessons with her Angel of Music.

The man had rescued me, and told Mother of the incident out of a sense of duty. He seemed to have no thoughts about me apart from my welfare, and yet... he frightened me. As I healed and returned to my daily routine, I suddenly felt that everywhere I went there were eyes upon me, that my every word was overheard, and that I could not find solitude anywhere but my own dormitory.

Figaro, apparently having got it into his head that I was the source of fish, since Christine and I shared the pie with him, followed me around the Opera House wherever he was permitted to go. He had arrived four months earlier, a scrawny stray, and been fed by the cook and some of us dancers. He had returned day after day, mewing pathetically until someone gave him food. We had named him Figaro after the main character of the opera we were rehearsing, and someone somewhere suggested that a cat in our midst was a lucky omen. When the opera was a sell-out success, the newspapers accredited it to La Carlotta the leading soprano, and the ballerinas to Figaro. He was our lucky charm and quickly established himself as a permanent member of the Opera House by sleeping in the stables, or even the dormitories of those who would allow it. He paraded the grounds with the air of an animal that believed it was the king of all it surveyed. Although the manager, Monsieur Lefevre, didn't like the idea of a communal pet, Figaro proved himself to be an excellent catcher of rats and mice. The fact that he would carry bits of them around or leave them outside your door as a sort of gesture of affection was a little squeamish, but since there is little that is less attractive than an entire ballet class screaming at the sight of one mouse, Figaro was considered a hero and excused his peculiar endearments.

I was chasing him out of the manager's office when I found the note. It was on the desk, white paper with black edging. It was tilted forward against something, and I realised it had a seal of red wax keeping the corners together and creating its own envelope. Lefevre's name was on the outside in black ink and neat handwriting. I picked it up and flipped it over to see the seal was stamped with a skull.

"Meg Giry, isn't it?"

I jumped, dropping the note back as Lefevre entered his office with a pile of paperwork in his hands.

"I'm sorry, Monsieur. Figaro was making a nuisance of himself again."

He frowned. "If that animal has scratched my desk then I will use his tail as a feather duster."

"Don't worry, Monsieur, I got him out of here before he could do any harm. I'll leave you to your work. Sorry to have disturbed you."

I turned, looking for the flash of ginger tabby fur and sulky green eyes that showed Figaro was lurking in an alcove.

"Giry?"

I looked back to see Lafevre frowning at the black-edged note in his hand.

"Monsieur?"

"Did you deliver this?"

"No... is something wrong?"

"It's... it's preposterous!" He spluttered. "Twenty thousand francs? Who does this madman think he is?!" He looked up at me, face the colour of claret, and made a visible effort to calm himself. "Please can you get the concierge—that is, your mother, and tell her I need to speak to her at once. And Monsieur Reyer... twenty thousand francs..."

I left him muttering over the note and fetched Mother.

"I will tell Monsieur Reyer that he is needed," she said firmly. "You stay out of the way. You will know soon enough all you need to know."

I thought about disobeying, but decided against it. Instead, I passed my day in a fever of impatience. Lafevre was well-liked among the company, a pleasant and calm man who respected everyone from the cleaning maids to the mighty diva La Carlotta herself. It took a lot to work him up the way I had seen him that morning, and I was keen to know what those few lines contained that had so alarmed and angered him.

I have many faults, but gossip-mongering is not one of them, so I was surprised to hear news of the note spreading through the company. The writer, signing himself as the Opera Ghost, had claimed to be the driving force of the House's success, and was demanding twenty thousand francs. He threatened unspecified disaster if the money was not paid.

"Of course, everyone knows about the Ghost," Lycette said as she tied her ballet shoes.

"Do they?" I was surprised; Mother and Papa had told me tales of the Ghost since I was a child, but I'd always thought of him as *our* Ghost, a fairytale. Suddenly, he was a tangible figure, properly haunting the Opera House, and being noticed.

"Of course they do," Lycette replied. "My grandmother has a spirit board we could use to talk to him."

"Do ghosts often write letters?" Christine rose elegantly from her stretch and lifted both arms above her head.

"All the time," Lycette assured us. "He's been around for years, one moment in the wings, and the next moment in the auditorium."

THE ANGEL'S SHADOW

I felt a shiver as I remembered my own encounter with him in the auditorium. I had seen him in the Boxes, but heard his voice coming from another direction entirely. Then I knew he had been behind me, so close that I could have touched him if I had dared. The Opera House had been my playground since I could toddle, I knew that there was no way down from the Boxes into the stalls without being seen. Yet, there was a whole world here that I knew nothing about. There was somewhere the two worlds met, but *where?*

Lycette was still twittering on about spirits, but my mind was focusing more on the natural rather than the supernatural.

"You were dreaming!" Mother scolded as I set the table in her rooms for the two of us to eat our evening meal. "If you want to become a prima ballerina, Meg, then you must focus all your attention on the dancing."

I was apt at drowning out this particular speech. Mother had been in her prime when a carriage accident had forced her to give up her career and turn to teaching instead, and I had no doubts that she wished to relive her glory days through me. This evening, the regular chiding prickled me.

"It's difficult to concentrate on dancing when the whole class is gossiping about the Opera Ghost. Which I never said a word about," I added, before she could accuse me.

"Yes..." She brought the dish of food to the table and began to divide it between our two plates.

"Three weeks ago I thought the Opera Ghost was a story," I said, sitting down. "And now... I've met him and he's real and a man... Mother, please tell me who he is."

She sat down opposite me, beginning to eat.

"He saved me," I pressed. "And he says he knows me. He certainly knows you. Have you and he... is he my father?"

She looked up, shocked. "Meg!"

"Well?" I challenged.

"Marguerite Giry, your father was Claude Giry, as you know full well, and no better man ever walked the Earth. And no, the Ghost and I have never..."

"He was exactly as you described him to me in the stories," I said, watching her closely. "The mask, the way he moved, everything. He'd been watching me. He must have been following me the whole night and I didn't have a clue." I shivered, unable to help it. "He dropped down into... into that alleyway as if he'd just fallen out of the sky. And where he lives... it is *in* the Opera House, isn't it? Or *under* it. The way he spoke about owning it... 'This is my Opera House', he said. He's a *real* person, and now..."

Mother sighed. "Yes, Meg, the Opera Ghost is a real person, and he

17

does live…" she hesitated, searching for the right word. "*Within* the Opera House. Do not ask me to tell you where, you are better off not knowing. He lays claim to the place because he has a *right* to it. He's been here a long time, and knows all its secrets."

"What's his name?" I asked. She raised her eyebrows at me.

"As far as you are concerned, you can call him 'sir'. He is *not* your father, Meg, but he does have something of a paternal interest in you and is worthy of your respect. He has watched over you for years."

"Why?" I demanded, appalled to learn that I had been the object of observation for far longer than I had ever suspected.

"Meg, you were born in this building. The first, and thus far the only infant born here. He regards you as part of the Opera House, and therefore belonging to him. Don't look so horrified," she added as she saw my expression. "It just means that he takes a particular interest in your welfare, that's all. He has no interest in *harming* you, quite the opposite."

I swallowed hard.

"It's not me he's interested in, it's Christine. He's teaching her to sing at night. Every night she leaves her bed and goes to him."

"Are you jealous?" She asked, and I blushed, not knowing whether I was or not. "Christine has a beautiful singing voice, even if her ballet skills are only average. With the proper training she could truly become an opera star, and he can teach her to sing the way no one else can. It is *music* that interests our Phantom, Meg. You know yourself the power of it. You've been enchanted by it since you were born." She smiled at me.

"I'm… afraid of him." I admitted, and she nodded.

"A degree of apprehension is wise," she said. "He's not like other men, he has not lived the life of an ordinary man."

"What about the note today? Monsieur Lafevre said 'twenty thousand francs', people were talking about bribes and threats…"

Mother sighed. "The Ghost does more for this Opera House than you know, why shouldn't he be paid for his time and his efforts?"

"Because he lurks in corners instead of showing himself openly?" I suggested.

"The world is not ready to recognise his genius."

"And for that he should get twenty thousand francs?"

"That is his request as a monthly salary."

"*Monthly*?" I was completely shocked. "Monsieur Lafevre makes twenty five thousand francs a *year* and he's the *manager*! Can the Opera House afford to give into unspecified blackmail without going bankrupt?"

"Enough, Meg."

"No, not enough!" I argued. "I care about the Opera House and the company, if it goes bankrupt then we can't continue playing and—"

"And you will have lost something you care about."

THE ANGEL'S SHADOW

"Something we all care about, including the Ghost. Why would he want that?"

"There is more to his request than just getting money," Mother said. "It's all part of his game."

"And he's moving us around like pieces on a board. Well forgive me if I don't want to be the chessman of someone who blackmails and frightens people into submission."

"And who saved your life."

"Why does he wear a mask?"

"Because he chooses to." She said, her tone suddenly turning cold. "If you want to remain under his guardianship I suggest you mind your tongue and control your temper."

I hadn't realised that my own tone had become heated and my cheeks flushed. We ate the remainder of our meal hardly speaking at all, tension swirling around us like an unfelt breeze, and I left to go to my own dormitory feeling unsatisfied. Had I learned any more about the man calling himself the Opera Ghost, or his intentions? The idea that he might view me as property chilled me, and even if his attitude to me was paternal in nature, what about his view of Christine? Both of us were turning from children into young women, almost completing our journey from caterpillar to butterfly, and Christine would be beautiful. What if his interest in Christine was not just because of her voice?

CHAPTER FOUR

The news of the Opera Ghost's financial demands made its way through the company like rain water trickling down a window pane and people starting referring to him as the Phantom of the Opera. A second note arrived, stating to Monsieur Lafevre in no uncertain terms that if he did not comply, the damage that would occur would cost far more than twenty thousand francs to repair. I don't know what Mother said, but Lafevre did submit to the demand. The manager began to look like a ghost himself, white-faced and tight-lipped with worry. I was worried too, anxious in a way I had never felt before. I had always felt absolutely safe in the Opera House, it was my home. Mother spoke of being under the Ghost's guardianship, and the feeling of being observed never left me. I was unused to the sensation and it angered me.

Figaro had been ignoring me since the day I chased him from Lafevre's office, but my lunch of fish pâté sandwiches five days later suddenly ensured his affections again. With the need for solitude rattling through me, Christine off to church and my mother in a temper, I chose the most deserted place I could think of for lunch; the corridor that led to the dressing rooms. The cleaners had already gone, and the cast would not be returning there until evening, so Figaro and I could enjoy our pâté in peace. It was lined with small alcoves, in each of which was a short pillar topped with a vase of flowers. The flowers were beginning to wilt and would be replaced within the next few days, as patrons often used this corridor to send bouquets, chocolates or champagne to the singers. The dressing rooms themselves were off this corridor, and mostly modest, apart from the one belonging to the prima donna. Christine, myself and the rest of the ballet girls had a dressing room at the far end, a room that would have been spacious had it not had between ten and twenty girls all jostling for space.

The cat happily shared the fish pâté, and then started pacing the corridor in his hunting stance, nose close to the ground as he tracked a mouse unseen to me. He threw himself into one of the alcoves after his imaginary rodent, scrabbling at the base of the pillar, and I heard a click. The wall in Figaro's alcove moved as the cat's back leg hit it. I caught my breath and stepped forward. There was, without a doubt, a door there, the width of the alcove and about three feet in height. I couldn't see any hinges, but the door swung inwards and I saw nothing but darkness beyond. If there were places where the world of the Ghost and my world collided, this must be one of them. Warning bells rang in my head, but I ignored them as the cat turned his attention to the revealed door, ears pricking up in interest and nose twitching.

"Here there be mice," I murmured, running my hand along Figaro's back. I pushed the secret door inwards and the two of us slipped into the passageway beyond. I felt strangely comforted to have Figaro by my side, even if what was driving him was simply the scent of vermin; if this was indeed one of the entrances to the Ghost's realm, I had no desire to explore it alone.

I used my fingers to pull the door to behind me, not finding a handle on either side, or a switch to open it from the inside. The switch that opened the door on the outside must have been on the base of the pillar Figaro had pressed a paw against on his mouse hunt. I slipped off one of my boots and pushed it into the gap so that the door could not close completely behind me, for I had no desire to be shut in the darkness with no known means of escape.

The only light came from that one crack where the door was propped open, illuminating a dust-covered floor to which the cat pressed his nose. The passage was as narrow as the alcove itself, and reaching out I could easily touch both sides. The walls were rough stone, and I use them to guide my way forward, heart pounding, almost leaping out of my chest altogether when the floor beneath my feet suddenly disappeared. A flight of steps, leading downwards. The cat was ahead of me on silent paws, the details lost to my light-accustomed sight. Eight steps, nine, ten, eleven, twelve... I counted the stairs, feeling the air grow colder the further I went. The walls on either side of me vanished, the passage widening or disappearing altogether. The silence was frightening in its depth, the darkness impenetrable... surely only the supernatural could see down here with no light source. The noise of my own heart filled my ears, and then the cat hissed. Tension pulled my body as taught as a violin string, my blood hummed through my veins, the cold made me shiver. Someone else was down here in the darkness with me. Figaro pounced forward, emitting a hiss that was almost a growl, and I lost my courage altogether. I turned and fled back the way I had come, up the stairs that seemed longer than on the way down, my hands groping the wall, eyes seeking desperately for my salvation, that sliver of light that showed the opening into the real world. When I saw it, it was like a blessing. I flung myself towards it as if into the arms of an angel, seized my boot from the floor, almost screamed as a shape brushed past me into the light of the corridor. Figaro, holding a still-squirming rat between his teeth. I nearly hit my head on the low doorway as I exited and slammed it shut behind me, squeezed myself around the pillar, knocking the flower arrangement onto the floor, and sank down against the opposite wall, my breath tangled and choked by unknown terror.

I was born here! My frantic mind insisted. *There is nothing here to frighten me!*

In the last month, everything seemed to have changed, my perceptions of reality and imagination entwined. There *were* things here to frighten me, to hurt me, and they knew me better than I ever supposed. I sat panting, staring at a wall that looked as solid as every other, and the shattered vase on the ground.

An evening out in Paris was a special occasion, and this one was due to Giselle's birthday. She had invited Christine, myself, and half a dozen of the other dancers out for a meal in a restaurant that Giselle described as "inexpensive but friendly". It seemed that some extended family member worked there and had reserved a table for ten people, and we were allowed to go as long as we were chaperoned. Madame Soirelli, one of the wardrobe mistresses, would be accompanying us on our night out, making sure that we were home before midnight and behaved ourselves. I didn't need reminding to behave; the incident with Jacques was not going to fade from my memory.

Mother kept Christine back after the day's dance lesson, so I went to get changed for the evening alone. Figaro joined me outside my dormitory, rubbing himself against my legs.

"I haven't got any fish," I told him, opening the door.

The cat flashed past me and leapt onto my bed, and I sighed.

"I am going to echo Monsieur Lafevre's warning," I said sternly. "Scratch anything and your tail becomes a feather duster."

He walked in a circle on the foot of my bed, and then curled up. I crossed the room and opened the window, to release some of the stuffiness and let in the cool evening air. The light of the setting sun slanted across the room, red and orange, like rubies and amber from a treasure chest. I lit the candle beside my bed, then opened the wardrobe and considered my gowns as I let the rehearsal dress slip off me to pool at my feet. There wasn't much to choose from; the dresses Christine and I owned were hand-me-downs from other dancers and actresses within the company, hemmed and un-hemmed, taken in and let out, but always done with care to get as much wear out of them as possible. However, it was a tired-looking collection, and I sighed, placing my hands on my hips.

"Such dilemmas you young ladies face."

I spun around. The Phantom of the Opera was sitting on my bed, back against the headboard, legs stretched out and crossed at the ankle, Figaro purring treacherously in his lap.

"How did you—" I began, and he tilted his masked head towards the open window. He was immaculately dressed in a black tail coat, white winged shirt, black trousers, white bowtie and waistcoat. I was standing in nothing but my corset and petticoat. He rolled his eyes as I grabbed at the dressing gown at the end of the bed and held it against myself defensively.

"It's not nice to have one's personal space invaded is it, Meg?" He said, caressing Figaro as the cat arched his spine to meet his fingers. "To know that someone has been snooping around places that should be private."

"No," I admitted, then with forced bravado: "We're back to 'Meg' now, are we? No more 'Mademoiselle Giry'?"

He lifted Figaro off his lap and swung his legs off the bed.

"If I were you I would not do such a stupid thing again." He picked up the book on my nightstand and flipped to the title page. "*The Masque of the Red Death and Other Stories* by Edgar Allan Poe. Well, well. Hardly what I would have thought would be to your taste, Meg."

"How did you know it was me?" I asked, trying to disguise the tremor in my voice.

"Your footprints, obviously. Well, one footprint and one boot print to be exact. And some paw prints from your friend." He looked down to where Figaro was winding himself around his ankles. I shifted my tense stance and his head snapped back up to me as though I had tried to run. He stood and took hold of the dressing gown I clutched. "I'll take that back, thank you."

"Why *do* you have—"

He raised a finger, holding it up to my lips without actually touching me, startling me into silence.

"Do not finish that question, girl," he advised. "You won't like the answer. Turn around."

"What?"

"Turn around, face the door."

I swallowed hard, fear pricking my skin. I did *not* want him behind me. His mismatched eyes focused on mine, and he made a twirling motion with his finger. I turned to face the door and felt his hand on my shoulder, guiding me closer to it and making me flinch.

"You're cold." I said. He didn't reply, moving my blonde curls over my left shoulder. The sunset threw our shadows onto the door, his obliterating mine as his long, chill fingers brushed over the skin of my back that the corset left exposed.

"No marks at all," he said, his hand leaving me. "Very good. I am pleased to know I remembered the gypsy recipe correctly."

"Gypsy recipe?" I spun to face him. "That herbal stuff Mother put on my back after she beat me? That was from you?" He didn't even twitch. "Who *are* you?"

"I hear they are now calling me the Phantom of the Opera," he said. "The Opera Ghost, and to some, an Angel of Music. To you I am not someone to be trifled with and you *will not* attempt to infiltrate my home again unless you want to end up at the wrong end of a rope."

"What do you want with Christine?" I asked before I could stop myself and his eyes flashed.

"That is no business of yours."

"You are working her to exhaustion with your late-night singing lessons. Christine needs her sleep, she's having trouble with her day-to-day activities because of you."

"Thank you for the advice," he said coldly. "You need rest too, it seems. How *have* you been sleeping? No more nightmares I trust?"

I swallowed and looked away. He took a step towards me and I instinctively backed up against the door.

"Did you know," he put a hand against the door on either side of my head and leaned forward so that I was trapped by his arms. "That you sing in your sleep?"

"What?" My horrified voice came out as a whisper.

"Oh, yes. Christine talks in her sleep, and you *sing*. Badly." He added cuttingly.

"How dare you! You creeping p—"

"And how dare *you*, Meg. I've given you fair warning. Continue prying into places that do not concern you and you will arouse my *anger*. It's not a sight you will find pleasant, little dancer. Now get out of my way." He stepped back, jerked his head sideways and I obediently stepped from in front of the door on trembling legs. He opened it, exited and closed it firmly behind him, inciting an annoyed mew from Figaro who had tried to follow him out. I sank down onto the end of my bed, wrapping my arms around myself as goose bumps erupted all over my exposed skin.

He is just trying to frighten you. I told myself. *He hasn't been in here. He hasn't watched you sleep.*

But it was certainly true that Christine talked in her sleep, sometimes in French and sometimes in Swedish. He had known where my dormitory was without me having to tell him the night he had guided me back to it, blindfolded and helpless.

I jumped as the door opened again five minutes later and Christine entered, almost tripping on the cat who rushed out past her, slightly red in the face from the long stair climb to the dormitory.

"Hard work pays off," she said with a smile. "Madame Giry says the extra practice I am putting into *Ophelia* is showing. She's impressed."

"Congratulations," I said numbly. Christine looked at me, tilting her head to one side.

"Are you all right? It's getting cold in here." She went to the window and closed it, before lighting the candle on her own nightstand. "You look a bit pale... are you feeling unwell? Are you worried about going into Paris this evening?"

I looked up to meet her concerned gaze.

"Meg... after what happened with that suitor of yours, even if you did manage to fight him off... you don't have to come into Paris tonight if you don't want to. I'll stay here with you and the others can just... carry on without us."

"They'll be a whole group of us and we'll be chaperoned," I said. "I'm not going to let one bad experience keep me inside for the rest of my life, afraid to go anywhere."

"If you're sure..."

"Christine? Do I... sing in my sleep?"

"Not that I've ever noticed," she replied, surprised. "Why?"

I shook my head.

He was lying to you. He was lying and making you fear him.

"Did you pass anyone on the stairs? A patron, maybe, someone in white tie?"

"Patron? No, of course not, there's no show this week. Meg..." she reached out and placed a hand on my forehead. "You're all clammy. Maybe you should stay home tonight."

I shook my head adamantly. *Damn him!* I was not going to let him get inside my head, with those eyes and that voice, and a presence that seemed to make me want to be under his protection and as far away from him as possible. Was that the effect he had on Christine? Had she ever seen him, and if not, then why was he showing himself to me? Let him intimidate and threaten and rescue me, let him contradict himself by word and action. I could do the same.

I tried to act as normally as I could through Giselle's birthday meal, thankful that it was nowhere near the alley where I had been assaulted, and encountered the Opera Ghost. Christine sat beside me, talking and laughing, and gently took my hand under the table.

As we returned through the night streets like a gaggle of geese herded by our chaperone, we passed a man in a long cloak and broad-brimmed hat, his face hidden by the brim and a scarf wrapped around his neck, playing the violin. Christine paused, gazing at him, and I wondered if she knew the tune, if perhaps her violinist father had played it to her when she was small.

"Christine?" I said gently. "Are you all right?"

"Christine! Meg!" Madame Soirelli clapped her hands at us. "Stay together, please!"

We trotted to join up with the other girls again, just in time to hear Giselle's pronouncement.

"It's still my birthday for another hour and a half, so I've decided what we're going to do. You're all going to come to my dormitory and we're going to have a séance. We're going to contact the Opera Ghost."

CHAPTER FIVE

"We can't hold a séance." I sighed as Christine and I moved to the centre of the group of girls.

"Why not?" Giselle asked.

"We'd need a medium."

"Lycette can be the medium." She gestured to her friend. "She's borrowed her grandmother's spirit board."

"Can you really do that?" Christine asked, falling into step beside Lycette.

"Christine," I said, surprised. "Wouldn't you think that ungodly, good Catholic girl like you?"

She smiled.

"When was the last time you went to church, Meg?" She asked with her familiar twinkle. "And where's your sense of adventure?"

"I lost it about a month ago," I scowled.

Christine blushed and mouthed an apology, but stayed by Lycette.

"A spirit board does not a medium make," I argued. Giselle frowned at me.

"Why are you so resistant to this?" She asked. "You're not... frightened, are you?"

I shrugged, adjusting my cloak against the growing night breeze. Frightened wasn't the word I would have chosen. Apprehensive, perhaps. There was no way of contacting the Opera Ghost with a spirit board; despite his apparent ability to move through walls, I knew him to be a man of flesh and blood. The night of my rescue he had carried me in his arms, and I had felt his heartbeat, smelled his sweat. I knew Christine was hoping that Lycette could bring her a message from her father... I had no desire to get one from mine. If Christine's beliefs were right, Gustave Daaé was indeed in the company of angels, but Claude Giry would not be with him. Hell was his eternal location now and I had no desire to hear from it.

I fought with the over-riding memory of my father, smiling at me in the mirror with tears in his eyes and a pistol pressed to his temple.

Fifteen minutes later, all nine of us were seated in a circle in Giselle's dormitory. It was one of the largest in the Opera House, containing three bunks. The room I shared with Christine may have been tiny—two wardrobes, beds and nightstands took up almost all the floor space—but at least it was marginally private with just two occupants. Sleeping in the company of five other girls seemed extremely uncomfortable. The group was seated on the floor around a piece of wood about the size of my mother's chopping board. The letters of the alphabet were written along the top, and the words "*Yes*" and "*No*" in the lower corners. A small pointer on wheels was in the centre of the board. The window was open and the flames of the candles that illuminated the room flickered. When I complained that it was cold, Giselle said it created 'atmosphere'.

"What's going to happen?" Asked Aimée, one of the youngest of the group.

Lycette cleared her throat.

"We all put a fingertip very lightly on the pointer, but be sure not to actually push it or move it deliberately. I'll ask the questions, and the spirits will answer by using the pointer to spell out words."

I scoffed under my breath.

"Meg can write them down," Giselle said, passing me a piece of paper and a pencil.

"Why me?"

"You have the neatest handwriting," she replied simply. I sighed and shrugged, placing the paper on the floorboards.

"All join hands and we'll say the Lord's Prayer."

I took the hands Christine and Aimée offered me and bowed my head.

"Our Father, who art in Heaven…" I chanted the words with the rest, so familiar that they had lost their meaning. But somewhere a voice told me that it wasn't familiarity that robbed them of meaning but my own doubts and rage.

"… but deliver us from evil…"

Wind swept through the dormitory and I felt Aimée jump beside me as three of the candles went out.

"Amen."

"Everyone put a finger on the pointer," Lycette commanded. "And stop giggling, this is serious."

I rested a fingertip on the pointer and hoped that this was just a game. Christine smiled at me as she pressed a finger next to mine. Lycette took a deep breath, crossed herself, and said into the air:

"Spirits, we call you. Hear us tonight and enter our circle. Is there

THE ANGEL'S SHADOW

anybody there?"

I rolled my eyes, but the pointer quivered under my finger and there was a gasp throughout the room.

"Is there anybody there?" Lycette repeated.

The pointer quivered again, then began to slide across the board.

"Who's pushing it?"

"No one's pushing!"

The pointer stopped.

"Are there any spirits here with us tonight?"

T — R — O — I — S

"Three," I repeated, and Lycette gave us all a triumphant look.

"Do any of you have names?"

I felt Christine tense beside me, waiting. Very slowly the pointer travelled across the board, and I watched, the pencil in my left hand, ready to the write down the letters.

C

C... for Claude...

I swallowed hard, desperately hoping that it was just a coincidence. The pointer wasn't moving any further. Lycette glanced around at all of us, then asked:

"Do any of you have a message for us?"

Yes.

"What is your message?"

The pointer trembled and I wrote down the letters as they appeared.

C — U — R — I — O — S — I — T — E

"*Curiosité.*" I repeated, staring at the word I had written down. "Curiosity. The message is 'curiosity'. What sort of message is that?"

"Shh!" Giselle frowned at me. I could sense that Christine was disappointed beside me. Lycette's neighbour whispered in her ear.

"Spirit, how did you die?"

The pointer swept across the board and I felt my hand go with it as if affixed.

S — U — I

Oh, God... The memory flashed through my head again, my father smiling through his tears, gun against his head.

"Look after Mama."

Suicide.

I stared at the word I had written down. Christine looked at me, face pale.

"We shouldn't be doing this."

"Spirits," Lycette spoke clearly over Christine's whisper. "Is one of you the entity that calls itself the Opera Ghost?"

No.

"Is the Opera Ghost in this building tonight?"

Yes.

Another draught swirled through the room and the remaining candles were extinguished. It wasn't total darkness since moonlight flowed strongly through the window, but nevertheless there were some shrieks.

"We must end this now." Christine said firmly.

"Everyone stay where you are," Lycette sounded perfectly calm. "Don't break the circle. We have to finish this properly." She cleared her throat. "Spirits, thank you for speaking to us. We release you from our circle and wish you goodnight."

The pointer responded.

A — U — R — E — V — O — I — R

"Goodbye," I repeated, and the feeling that my finger was glued to the pointer subsided. Giselle relit the candles and handed one to Christine and one to Aimée.

"You'd better get back to your dormitories before someone catches you."

"Or something," I muttered sarcastically.

"Shh!" Christine gave me a reproachful look and nodded to Aimée and her little roommate. I sighed.

"Come on, you two. We'll walk you back to your dormitory."

They stayed close, pressed tightly together as if expecting phantoms to jump out of the walls and spirit them away. I wished I could remember the other girl's name but I was drawing a complete blank.

"Listen," I said to them. "The only thing you have to be afraid of is Madame Giry or Madame Soirelli catching you out of bed after hours. There aren't any ghosts here, believe me, I've lived here my whole life. It was all a trick, the other girls were moving the pointer. Giselle was just trying to scare you."

The two girls nodded, a little reassured, but did not look completely happy until they were safely back in their dormitory. Christine and I continued upwards to our own beds.

"That was the biggest load of tosh I've seen all year," I said, kicking my dress across the floor. "It was cruel of Giselle to try and frighten us like that even if it is her birthday."

Christine didn't reply as she changed into her night gown and I struggled with the laces of my corset with fumbling fingers.

"God damn it!" I exploded.

"Meg!" Christine cried.

"Sorry." I sighed, wiping a hand across my forehead. "I know you don't like it when I… blaspheme, I'm sorry. I just can't get this wretched thing off!"

"I'll do it," she said, coming over to me. "Turn around, face the door.

What?" She asked as I stared at her. "Why are you looking at me like that?"

"Nothing." I shook my head and turned to face the door. Her warm fingers brushed my hair over my left shoulder so that she could reach the laces, and I remembered the Phantom's cold ones doing the same that evening, searching my back for scars.

"You've got yourself in a real tangle back here," she murmured.

"I was in a rush."

"Meg?" She tugged at the laces. "Did you really mean what you said to Aimée and Maria?"

Maria! That was the girl's name, Maria!

"Did you mean it, that there are no ghosts here?"

"Christine," I craned my neck to look at her over my shoulder. "There are no such things as ghosts. Anyone who tells you otherwise is trying to trick you."

She sighed and gave another tug, and I let out my breath in relief as the corset strings loosened.

"Oh, thank you."

"You're welcome." She climbed into bed without looking at me again.

As it turned out, I was right to warn the Phantom about Christine. We were having a music rehearsal on the stage with Monsieur Reyer two days later, divided into blocks according to our vocal range. It was one of those tedious but necessary rehearsals that Reyer called 'note-bashing', and which involved singing phrases over and over until everyone got them right.

"One of the sopranos is still sharp," he complained. "Mademoiselle Giry, is that you? Can you give me that E again please?"

Reyer had an astonishing ear for music, and I was amazed that he was able to pick out my voice among all the other sopranos. Embarrassed, I complied, and he nodded.

"Just a little sharp," he picked out the note on his piano. "Try again."

I listened to the sound and tried again, and this time Reyer smiled.

"Much better, well done. Altos, your line—"

I felt Christine's touch on my arm, but when I turned my face to hers she was already dropping downwards, eyes rolling.

"Christine!" I grabbed her just in time to stop her cracking her head open on the stage, someone else grabbing her on the other side.

"What's happened?"

"Is the child unwell?"

"Christine?" I shook her gently, then tapped her face. "She's out cold."

I tried not to panic, looking around wildly at my companions.

"Here."

A tenor knelt next to me and held a small bottle under Christine's nose, and she jerked, her eyelids fluttering.

"What…" she began.

"You fainted!" I cried, half relieved and half angry. "Don't frighten me like that!"

"Mademoiselle Giry, please help Mademoiselle Daaé to her dormitory," Reyer said. "Monsieur Dainier please fetch Dr. Forrester. Take a ten minute break, the rest of you."

Mother appeared from somewhere in the wings and together we helped the trembling Christine to our dormitory.

"Here," Mother said, holding a glass of water to her lips. "Sip slowly."

Dr. Forrester arrived within fifteen minutes, a stout bearded man in a dark brown suit, and although I dislike doctors on principle, he was very kind and gentle with Christine.

"All done," he said, after examining her. "There's nothing to be concerned about, Mademoiselle Daaé. You've just pushed your body too hard and it decided to push back. You are to stay in bed for the next three days and make sure you get plenty of water into your system. We won't have to resort to blood-letting or anything like that." He gave her a kind smile. "It's exhaustion, Mademoiselle, complete exhaustion. When did you girls start working so hard?"

Christine thanked him and I sat on her bed, stroking her hair until she fell asleep again.

What sort of a friend am I? I berated myself. *Not to have noticed that her cheeks were flushed and her eyes over-bright?*

I knew that she left her bed night after night and worked twice as hard as me during the day, and now she was suffering for it. And I had warned *him* as well.

"Dr. Forrester?" I joined him just outside the door, where he was talking to Mother. "Will she be all right?"

"Your friend will be fine, Mademoiselle," he said gently. "As I said, she needs to rest. I've left her a sleeping draught."

I spent the rest of the day with Christine, and as the sun set she began to seem anxious.

"I'm all right, really." She insisted. "I'm feeling much better."

"Christine," I replied. "You are not all right; you have to get a good night's *sleep* for once."

She blushed and didn't argue anymore, and I made sure she drank the draught that the doctor had left for her. I sat watching her through the darkness until the bells of the nearest church started to strike two o'clock in the morning. It was during this time that I had noticed that she was missing from her bed, learning from the Opera Ghost.

THE ANGEL'S SHADOW

I took up my candle and left the dormitory, moving as though I were a ghost myself in my white nightgown and dressing gown. I descended the stairs, trying to think of where Christine would go for lessons with her Angel of Music. I wafted barefoot through the Opera House, and had returned to the corridor where I had found the secret door, when my ears picked up notes. The beautiful strains of a violin, played with so much talent that I gasped, emerged from the doors opposite the dressing rooms, leading to the auditorium and the stage. I forced myself to inhale and pushed open the doors that led onto the stage as quietly as I could.

Standing far back in the wings, I saw that the auditorium was in complete darkness, and a single spotlight illuminated a circle on the stage like a full moon reflected in a lake. Everything else was black as pitch, as though nothing existed beyond it.

A voice joined the music of the violin, the baritone role from the song we had been rehearsing that afternoon, and it was filled with such purity, skill and raw emotion that I felt my breath catch in my throat and my pulse beat at double quick time. I knew that I had never heard another voice to compare to it, and the hairs on the back of my neck rose and tears pricked behind my eyes. To sing with that voice, to have it surround me, to *feel* that *passion*... It touched something in my soul that longed to join with that voice, and touched something in my body too, a tingling I had never felt.

Witchcraft... I told myself, and pinched my own wrist fiercely to pull myself together. Whatever that creature was he wouldn't have me under his spell so easily. I lifted my chin and marched into the puddle of light. The voice and music stopped abruptly and I blinked in the sudden dazzle.

"You!" The hiss was filled with such venom that it ran cold through my veins like a poison. I couldn't tell where it had come from, and before I could turn, something snaked out of the darkness to my left, a long piece of rope striking me so hard against my cheek that I saw red sparks. It knocked me off my feet and the candle rolled into the blackness, its flame extinguished.

"Do you intend to test my anger?! Do you have a death wish?!" His voice was booming through the darkness, terrifyingly close. "Allow me to grant it!"

The rope caught around my neck, a noose, inescapable. A body was against mine, pressing me flat, pinning me down, then hands turned me onto my back and against the bright glare that seemed to come from Heaven itself I saw his masked face and silhouetted shape. He snarled down at me with eyes full of fire, and pulled the noose tight.

"Meg Giry, prepare to meet thy God!"

CHAPTER SIX

The knot pressed against my larynx, the noose tightening around my throat. The Opera Ghost was straddling me, teeth bared, one knee on my left hand, my right hand trapped under my own body. He increased the pressure of the rope slowly and I realised that this was not going to be the quick snap of the neck I had seen him use on Jacques. He was taking his time, allowing himself to enjoy the act, and with dark spots beginning to dance at the edges of my vision, I choked out the one thing that might penetrate his brain.

"Christine!"

Air rushed into my lungs as the pressure against my neck was relaxed, but he was still holding the rope, still pinning me down with his body, still ready and willing to tighten the noose again.

"What did you say?"

"Christine!" I gasped, blinking tears from watering eyes. "She's ill! She collapsed during rehearsals today! That's why I came here, to let you know!"

"What has she said to you about me?" He roared, pulling the noose tight again.

"Nothing!" I choked. "She's doesn't speak to me about you! I worked it out on my own! I thought you should know!"

He stared, his masked face unreadable to me. Was he angry or concerned?

"If I find out that you've lied to me…"

"I wouldn't dare! Please! I don't want to die!" My tears ran into my hair and I begged him with my eyes. He looked at me, tilting his head to one side as if he could read my thoughts through them.

"Why did you come *here* tonight? Speak!" A quick tug on the noose to make his point, then it relaxed enough for me to obey.

"I heard your music! I followed the music! Christine was given a sleeping draught but I know what time of night she is absent from her bed! And I know she was afraid not to come to you tonight!"

God, I thought *What would this madman have done if she had been absent without explanation for three days?*

"Do you mean to tell me," he said slowly. "That you came here out of concern for Christine's welfare?"

"Yes!" I gasped. "I was afraid of... of what would happen if..." I struggled underneath him, but it was pointless. "Christine is on bed rest for three days."

"I wouldn't hurt Christine," he said quietly.

"You are hurting *me*!" I cried. "Monsieur, *please*!"

A flicker of surprise crossed his visible features, then he let out an impatient sigh and tugged the noose over my head, some strands of golden hair going with it. He stood with the grace of a cat and I rolled onto my side, pressing my freed hands onto the boards of the stage, and heaving in breath after uninhibited breath as the tears continued to run. Oh, to *breathe*!

His boots came into my line of vision, polished to a shine, and that foul noose with strands of my hair tangled in its rope work, glaring pale against his black trouser legs.

"You are a thorn in my side, Meg Giry," he growled, and the noose swung from left to right like a hypnotist's pocket watch. "Intensely annoying."

Sense begged me to hold my tongue, but as usual I did not comply.

"If I cause you so much trouble, you should have let Jacques have his way with me in the street."

"Never." He crouched, seizing my chin and turning my face so that my eyes were locked with his. "I will not have another man sully what is *mine*."

He leaned down, and for a moment I thought he intended to kiss me, but instead he pressed his unmasked cheek against mine, his sweat mingling with my tears as he whispered in my ear.

"Keep your hand at the level of your eyes."

Then he left me, striding out of the pool of light without a sound, coiling the rope in his hand. I stayed where I was on the stage, relishing my ability to breathe. Thirty seconds—or perhaps it was half an hour—after he vanished from my sight, the light above me went out, and I smiled. There was only one place he could be in order to turn it off; but I had no wish to see that temper again tonight and no desire to be strangled to death. I carefully found my way into the wings and then to Mother's bedroom. She answered my knock in her nightgown, her long dark hair in a braid down her back.

"Good God, Meg!" She cried on seeing me. "What happened to you?"

I hesitated.

"An accident," I said at last. "There was an accident."

The day after my near-death experience, Christine received a bouquet of red roses, an unsigned note wishing her a speedy recovery. When I climbed into bed that night, I found a white rose between the sheets. The note tied to it with black ribbon simply stated: 'With thanks'. The stem was absolutely covered in thorns and drew blood the moment I picked the flower up.

"A thorn in your side," I muttered. "Very droll."

I had hoped not to see the Ghost again, my curiosity crushed by the bruising to my throat, but that same night a black-gloved hand pulled open the dormitory window and his slim frame slid inside. I froze, my voice deserting me in panic. It was almost a relief to recognise the shape, and the mask.

"What are you doing in here?!" I hissed. "Get out!"

He raised a finger to his lips, then took off one glove and turned to Christine.

"What are you doing?" I repeated.

He ignored me, leaning over her and placing his hand on her forehead, and I realised he was checking Christine's temperature. Apparently satisfied, he straightened up and faced me again as I sat up in my bed, staring at him with wide eyes. His un-gloved hand went into the recesses of his cloak and he withdrew a bottle containing a liquid, the colour of which I could not distinguish in the moonlight.

"More of your gypsy potion?" I guessed in a whisper, and he nodded. "Ironic that the injury and the cure come from the same source."

"You're welcome." Were the only words he spoke to me that night, before leaving the room the same way he had entered it. I closed the window behind him, firmly pushing the bolt home. So we were back to invading each other's private spaces, were we?

My 'accident' at the hands of our Phantom was the first of many in the coming months. He demanded the sole use of Box Five for every night there was a performance, which Lafevre refused, on the basis that with a 'salary' of twenty thousand francs a month the Opera Ghost could afford to buy the Box. The next day, every one of the Boxes had their velvet seats and curtains slashed. Every one, except Box Five. The loss of nine Boxes containing up to four seats at two hundred and fifty francs apiece, was a huge blow to the Opera House, and then there was the cost of the repair work and replacement curtains. Monsieur Lafevre was looking worse than ever, stress showing in his haggard face and hunched posture. I couldn't help but worry about him, and I knew Mother was worried too.

The next note was addressed to Monsieur Reyer and demanded the sacking of the third violinist. When the man arrived the following day, his violin had been smashed beyond recognition and any spares that we might have had, mysteriously vanished. I imagined what the Ghost might do with them; sell them perhaps, or use them as decoration in his subterranean lair.

THE ANGEL'S SHADOW

Christine's vocals went from strength to strength, but her rehearsal times with her Angel had evidently changed; she would go missing for a couple of hours while everyone else was eating dinner, and get a full night's sleep. I still worried for her, even though she assured me she was fine. She never even saw her Angel, she said, only heard his voice as he coached her, sometimes to the accompaniment of the violin, sometimes without.

"He brings out a performance in me I never thought I could give," she told me, blowing out her candle as we settled down for the night. "The way he encourages me... he is strict, but his tutorage is doing me a power of good."

"But you've never seen his face?"

"No, I've told you, I only hear his voice."

"And that doesn't frighten you?"

She hesitated, then admitted: "At first, it did frighten me... and when he becomes angry, he can be terrifying..."

"Angry?" I repeated, alarmed. "What sort of angry? Christine, has he hurt you?"

"Of course not," she said softly. "Angels cannot hurt people."

"You said he becomes angry," I prompted and she sighed.

"The Angel of Music has high expectations, and when I do not fulfil them, he becomes enraged. He shouts, Meg, that's all... but it is terrible to know that I have disappointed him."

Although I burned with questions, I let the matter drop. It seemed that Christine was in no immediate danger; as long as the Opera Ghost maintained his distance, she was safe... And yet... he was manipulating her, playing on her faith and her belief in angels. Under his instruction, Christine was beginning to shine. Someday she would become a star, but what was in it for him?

The alarming thing about what happened was that there was no trigger, it just occurred as suddenly as a thunderstorm on a summer's day. Music no longer had the power to blanket my thoughts; dance no longer soothed my soul. My mood—which is temperamental at the best of times—grew dark for long periods, and it was increasingly difficult to keep my mind on what I was supposed to be doing. I knew the signs, for they had troubled my father, and the idea that his affliction had been passed on to me should have turned my stomach to ice. Instead I felt myself sinking into the idea like a villain into a quagmire.

Christine noticed, and so did my mother, although it was a still shock to hear them discussing me. I was walking past Mother's office when I heard Christine's voice from inside.

"Madame, I don't know what else I can tell you. Meg *does* seem to be...

unhappy at the moment, but surely that's just the stress of the upcoming opera? Maybe she's just feeling the strain from being given the solo in the ballet."

It took all my self-control not to march in through the door and demand an explanation of why I was the topic of conversation. Instead, I listened to Christine promise that she would keep an eye on me, and inform Mother if I did anything that seemed particularly out of character, such as try to venture forth into Paris alone again. I waited, hidden in the shadows until Christine left, then entered the office myself.

"Mother, why are you talking about me behind my back?"

She looked startled. "Meg… I'm just worried about you. This is more than just stress or… being a teenager. Ever since your father died…" she trailed off.

"This will pass, Mama." I said, using the childish endearment to please her. "I'm just… tired, that's all."

"I spoke to Dr. Forrester when he was here to tend to Christine…" Mother began.

"And I'm sure he recommended a short hospital stay." I cut in. "Nothing long-term, she'll be back in time for the next opera. We'll just do some tests and torture her the way we tortured her father."

Mother swallowed hard, her eyes glittering as if she were holding back tears.

"The doctors did not torture your father. They were trying to help him."

"They killed him!" It was an effort not to scream it at her, but I managed, and although my words came out vehement, they were still soft. "They killed him just as surely as if they put the bullets in the gun."

I rounded the desk and knelt, taking her hands in mine.

"Please… don't make me go there. *I beg you*. Don't put me through what he went through."

She sighed, and reached out to stroke my cheek.

"I'm so worried about you, Meg. I can't stand to see you suffer."

"I'm *not*," I insisted. "I'm just… on edge. If things get worse I promise I will tell you. Just… promise *me*… no doctors. Swear you won't send me into hospital."

She promised, and although I knew it was a promise she might break, it would suffice for now. I, in turn, had to drag myself out of the melancholia that had descended like a lead trunk onto my shoulders, and with a new goal in mind, I headed up to my dormitory and stood outside the door. I had stood here three months earlier, blindfolded despite the darkness, and a voice had informed me that I had left his world and entered my own.

"Retrace your steps," Mother always told me when I lost something, and now I intended to do just that. I closed my eyes and concentrated on that night, on the feeling of his fingers digging into my shoulders as he guided

THE ANGEL'S SHADOW

me, of his breath, cold against my ear.

"You have returned. Goodnight, Meg Giry."

I reversed the words in my mind, feeling his fingers move, his push become a pull, and I took a step backwards. Another. Another. We had walked along this corridor. I remembered feeling a slight breeze against my cheek and saw the light change through my closed lids as I passed a window. He hadn't been using a candle, I realised in surprise; his nocturnal vision must be extraordinary, no doubt an effect of living underground. Underground meant *down*. We hadn't used the main stairs to this floor, the wooden ones which creaked and the banister that wobbled alarmingly. I had felt stone under my feet.

My back hit a wall and I opened my eyes in frustration. Maybe ghosts could move through walls, but I couldn't, so there was no way that I could have been in this spot on that night. I'd lost count of my steps, and sighed, sitting down on the floorboards. What was I doing anyway? What was the point? I traced the lines of the wood grain with my fingertips, mindful of splinters. Christine was *safe*, we all were while the Phantom's demands were being met. When would a demand for the next installment of twenty thousand francs come? How long would it be before Monsieur Lafevre had to start selling off parts of the building in order to pay this ridiculous man his 'salary'?

The wood grain was running the wrong way. I blinked down at the floorboards between my feet, where the pattern had altered. One line ran horizontal across the floor where the others ran vertical and my heart started to thump. It was a work of art if nothing else, camouflaged as well as a stick insect might hide itself in the forest. But I had been standing on a stage since I was old enough to walk, and I knew a trapdoor when I saw one.

CHAPTER SEVEN

The first time I actually saw a trapdoor in use, it frightened the life out of me. I had been perhaps three, the youngest child in the company, and taking my first steps in ballet slippers. The scene being played out on the Opera House stage was set in a village, which was to be visited by an evil sorcerer who materialised onstage. It was the dress rehearsal when I saw this materialisation; the actor rising through the stage like a demon appearing out of hell, and I screamed the place down. My father scooped me off the stage and I spent the rest of the rehearsal sitting on his lap in the orchestra pit as he played the piano. The conductor at the time was not especially happy to have me there, but captured between pianist and piano, turning the pages of the score for him whenever he nodded for me to do so, I caused no trouble. Afterwards, Papa took me under the stage to show me how the trick was done, where the trapdoors were located, and meet the stagehand who operated them. The doors were so well hidden that they were hard to see even when you stood right on top of one, and it became an established prank to open a trapdoor when a new member of the company was standing on it.

This trapdoor clearly worked along similar lines... so how did you open it from this side? I dug my fingernails into the near-invisible edge of the trapdoor and tugged, achieving a broken nail but nothing more. The entrance by the dressing rooms opened by a button, concealed from prying fingers; presumably this worked the same way.

First thing was first, though. I fetched the candle and a box of matches from my dormitory, along with a chunk of chalk, usually used for marking dresses where they needed to be hemmed. I had been an avid reader as a child, and among the hand-me-down books had been a collection of Greek myths. One of the stories involved a hero entering a labyrinth, and using a ball of twine to guide his way back out. Without a ball of twine, chalk would have to suffice; I'd just have to remember to erase it on my return. A lantern would be better, but I didn't have one to hand, so I put the candle in one pocket of my dress, the box of matches and chalk in the other.

THE ANGEL'S SHADOW

Now, to think... If I wanted a switch that I could access at will, but would not be pressed by accident, where would I put it? That in itself ruled out the floor and the window, where cleaners carrying out their work with unusual efficiency might find it. Higher, then; another problem for me since the Opera Ghost must be at least seven inches taller than my five foot one. My eyes travelled along the corridor as I revolved on the spot, like a clockwork ballerina on a music box, despite the fact that I was wearing a simple grey dress and not a tutu. It was a bland sight. The staircase that led down was in the centre, the arms of the corridor branching out from it in a T shape. If you went up the stairs and turned left, you faced the dead end where I was now standing, with the window in the wall. Look out of the window and you saw another wall jutting out over the stables; the dormitory Christine and I shared. That was the first door if you went right at the top of the stairs, the second a bathroom. The walls enclosing the T shape had small pictures on. I stared at the one closest to me; it was a copy in chalk and charcoal of a painting by Simon Vouet, and featured a young man in strategically placed robes playing a lyre. He might have been Apollo, but if I ever knew the identity of this youth, I couldn't be certain of it now. He had vines or some sort of wreath in his hair, that for all the world looked like a halo, the billowing robes around him almost representing wings. *No...*

I stepped towards the picture. The frame was wood, plain, with no decoration that could hide a button. There was no disturbance in its surface, but when I tried to pull it off the wall, nothing happen. I twisted, something clicked, and the trapdoor slid open.

Don't go down there, my sense insisted, but with my heart beating a rhythm in my head and my fingers trembling, I lit my candle, holding it in my left hand, the chalk in my right, and gazed at the stone staircase that was now revealed to me. With the determination of Theseus, I took the stairs down into a world where I knew I was unwelcome.

The journey I made into the hidden passages of the Opera Populairé was certainly educational. I was creating a picture of the true building. On every floor, it seemed, there was a secret route around. I kept to the one staircase for the most part, but paused to investigate light sources. The mirrors were the most shocking discovery. Not *all* of them were double-sided, allowing someone to use them as windows into my world, but enough of them were to give me a nasty fright. My paranoia edged up a notch—from the other side there was no indication that you were being observed, you would see only your own reflection.

I found in the course of my prying that I could get all the way up to the roof without the use of a conventional staircase, but there was only so far I could go down. There were five cellars to the Opera House and a further sub-basement that had been completely flooded, presumably by the waters of the Seine. It gave the impression of a mighty lake deep under the building. Although I had followed only one route from the trapdoor by my dormitory to this lake, a network of tunnels indicated there were plenty more ways to get here. Time enough for investigating those; for now I was cold, damp, filthy dirty and at a dead end. The Opera Ghost, it seemed, did not take much pride in the housekeeping of his catacombs. There seemed no way to cross the lake and no way of measuring its depth; it might only come up to my knees, but it might come way over my head, I couldn't swim, and didn't want to bet my life on its shallowness.

Hidden passageways did at least mean that I could return to my dormitory without anyone seeing the state I was in; the grey dress covered in slime and dark muck from the walls. My hands were also covered where I had erased my own chalk trail. Back in the daylight, which seemed dazzling to candle-adjusted eyes, I pushed the picture of Apollo or whoever he was supposed to be straight, and saw the trapdoor remerge as if the hole in the floor had never existed.

Christine was stretched out on her bed reading a book, and stared at me in astonishment when I entered the dormitory.

"Meg... you look like you've been... rolling around in the forest."

"Don't say anything to my mother!" I begged, and she smiled.

"Of course not... you'd better get out of that and rinse it thoroughly to make sure there aren't any stains." Her smile widened. "What's his name?"

"Who?" I looked at her blankly.

"The boy... the one you've been in the forest with. You are being careful, aren't you, Meg? You won't let him take advantage?"

I felt the blush stain my face from hairline to chin, and every male name I had ever heard fled from my mind.

"Patrice," I invented, wondering whether I should be relieved or insulted by her assumption. Since meeting the Phantom and witnessing a murder, men had not been foremost in my mind. On the other hand, I was propositioned far more often than Christine, who despite her beauty and burgeoning talent, seemed to fade into the background when it came to courting.

I changed as quickly as I could and rinsed my dress in the bathtub of the communal bathroom used by the people living on this floor and the one below. No two-way mirrors in here, I hoped, and that did little to improve my state of mind. Whatever he was, the Phantom was an intelligent man. Even having wiped away my chalk markings and scuffed up my footprints, I knew there were a dozen ways in which I had given my identity away— chief among them that there was probably no one else stupid enough to ignore two warnings and a death threat.

THE ANGEL'S SHADOW

Days passed, rehearsals for the opera continued, opening night came and went. Eight times a week I danced my ballet solo in *Ophelia*, the only time I was truly lost in the music and the movement.

I drew crude maps of the secret passageway I had investigated, causing a curious Christine to ask if I were thinking of becoming an architect when she caught me at it. I just smiled guiltily and changed the subject.

Eight times a week I listened to La Carlotta sing her way through the performance, and when I sang in the chorus beside Christine, Carlotta's voice became just so much caterwauling. I was astonished by how much Christine's singing had progressed in the last few months, and that no one else seemed to have noticed. She truly sang like an angel. The rest of the time, I was acting my tutu off so that others wouldn't know I was a nervous wreck. I kept my eyes firmly away from Box Five; he wasn't there at every performance, and I never saw him on the nights he did attend, but I could *feel* his presence, as if there were additional harmonics humming through the auditorium. On such nights, Christine seemed to glow as if caught in her own personal spotlight.

Mother was the only member of the Opera House staff with a key to Box Five, and she insisted that she never saw the Opera Ghost. He left her notes asking for whatever he wanted—refreshments, opera glasses, a programme. Whenever she went in, she said, the Box was empty of people. Sometimes he would leave her a gift after the performance was finished—a bouquet of flowers, a box of chocolates, once a fan edged with black lace. When I told her she had an admirer in the Phantom, she told me the suggestion was daft.

I waited with tattered nerves for the day my trespass into his realm was discovered, but days turned into weeks, *Ophelia* ended, rehearsals for *Hannibal* began, and there was nothing aimed in my direction. Gradually, I felt myself start to relax. There were more notes, of course, suggestions, bribes, threats, demands, but none of them came with my name on the wax-sealed envelope. I allowed the stress and depression that had been pressing on my shoulders to lift, and indulged the other dancers with tales of the Opera Ghost, careful to keep them ridiculous and away from the ears of those who might believe them or find them too close to the truth. Joseph Buquet in particular listened with wrapt attention, but simply laughed and turned away with the others. I had told the younger ballerinas that ghosts did not exist, and now they were angry with me for telling stories about one, but I did not fear their small rage.

Of course, it wouldn't last, and I was in the place that most reminded me of my childhood when the shadow of a deadly angel hung over me again.

It was one of the many rehearsal rooms used for the musicians to

43

practice in, and the one that my father had favoured because of the dark mahogany piano. I would never understand the instrument the way he had understood it, but he had told me that of all the pianos in the Opera House, this one was his favourite because of its character. To me, it was simply an upright piano, decorated with a few trailing flowers and vines. I traced my fingers over the black and white keys, picking out a simple tune, then sat on the bench, back straight, the way he'd taught me, and closed my eyes. Christine believed that Gustave Daaé had sent her an Angel of Music, and although Claude Giry could not send me anything, I could pretend just as well. I was six years younger, and he was sitting by my side, one arm over mine, and as I played the piece that we had always done as a duet, I heard his notes join with mine. He was a virtuoso, a better pianist than I would ever be, even if I gave up the ballet and practiced until my fingers bled, and yet it was a joy just to be with him, here in this place, in this music. Memory surrounded me like a cloak, imagination filling in the missing senses. I could feel him sitting next to me, smell his cologne, hear his breathing, his fingers lightly brushing mine at places where our notes crossed.

"Meg?"

My eyes opened and the illusion was gone. I was alone, playing a mahogany upright piano in a high octave and with mediocre skill. Mother entered the room, holding a letter written on black-edged paper.

"There you are," she said, her gaze meeting mine. "*He* wants to see you."

"*He?*" I repeated. "I'm sure Christine would tell you that there is only one *He* worthy of a capital H, and unless He wants to apologise for Papa's untimely end, there is nothing else I need to hear from Him."

Mother sighed. "Meg Giry, you are becoming more insolent with every day. You know very well who I mean. He wants to see you in Box Five, immediately."

I sighed and stood up.

"The note doesn't say what this is about?"

"No." She narrowed her eyes at me. "Is there something you should be telling me?"

I shook my head and left the room as swiftly as I could. Here it was then. He knew I had been snooping around was preparing to dish out my punishment. I wondered what form it would take, and why I wasn't more scared as I climbed the stairs to enter the auditorium at the third level, walking along the plush red velvet corridor to the door of Box Five. It was locked, of course, and Mother hadn't given me the key.

He's already in there, my mind whispered *The Phantom of the Opera...*

I hesitated, then knocked. There was a click.

"Enter."

I tried the handle and the door opened silently. The interior of Box Five was full of more red velvet, picked out with gold finishing. There were only two chairs in this Box, the privacy and view of the stage it offered making it one of the most expensive Boxes in the Opera House. The Phantom was sitting in one of the chairs, dressed in his customary black suit and white mask, with a white shirt, gold waistcoat and cravat. He acknowledged my presence with a wave of a thin, pale hand.

"Ah, Meg Giry. Take a seat."

"I'd prefer to stand."

"In third position, I see."

I blinked and looked down at my feet, seeing that I had indeed placed them in what was known as 'third position' in ballet dancing. I shrugged.

"It's a habit for a dancer."

"I know." His tone sharpened to an order. "Sit down."

I sat, feeling like a child in the presence of her tutor, while his posture in the chair was like that of a king on a throne. He wasn't wearing a cloak, which presumably meant there was no noose on him at this moment in time.

"No, I don't have it with me." He answered, and I jumped, causing him to chuckle. "I can read you like a score, Meg. You are safe from my Punjab lasso for now. I don't need it anyway, there are several ways I could kill you that require no weapon at all. Oh, relax, child! I did not ask you here with murder in mind."

"You did not *ask* me here at all," I said, unable to release the tension from my shoulders. "You *summoned* me as if I were a dog."

"Everyone needs a pet. You have a cat, I believe."

"Figaro is not *mine*, he belongs to everyone. Or we belong to him, I'm not sure."

"Stop rambling, girl. Asked or summoned, you are here for a specific reason and that reason is the dress rehearsal of *Hannibal*."

I stared at him in confusion.

"What about it? It's not for another week."

"I know very well when it takes place. There is a task that you will perform for me. Make sure you keep Christine downstage right during the aria of the third act."

"But we're supposed to be—"

"I *know* where you're supposed to be, but for this rehearsal you will do as I say. Where will Christine be?"

"Downstage right," I said, shaking my head, and he nodded.

"Good girl. And should anything occur that might cause La Carlotta to storm off in a huff, you are to volunteer Christine for the role of Elissa."

He suddenly moved, turning towards me and leaning forward, causing me to shrink back.

"And, since we were talking about pets, I owe you a *lesson*. A lesson in what happens when people ignore the warnings of spirit boards and the threats from their master."

"*Master*?!" I repeated in indignation. "Who do you—"

He raised his hand and I flinched, anticipating the slap that did not come.

"I could, of course, simply ask your mother to give you another beating, or indeed administer it myself, but it seems that such punishments have little effect on you. I have been on the receiving end of many such beatings and I know that they are sometimes inefficient."

His hand reached out and grabbed me around the wrist, his voice dropping to a hiss.

"You have once again ignored my strict instructions and *invaded* my personal space. I cannot fathom whether it is stupidity or intelligence on your part, but whichever it is, it ends *here*."

I couldn't break my eyes from his blue-green gaze, the mask doing little to hide the fury that I could sense shimmering just beneath the surface of his words.

"Return to your dormitory. *Do not* attempt to use the hidden passageways, but pray to God, Meg, that you reach there before I do. Run, little Meg!" His voice became a bellow, a command. "*Run!*"

I wrenched my wrist from his grasp and ran, hearing laughter follow me as I exited Box Five and pushed open the door of the auditorium. Get back to my dormitory—which way was the quickest? Backstage, through the ballet rooms, into the domestic apartments and up from there. I ran as if he brandished a whip behind me, pushing through crowds that seemed to appear from nowhere, through familiar rooms where ballet classes were in mid-progression, away from the decoration and glamour that the opera patrons saw and into the more sparsely decorated living areas. I had no idea what awaited me, but this was one order I did not dare to disobey. On! On! Up!

Here was the staircase that led all the way up to my dormitory, with its dangerous handrail that I paid little heed to as I took the steps two at a time. I could hear a banging sound when I was on the second landing and my mind filled with visions and questions. The banging noise grew louder the further I went up the stairs, and I felt the chill that told that the corridor's window was open. I reached the top of the stairs, panting, looking both ways along the corridor. Something was suspended outside my dormitory door, swinging in the breeze from the window and banging into the wall. Despite the sweat running from me, I went cold when I saw what it was, hanging there like meat in a butcher's window. Figaro had a noose around his neck, his eyes open and blank as glass marbles in his face, jaw dropped, and his belly… God, his belly. The cat had been gutted, his entrails hanging out of him. On the wall beside the door there were

THE ANGEL'S SHADOW

smudges, which my horrified gaze realised were spatters of Figaro's blood. As I came closer, sick with horror, I saw that the blood was not just random, but formed letters, spelling out a word.

CURIOSITÉ

I don't know how long it was before I started to scream.

CHAPTER EIGHT

I remembered screaming. I remembered the hysteria rising through my body as I stared at the horrific message left for me outside my dormitory door. No... not mine, the dormitory I shared with Christine... Where was Christine? God, if he'd hurt her...

"I would never hurt Christine," he had told me once, while pinning me to the stage. How could I trust that? To see an attempted rapist killed quickly in front of me was one thing. This was something else... an innocent creature, displayed in blood and gore...

The bed I was in was not my own. It was bigger than mine and smelled different, but familiar, safe. Mother's bed. The heaviness of an extra blanket over me told me that when she had brought me here I must have been shivering. I fervently hoped that I hadn't vomited up there on the landing. My head felt light and my eyes wouldn't open; I felt as if I were drifting.

"Of all the things you could have done, that was incredibly cruel."

I could hear my mother's voice, near and yet far away at the same time.

"It was necessary." Another voice, golden and yet cold, *his* voice. God! Why was he here? Why couldn't I move or open my eyes or scream again? "Although I have to admit I did not anticipate such an... extreme reaction."

"Extreme? Perhaps if you'd been through what Meg has been through, your reaction would be the same!"

"Do not presume to lecture me on torment, Madame." The tone was dangerous. "I did what had to be done. The lesson needed to be taught, and by God if this one doesn't hit home I will devise something more terrible."

"When I lost my husband—"

"Many wives lose their husbands, Madame, and many children lose their fathers."

"He did it in front of her! And now you terrify her with the corpse of a domestic animal that has shown her nothing but affection!"

There was a long silence. I could hear my pulse beating like music in my head.

"That I *was* unaware of."

"Leave Meg alone."

"I *must* be cruel to be kind, it seems, when dealing with your daughter. I am to be punished for my one act of kindness in taking her to my house the night she was assaulted. I warned her, more than once, not to seek out my home, and yet she still does. There are traps in my catacombs, Madame, some of which are fatal. If you do not wish little Meg to disappear into one of them then I suggest you talk some sense into her where I have failed."

"After all I've done for you, you would threaten the life of my daughter?"

He let out an impatient sigh, and I heard his footsteps as he paced the bedroom, up and down in front of the fireplace. Was he still dressed as I had last seen him, in black and white and gold? My head swam...

"I am telling you *facts*, Madame Giry. Meg is very *lucky* that so far the only two entrances she has found do *not* contain lethal traps. Do you see? If she continues to pry about in the way that she has been, then she may well end up injured or killed. So *make* her *stop*, if the death of the cat has not already done so."

"She was lucky not to fall down the stairs."

"That was not my intention either; I meant no physical harm to the girl."

"No, you just meant to cause her psychological damage," she spat in return. "That may be far worse than you intended with your little stunt."

His footsteps ceased. "What did the doctor say?"

"He gave her something to help her sleep, and said to observe her closely. She should rest until tomorrow afternoon. There is a week to go until the opening night of the Gala, Monsieur, and if she has to miss it on account of what happened today I do not think even I can stop her from hunting you down."

"She is certainly persistent. But *why*? It's incredibly frustrating." The thump of a hand against the mantelpiece. "Whenever I have had to face this problem before it has been easily dealt with. Your Meg is something I do not understand. No one has ever faced my wrath and returned for more."

"Except Claude," Mother responded. "Meg is her father's daughter, and she loves Christine. All the while she thinks you are a threat to her, she won't stop trying to protect her."

His breath heaved in a sigh again and his footsteps resumed.

"The Angel of Music intends no harm towards Christine. How many..."

If I heard more, the subsequent drifting in and out of sleep has robbed it from my memory. Footsteps beat in my head with the rhythm of drums, the rhythm of my heart. There was singing in darkness and a kiss against my temple that felt strange, light, cold, the kiss of a ghost. *Papa?* Someone was stroking my hair gently and I felt the world reclaim me, mind and body reconnect. I opened heavy eyelids to find Mother sitting on the bed beside me.

"Welcome back," she smiled. My entire body went tense.

"Where is he?"

"Who?"

"The Phantom!" My eyes travelled wildly around the room, seeking out his shape, his mask. "He was here, I heard his voice!"

"Shh…" Her hand stroked my hair again. "Calm down, love. He was here, but he's gone now. You've been asleep for hours."

"He… he killed…"

"I know." She replied. "That was cruel."

"Where's Christine?" I suddenly panicked.

"Hush, Meg. Christine is having a costume fitting, she is perfectly safe."

I sat up slowly, realising that I was clothed in one of my mother's nightgowns.

"How long was I out?"

Mother glanced at the clock on the mantelpiece.

"Almost twenty four hours. Christine has been very worried about you."

"She didn't see—"

"No, no… Joseph Buquet cut… cut it down and cleaned away the… the message before Christine could see it. It was him who found you up there. He said you seemed to be having a fit…" Her hand traced the line of my cheek. "Meg…"

"No!" I snapped. "No doctors, no tests! I didn't have a fit, I just… I fainted." I felt the shiver go all the way down my spine, making my limbs tremble. "When I saw… I fainted."

Mother had brought a change of my clothes into her bedroom, and after I had washed, dressed and had a bowl of chicken soup, I felt much better. There was warmth here, and kindness…

Figaro strung up and disembowelled, a noose around my own neck, a masked man leaning over my sleeping friend…

I shook my head, blinking hard, trying to banish the darkness that swirled in my thoughts. It was dragging up more images that were to remain hidden, that were not to taint my present. Mother was watching me, her expression sad and firm.

"We can't go on like this," she said quietly.

"What do you mean?"

"You're afraid, Meg. Every waking moment, you are afraid, and I'm not saying it's not without good reason… the Opera Ghost has gone out of his way to protect his secrets, but yesterday he went too far… And yet, your fear does not seem to deter you from seeking him out… He has an… invitation to extend to you."

"An invitation?" I repeated. "What sort of invitation?"

THE ANGEL'S SHADOW

"He has offered to show you this home that you are so eager to see, in order to calm your fears and cease your prying."

"And he made this invitation of his own free will?" I asked doubtfully. The Opera Ghost who had laid commands, threats and violence at my feet in order to keep me away from his home was suddenly inviting me into it?

"He makes it at my request," Mother sighed. "And I request that you accept it. These last few weeks… things can't carry on in that way. I saw the effect it was having on you."

I shook my head. "No. He has made his point perfectly clearly, I am to keep away from his home and all the little tricks that seem to be scattered about this place."

But, oh God, Christine…

"He can continue his… haunting without my interference."

"And how long will that last, hmm? How long before your curiosity once again gets the better of you? What if this time you end up drowning yourself in the lake—"

"You know about the lake…" I said quietly, and the faintest pink coloured her cheeks. "Oh, Mama, what haven't you been telling me?"

Mother was the middle man between the Phantom and I. She begged and argued with me, and with him I think, before we both agreed that I would be shown the home he lived in beneath the Opera House, across the lake. It was to be on Sunday, when Christine—and many other members of the company—would be absent from the building, for Mass if not for the entire day. He would provide me with a meal and return me to my dormitory. Every week Christine tried to talk me into attending Mass with her, and every week I refused, Christmas Day being the only exception.

That Sunday I bid Christine goodbye as she left for church, then stood outside my dormitory door, keeping my eyes firmly away from the wall where Figaro had been displayed in such a gruesome fashion. The wall had been freshly painted and the odour still hung in the air, a reminder in itself of what the paint was concealing.

The trapdoor at the end of the corridor opened with barely a sound, a square of light seeming to emerge from the floor, and with my heart hammering, I walked slowly towards the it and began the journey down once more, descending the steps towards the glowing light. The Phantom was standing at the bottom of the first flight, holding a lantern. He nodded to me, a stiff inclination of the head, and held the lantern out to me.

"Hold this, please."

I took it and he swept past me, up the stairs I had just come down. An instant of panic pulled a gasp from my lips as I divined that he meant to leave me here in the dark; indeed, the trapdoor at the top of the staircase

51

was closing, the natural daylight banished into the gold flicker of the lantern. The thought had no sooner crossed my mind, however, when I heard his footsteps again and saw him returning.

"What's wrong?" He demanded, seeing my expression.

"I thought, just for a second, that you were going to trap me here."

"What must I do to earn your trust, Meg Giry?" The question came out as a snap.

"Stop trying to frighten me?" I suggested.

"Watch your footing," he said after a moment. "Some of the steps are uneven and you wouldn't want to twist an ankle."

"You're not going to blindfold me again?"

"There is little point," he growled. "Since you have seen the route already. Keep hold of the lantern."

"You don't need it?"

"My eyes are accustomed to the dark. Come."

I followed him carefully down the stairs, my eyes flicking between the back of his head and my own feet. I found myself wondering how he kept the mask on, as there were no fastenings that I could see, but did not have the nerve to ask. He did not speak as we went deeper into the hidden underworld of the Opera House, his pace steady but swift, not allowing me more than a passing glimpse of further tunnels, corridors and staircases. I stumbled at one point, sending the lantern light skittering across walls and ceiling, and his arm flew out to prevent my fall.

"I told you to watch your footing!"

"I'm sorry. I'll be more careful."

We continued downward, my mind wandering as I lost count of the floors we had passed, until we reached the underground lake. There was a boat bobbing on the surface, tied to an outcrop of rock. The Phantom took my hand, helping me into it like a gentleman in a romance novel, indicated with a jerk of his chin that I should set the lantern in the bow of the boat, then climbed in himself and took up the oars. His silence was beginning to unnerve me as we were propelled through the water with apparent ease.

"How am I supposed to address you?" I asked, swivelling to look at him. "And please don't suggest 'Master'. Even if I were in service I don't think I could abide it. It makes me think of chains."

His eyes flicked to mine, then over my head to the route, rowing methodically as if in response to a drumbeat only he could hear.

"'Monsieur' is, I believe, the appropriate way for a young woman to address a stranger."

"You are not a stranger."

"Am I not?" A quirk of the eyebrow.

"I have heard about you from childhood, Monsieur."

"And yet you still show me no respect."

I sighed. "One of my many faults. When the highest of all authorities fails you, you lose faith in all others as well."

I pressed my lips together, and his head tilted like a bird's.

"You are a most perplexing girl."

"The mighty Opera Ghost, and he thinks of me as the riddle?"

We didn't speak again as he guided the boat expertly towards a huge portcullis.

"Eyes front!" He ordered as my curious gaze sought for the mechanism to open it. I obeyed, and watched as the portcullis rose ahead of us and the boat glided underneath. He manoeuvred the boat into the small harbour, illuminated by a few candles alight in candelabras, and stepped out to tie it off onto a wooden jetty. The small vessel rocked as his weight left it, and once it was secured, he reached out to help me disembark.

"Thank you," I said, genuinely grateful to be back on firm land. "You do that every time you want to leave or arrive? It seems rather elaborate."

"It is an efficient way of keeping others away."

"But it can't be the only way of getting here…"

He gave me a sharp look and I closed my mouth, wondering if he were considering pushing me into the lake. Instead, he gestured for me to follow, walking off the jetty and past uneven stone walls, around the corner to where there was an honest-to-God front door. He pushed it open, and stepped back to allow me through.

"Welcome to my home."

The room I entered looked like a cross between a cave, a stage set, and the drawing room of a manor house. Rough stone walls were hung with pictures and tapestries, including some drawings that I presumed to be the work of the man now standing behind me. Gas lights were affixed to the walls at regular intervals, looking surprisingly modern against the stone. There was a large fireplace in one wall, and I realised that the chimney must connect to another fireplace further up. I had lost my bearings on the journey, and for all I knew this fireplace might share a chimney with the one in Mother's office. There was a rug in front of the fire that may have been Persian, two small tables each holding an oil lamp, a third holding a vase of red and white roses. The chairs were an odd assortment; two armchairs, an ottoman and one huge throne-like seat. There was a grand piano in one corner, facing out into the room so that the pianist would be looking towards his audience, sheets of music scattered over it. I chuckled when I saw two violins on the wall, one on either side of the fireplace, their bows crossed above the mantelpiece the way swords might be hung in a gentleman's home. Against the wall opposite was a sideboard holding decanters and glasses, and a bookcase absolutely crammed with titles.

The Phantom stepped around me and opened a door, opposite the one I had entered through. A dining room greeted me, gas-lit again, the table set for two.

"You can cook?" I asked, surprised. He gave me a look that seemed to be questioning my intelligence.

"I live alone, girl. Who do you imagine would prepare my meals if not myself? The kitchen is through there, the pantry beyond it." He gestured to my left. "And the doorway on your right leads through to the hallway. Off that is the bathroom, my bedroom, and the Louis-Philippe… my music room."

"Music room?" I repeated, my interest peaked further. "May I see it?"

"You may not. I have invited you here today in order to assuage your curiosity, but that does not mean I am losing all my privacy to you."

I blushed under his glare, honestly ashamed by my rudeness.

"How many instruments do you play?" I asked, hoping to get onto a safer topic. He paused, his eyes glazing over for a moment as he pondered the question.

"At least four," he replied. "Without counting the human voice as an instrument. I never learned to play a wind instrument, though… perhaps I should look into the purchase of a flute…"

He was looking at me without actually seeing me, until I shifted uncomfortably and his eyes regained their focus.

"And you, Meg? Do you play any instruments apart from the piano?"

"How did you…? Of course. You have been observing me since infanthood, and in that case, Monsieur, you already know the answer to that question."

"Just the piano, then." He said and gave a small sigh. "Do be seated. I will bring the food through."

I sat, and he returned carrying a covered dish, a couple of cloths protecting his hands from the heat, with a plate of bread balanced on the lid. His posture and movements were so graceful that the plate did not even wobble, and I found myself wondering if he had ever been a dancer as well as a musician.

The meal turned out to be a stew of beef and vegetables, and we sat opposite each other in uncomfortable silence, my eyes scanning the room as I chewed.

"What are you thinking?" He asked at last, sounding irritated.

I hesitated, trying to find the best way to phrase my reply.

"I am thinking… that this is not how I expected the Opera Ghost to live."

"Oh? And what were you expecting, pray? Dark, damp caverns illuminated by dozens of candles and no modern conveniences?"

I shrugged and nodded, and he gave a small smile and shake of the head.

"Such accommodation would not be conducive to adequate living conditions."

THE ANGEL'S SHADOW

"No," I agreed slowly. "I suppose not." My eyes travelled the room again. "This is… a house, a home like that of a gentleman… Not that I've seen a gentleman's home…down here in the Opera House. I suppose the gas pipes go through the whole building, the fireplaces must connect to other chimneys… Someone designed and built this to be a home, it's not like you've just converted some unused cellar space, this place was always meant to be lived in… and the building is… what, twenty five years old?"

He was no longer eating, his eyes boring into mine.

"I suppose I am wondering what sort of person would choose to design and build a home beneath an Opera House in the 1870s, and then to hide it away with trapdoors and hidden passages."

"If you have finished eating, perhaps we should retire to the drawing room."

I nodded, dabbing at my lips with my napkin, knowing he was not going to divulge any further information. It was frustrating, to be right here in the heart of his domain, and yet still know so little. At the same time I did not want to cause him to lose his temper.

I followed the Phantom into the drawing room, and watched him as he moved to the sideboard.

"Wine?"

"Yes please."

I listened to the clink of glasses as ran I my fingers over the spines of the books crammed into the bookcase.

"French, English… Italian… is this one in Spanish?"

"It is." He came over with my glass of wine, a tumbler of brandy in his other hand. "*Come è il tuo italiano,* Meg?"

"*Abbastanza buono,*" I replied, concentrating hard. "*Per capire La Carlotta quando lei ha… una vestibilità.*"

"'A fit'?" He repeated. "'To understand La Carlotta when she has a fit?'"

"Of temper." I clarified. "A tantrum."

"Ah. *Una crisi di nervi.*"

"If you say so."

"I didn't think you would be interested in languages, little dancer."

"Well, we're a multi-lingual company." I took a sip of wine. "And I learned that it is better to understand what is being said before repeating it." I stared unseeing at the books in front of me. "The last time my father took his belt to me was when I said something to him in German that turned out to be one of the worst insults under the sun."

"What did you say?" He asked with a spark of interest, and I looked up.

"Something I'm not going to repeat in front of you. What's this… squiggly language?"

"That is Arabic. It's used in the Middle East."

"And you can read it?"

"No." He rolled his eyes. "I think the patterns are aesthetically pleasing. Of course I can read it."

He sat down in the throne-like chair in front of the fire, as I blinked at him in surprise. Sarcasm? It was new to hear sarcasm from him without a hint of anger. I chose an armchair, watching the flames reflected in his eyes.

"Christine is teaching me Swedish."

"*Ja? Och hur går dina lektioner?*"

"Is there any language you *don't* speak?" I asked with a hint of annoyance, and the ghost of a smile crossed his lips.

"Chinese."

His posture had changed at the sound of Christine's name; he seemed to have tensed, his fingers moving restlessly on the arm of his chair.

"You are a great teacher to her, Monsieur. Her voice gets better every day. And so does her confidence."

He inclined his head at the compliment.

"She is a natural star, and has a shining future ahead of her."

He shifted in the chair and I looked away, into the fire, embarrassed.

Just from speaking of her? What sort of power does she have over him?

His fingertips beat out a rhythm.

"May I play your piano?" I blurted, and immediately wished I hadn't. I couldn't play in front of him. He looked at me in surprise, but nodded.

"If you wish. Do you play for Christine?"

So much for changing the subject.

"She asks me to sometimes, when she is practicing." I replied, moving across the room to sit on the piano bench.

"Good," he followed me and I wished he had remained seated. "I am glad to hear she is practicing outside of her lessons."

"She works very hard," I began to say, but then, as he stood by the instrument, hands behind his back, I noticed a line of red running down towards his lip. I stood, reaching out.

"Your—" A gasp cut off the rest of my words as he seized my wrist in mid-air, his grip so tight my skin went white around his fingertips.

"Attempt to remove my mask and I will attempt to remove your arm. Do you want to go first?"

CHAPTER NINE

"I wasn't going to—"

"*Liar!*" His eyes were blazing with fury. I stayed very still, as if he were a rabid dog.

"Your nose is bleeding."

"What?" Confusion flickered over his rage.

"Your nose is bleeding," I repeated. "Left side. That's why I reached out."

He stared at me as we stood in front of the piano, his hand vice-like around my wrist.

"Your nose is bleeding and I am losing the feeling in my fingers."

He let me go, his hand going to his nose, a look of surprise coming over him when he saw the blood on his fingers. I rubbed my wrist, knowing there would be bruising. I wondered if he had intended to hurt me, or if he simply didn't realise how strong his grip was.

"Excuse me."

He stalked from the room, through the door that led into the dining room. The abruptness with which his mood changed was what worried me the most, the snap from fluid grace to sharp violence. If he was truly unaware of his own strength, he could hurt Christine without meaning to. With a little trepidation I crossed the room and drained my wine glass, before returning to the piano and sinking down onto the bench. I ran my fingers gently over the keys, wondering how much it cost and how it had been transported here. There had to be another way apart from crossing the lake; the grand piano would never have fitted in the Phantom's boat. I picked out a few notes, breathing deeply, and as I calmed I found my way back into the familiar tune my father had taught me, half a duet that could never be whole again without him.

"Claude Giry taught you well."

I jumped, stopping mid-bar. I had closed my eyes, letting the music surround me, and lost track of how long I had been playing the piece. The

Phantom was leaning against the doorframe of the dining room, the blood cleaned from his face. He was holding a cloth and a bottle of that now-familiar gypsy potion.

"That's kind of you to say, Monsieur, but I will never even be half the pianist that he was."

He approached slowly, and I realised that I had tensed again, that the leisurely pace was intended to calm me. I rolled my shoulders self-consciously.

"Your father was an exceptional musician."

"Did you know him?"

"A little." He placed the bottle and cloth on top of the piano. "You are very much like him."

"I've been told that before," I nodded. "I inherited his hair colouring, his skin tone, his eyes… even his jaw line. Mother certainly sees him in me."

"True, but I wasn't referring to your physical characteristics." He rounded the piano bench and then sat on it beside me. "Like you, he was a person who pried about where they weren't wanted. He and I did not get on."

My heart was pounding again. Gently, very gently, he lifted my hand from the keys, turning it over to inspect my wrist. I wanted to clench my fingers together and pull away, to do something that would distract from my sudden fit of trembling. He passed a cold fingertip over the marks that were to become bruises over the next few hours.

"Forgive me."

I wondered what he was asking forgiveness for; these bruises, or the ones flaring anew within my soul. He upended the bottle of liquid over the cloth and began to dab at my wrist.

"What did you do to my father?"

"Do? Nothing. I may have sent a threatening note or two, but he never found the secret passageways you found, girl. He never made it into my realm."

"Why are you doing this?" I asked.

"Doing what?"

"Trying to repair the damage you caused me? With this potion of yours?"

"Because, Meg, this is damage I did not intend to cause. Had I realised you were not intending to remove my mask I would not have grabbed you the way I did."

"You certainly go to extreme lengths to protect your anonymity."

He paused, looking up from my wrist with a surprised expression.

"You think that is why I wear a mask? Because I want my identity to remain unknown?"

"Yes…" I said, uncertainty clouding my assumption. "And because you won't tell me your name. In the operas, people who wear masks and won't reveal their names are always trying to keep their true identity a secret."

"Operas…" He repeated the word in an amazed tone of voice, shaking his head as if he could not believe what I had just said to him, then went back to bathing my wrist. I was annoyed by his tone but forced myself to remember that I was supposed to be on my best behaviour.

My free hand went back to the piano keys, picking out the notes of an old song. Another moment and he let go of my hand, re-corking the bottle of potion, and my fingers went back to the piano, picking up the melody, the feel of the music.

"You wear the same cologne." I said.

"Cologne?" I didn't have to look up; the confusion was there in his voice.

"As my father." I kept my eyes fixed on the piano keys, simple, black and white, and yet able to produce such complexities. "It's what I remember most about him. It's what remains of him. Mother still has the cologne in her bedroom, she still has some of his clothes in the wardrobe. I remember Papa's voice, his smile, what he looked like… but his smell is what I remember the most. Does that sound strange?"

"No, Meg."

I still didn't look at him, but his own hands came down on the piano keys and I realised I had started to play that incomplete duet again, memory guiding my fingers without my conscious mind noticing. He was playing as well, the lower part my father had played, playing it by heart. The music was lulling, the wine I had consumed muddling my thoughts, loosening my tongue.

"This was one of his favourite songs. It's from *The Bohemian Girl*, and he used to sing it to me… it's beautiful and sad at the same time… like him…"

My eyes closed and I breathed in the scent of the man beside me… different, yes, but familiar, the cologne a thread to my past.

Stop this, Meg… stop playing, stop talking…

"He was happy when he was involved with music… he was happy with Mother and I… he would play with me, laugh with me, teach me… but then it would all go wrong… He would suddenly… stop being himself. He didn't want the music anymore, he didn't want Mother or me… and he was so sad or angry… and I never knew why, or what caused him to change. One day he was happy, the next he was sad… and then a little while later he was happy again."

I had longed for those happy days, delighted in them, relished every moment that we had together, always afraid that the strange anger and sadness would snatch him away from me, like a demon pouncing on him from out of the darkness.

The music had stopped, my hands were frozen on the piano, and the Phantom's voice, when he spoke, was soft and lyrical.

"Is that when you swore at him in German? During one of his... sad times?"

I nodded.

"He'd been so distant for days... not speaking, not eating... I don't even know if he slept. It was like we weren't a part of his life anymore, and I tried everything I could think of to reach him, to bring him back to us. The German... I don't know what came into me. He was sitting on his bed, staring at nothing, and I just screamed it at him, knowing it was vile, even if I didn't know the literal translation..."

"And what happened?" His voice was so soft...

"He... he stared at me as if he didn't know me... and then he grabbed the belt that was on his nightstand, and... I've been punished before, of course I have, and what I said... God knows discipline was deserved ... But never like that. Never in such anger, with such force..." I remembered the sounds of the belt going through the air, and of my own screams. "Mother stopped him. She took the belt away from him and threw it on the fire, and he turned and was going to hit her... and then he just broke down, started crying... I'd never seen him cry before... It was after that... he went into hospital. The doctors said they could make him happy, make him... normal... but they tortured him!" I could feel myself shaking; I had pulled at the thread of my past and now everything was unravelling. "They *tortured* him! He told me what they did to him, what they called treatment and medicine... and when he came home... it was as if they'd sucked out his soul..."

"Meg," cold hands were taking hold of mine. "Meg, stop. I shouldn't have asked—"

"I'd left my ballet slippers in their bedroom and I went to find them, and he was sitting there on the end of his bed, the mirror in front of him... and he had a gun. Where did he get a gun? He was... praying and crying, with the gun up against his head, and then he saw me in the mirror. I... I was just standing there, staring... and he smiled at me. He smiled at my reflection in the mirror, and he said 'Look after Mama', and then he—"

"Stop it!" I was being held, shaken roughly by the shoulders. "Meg, look at me!"

The past swam in front of my eyes, and there was a masked man with one blue eye and one green eye, shaking me by the shoulders in a drawing room lit by fire and gaslight.

I twisted out of his grasp and stood in the middle of the Persian rug, trembling, staring at the Phantom still seated on the piano bench.

"Where were you?!" I screamed at him.

"What?" He stood up. "Meg, what are you talking about?"

"The day he died! The sixteenth of November 1886! The day he blew his brains out in front of his ten-year-old daughter! Where was the great Opera Ghost then?! Where was your protection, your intervention, your regard for my welfare? If I am your property, Monsieur Phantom, then why didn't you protect me from *that*?!"

I stood there, my breast heaving as my breath escaped me in choking sounds I only slowly recognised were sobs. The tears were running hot down my cheeks and my chest constricted as I clenched a fist against my heart.

"Dear God..." I moaned, and suddenly he was in front of me, his arms steadying me as I sank to my knees on the rug. "What have I said? What have I *said*? God, don't!" I tried to push him away. "Don't touch me!"

He withdrew slowly, watching me, and I pressed my hands against the rug, closing my eyes against the pattern that suddenly seemed nauseating. I could hear him moving, and after a moment there was a cold glass against my lips.

"Here, drink... it's just water, drink..."

I sipped the water, eyes still closed. My darkest secrets, my most terrible memories, ones I had been fighting to keep at bay for so long... and they had all come flooding out amid music, into the ears of a man who would surely use them to manipulate and control me.

"You said there was a bathroom?" I managed.

"Through here," his hand was on my arm.

"Don't!" I shook him off, blinking away more tears. "I'll find it myself!"

I ran from him, through to the dining room. The door to the left, he'd told me, into the hallway, and one of these doors. One a bathroom, one a bedroom, one a music room. I fumbled with the handle of the nearest door, pushing against it. It wasn't the bathroom, but a bedroom, and not the one I had seen on my previous visit. This room was beautiful, elegant, the walls covered with a paper of pink roses. Mahogany furniture filled it; a double bed, a wardrobe, a chest of drawers and a vanity table with a large oval mirror. It was all by the designer Louis-Philippe, which was presumably why the Phantom had begun to call it the Louis-Philippe room. The bedroom was intended for a woman, all the furnishings from the bedspread to the carpet shades of pink. I was clutching the doorframe, my eyes wildly searching. I could hear the Phantom's footsteps behind me, his voice raised in anger, but I didn't care, I had found what I was looking for. I staggered across the room and seized the chamber pot partially hidden under the bed, just in time for my rebelling stomach to empty itself.

When I had finished vomiting, I looked up to where the Phantom was standing in the doorway, his entire body tensed with barely controlled fury.

"Wrong door," I muttered, getting shakily to my feet with the chamber pot still clutched in my hands. He stepped aside to let me pass and pointed to the door at the end of the hallway.

"The bathroom is there. Clean yourself up and get back to the drawing room."

The bathroom was amazing, the way I imagined one in a hotel. There was a toilet, a sink and a full-sized bath, both with hot and cold running water, the walls covered in white tiles. I washed my hands and face, rinsed out my sour mouth, emptied the chamber pot down the toilet and rinsed that out as well.

When I returned to the drawing room, the Phantom was seated at the piano, pounding out chords as if the instrument had been refusing to comply with his musical wishes. He didn't look up as I entered, but just said:

"Oh, Meg Giry, what am I going to do with you?"

"I think you should take me back." I replied.

"Is that so?"

"I think that if that room you didn't want me to see is indeed a prison, it was not one intended for me."

There was an ugly discord from the piano.

"It is not a prison!"

"Then what is it?" I crossed to him, being sure to keep the instrument between us. He was breathing hard, his teeth clenched.

"It is a guest room."

"For Christine."

He stood up abruptly, but I stayed where I was, fighting the instinct to run.

"I'm not stupid," I said. "And I'm not as naïve as you think I am. The way you talk about her, the way you... react to her name... Christine *believes* that you are an angel. Even if she didn't, you're her teacher, and you're old enough to be her father."

"I don't need a lecture on morality from you, Mademoiselle!"

"Monsieur, please!" I begged. "Whatever plans you have for Christine's future... whatever your feelings are towards her... please don't try and—"

"Rape her?" He snapped, and I flinched, not having expected him to put it so bluntly. He looked at me in complete disgust. "Do you really think me capable of that?"

"I've seen you kill..." I whispered.

"To save *you*, you ungrateful harridan! To prevent *you* from being raped! Come here!" He rounded the piano and I darted away from him. "*Come here!*" He seized me by the upper arm. "Come on!"

He marched me though the dining room, through the hallway and into the bedroom designed for Christine. He slammed the door behind us and swung me around to face it.

"Now look!" He ordered. "Use those accursed eyes properly and look!"

THE ANGEL'S SHADOW

I stared at the door, trying to see what he wanted me to see.

"The lock!" He bellowed, when I took too long.

My gaze focused on the lock. The door handle was an elaborate gold affair with an ornate keyhole, and just below it, a bolt and chain. Once they were drawn, not even the Opera Ghost would be able to enter.

"Oh," I said weakly.

"'Oh'," he mimicked. "'Oh', yes, 'oh'. Your experience of men may be limited, girl, but I trust you will think better of me in future." He touched my chin, tilting my head to meet his eyes. "I have been called a monster, Meg, but I do have some moral boundaries. I would never force myself on Christine, or on any woman. Do you believe me?"

I looked at him for a long moment, considering.

"I believe you," I replied quietly. "Please take me home."

CHAPTER TEN

I lay in the darkness of my dormitory, listening to Christine's peaceful breathing. There was another far more luxurious bedroom for her beneath us, but only if she chose to use it. The Phantom was going to meet Christine face to face for the first time; he wouldn't say when, but I knew it would be soon. He would invite her to his home, and would not overstep his role as singing teacher. He promised me no harm would come to her. He promised.

I watched the patterns the moonlight made as it trailed through the thin curtains over the dormitory window. Sleep was pulling at me and yet I was afraid to submit; the memories that had been wrought from me today had been terrible and I was afraid of the dreams they would bring.

The only person I had told about my father's suicide was Christine. Of course, others within the company knew that Claude Giry had taken his own life, but none knew that I had been watching. There had been shock and sorrow all round, and Monsieur Lafevre had helped Mother pay for the funeral. And now I had told the Phantom.

"He did it in front of her!"

My eyes shot open. I had been dozing, and the words Mother had said to the Phantom after he'd killed Figaro, that I had overheard in my strange half-sleep, had suddenly rung loud in my mind. He had known about Papa's suicide, known that I had witnessed it, and made me tell him anyway. Or had he? No... he had told me to stop, and yet somehow the grief I had kept bottled up for six years had come pouring out of me. I rolled over in bed and pounded my pillow into a new shape, wondering what on earth had gotten into me. The past should stay dead and buried, not coming looming up out of the dark like a ship through fog. I had more important things to worry about.

THE ANGEL'S SHADOW

I slept in snatches that night, my dreams an intangible muddle, and both Christine and I woke up late. Today was the dress rehearsal for *Hannibal*, and it was as we were scrambling into our costumes for the first act that Christine gasped.

"Meg, what happened?"

"What?" I looked up from trying to untangle the ribbons that made up the skirt of my slave girl outfit.

"Your arm." She reached out to touch my upper right arm, and I saw a fresh bruise there.

Damn. It must have been from the Phantom dragging me for a second look at Christine's bedroom.

"It's nothing." I reached for the stage foundation in the drawer of my nightstand and dabbed it on carefully to conceal the bruise.

"Meg, has someone been hurting you?" Christine asked worriedly. "This... Patrice of yours? Surely not Madame Giry?"

"I said it's nothing." I told her. "Please, Christine... please don't ask questions. I swear to you there's no need to worry. This bruise was accidental."

I'd forgotten about my imaginary boyfriend. I was suddenly grateful that we were running late; there wasn't time for Christine to interrogate me. We hurried to the stage where the other dancers were already warming up. Mother gave us both an angry glare and I knew there would be lecture as soon as time permitted. We were midway through the first act of *Hannibal* when Monsieur Lafevre came walking onto the stage. Monsieur Reyer had already paused to correct the pronunciation of Ubaldo Piangi, but was nevertheless not pleased to be interrupted. He was always stressed just before an opening night.

"Monsieur Lafevre!" He reproached. "This is the muddle of a rehearsal!"

"Monsieur Reyer," Lafevre acknowledged the musical director, then my mother. "Madame Giry, ladies and gentlemen, I apologise for the interruption, but please give me your attention."

We all stopped, intrigued, and I realised that there were two other men with him.

"For some weeks now, people have been spreading rumours about me retiring as manager of the Opera Populairé. I can now confirm the truth of these rumours, and have the pleasure of introducing you to your new managers," he indicated each man as he spoke his name. "Monsieur Richard Firman, and Monsieur Gilles André."

Firman was a dark-haired man with an impressive moustache and an equally impressive build. According to the wardrobe mistress, the average height of the male performers in the company was five foot six inches, and a quick up-and-down glance estimated Firman to be about six foot. I could hardly remember seeing anyone else so tall... except, now I came to think about it, the Phantom.

There was a shifting of shadows over my head, in the flies, dust floating onto my shoulder. I looked, but saw nothing, except perhaps the ghost of movement.

André was of much more average height, grey hair thinning, but he had twinkling eyes and a friendly smile.

"You may be aware of these men," Lafevre continued. "Due to their success in the junk business—"

"Scrap metal, actually." André corrected.

"—Which has amassed them a great fortune."

"They must be rich," Lycette whispered excitedly.

"And it is our great honour to introduce a new patron," Firman said. "The Vicomte de Chagny."

The young man who walked onstage was quietly but expensively dressed. He had shoulder length blonde hair and blue eyes, and I judged him to be around twenty. At my side, Christine's attention was captivated.

"Raoul," she breathed, and I looked at her. Her face was alight, the way I saw her after an especially successful singing lesson. "We knew each other as children, when Father and I lived by the sea. You could say we were childhood sweethearts. He called me Little Lotte."

"Christine, he's so handsome..." I said truthfully, and I wasn't the only one who thought so. Every female eye in the room was turned to the Vicomte, and I could almost hear the collective heartbeat speeding up, the quickening of breath. I found myself wondering what I would look like on his arm. Poor, I decided with an inward sigh. Beautiful, perhaps, if looked at in the right way, but poor and uneducated.

"The Opera Populairé is world-renowned as a seat of operatic excellence," Raoul, the Vicomte de Chagny said to the assembled company. "And my brother, the Comte de Chagny and I, are proud to patronise it."

World-renowned? Lafevre must have done some sweet talking to these new managers and their patron. The Vicomte was introduced to Carlotta and Piangi, then graciously apologised for interrupting the rehearsal, and left without another glance at the ballerinas. I felt Christine's disappointment radiating from her like heat.

"He wouldn't recognise me," she said, more to herself than to me.

"He didn't see you," I assured her.

Mother indicated that the ballet should continue, and ushered our new managers out of the way. I could hear them discussing me as I danced, calling me 'that little blonde angel'. I'd never been referred to as angel before, but then they were distracted by Christine.

We finished the number, unashamedly lapping up the attentions of Firman and André, which did not impress La Carlotta in the slightest.

THE ANGEL'S SHADOW

"Why am I here?!" She cried in her melodramatic Italian accent. "All they want is dancing!" She stormed over to where Lafavre was telling Firman and André how much the Vicomte was looking forward to the Gala.

"I hope," she snapped. "That he is as excited by dancing girls as your new managers! Because I *will not be singing*!"

I looked at Christine and saw my own worry reflected in her face as Carlotta swept past us waving her arms.

Firman and André scurried across the stage after the soprano.

"Monsieur Reyer," André cried hurriedly, "Isn't there a beautiful aria for La Carlotta's character in the third act?"

Panic flooded me as I remembered my instructions. I glanced upwards, but still saw nothing, no black-clothed figure, no white half-mask. I tugged on Christine's arm, murmuring:

"Come on."

"Where are we going?"

"Just… come."

I led her downstage right as Carlotta started to sing. There was a rattle over my head and one of the backdrops plummeted down. I gave a shriek of fright, darting forward just in time to prevent it clipping my shoulder, pushing Christine ahead of me. Carlotta was not as lucky. The backdrop caught her against the backs of her legs, causing her to fall flat on her face with a cry.

"My ankle!"

"The Phantom of the Opera!" I blurted it out without thinking. Lafevre, Firman and André were gathered around Carlotta.

"Buquet!" Lafevre yelled into the flies. "What's going on up there?! For God's sake, someone could have been killed!"

Joseph Buquet marched onto the stage from the wings, passing me.

"Messieurs, I cannot tell you," he cried. "I'm afraid I wasn't at my post. There's no-one there, and no one could have passed me without being seen." His eyes met mine. "Unless he was a ghost."

"Signora," André struggled. "Accidents happen…"

It was the last straw for the soprano. She turned to the new manager, mimicking his words in a high-pitched tone.

"Until you find a way to prevent these accidents, you will not hear my voice in your precious arias!"

With a cry of farewell in Italian to her husband, she turned and swept magnificently off the stage. Say what you wanted about La Carlotta, she knew how to make a good exit. Piangi paused to throw one last insult at our new managers.

"Amateurs!"

Lefevre pursed his lips.

"I don't think there's much more I can do to assist you, gentlemen. Good luck. If you need me, I will be in Frankfurt."

The men looked into the wings, faces lined with worry and confusion. It struck me that this was not the best start to their first day of ownership. Mother approached the two bewildered men, holding a familiar black-edged envelope with a skull moulded of red wax.

"I have a message, Messieurs, from the Phantom of the Opera."

"The *who?!*"

"Our resident ghost," Mother explained. "If you please him, then the Opera Populairé will continue to thrive. He welcomes you to his Opera House—"

"*His* Opera House?!"

"—and commands that you continue to leave Box Five empty for his use..." she pointed to it with her cane. "And reminds you that his salary is due."

"His *salary?!*"

"Yes. Monsieur Lafevre used to give him twenty thousand francs a month."

"Twenty *thousand* francs?!"

"If you refuse his demands, then the Opera House and its patrons will suffer."

"Madame Giry," Firman snatched the letter from Mother and began ripping it up. "We were hoping to announce the new patronage of the Opera Populairé tomorrow night when the Vicomte de Chagny was to watch the Gala with us! But now we are going to have to cancel it as we have lost our leading lady!"

"There must be an understudy..." André looked around as though expecting a secondary diva to pop up from the orchestra pit.

"Understudy?!" Monsieur Reyer looked like he was about to have a nervous breakdown. "La Carlotta has never allowed us to insult her with the presence of an understudy!"

"We're going to have to refund every seat that has been sold, André!" Firman cried. "Every single seat!"

"Christine Daaé could sing it, Monsieur." I said, and they turned to look at the two of us.

"A chorus girl?" Something about Firman's patronising tone make my hackles rise.

"She's been taking lessons from a great teacher."

"Who?" He demanded, and Christine stared back at him.

"I don't know his name, Monsieur." She said eventually.

"Let her sing for you, Monsieur." Mother insisted. "She has been well taught."

"Meg, I can't sing it!" Christine gasped. "I haven't warmed up properly, the cadenza will be awful!"

"Christine," I took her hands. "You *can* sing it, beautifully. I know you can. And *he* knows you can."

"From the beginning of the aria then, Mademoiselle." Reyer instructed, and with a last nervous look at me, Christine moved centre-stage. Any doubts about her capability to play the role of Elissa had vanished by the time she had finished the song.

"A word with you, Mademoiselle Giry."

Joseph Buquet seized my elbow and drew me against the wall in the darkest part of the wings. After her song, Christine had been swept off to attend a fresh wardrobe fitting. Then, Reyer would want to go through the music with her. *Hannibal* was mostly an ensemble piece, the aria Elissa's only solo, but I was in no doubt that the Phantom would also want to spend time with his pupil.

"What do you want, Buquet?" I asked. "Blaming the Opera Ghost for your clumsiness, that's low even for you."

"I'm glad you mentioned that," he said.

"Your clumsiness?"

"The Opera Ghost." He leaned towards me and I could smell the gin on his breath. "I saw you."

"What are you talking about?"

"Yesterday, little Giry. I saw you in the company of the Opera Ghost."

I stared at him, unable to form a reaction, which was probably an admission of guilt in itself. I thought back, trying to work out when he could have seen us together. The previous day, the Phantom and I had stood in the Louis-Philippe room, staring at each other.

"I believe you," I told him. "Please take me home."

He had frowned down at me, and for a moment I thought he would refuse, but then he nodded and swept me through his home and to the boat. He had rowed me across the lake, mooring the small vessel where he had originally docked, and to my surprise, had headed into a different catacomb to the one that led straight up to the floor of my dormitory.

"Where are we going?" I asked, grabbing the lantern and hurrying after him.

"Assuaging your curiosity, little dancer."

He led me through another corridor, bereft of decoration apart from a gargoyle carved into the stone. I watched him, treading in his footsteps, observing his gait, his elegance. It was only a suspicion on my part, but if the Phantom had not designed these passages, he was close to the man who had. There was dust on the floor and with a start I saw a track in it, the paw prints of a cat.

"Yes." My companion turned to me and was watching me. "This is the passageway you found with your feline friend." The feline friend he had murdered, hung and gutted. "The staircase ahead leads to the concealed door you found."

"The one by the stage?"

"Quite so. You can find your own way from there?"

"Of course." I nodded, raising my eyes from Figaro's paw prints to the Phantom's face. He led me up the stairs and paused, listening intently. When he was satisfied that there was no sound from outside he opened the door, using his body to shield the mechanism from me. The light seemed blindingly bright, and I put down the lantern and stepped into it thankfully. He followed me out, raising himself from a crouch to his full height and closing the door behind him. He frowned, then reached out and started plucking at my hair.

"There is a cobweb in your hair," he said in response to my startled expression. "There." He blew it from my curls. "It seems my housekeeping leaves something to be desired."

"Why do you do that?"

"Do what?"

"Treat me like… I don't know. Sometimes you treat me like an enemy, sometimes like a pet, sometimes like… a daughter…"

He looked down at me, his face completely expressionless, and I swallowed hard, scrambling back onto firmer ground.

"I'm sure blackmailing Monsieur Lafevre and coaching Christine takes up much of your time." I said, and he gave a slight bow in acknowledgement of the mild rebuke. "Thank you for the meal."

I turned away and headed towards the backstage area, but his golden tones stopped me.

"Meg?"

"Monsieur?" I faced him once more and he approached, gazing at me intensely.

"You asked why I wasn't there the day your father died, why I didn't prevent you witnessing it. Those are questions I cannot answer. But I have one for you." He paused, his eyes searching mine. "Do you blame me for Claude Giry's death? Do you hold me responsible?"

I stared at him, knowing the question demanded an honest answer.

"I don't know." I said with a shake of my head. "I really don't know. Perhaps. Some days I blame the doctors at the hospital. Most days I blame myself."

"Meg!" He called my name as I started to run down the corridor away from him.

"Goodbye, Monsieur!" I called back without looking round, knowing he could easily catch up with me if he had wanted to, but he hadn't.

"Not denying it, are you?" Buquet's alcohol-laden breath rasped over my face. "Not denying that you and he were together?"

"You're absurd, Buquet." I said, pulling my arm free of his hold. "As if the Opera Ghost would want anything to do with me. I had no influence over Lafevre and I have none over our new managers. Whatever you have seen, I expect it was through the bottom of an empty bottle."

"I saw you," he insisted. "I saw the way he touched your hair. Been touching other places has he?" He pressed against me, a hand claw-like against my left breast. "Have you been honing your skills with that monster for the opening night in order to impress the punters?"

"I'm not like that!" I hissed. "I know... some of the girls do... lavish their attentions on the men who come to the operas, but not me! Do you really think so lowly of me? Or is it just your perverted view that any girl old enough to have breasts must be baring them for every man in her path?"

I shoved him away from me and he gave a little chuckle.

"*I'm* perverted?" He said. "I'm not the one letting a beast touch me."

"You've never described yourself so accurately before."

"Not *me*, little Giry. *Him.* Your Opera Ghost, your Phantom. Are you telling me you've never seen him without his mask? Does he keep it on when he takes you? Or are you telling me that you find such a twisted excuse for a face attractive?"

"Shut up."

"Ah, so it's *The Beauty and the Beast.* But this is no fairytale, little Giry. If you carry on like this, he will kill you."

"Let us assume," I said slowly. "That what you say is right, and I am sleeping with the Phantom of the Opera. How do you think he would react when I tell him that your filthy hands have been touching me? That you've made suggestive remarks? It's not my life you should be concerned for, you drunken old fool. It's yours." I shoved him hard again and strode past him, pausing only to issue one more threat: "Keep your hand at the level of your eyes."

CHAPTER ELEVEN

My hands clenched and unclenched as I marched away from Buquet, the burning filling my throat and eyes. I was *not* going to cry, Buquet was not worth my tears, and his assumptions were shared by half the men who attended the opera. No matter how much skill and training it took, women who performed onstage were viewed as little higher up the social ladder than whores, and indeed some women, flattered by the attentions of their rich spectators, did exchange their bodies for the attention. From there, many slowly sank into the dark underworld of prostitution. I prayed that such a fate did not await me, but I knew that I would have to deal with unwanted attention my entire life. I could not let men like Buquet upset me so.

We ran the entirety of *Hannibal* again with Christine in the role of Elissa and a man named Tobias singing the part that Piangi had abandoned. Her absence from the *corps de ballet* did not have any negative impact upon the dances and the aria of the third act was the highlight of the rehearsal. Reyer, Mother and the director made us go through the numbers again and again, and by the time six o'clock arrived I was exhausted. When we were dismissed at last, I helped Christine carry her new costumes from the crowded ballerina's dressing room, to the private one that Carlotta had vacated. It was almost as big at the one fifteen ballerinas shared, and contained a vanity table, chaise longue, a rail upon which to hang the costumes, and a number of small tables. Every surface was covered with roses, red, white and pink, arranged in vases. Against the far wall was an enormous mirror, the same size as the door. No doubt it was there at Carlotta's insistence, but it made me nervous; I no longer trusted mirrors to be what they appeared to be.

With the costumes hung on the rail, Christine gazed around the room.

"Oh, Meg," she murmured. "This is all happening so fast."

"It is," I agreed. "But you are the perfect Elissa, and I have no doubt that this role will lead to others." I hugged her tightly. "Have confidence,

Christine. I know you'll do wonderfully."

"*Christine...*" The musical whisper seemed to come from all around us and I let go of my friend.

"I should go," I said. "You'll want some time to rehearse, I expect. I'll see you tonight in our dormitory."

Christine hesitated. "I might be late..."

"I'll wait up," I told her firmly, glancing at the mirror. "See you later."

And with those words, I left Christine in the company of her Angel of Music.

It was gone eleven by the time Christine returned to the dormitory. As I had promised, I was sitting on my bed, reading by candlelight, in my nightgown with a shawl wrapped around my shoulders. Christine gave me a tired but genuine smile.

"You didn't have to stay awake for me, Meg." She said.

"I wanted to." I swung my legs off the bed and passed her a plate of bread, cold meats and cheese. "I thought you might be hungry."

"I am, thank you." Christine took the plate and sat on the edge of her bed. "When I'm having a singing lesson, I forget about everything else, including food. The music just... takes over."

"I know the feeling." I said, and she smiled. "How did the lesson go? Do you feel more confident now?"

"Much," she nodded, still smiling. "He made me work hard, but it is worth it. He wants the best out of me tomorrow night, and when he praises me..."

I raised my eyebrows at the dreamy expression on her face. She finished eating, dressed in her nightgown, and had just climbed into bed when I sat on the end of it.

"The entire Opera House is buzzing about our new patron, and it appears you've met him before..."

She smiled, starting to work her dark curls into a braid over her right shoulder.

"And you want to get ahead of the gossip?"

"Tell me about the Vicomte de Chagny. You said you were childhood sweethearts?"

"In a way." She looked into the middle distance, arranging her thoughts as her fingers continued to braid her hair. "It was just before Father died. We were living in a cottage on the coast of Northern France, our money earned by Father's music. He would play the violin and I would sing. The locals called us 'The Swedish Songbirds'." She smiled at the memory. "Father liked to paint, with watercolours, and we would go to the beach when we weren't working. That summer, the de Chagnys were holidaying there—they'd bought a villa in the area. The boys—Philippe and Raoul—had a Swedish tutor, who approached us when he heard that we were speaking his language."

"How old were you?"

"Six. Raoul was ten and I think Philippe had just turned fifteen. Raoul and I were playmates that summer. I remember I had a red scarf... Father had written a song called *The Girl with the Red Scarf* that we would perform, and he'd bought me this scarf as a prop. It was so rare to get something brand new, I loved it. One day, on the beach, the wind whipped it away and into the sea. I was devastated, so Raoul ran into the waves, fully dressed, to fetch it back. He got quite a beating for ruining his suit. I saw the bruises..." Her voice trailed off.

"And... Little Lotte?" I prompted. "I would have thought Lotte was short for Charlotte, not Christine."

She tied the braid off with a ribbon, and hugged her knees through the blankets.

"When the weather changed, we would go into the attic of our house, and play or read. Raoul would tease me because I could never decide which I preferred: dolls, goblins, shoes, riddles, frocks, chocolates..." she gave a little laugh. "It changed every day. We would have picnics up there and Father would play the violin... and he would tell us stories about a girl called Little Lotte. Little Lotte had a heavenly voice and was visited by the Angel of Music... Raoul told me that I was Lotte, and Father promised he would send me the Angel of Music..."

I swallowed. "And so... Little Lotte became his pet name for you? Because of the stories?"

"Yes." She nodded.

"And that was the only time you met?"

"Yes... but it was a memorable summer. We haven't seen each other since. Father died that winter, I came here, Raoul joined the navy. That's all I know... I don't know what happened to Philippe, or their parents. It's strange, to see him after so long."

She was silent for a long moment, and I rose to my feet.

"We should get some sleep. Big day tomorrow."

She nodded, and I leaned forward to hug her.

"Sweet dreams."

I blew out my candle as she was crossing herself, and lay down just as her voice began murmuring:

"*Vår far, i himlen...*"

I slid the last of the hair crystals into Christine's curls and smiled at her reflection in the mirror on the vanity table.

THE ANGEL'S SHADOW

"There. Finished."

Christine looked stunning. The costume she wore in the third act had been meant for Carlotta, but hadn't been finished in time for the diva to wear it. Nevertheless it had been the work of a sleepless night to alter it to fit Christine's frame. It was a white corseted dress with a full skirt, decorated with silver stars. Her earrings and the crystals in her hair were also star-shaped, and she seemed to glitter with every movement.

"Thank you, Meg." She whispered, and I put my arms around her shoulders, hugging her from behind.

"You look so beautiful. Like a fairytale princess."

She rubbed my arm, smiling at me.

"Are you ready?" I asked.

"Yes," she took a deep breath. "Oh, Meg…"

"Butterflies?"

She nodded. "The rest of the show has gone so well…"

"And your solo will be the jewel in the crown." I kissed her on the cheek as she turned to me. "Good luck, Christine."

She kissed my cheek in the return and we left the dressing room together. I watched from the wings as she performed the aria, Mother behind my shoulder, stroking my hair. Christine belonged in the spotlight, not hidden amongst the ballerinas; she shone. I had looked up towards Box Five during the opening act, and had been surprised to see that it was occupied, and not by the Phantom. Instead, the Vicomte de Chagny had been sitting in the Box, gazing down at the stage, accompanied by a man who was very similar in appearance, but older and with a fair moustache, and I presumed this was Philippe, the Comte de Chagny. I found my eyes travelling around the small part of the auditorium I could see from my place in the wings, and hoped that the Phantom was watching from somewhere, and appreciating his pupil's performance. She deserved his praise and his admiration. Even if he were not satisfied with it, the audience were on their feet, applauding wildly. Christine looked surprised for a moment before dropping into a deep curtsy, and as the curtain came down, all the ballerinas rushed over to congratulate her. We had to abandon our hugs and words of encouragement when the curtain rose again, and Christine blinked in the fresh glare of the lights before acknowledging the continuing applause. Someone pressed a bouquet of roses into her hands. We fell on her again once we were sure that the curtain call was over, and I managed to get one hug in before Mother came marching onto the stage.

"Yes, you did very well," she said to Christine, scattering the rest of us like doves in our white tutus. "He will be pleased with you. And *you!*" She rounded on us with venom in her eyes. "That performance was absolutely *disgraceful!* Have you learned *nothing* during our rehearsals?! Well, we shall continue to rehearse until you get it right! Come along, *now!*"

75

It was an hour before I could get away from my mother's scolding and her biting glares, and another ten minutes before I discovered Christine in the Opera House's small chapel.

"*Christine...*" I heard his voice as I entered the room, but Christine was alone in the circular space. She was kneeling on the floor, her white skirts billowed around her, holding the charred taper she had used to light the candle. Gustave Daaé's portrait was attached to the candle holder, showing a dark-haired, handsome man with beautifully defined cheekbones, who looked too young to have left this world.

"So this is where you've been hiding." I knelt beside my friend and gave her a hug. "You were perfect tonight, Christine, absolutely perfect. If I could sing like you..." I smiled.

"It's thanks to my tutor... to the Angel of Music..." she smiled back. "He's here, now. I can feel him."

I could feel his presence as well, a faint humming in the air around us as if someone were playing a violin too high-pitched to hear. I took Christine by the hand and helped her to her feet.

"Have you seen him yet? Have you met your Angel?"

She shook her head, letting me lead her to her dressing room. I unlaced the ribbons binding her into the costume and helped her step out of the skirts, gathering the outfit up in my arms and hanging it up on the rail as she pulled on a dressing gown.

"I'm not crazy, Meg." Her voice was quiet and I turned to her in surprise.

"Christine, I never implied you were. I believe what you're saying."

She picked up a red rose that was lying on her dressing table, with a black silk ribbon tied around the stem.

"I think it's my father. He told me that when he died, he would send the Angel of Music to me. He promised."

My heart broke for her; to have her believe in an Angel was one thing, but to let her believe that the spirit of her father was communicating with her from beyond the grave was more than I could bear.

"Christine... no..." I began, but before I could say more the dressing room door burst open. Mother stood there, cane in hand, glaring like an angry raven. Christine and I both instantly stood to attention, backs straight, heels together.

"Meg Giry, are you a dancer?" She demanded and I gave a nod. "Then come and practice."

I slipped past her and out the door as she approached Christine.

"My dear, I was asked to give you this."

She closed the door behind her and followed me back to the practice room.

THE ANGEL'S SHADOW

* * *

Bed, I told myself as I climbed the stairs to my dormitory, the muscles in my legs protesting with every movement. *A wash in some hot water, and then to bed.*

The entire *corps de ballet* had worked extremely hard, knowing that the opening night of the Gala was the night we must be at our best. Those who came were the ones who would invest in the Opera House's future, and Mother demanded perfection from her dancers. She had been immensely displeased at what she termed our "sloppiness" and worked us until the bells of the nearest church were striking midnight. I wondered if it was just because I was her daughter that it felt like she was singling me out for more criticism than any of the others, whether it was all in my imagination or whether that was truly what she was doing. I hoped that the Phantom had been more lenient with Christine than Mother had been with me. From what I had seen from the wings, he had no reason to be displeased with her, but I had also seen his temper and hoped she would not trigger it.

I washed away my stage makeup and carried a bowl of cold water to my dormitory. When I opened the door, I was surprised to find Christine's bed empty. Surely the Phantom was not tutoring her this late into the night, even if he demanded the same level of perfection as my mother, and then my mind caught up to my aching body. Their introduction would be tonight, when she would at last see the masked face of her mentor. How would she react when she learned that her Angel and my Phantom were one and the same? Would he keep his promise to me and leave her unharmed?

I sat on my bed, peeled off my ballet slippers and sank my feet into the bowl of cold water, almost groaning with the relief it brought. With difficulty, but unwilling to stand again, I pulled my costume off over my head and reached under my pillow for my nightgown. My fingers touched thick paper, and with a sinking heart I pulled a black-edged envelope out along with the cotton nightwear.

Mademoiselle Giry was written on it in familiar, neat handwriting. I opened it and read the note inside.

Meg,
Your dancing was a lamentable mess.
O.G.

I scrunched the paper into a ball and threw it towards the window, calling the Phantom a name that would have earned me a clip around the ear if either he or Mother had heard me. What did he know? He may have been a superb violinist, pianist, vocal coach and master of any other unknown talents, but I did not think that dancing was one of them.

There was a shout outside and the dormitory door burst open.

"Christine?!"

The Vitcomte de Chagny was standing in the doorway, looking frantically around the room before his eyes landed on my half-clad form.

"Where is Christine?!"

CHAPTER TWELVE

"Monsieur le Vicomte!" I cried, grabbing at my nightgown to cover my modesty. The young man blinked, then blushed as red as a maiden, and turned his back.

"Mademoiselle, forgive me! I was given to understand that Mademoiselle Daaé lived up here."

"You were not misinformed, Monsieur." I replied, pulling the nightgown on over my head and wrapping my shawl around my shoulders. "But this is not the place to discuss my roommate." *Nor the time*, I added silently. "Please, give me five minutes to attire myself properly and I will join you in the foyer."

"Thank you, Mademoiselle."

Without looking back at me, he made his way to the staircase. I sighed deeply, took off my nightgown and pulled one of my day dresses over my head. I was tired and aching, and wanted nothing more than to crawl into bed and sleep, but the urgency in Raoul de Chagny's voice had tugged on my own thread of worry when I found Christine was absent.

I heard a voice as I entered the foyer, deep and berating.

"For God's sake, Raoul! It's gone midnight and you're waking up a poor ballet dancer because of some girl you met once when you were ten!"

"Christine recognised me, Philippe, she was pleased to see me! She wouldn't just abandon me!"

I cleared my throat to alert them of my presence.

"The Comte de Chagny, I presume?" I asked, joining them. The older man, slightly shorter than the Vicomte, turned and bowed to me.

"Mademoiselle, I must apologise for my brother's appalling invasion of your privacy tonight." He glared at Raoul. "He is not usually so ill-mannered."

"Apology accepted," I said with a tired smile. "How can I help you, gentlemen?"

"It's about Christine," Raoul explained redundantly, his blue eyes earnest. "I recognised her the moment I saw her onstage tonight, I sent her a note reminding her of our childhood together and she admitted me into her dressing room. We talked a little, discussed our past, and I invited her to dinner. I gave her some time to change, but when I came back, her dressing room door was locked. I thought perhaps she intended to meet with me here," he gestured around the darkened foyer. "Or perhaps outside... but I heard a voice through the door, a man's voice talking to Christine. I need to know she is safe!"

"I am sure she is," I told him gently. "When you invited Christine to join you for supper, what exactly did she say?"

"She... she made some excuse. Something about an 'Angel of Music'." He gave a strained smile. "It's a childhood joke between us, nothing more, but she seemed..." He shook his head.

"I know the story," I said. "The Angel of Music is the spirit of music incarnate, yes?"

"Yes..."

"It is also the name she gives her tutor. Monsieur, Christine's performance brought her to the attention of many people, all of whom will have wanted to speak to and congratulate her. One of those people is her tutor, and I have no doubt they are reviewing her singing this evening. She is in no danger, Vicomte, and will doubtless contact you tomorrow."

I spoke with far more confidence than I felt, but along with his brother urging Raoul to leave the Opera House, my words seemed to have the desired effect. Philippe apologised to me again and ushered his brother out of the building.

His concern had more effect upon me than I liked, however, and I found myself going to Mother's room and picking up the ring of keys she kept; keys that fitted every door in the Opera House. I went to Christine's dressing room and unlocked the door, opening it slowly.

"Christine?"

The room was empty and dark. I walked through it slowly, placing the keys on the vanity table, before my eye was caught by a narrow line of light at the far end of the room. The mirror, as I had feared, was not all it seemed to be. The glass seemed to have moved away from the left side of its frame, and as I put my fingers on the exposed edge of glass and pushed, it slid into the right side of the frame. I glanced behind me, and saw a red rose tied with a black ribbon lying on the floor in front of the mirror as if it had been dropped. Heart pounding, I stepped through the mirror's frame. On the other side, I found I could see straight through the glass like a window. He had been watching her, without her knowledge, and I felt my stomach knot as I remembered the other windows I had discovered in his catacombs. I was a fool not to have realised that this was one of them, and not just a window, but a door.

THE ANGEL'S SHADOW

The corridor beyond was damp, the walls covered in cobwebs which trailed over the brackets on the walls that held torches. One, further along, was still burning, and I headed towards it in the hope that light meant safety. Something touched my foot and I shrieked as a rat scuttled across my path, my heart almost stopping altogether when a hand came down on my shoulder.

Mother took me by the hand and marched me from the passageway without saying a word. I had no choice but to return to my bed, trying to convince myself of Christine's safety. He promised he wouldn't harm her. He promised.

I woke the following morning to find that Christine's bed had not been slept in, and by ten thirty the Opera House was in uproar. The role of Elissa was cursed—one actress had stormed out, the other had vanished into thin air. Although there was not another performance for a week, the managers were furious. The evening newspapers had discovered the story and questions were being asked that they could not answer. The Vicomte prowled the Opera House like a predatory animal, the night came and went, and still Christine had not returned. By the time a third day had come and gone, there was talk of involving the *gendarmes*; the de Chagnys had money, and it seemed Raoul wanted to invest his in locating Christine. For myself I had gone from being mildly concerned by my friend's absence to worried sick. There had been no sign from her, no word. What if she was unable to return? What if the Phantom's promise to leave her unharmed and unmolested had been nothing more than words?

It was just gone six o'clock in the morning on the fourth day of Christine's disappearance that I decided I could stand it no longer. I used the trapdoor by my dormitory, lantern in hand, and headed down until I reached the underground lake. Perhaps if I shouted, the Phantom or Christine would hear me; perhaps the lake was not deep and I could wade through it; perhaps...

The Phantom's boat was moored on my side of the lake. I stared at it, wondering why it was here; perhaps the Opera Ghost was stalking the corridors of the House again, perhaps he was even now returning Christine to her place among us.

I stepped into the boat, hung the lantern in its place, and picked up the oars. They were heavier than I was expecting and unwieldy, and the boat rocked as I struggled to make it move. After a few moments, I picked up the rhythm and began to row myself over the calm water, only disturbed by the ripples the oars were causing.

I was in the centre of the lake when my ears picked up on the music. It was a light, whispered singing that made my skin erupt in goose bumps and

81

seemed to come from the water itself. I found myself once again thinking of the book of myths I had read as a child, remembering a creature of such beauty that it lured sailors to it with its song, before drowning them. A siren… surely the Phantom did not have a siren guarding his lake? The music followed me, surrounded me, not alarming, but sweet and enticing, and I dropped the oars, leaning over the side to seek out its source.

I leant, the boat tipped, and before I could correct the balance two thin hands shot up from out of the water and grabbed me by the throat. I gave a brief scream before tumbling into the black, freezing lake, the hands around me dragging me down. Blind in the darkness, I struggled and kicked, trying to dig my nails into the fingers tightening around my neck, but my clothes were weighing me down, the skirts and petticoats constricting the movements I could make. The surface was far above my head and I couldn't touch the bottom of the lake with my feet. My lungs were on fire and with the dizziness engulfing me, I opened my mouth for air, and felt the water flooding into my lungs.

My chest and throat burned as I coughed and spluttered, water coming from my lips and running down my chin. I was lying on my back on the shore from which I had come. The Phantom was leaning over me, one hand on his mask as if he had just replaced it. He was fully dressed and as drenched as I was, and the moment my eyes opened he pushed me onto my side.

"Fool!" He bellowed, punctuating each word with a violent slap to my back, forcing me to cough up more water. "Stupid! Insolent! Disobedient! Child! I invited you to my home *once* at the request of your mother! That invitation did not mean you are free to come visiting whenever you wish, as if we were bosom friends! What in the name of the devil did you think you were doing?!"

"Looking for you!" I choked. "I didn't imagine that you would have a siren guarding your lake!"

"Siren?" He laughed and showed me a long hollow reed. "Here is your siren, little dancer! A silly trick I learned from a Tonkin pirate, which allows me to breathe and sing underwater."

I rolled onto my back, staring at the ceiling over my head, once again relishing my ability to breathe as the sheer joy of being alive raced through my veins.

"A 'silly trick' that nearly killed me!"

"Yes," he said, still smiling as he rose to his feet. The water dripped off him and onto my sodden form. "It seems that you owe me your life for a second time."

"Having almost been murdered by you for a second time!" I sat up, my entire body trembling. "In this accursed lake, and on the stage with your bloody noose around my neck!"

"It is not a noose, it is a Punjab lasso. And I do not appreciate such language from a lady." His smile vanished. "Think of that the next time you contemplate paying me a visit, my dear. I should hate to have to dedicate my Requiem Mass to you."

I struggled to my feet, furious with him beyond sense.

"I expect," I snarled. "That you have already dedicated it to Christine!"

"How *dare* you!"

"She's been missing for four days! What do you expect me to think?! You've either killed her or you're keeping her a prisoner!"

"Christine stays with me of her own free will! She *loves* me, Meg Giry! She can come and go as she pleases!"

"I don't believe you," I shook my head, and ruined the effect by sneezing violently.

"Your opinion is of no relevance to me." He turned and climbed into the boat. "Go back and dry yourself off, before you catch your death."

"Take me to Christine!" I demanded, rushing forward and grabbing at his arm. The boat rocked and he shoved me away.

"Go home, Meg, before I rethink my actions and finish my interrupted drowning of you!"

"Others will come looking for her!" I threatened. "The *gendarmes* have already been summoned. They will find you! Take me to Christine!"

He growled and lifted the oars in his hands.

"And how would your seeing Christine influence the actions of the *gendarmes?*"

"They are coming by request of the Vicomte de Chagny. They are coming because I was unable to prove to him that Christine is safe!"

He cursed under his breath.

"Get in."

I stepped into the boat, sitting at his feet as he rowed us across the lake, still muttering too low for me to hear. When he reached the lake house, he opened the door with a violent shove of his shoulder and strode inside, leaving me to follow in his wake. He went straight through the living room and dining room, into the hallway where he knocked on the door to Christine's bedroom with more gentleness than I expected of him.

"Christine?" He murmured. "Christine? Are you awake, angel?"

I stared at him, surprised by his tone and his endearment. Where was the Opera Ghost, all darkness and menace? I stood there, wrapping my arms around myself, shivering as the water dripped from my hair onto the carpet.

"Erik?" The door opened slightly and I heard Christine's voice. "Are you all right? You're—you're soaking wet..."

Erik? His name was Erik?

"I am fine, Christine," he assured her. "I'm sorry to disturb you so early. Your friend requires a change of clothes."

He stepped to one side so that Christine and I could see each other. She was clothed in a nightgown and dressing gown, and looked astonished when she saw me.

"Meg... what happened?"

"She fell in the lake," the Phantom replied smoothly before I could speak. "She came to look for you, it seems. I saved her life." He turned and gave me a glare, although his voice maintained its calm tone. "I must change. Excuse me, Christine. I will have breakfast prepared for you in twenty minutes."

I couldn't believe what I was hearing, and sneezed again. He swept past me and I felt Christine take my hands in hers.

"Come in," she said, drawing me into the Louis-Philippe room, closing the door behind us. She didn't lock it, I noticed. "Meg, you're shaking..."

She grabbed a blanket from her bed and wrapped it around me, rubbing my arms, sitting me down on the stool in front of the vanity table before going to the wardrobe and pulling out a blue dress.

"It'll be a little long for you, but it should do."

I tried to stop my trembling as I stripped off my wet clothes. I was astonished to see that the wardrobe was full of dresses, finer than anything either Christine or I had ever owned. She handed me fresh under garments, the corset in the style that laced at the front so that Christine would not need help to fasten it. I tried to imagine the Opera Ghost going into a ladies' outfitters in Paris and purchasing all these items—perhaps that is what the ludicrous twenty thousand francs a month he demanded was spent on—but the notion was just too bizarre. He must have someone else do his shopping for him... and the most obvious person would be my mother.

"Meg," Christine was gazing at me, her blue eyes radiating concern. "You're still shivering... come and sit by the fire in the drawing room."

I clenched my chattering teeth together as Christine took the hairbrush from her vanity table in one hand, my hand in the other, and led me into the drawing room. Someone, presumably Erik—*could that really be his name?* —had stoked up the fire and it was blazing brightly, filling the room with light and heat. I did as Christine asked, sitting on the Persian rug in front of the fireplace, and she began working the brush through my wet hair. I watched the flames, trying to organise my thoughts, looking for the subtlest way of finding out what kind of spell he had over her.

"Christine, what are you doing here?"

"He came to me after the Gala," she said, and I could hear the smile in her voice. "And he brought me here. He's been giving me more singing lessons, and I've been improving so much."

THE ANGEL'S SHADOW

"You know he's not an angel?" I asked, and twisting around to look at her. "Christine?"

"God works in mysterious ways, Meg." She said. "My father promised he would send me the Angel of Music, and he has. My angel has come to me in the form of Erik, a man."

"A man?" I repeated. "Christine, he's the Opera Ghost, the Phantom of the Opera."

"I know." She said quietly.

"And you're not afraid?"

"Why would I be? He has shown me nothing but kindness, Meg. I'm not his prisoner; Erik is not going to harm me."

"How can you know that?" I cried, unable to believe her naivety, and she put down the brush, taking both my hands as I turned to her, and rubbing the backs of them with her thumbs.

"Because he could have done already," she said. "I fainted just after he brought me here. If he had wanted to... to harm me, he would have done so while I was unconscious."

"No one knows where you are!" I told her, trying to keep my voice low. "Everyone is worried about you, there's talk of the *gendarmes* being called in to look for you." I studied her face, my mind registering what she had just said. "Why did you faint, Christine?" She looked away from me and I clasped her shoulders and gave her a little shake. "Christine! What did he do to you?"

"He didn't do anything," she insisted. "He... he showed me a mannequin in his bedroom, that's all."

"A mannequin?" I repeated, frowning. "Why would a mannequin make you faint?"

"It... it looks like me."

I stood up, feeling sick.

"In his bedroom?"

"Meg!" Christine stood up. "Meg, don't! Don't go prying around! It's his private space, I'm not allowed to go in there."

"Your tutor has forbidden me no such thing!" I snapped, and marched back through to the hallway, pushing open the one door I had not tried on my previous visit. The room looked the same as it had months ago, when Christine's angel had tended to my injuries. The rough stone walls, the bed, covers rumpled, that peculiar toy monkey holding cymbals, that looked completely out of place given what I knew of its owner.

A heavy, red velvet curtain hung across a space of wall where, had this been a normal home, there might have been a window.

"Don't..." Christine whispered from the doorway as I approached it, but I ignored her and drew the curtain aside.

In the alcove it concealed, there stood a mannequin like one in a shop window, but the face… the face was Christine's, recreated in some kind of wax so faithfully that it might have been a photograph. The wig he had used for her hair was slightly shorter than hers, but was of the same texture and colour. Or so I assumed. The mannequin had a veil over its head and was attired in a beautiful white bridal gown, all ruffles and beading, silks and lace. At that moment, it was the most horrific thing I had seen.

"Mother of God…" I whispered, and my own voice was drowned by Christine's cry.

"Erik, don't!"

I didn't hear the Phantom behind me, and before I could turn there was an arm around my waist, lifting me off my feet.

"*Out!*" He roared, dragging me across the room. "*Get out!*"

Instinctively I thrashed, trying to free myself, but his other arm clamped around me, pinning my arms to my sides. He half-carried, half-dragged me back into the drawing room, repeating vile oaths in my ear. Christine hurried after us, sounding terrified.

"Erik, don't! Don't hurt her, please!"

"Why not?!" He threw me down, the wind knocked from me as I hit the Persian rug. "This little snake has attempted to cross swords with me too often before!"

He towered over me, fist raised, but Christine grabbed him by the wrist, her other hand going to his unmasked cheek.

"Erik," she murmured "*Angel… please.*"

CHAPTER THIRTEEN

Christine moved between the Phantom and I, her soft touch on his cheek making him look at her.

"Meg is foolish," she said softly. "But she meant no harm. Leave her be, Angel."

Her fingers stroked the inside of his wrist, where I could see his pulse jumping, and he drew in a sharp breath, eyes closing. Her other hand caressed his cheek and she whispered something in his ear. I swallowed hard, watching his face and hers. Her eyes flicked to mine, and I saw fear and compassion. The Phantom's hand dropped to his side and his eyes opened.

"For you, Christine." He said, the words sounding slightly strained. "You know I would deny you nothing."

Christine still had her fingers on his wrist, almost as though she thought she could restrain him.

"Get up!" he snapped, and I obeyed. Christine let go of his wrist and came to me, wrapping me into a tight hug.

"It's all right," she murmured. "Hush… Don't be afraid…"

I stayed locked in her arms for a few moments, thinking hard, then slowly pulled back and turned to the Phantom.

"Forgive me, Monsieur." I kept my voice low, polite, respectful. His jaw clenched.

"Christine," he said quietly. "I need to have a short conversation with Mademoiselle Giry before I return her above. Eat your breakfast in the dining room, and once we've left you may use the piano to begin your vocal warm-up. We have a lot of work to do today, but this is a conversation I must have in private."

"One moment, Angel." Christine took my hands, drawing my attention from her dark angel to her deep blue eyes. "You can see I am unharmed, safe and well. Erik is not going to hurt you." A quick glance in his direction. "Tell them that I was called away on the night of the Gala—tell them

Madame Valerius sent for me, that I'll return soon."

"When did you learn to lie, Christine?"

I was surprised to hear that the question, which had been on my own lips, came from the Phantom. Christine's shoulders rose and fell in a shrug.

"Meg is right, Erik. If they have no word from me then they will summon the police. This way, we need not fear their intrusion."

He made a small huff of acknowledgement. Christine hugged me again, and pressed her lips to my forehead.

"I will see you soon. Tell the others… give them my love."

"I shall." I told her, and she smiled and let me go. I wanted to beg her to stay, not to leave me alone in the presence of her mentor. Perhaps she sensed my growing fear, for she stopped beside the Phantom, before the door to the dining room.

"Erik. Promise me you won't harm her."

"You have my word." He replied, and then she was gone, closing the door behind her.

Erik, the Phantom of the Opera, stood not five feet away, his eyes on mine.

"You have invaded my home three times." His voice was soft, matter-of-fact, and dangerous. "And you are annoying me. I tell you, all this will end very badly and you will have brought it upon yourself. I have been extraordinary patient with you. I spared you, saved you today. I had intended to drown the intruder who commandeered my boat, to grab him by the throat and hold him under until he was gone from this world. When I realised that my intruder was you, I dragged you to the shore and ensured the breath of life remained in your lungs. This is your final warning, little girl." He took a step towards me. "Don't let me catch you near my lake again. If others notice your reckless prowling then they will start to wonder what you have discovered, and then even their unintelligent minds may begin to knot threads together. You have seen me kill, my child. Men, women and children have met their maker at my hands. Must you force me to take the life of someone you love? Your mother? Because that is what *will* happen, if your meddling means that my secrets cease to be my secrets. Not even Christine's pleas could restrain me then. Do you understand what I am saying to you?"

"I understand." I nodded, my mouth too dry to say more. There was something about his eyes, about the vein that jumped in his throat, which made me realise that I finally pushed him too far.

"Good." At last he turned away, and I felt as though a grip around my neck had been released. My eyes focused on the Persian rug, and I allowed myself to remember Figaro's gruesome end, and then to picture Mother in his place. The hole it tore in my chest made me tremble, and I knew that the Opera Ghost would do it. I heard the clinking of glass and he was beside me again, walking around me.

"No, stay still." He ordered when I tried to turn and follow his movement. "How is your breath control?"

"What?" I whispered.

"When you sing, Meg, do you breathe correctly? It is an error I have had to correct in Christine." He was standing behind me and his hands went to my shoulders, then down my arms, one resting on my side, the other against my waist. His voice was a golden whisper against my ear. "*Breathe.*"

I inhaled, feeling his body pressed against mine, suddenly understanding how Christine could find her mentor appealing. Yes, he was frightening, but his voice was also seductive, hypnotic, mesmerising…

He has threatened your mother's life.

My breath became a sharp gasp. He tutted in my ear.

"No, no, that won't do at all. You must know how to breathe for singing or you will produce nothing more than a mouse's squeak. Now *breathe properly.*"

His left palm pressed against my stomach, the fingers of his right hand pushing against my ribs. I understood, and drew the next breath into my abdomen, breathing from my diaphragm, the breath I would need when I sang on stage.

"Again." He ordered, and I obeyed. "*Again!*"

His hands moved; pulling me still closer with the left, the right leaving my ribs and clamping a cloth over my mouth and nose. I was mid-breath, tried to scream Christine's name, smelled a sickly sweet vapour, and immediately my head began swimming. The Phantom held my body tight against his, fighting my struggles, his firm pressure over my mouth muffling my attempts to cry out. Had I known what was on that cloth, I would have stopped, feigned unconsciousness, but I was ignorant of it, and panicking. I kept trying to struggle, panting in breath after tainted breath, and the world dissolved in a diamond's facets of colour.

I was being carried in the arms of the Opera Ghost through the streets of Paris… he was sitting on my bed, Figaro in his lap… in Box Five, gripping my wrist over the piano keys, pinning me to the stage…

I awoke feeling groggy and a little nauseated. I was lying on the chaise longue in Christine's dressing room, illuminated by a few candles, still wearing the blue gown she had leant me. I sat up, feeling my head whirl for a few seconds before the world stabilised again; the movement caused something to fall from my skirt and onto the floor. I leant down and picked up a folded sheet of paper, opening it to be greeted by Christine's neat, curling handwriting.

Dearest Meg,

Do forgive me for leaving on the night of the Gala without a word to you. I received word that Madame Valerius, the widow of my father's benefactor, had fallen ill and sent for me.

It went on, a long stream of lies, a promise to be back at the Opera House within a few days. I knew that the managers and Raoul de Chagny would believe the words, that they had no reason not to, but they rang false to my senses. I folded the letter and stood, carefully making my way out of the dressing room and through the corridors where people were already moving, talking, laughing, arguing. I wondered what the time was. It had been just after six o'clock in the morning when I had descended into the catacombs of the Opera House, and when I entered my mother's office I saw the clock on her bookcase said ten thirty; lessons and rehearsals had already started.

I sat down at Mother's desk, folded my arms on it and rested my head on my arms. If I had not ventured into Paris on that fateful night, frustrated at being sixteen and not having experienced so much as a kiss, then the Phantom could have continued his coaching of Christine undisturbed. I wouldn't have taken as much notice of my friend's words and actions, certainly would not have been searching the Opera House for secret entrances. I would have continued believing that the Opera Ghost was just a story, and been as afraid of him as the rest of the *ballet de corps* when his notes began arriving.

Instead, fear had been surpassed by terror. I knew more than I wanted to know, and yet still felt so ignorant of his intentions. I had almost been killed, twice, been traumatised, revealed my darkest secrets, and now had a death threat hanging over my mother.

I blamed Giselle entirely for bringing up the unwanted memories of my father. If she hadn't insisted on using Lycette's spirit board on the night of her birthday, my thoughts wouldn't have been drawn to him and the manner of his death.

I had lied to Christine.

"Where on Earth have you been?" Mother's angry voice made me raise my head from the desk, and she slammed the door shut behind her. Slamming was a good sign; she was angry, yes, but not furious.

"I was with Christine." I said and she stared at me. "She's been gone for days, I had to make sure she was safe! I thought he'd killed her!"

"And?" She asked quietly, and I took a deep breath, then told her everything. Starting from that night in Paris, I related all that had happened in the past few weeks. By the time I had finished, she had drawn me to my

THE ANGEL'S SHADOW

feet and wrapped me in her arms. I felt like I was seven years old again, seeking her comfort after a nightmare.

"Why didn't you tell me sooner?" She whispered, stroking my hair. "Oh, my poor little Meg…"

I don't know when I had started crying, and despite my desire to become a woman, I was snivelling like a child. For all it was undignified and immature, I felt better when my tears had stopped flowing and I was sitting again, sipping a glass of water. Mother had taken the letter from Christine and read it.

"You leave the Vicomte and the managers to me. And don't worry about my wellbeing. The Opera Ghost owes me too much to take my life in an act of spite against you. Are you sure you're feeling steady now? It sounds like he used chloroform to knock you unconscious. You should get some rest."

"I don't want to rest." I said.

"Then go and find Monsieur Reyer. He was looking for you." She stroked my hair gently. "Meg, you needn't hide such things from me. I love you more than anything else in this world, do you understand that?"

"I understand."

Love is such a strange thing. It makes us do things to the ones we love that we wouldn't do to others; deceive and hide. How long had my mother been in the Phantom's service, and why would she not take the opportunity, now, to tell me of the bond between them?

I found Monsieur Reyer in his office, humming as he rustled through piles of paperwork. He had his own filing system, he said, but to me it looked like a strange children's game; how many sheets of paper could you balance on top of one another before they all tipped over?

I knocked on the open office door.

"Monsieur?"

He looked up and smiled.

"Hello, Mademoiselle Giry."

"Mother said you wanted to see me?"

"Yes, please, do come in." He moved a batch of scores off a chair. "Take a seat."

I sat, feeling curious as he routed among them.

"Messieurs André and Firman have agreed that *Il Muto* will go ahead, and I wanted to know if you still wished to take a principle part?"

"I'm sorry?" I blinked at him.

"*Il Muto*," he prompted. "You auditioned back in March, remember?"

"Yes, of course." It had been on a whim, and having heard nothing I had assumed I had been unsuccessful.

"I'm afraid I can't offer you the role of the Countess, it's still out of your range, but I wondered if you would like to play the maid, Nicciola? She has a few solo lines and is part of the Greek Chorus, and should also enable you to perform in the ballet."

I felt a smile touch my lips, lightening my heart in a way I had not felt since Christine's disappearance.

"I would be delighted, Monsieur," I said. "Thank you."

He nodded. "I'll get a rehearsal schedule to you shortly."

"Does Christine Daaé have a role?" I couldn't help asking.

"Mademoiselle Daaé did not audition," he replied. "And as far as I know, she remains absent." He sighed. "Such a pity; she has quite a remarkable talent."

I left him, a copy of the *Il Muto* libretto clutched to my chest. The news that I had secured a role, albeit a small one, in an upcoming production, was a surprise and a delight, as well as a reminder that life went on, no matter what mysteries clouded my mind.

The routine was so familiar to me that I did not need the music, even though it was a role I had never played. I had watched Fabienne Moineau dance it so often before her retirement, entranced by her power and her grace, that I had memorised every motion. I didn't need Tchaikovsky's music actually playing, for it filled my head, every note, every beat. The music of *Swan Lake* was entrancing, but it was the character that I allowed to fill me from pointe shoes to high bun.

Odile, daughter of the sorcerer Von Rothbart, and willing to do anything to please him, felt so distanced from my own world that she was the perfect form of escape. She was beautiful, dark, enchanting, and seductive to the point that not only did she charm a whole court, but also persuaded a lovesick prince that it was she who could fulfil all his desires. Brought to the palace by her father, Odile manages to trick Prince Seigfried into mistaking her for his true love Odette, despite the fact that she is in black rather than Odette's innocent white. When I had watched Fabienne dance the scene, I had wondered about Odile. *Why* did she agree to trick the prince? Was she in love with him? Had she watched him from the shadows and imagined herself as his bride? If Von Rothbart had not gloated and shown Siegfried his mistake, could he and Odile have been happy together?

I had no Siegfried to dance with me, no black tutu. Instead, I had to make do with my rehearsal dress; white corseted bodice that exposed more cleavage than I was comfortable with—I would have to look into the purchase of a new one—and tulle skirts that mimicked the tutu's spread. I imagined the arms around me, the music, and the applause. Odile would not have felt embarrassment that the outfit revealed her breasts to the eyes

THE ANGEL'S SHADOW

of the court and the prince, she would have rejoiced in it, used it to her advantage. I stopped pirouetting, panting, when I realised that my imagination had given Siegfried a shape, that Von Rothbart had been watching us with pride and triumph in his eyes, and that his face had been covered with a white half-mask. I looked at my own reflection in the long mirrors of the practice room, face flushed, breast heaving, tendrils of blonde hair hanging around my face where the energy of the dance had loosed them from the bun. Any one of them could be a window into the dark underworld of the Opera House. Anyone could be watching.

"Meg?" Mother's voice called my name from the corridor, and I went to the doorway to see her approaching. "It's today. He's bringing her back."

She held out a black-edged note, short and direct.

Antoinette,
Christine returns today at eleven o'clock. Meet her in her dressing room.
O.G.

"Do you want to come with me?" She asked. I hesitated, then nodded.

CHAPTER FOURTEEN

We sat on the chaise longue in Christine's dressing room, side by side, Mother taking my hand in hers. The air smelled of the dying flowers that had not been taken away

"He called you Antoinette," I said, without taking my attention away from the mirror.

"We have known each other a long time," she nodded. "We are familiar enough to be on a first-name basis."

"Christine called him Erik."

Mother gave me a look, raising an eyebrow. "I wouldn't follow her example if I were you, Meg. You said he asked you to call him 'Monsieur'."

I nodded, but couldn't help adding. "He doesn't look like an Erik to me."

We lapsed into silence, waiting, and I found myself listening intently for Christine's return. It was extremely quiet in the dressing room, as if we were somehow cut off from the rest of the Opera House and its hustle and bustle.

The mirror slid silently into its frame and I stood quickly, watching the two figures cross the threshold into the dressing room. The Phantom was dressed in sombre colours, his hands covered by black gloves, a black cloak around his shoulders. Christine was also wearing a cloak, light green, over a cream dress.

"Christine," Mother took her hands and gave her a kiss on the cheek. "How are you?"

"I am well, Madame Giry," Christine smiled. She looked a little tired, but otherwise in perfect health as she came over to me and we embraced. It wasn't until she pulled back from the hug that the light caught the tearstains on her cheeks; she had been crying.

"Madame," the Phantom bowed his head to Mother, handing her one of his distinctive envelopes. "You will do me the courtesy of delivering this to those two fools who run my theatre. You have told them about the Opera

THE ANGEL'S SHADOW

Ghost, as I instructed?"

"I have," she replied. "But they do not credit me on my word."

"That is perfectly clear. I shall have to teach them some respect. Have rehearsals begun yet for *Il Muto*?"

"Not yet, the cast list has only just been announced."

"Excellent." He gave a humourless smile. "I observed La Carlotta's return this morning, but the role of Donna Bianca should be sung by someone who can actually convey the character instead of just shrieking through the high notes."

"Erik?" Christine's voice was timid and he turned his head to look at her.

"Yes, Christine?"

"Perhaps... perhaps La Carlotta should sing the role... An Italian actress in an Italian—"

She stopped speaking, and one look at his face told me why; the Phantom was furious.

"How dare you!" He seethed.

He didn't raise his voice, but he didn't need to. Christine was already shrinking into her cloak. Standing beside her, I reached out to take her hand in mine. Her fingers were cold, and she trembled as he continued to berate her.

"Do you think we have been working day and night for the past week for my *amusement*?! You could be great, Christine, a true prima donna! I offered to teach you greatness and you throw it back at me like a spoiled child?!"

"Please," she whispered. "I'm sorry—"

"*Sorry*?" He took two steps towards us and Christine's hand tightened painfully around mine. "You don't even know the meaning of the word! You are my student and will do as I say! The managers don't know what to do with you; they'll just push you back into the chorus while Carlotta has sway of them with her bitter jealousy! Yes, jealousy! She knows you have a superior voice, Christine! I'll not have you lost among a gaggle of ballet rats, mocking your talent with notes even the Giry girl could hit and never getting a principle part!"

"That's not fair!" I interrupted before I could stop myself. "I *do* have a principle part in *Il Muto*, and I got it without your help."

His fiery gaze went from her to me, and I had the strong notion that he had only just noticed I was there.

"As the mute, no doubt." He sneered.

"No," I replied, bristling. "I'm playing—"

"Be silent!" He snapped, and looked to my mother. "What is the girl doing here?" He made a swift, cutting motion with his hand, and Christine flinched. "Never mind! To think, after all I've done for you, Christine, you

95

would behave so ungratefully. I would never have believed it of you, and I will not tolerate it!" He shook his head at her, his tone bitter. "I would never have believed you would be such a disappointment to me."

He turned away and Christine's inhalation was a gasp, as if he'd struck her. Tears were running down her cheeks; she let go of my hand and followed him across the room as he returned to the mirror's empty frame.

"Angel, please, I'm so sorry! Of course I'll sing the role. Please…"

His shoulders sagged and he turned to her, one hand cupping her cheek.

"As am I, Christine. I know you think I am pushing you too hard, even beyond your limits, but it is what I must do as your teacher. The world deserves to hear your voice, and the best performance I can pull out of you. Remember, your music comes from your *soul*, don't be afraid of what you can accomplish. Don't be afraid." The last three words were a whisper and he traced the line of her jaw with one gloved finger. He stepped back, straightening to his full height. "I will collect you here at seven o'clock sharp, and we will continue our work on the role of Donna Bianca. Do *not* be late."

She ducked her head in a nod. "Yes, *maestro*."

He touched her shoulder, nodded to my mother, then turned and walked through the mirror frame, the glass sliding into place behind him without a sound. Christine stood gazing into the mirror as if she could see through it from this side and watch him go. Mother gently took hold of her arm.

"Come, Christine. You need to rest."

She nodded, allowing Mother and I to lead her back to the dormitory. Exhaustion seemed to have descended onto her shoulders the moment the Phantom left her, and she struggled to remove her cloak and dress. Mother and I helped her into a nightgown, and Christine climbed into her bed, curling up like a child. I waited until we were out in the corridor, the dormitory door closed behind us, before saying quietly:

"She has bruises. On her arm, on her side. He hurt her when he *promised* me—"

"Shh!" Mother shook her head. "Don't speak of it, Meg. You know his strength, and his difficulty in controlling it. He wouldn't have harmed her deliberately."

"He promised," I repeated helplessly. Mother reached out and brushed a stray tendril of her behind my ear.

"Come on. I have a note to deliver, and you, my girl, need to calm down."

"Calm down?" I looked at her in surprise as we went down the staircase. "I am calm. I've been calm the whole time, even when I was called a 'ballet rat'."

"You're shaking." She said, her voice gentle. "You've been shaking ever since you saw those bruises on Christine."

I hadn't even realised, but it was true. The thought of him breaking that one promise, that he would use physical violence towards my best friend, made my blood boil. He had no right! He wasn't her father or her husband, he had no right! I took a deep breath, seeing Christine's bruising in my mind again. They were finger marks, where he had gripped her. He had done the same to me, and the marks were most likely accidental. The bruising on her side was something else entirely, like she had been hit hard. The closest I had seen on myself came from losing my balance during a dance routine and hitting the floor with considerable force. Maybe Christine had fallen... or been pushed.

We found both managers together, but not in the office where we had expected them. Instead, they were in the Opera House's main foyer, halfway up the stairs, surrounded by Carlotta Guidcelli, Ubaldo Piangi and the Vicomte de Chagny.

Each of the managers was holding two notes, and Firman was speaking.

"... all we've heard about since we arrived is Mademoiselle Daaé."

"Mademoiselle Daaé has returned to the Opera House," Mother said, standing at the foot of the enormous staircase. I hovered behind her, the tension in the air causing my skin to tingle.

"In that case, I think our meeting is over," Firman said.

"May I see her?" Raoul de Chagny started down the staircase towards us.

"No, Monsieur," Mother held up her hand. "She is not seeing anyone today."

"Is she going to sing?" Carlotta demanded.

"Here, I have a note."

"Let me see it!" They all made the demand at the same time.

"Please." Firman took the envelope from Mother's hand. He opened it, pulled out the letter and began to read aloud.

Messieurs,

This is the latest of several notes I have sent you containing instructions on the running of my theatre. You still persist in ignoring my instructions and have just one more chance to appease me. Mademoiselle Christine Daaé will be cast as Donna Bianca in the upcoming production of Il Muto. *Her aptitude for singing and genuine warmth will charm the audience and ensure that her fame spreads, bringing you further business in the future. As for La Carlotta, she will be cast as the mute pageboy. This should appeal to her vanity as it is, after all, the title role of the production. I shall be watching the performance from my usual Box, which you will have empty and prepared for me. Should my commands be ignored, a disaster beyond your imagination will occur.*

97

I remain, Messieurs, your obedient servant.
O.G.

"Christine," I murmured. No wonder the Phantom had been so angry when she had suggested allowing Carlotta to take the role; he clearly has her career mapped out ahead of her.

"Christine!" Carlotta shrieked. "This is all intended to thrust Christine into the limelight! Do not think I do not know who is behind this!" She thrust a finger dramatically at Raoul de Chagny. "Her lover!"

"That is ridiculous!" Raoul responded indignantly.

Carlotta swept past me in a billow of silk skirts and furs, André and Firman hurrying after her like puppies after their mistress.

"We have no intention of being bossed about by this lunatic!" They insisted. "*You* will have the leading role of Donna Bianca, and Mademoiselle Daaé shall play the mute!"

I trailed after the group as La Carlotta and Ubaldo Piangi continued to complain about their hurt pride. Their voices were a great discordant mass as the two managers tried to talk Carlotta into accepting the role of Donna Bianca. Maybe it was because my mind was still on Christine, or because Carlotta and Piangi switched between French and Italian too fast for me to interpret, but I found myself at a loss. Carlotta, it seemed, had received a note telling her that her place as prima donna at the Opera Populairé was to be taken over by Christine, beginning with the role of the countess in *Il Muto*.

The managers had assured her this was not the case, that they wanted, *needed* her to play Donna Bianca, but now Carlotta was rejecting the role. I didn't understand the attitude of the Opera House's new owners. Even if they did not believe that the Phantom was capable of carrying out his threats, with Carlotta refusing to sing, why not let Christine take her place? The reaction to her performance at the Gala had proved that Christine was a star, news about her would spread, and she would bring in as large an audience as Carlotta. Perhaps larger, since Christine was talented, young and unmarried.

"Do not defy the Opera Ghost," Mother advised. "He sees and hears everything!"

Her words were completely ignored. I didn't add my own voice to the cacophony, keeping back, and was surprised to find the Vicomte de Chagny had fallen into step beside me.

"I have something to show you, Mademoiselle Giry," he said quietly, and passed me a sheet of paper. The handwriting was all too familiar.

Vicomte,
Have no concern for the welfare of Mademoiselle Daaé; she is under the watchful eye

THE ANGEL'S SHADOW

of the Angel of Music. Do not attempt to see her again.

"As you can see, Mademoiselle, this note is unsigned... but a quick glance at the note Messieurs André and Firman have just received is enough to see that they are both written by the same man. Wouldn't you agree?"

Over the past week, Raoul de Chagny had spent long hours in the Opera House, and although he had not spent much time with me, it was clear that he had found out who I was and what my relationship was with Christine. I shrugged, blushing as he looked down at me and wishing I was more modestly attired.

"I know Mother has shown you the letter I received from Christine when she visited Madame Valerius, and now she is home again, safe and sound. I really don't know what else I can do for you."

"Mademoiselle?" He reached out a gentle hand to stop me, and then looked ahead at the arguing group. "There is nothing you or I can do about the operatic politics taking place. Is there somewhere we can go to have a cup of coffee and talk? Please?"

I hesitated, then nodded. "Follow me."

The Vicomte and I sat in my mother's office, sipping the scalding beverage. I took my coffee black, but he preferred milk and sugar. I felt lowly, sitting in the untidy office in his company, especially because I had struggled to find two cups and saucers that matched.

"Now," he said after a moment, placing his cup on the saucer. "I know that you care for Christine very deeply, and *you* know that she and I knew each other as children and that I am keen to renew our relationship." His clear blue eyes held mine. "And I think we both know that the letter you received from Christine two days ago is as false as the gold you use in your productions."

I didn't reply, my shoulder tensing. He waited, and I finally said:

"Forgive me for my impertinence, Monsieur le Vicomte, but I must ask a question. Why do you care so much where Christine has spent the last week?"

He smiled.

"Because, Mademoiselle Giry, that summer I spent with Christine was one of the most memorable of my life. I know we were both children and the friendship could be easily dismissed... but now she is a part of my life again. When I saw her onstage and remembered what affection I had for her... That affection has grown over the years. I never thought I would see her again, but if Fate has reunited us then I do not intend to snub it. I wish to know where our relationship may take us now that we are grown."

I gave a nod, and considered his original question.

"Christine is home now, that is all that matters."

"Hardly. Why did Christine leave me on the night of the Gala without a word? Why does she refuse to see me now? With you and Madame Giry behaving like guard dogs, I have been unable to say more than a few words to her. You yourself, Mademoiselle, told me that Christine refers to her tutor as the Angel of Music, and then I receive a note telling me that this aforementioned Angel is watching Christine. That rather contradicts her claim to be in the company of Madame Valerius, does it not?"

I bit my lip and he leant forward, placing his hand on mine.

"I think you and your mother know where Christine had been for the past week, and that is not with Madame Valerius. Am I right?"

"Please, Monsieur," I said quietly. "Please don't ask me questions I can't answer."

The Phantom's threat to murder my mother hung like a thunder cloud over my head, so heavy that it felt almost visible.

"Can't or won't?" He returned.

"Does it matter?" My fingers clenched under his.

"Mademoiselle, why are you so frightened?"

I took a deep breath.

"Vicomte, Christine is home now. She needs *rest*, that is why I cannot take you to her right now. Where she has been... that is for her to tell you. And I'm sure she will, after she has rested."

He nodded and sighed softly, withdrawing his hand from mine and taking another sip of coffee.

"Who is this Opera Ghost who sends notes containing orders and warnings?"

"He is the ghost that haunts the Opera House. He watches every performance... and he brings us luck."

"Luck?" The Vicomte's eyebrow rose. "From what I have seen, he seems to bring you bankruptcy."

"When he is pleased with us, the Opera House prospers. Angel or madman, the Ghost will strike back when he finds out that his demands have been rejected."

He would know before long, if I were any judge. Nothing seemed to happen in this place without his knowledge, and my biggest fear was that he would take out his temper on Christine. I heard the Vicomte's cup clink against its saucer.

"Are you telling me that the Opera Ghost and the Angel of Music are the same man?"

"No!" My eyes widened in fright as I realised that was exactly what I had said. "No! That would be ridiculous!"

"Christine talked about an Angel..." His eyes were unfocused as he thought allowed. I cursed my own stupid words.

"Excuse me, Vicomte." I stood up, hastily slamming my own cup down so hard that hot coffee splashed onto my fingers.

"Mademoiselle," he rose to his feet as well. "It is clear that there is something going on in this Opera House that has you, and it seems a good many others, frightened half to death. But no phantom, angel, tutor, or madman is going dictate to me that I cannot pursue a relationship with Christine."

CHAPTER FIFTEEN

I opened the door to my dormitory, balancing a tray on my other hand. Christine was just finishing getting dressed, fastening the clasps at the front of her gown. I set the tray down on her nightstand and spoke softly.

"Hello," I said. "I expected you to still be asleep, but it's gone one o'clock. I thought you might want some lunch."

It was a simple fair, cold beef sandwiched between two thick slices of bread, two helpings for each of us. She gave me a tired smile.

"You're so kind to me, Meg."

Her smile became a frown when she saw the sheet of paper on the tray. "What's this?"

"It's… from the Vicomte de Chagny. He asked me to deliver it."

"Raoul was here?"

"Christine…" I sat on the edge of her bed. "He's been here all week. It was he who was talking about calling in the *gendarmes*. He's been very worried about you."

She unfolded the short letter, read it through, and then folded it again and placed it on the nightstand under her candlestick.

"You were worried about me too, weren't you Meg?"

"Of course I was," I said, trying to hide the hurt in my tone. "Not a word, Christine, not a single sign! I honestly thought he'd killed you!"

"And that thought was unfounded. He wouldn't kill me Meg, he means me no harm."

"Oh, really?" I took her hand and turned it palm upwards, pushing her sleeve up so I could see the bruises colouring her wrist. "Then what is this?"

"It's nothing." She pulled away from me. "An accident."

"As I said to you the day of the dress rehearsal, you remember? You saw that bruise on my arm and asked what had happened, if someone had been hurting me?"

Her eyes went wide.

THE ANGEL'S SHADOW

"You mean... you and Erik..."

"We have butted horns a few times," I said, and looked down at my hands. "The night I went into Paris... the time Mother beat me for going out alone... Christine, the suitor I fought off... I didn't fight him off. He tried to..." I took a deep breath. "He tried to rape me, Christine. And the only reason he failed is that the Pha—your Erik saved me."

She sat down on the bed beside me, pulling me close, and I told her about that night, about seeing the Phantom kill in front of me, and being taken to his home. Our heads were together, her chocolate curls mingling with my gold ones.

"Oh, Meg," she murmured against my temple. "We have been keeping too many secrets from each other."

"I'll tell you mine," I said. "If you tell me about this Erik of yours. I'll tell you about my encounters with the Opera Ghost if you tell me about your encounters with Erik."

She nodded slowly.

"All right... it is time I should tell, I need to speak it out loud." She glanced around the room nervously. "But not here."

"Why not?" I asked, surprised.

"I have been underground for week," she sighed. "I need *sunlight*, I need *air*. Come on." She took my hand. "Put on your cloak, and bring the sandwiches. We'll go and sit on the roof."

We climbed up to the rooftop of the Opera House using the spiral stairs behind the stage and out through the doorway that opened onto the flat part. The statue on the very top of the Opera House was known as Apollo's Lyre, and depicted the Greek god, naked apart from a cloak slung over his shoulders, holding the gold lyre up over his head like a trophy. On either side of him sat a woman, the Muse of Poetry, writing in a large volume on his left, and the Muse of Music on his right, holding a tambourine. The statue sat atop a dome, edged with gold theatrical mask-like faces in expressions of anger, demonism, sadness and despair.

The sky over our heads was a deep, cloudless azure, the May sunshine beaming down on us, and Christine raised her face to it, eyes closed against the glare, her expression one of bliss. On anyone else, it might have looked melodramatic, but my friend was a creature of light, and spending seven days away from the sun must have taken its toll on her.

Christine was wearing the pale green cloak she had worn in the dressing room, and I wore my grey one. The afternoon was sunny, but the wind was strong up here, bringing with it an unseasonal chill. We walked side-by-side through the zinc streets and leaden avenues; there were plenty of statues up here, most of them adored with wings, so that we seemed surrounded by angels. We sat down against on one of the plinths, and I unwrapped the sandwiches from a clean handkerchief and handed hers across. While we

103

ate, I told her about finding the two secret entrances to the Phantom's lair, about going to the stage to tell him she was unwell, about my second visit to his home, but left out the darker elements of my tale until I knew how much she knew of his darkness already. I omitted my near-strangulation on the stage, his threats and warnings, and his murder of Figaro. I knew that my accounts caused her pain, and I felt sorry for that, but I had to tell her.

"So that's how I met the Opera Ghost." I finished. Christine was watching me, her eyes shimmering as if she were about to cry.

"A few short weeks," she said softly. "And you've been through so much. I had no idea, Meg, I'm so sorry. I've been so wrapped up in myself and in the music that I didn't realise how much you have suffered."

I shook my head. "Don't blame yourself, Christine. I've been hiding things from you, and from my mother. I've been… ashamed and afraid. I should have told you."

She hugged me tightly and I returned it. As we broke apart, she gave a long sigh.

"It's my turn for truths."

I took her hand in both of mine.

"Tell me, Christine. Tell me what happened."

She took a deep breath.

"He came to me on the night of the Gala. For months I'd only heard his voice, his singing all around me, coming out of the very walls. When I spoke to that voice, he answered my questions, but I could not believe such a voice, such beauty, belonged to a man. I remembered my father's stories, the promise he had made to me, and I asked the voice if he was the Angel of Music."

"And of course, he said yes." I sighed.

"He did, and from then on we were… friends. He offered to give me daily singing lessons, and I agreed, although he insisted they should be in the dead of night so we wouldn't be disturbed. I never once missed a lesson with him… until I fell ill. When I recovered and our lessons resumed, I was terrified he'd be angry, but he wasn't." She gave me one of her most beautiful smiles. "I suppose I have you to thank for that, for telling him I was ill. His teaching his firm but thorough, and when he sings… Oh, God, Meg, you've heard him speak and yet you can have no idea what those lessons were like."

I paused, choosing my words carefully.

"I have heard him. I heard you both. I heard him praise you, and heard you call him the Angel of Music."

"When?" She asked in surprise, but I shook my head.

"That is for another time. Go on with your story."

"He would have musical accompaniment, sometimes a violin, and because I never saw him, it seemed to come from nowhere. Erik understood me so exactly, Meg. It was as if he knew where Father had stopped teaching me, and the progress we made... I honestly believe that my singing improved more under his tutorage in those weeks than it would have done in *years* under anyone else's instruction. I could hardly recognise my voice when I sang." She shifted uncomfortably. "It frightened me... it was as if it was some other creature's voice coming from my lips, like witchcraft."

She paused, looking at me as if she was expecting me to laugh. I didn't, remembering my own feeling of enchantment when I had heard him sing.

"We had our lessons in the auditorium; he told me I had to get used to the acoustics, to projecting my voice. He also told me that my progress must be kept secret, so I spent every rehearsal with the rest of the chorus repressing what Erik had taught me. He said he had a plan for me, that we were going to astound all of Paris."

"He was right," I smiled. "When they heard you sing, I think a few jaws were broken when they hit the floor."

She giggled, blushing, and then passed her free hand over her eyes with a sigh.

"The night of the Gala, Raoul came to my dressing room. Talking to him, sharing the memories of our childhood... oh, Meg... it was as if no time had passed at all, and yet, the feelings I had were certainly... adult."

Her blush deepened and I fought not to smile. My beautiful, sweet, innocent Christine. I hoped that someday I would too experience the rush of romance that she had obviously felt.

"Raoul told me he was going to take me to supper." She frowned. "He didn't ask so much as... demand. I told him I couldn't go, that the Angel of Music was a strict teacher, but he just laughed at me." A flicker that might have been betrayal crossed her face. "Raoul has never laughed at me before..." She sighed and shook her head. "Raoul left the dressing room, and then I heard my Angel's voice... he was angry. He called Raoul an insolent boy who was basking in my glory and in his triumph. I begged his forgiveness, begged to see him... He came to me through the mirror, Meg. The moment I saw his face... his mask... I knew I was the pupil of the Phantom of the Opera."

I squeezed her hand.

"Were you afraid?"

She seemed surprised as she considered the question.

"No. Not even when he took me through the mirror. I felt... safe. Spellbound. He led me by the hand, and he sang to me. I felt peaceful, Meg, even when I thought I saw demons in the darkness. I knew I was protected... I don't know how long it was before we reached the lake... it might have been minutes... it might have been forever..."

Her eyes were unfocused and the blush had gone from her cheeks, leaving her looking as white as porcelain.

"Christine," I released her hand and stroked her hair. "You don't sound like yourself; you're not making sense..."

She swallowed.

"You've been inside Erik's home. The drawing room was full of flowers, every surface covered with them. He stood in the middle of them, and told me not to be afraid. He said I would be in no danger as long as I did not attempt to remove his mask. It was the one rule he imposed on me, Meg."

"And you broke it?"

"Not then." She shook her head. "He sat me down in a chair and took my hands... he knelt before me, Meg, as if he was humbled by me... and I started crying. He soothed me, and said: *It's true, Christine. I am not an angel, nor a ghost. I am Erik.*"

"Just 'Erik'?" I enquired. "He gave no surname?"

"No," she replied, and then admitted. "I never thought to ask."

"Go on."

"I asked him: *Why? You made me believe you were an angel, sent from Heaven by my father! Why did you deceive me?*'

He knelt at my feet, holding my bare hands in his gloved ones.

I beg your forgiveness, Christine,' he replied. *It was out of fear that I could not approach you openly. From the very first moment I heard you sing, I knew I needed you... Ah, Christine... You are my inspiration. You are my Angel of Music.*'

And he sang to me, Meg... he showed me around his home and he sang to me. He told me that music, its power, its majesty, could be found in the light, but that its soul dwelt in darkness. He told me not to be afraid of it, to embrace it. He called it the music of the night."

She gazed out over the splendour of Paris, laid out before us, but did not see it.

"He showed me the mannequin you have seen, and I... I fainted."

"It frightened you?" I asked gently, remembering how much it had disgusted me, but she shook her head.

"Not fear, I wasn't frightened... it was just... too much, on top of everything that had already happened that day. When I came to, I was in the bedroom Erik had designated as mine, lit by a lamp on the chest of drawers. There was a note beside it, which said:

My dear Christine,
You need have no concern as to your fate. You have no better or respectful friend in the world than I. You are alone at present, in this home which you must consider yours. I have gone out to fetch all the things that you may need.
Erik.

Since it was my home, I saw no harm in trying to find a way out, but

THE ANGEL'S SHADOW

there was none! Still in my nightdress, I explored my new abode. Every door opened to me, except the one to his bedroom and the main one, which leads from the lake into the drawing room. Those were both locked. It was only then, when I realised I was a prisoner, that I became afraid. I started cursing myself for being naïve, for allowing myself to be caught in his trap. I couldn't settle and paced the drawing room, back and forth like a caged animal. I didn't know whether to laugh or cry, and I found myself doing both at the same time."

Her eyes met mine, and I knew that she was remembering, as I was, the time shortly after my father's funeral, when a throw-away comment by a ballerina had caused me to collapse into just the state Christine was now describing.

"I was still like that when Erik returned," she continued. "I heard three taps that came from nowhere, and then, I swear to God, he walked in through the wall like the ghost he claimed not to be. It turned out, the doorway was concealed by the bookcase, but I was in no frame of mind to notice."

Ah. No wonder he had stayed so close to me when I had been examining his books; another of his hidden entrances.

"He had his arms full of boxes and parcels, and he set them down on the floor while I hurled abuse at him. I told him to take off his mask, and when he refused, I hurled myself at him like a wild thing. I don't think you would have recognised me, Meg, I didn't even recognise myself. Erik seized me by the wrists as I attempted to claw at his mask, then pinned my arms to my sides and spun me around so that my back was against his chest.

'Breathe, Christine,' he told me. *'Just breathe... breathe and be calm... Breathe in... and out... and in... and out... there's my girl...'*

"I couldn't disobey that voice, so I did what he told me and breathed... And when I had calmed and stopped crying and laughing, he led me back to my bedroom.

'Well, Christine, this is not a good start to our first day together. It is gone two o'clock in the afternoon and you are not yet dressed. I shall give you half an hour to attire yourself properly, and then come to the dining room and we will have some lunch.'

'And who am I eating lunch with?' I demanded of him. *'The Phantom of the Opera or the Angel of Music?'*

'With Erik,' he replied serenely. *'You will never see my face, Christine. Make your peace with that now and do not raise the subject again.'*

He left my bedroom and I slammed the door behind him in a fit of temper. *That* is unlike me, Meg, but I just felt... he made me angry."

"Yes," I agreed. "He does that."

"I must admit that I did feel better once I had bathed and dressed. Erik had provided a multitude of gowns for me to wear."

"I noticed."

"He gave me lunch as he said; prawns, chicken and some tokay. He said he'd brought that from the Konigsberg cellars, and then he said that our time together would be devoted to music.

'How much time?' I asked him.

'Five days,' he replied. *'And then you will be free, Christine, to return above and only see me when you desire it. Of course,'* he gave a great sigh. *'If you are not even willing to give five days in my company a try, I do not know that there is much I can teach you with regards to your music. You must not believe yourself to be a prisoner here, Christine. You are a guest, and we will use the time well.'*

And so I agreed to stay. I was… intrigued and tempted by his promise of music, of bettering my own skills. We talked a little more, and I asked him if he were Scandinavian, since Erik is a Scandinavian name. He said no, he was French, and the name had been given to him by a priest when he was small. What his name was before that, if he even had one, he had forgotten. I thought it was a strange thing to say but I could also tell that the topic made him uncomfortable, and so I let it drop."

Christine had more self-control than I did; if I had the man sitting opposite me and answering questions I would have probably submitted him to an interrogation.

"We spent the rest of the day lost in the music," she smiled softly. "Most of the time we spent together was spent rehearsing. It was different to actually see him watching me when I sang…" She blushed again. "He can be a bit… distracting, but he is a great teacher and we really did progress wonderfully. The day before you came to the house, I went into the drawing room to find him sitting at the piano, playing a tune I did not know.

'Christine,' he looked up at me in surprise. *'I thought you had retired for the night.'*

'I couldn't sleep,' I replied. *'I'm sorry if I disturbed you.'*

'No,' he said. *'My home is your home, as you know.'*

I sat down in an armchair and asked him to continue his playing. I was surprised when he refused.

'I've never heard that melody before,' I said.

'It is my own,' he told me. *'I compose sometimes; I am working on an opera called* Don Juan Triumphant.*'*

'Will you play something from it for me?'

'No,' his voice was stern. *'You… must not ask that, Christine. It… it is not finished. I will play you some Mozart, if you like, which will make you weep… but my Don Juan, Christine, burns and yet is not struck by fire from Heaven.'*

'I don't understand.'

'You think you know the power of music, Christine Daaé, but you have barely touched it. There is some music so terrible that it consumes all those who approach it. You are fortunate you have not come across it yet, for when you do, no one will recognise

you.'

He played music for me that night, but not his own compositions. The following morning was the day you... visited us."

I glanced down, letting the wind catch my hair so that it hid my face.

"I angered him. I'm sorry." I looked up, eyes wide as I had a sudden horrible thought. "That bruising... Was it my fault, Christine? Did he hurt you because he was angry? Did he hurt you because of me?"

CHAPTER SIXTEEN

Christine looked at me, her eyes surprised and then pitiful.

"Meg," she said softly. "You were not responsible for Erik bruising me. All right? These bruises occurred this morning."

"This morning?" I repeated. "Christine, please…"

"I'm getting to it. I knew that he was going to return me above ground; he told me as much the night before. This morning, when I had bathed and dressed, he suggested a last singing lesson, and of course I agreed. We went through the vocal warm-up, and then began the duet in *Othello*. I knew that something was different, I sang Desdemona with a despair I had never displayed before, and his voice thundered with every note. Love, jealousy and hatred burst around us with the music. As we sang, as his voice filled my spirit, I felt the desperate need to see the face belonging to that voice, to find out what lay behind his mask. I was just so curious… I edged around the piano until I was standing behind him and put my hands on his shoulders. I felt all his muscles tense and relax under my fingers. God, Meg, I… I took advantage of him…"

I stared at her, mind boggling. Took advantage? Christine Daaé? Christine just wasn't the type to take advantage of anyone.

"What did you do?"

"I… I felt like I'd lost all control of myself and I… I tore away his mask, and… oh, God!"

"What, Christine?" My own curiosity was getting the better of me and I was eager for the details. "What is it?"

"His face, Meg!… His face!"

"What about his face? I mean, I know I've only seen half of it, but that half is handsome. I mean—" I felt myself blushing furiously. "To some people, he might be considered handsome."

Christine was shivering and she pulled her cloak tight around herself.

"What is under that mask isn't handsome, Meg. It's… distorted, deformed… hardly a face at all…" She swallowed hard. "As long as I live I

THE ANGEL'S SHADOW

won't forget it. His skin is... yellow and shrivelled, like a rotting corpse's, and some of it is missing, showing parts of his inner flesh and skull... It almost looks as though his brain is exposed to the air. The right side of his nose is simply... not there, and there's just a hole. What looks like scar tissue or some kind of fungus twists his upper lip and continues over his cheek. His eye socket is deeper on that side."

Her own eyes were glittering with tears, and I watched one fall, but I was remembering the Phantom looking at me with surprise and incredulity when I had told him I thought he wore a mask to remain anonymous. Ever since I was tiny and Mother had told me stories of the Opera Ghost in his white half-mask, I had never thought it was to hide a deformity such as the one Christine was describing; the visible side of his face just looked so... normal.

"I screamed when I saw his true face," Christine continued. "But he was screaming too, a roar of... rage and grief. I tried to run from him and he lashed out, catching my ankle and making me fall with his mask trapped under me.

'Damn you!' He bellowed, leaning down over me, turning me onto my back and grabbing my wrists. *'Is this what you were so anxious to lay your eyes upon?! Then look at me! Feast your eyes, glut your soul on my accursed ugliness! Don't you dare look away, Christine, look at me! Oh, you women are so inquisitive! Well, are you satisfied?!'*

He got up and pulled me to my feet, and I was shaking so much I could hardly stand. He hissed at me:

'Oh, I frighten you, do I? But perhaps you think this is another mask? Well!' He roared, *'tear it off as you did the other! Come! Come along! I insist! Your hands! Give me your hands, you little viper!'*

And he seized my wrists again and forced me to drag my nails along his ruined flesh so I could tell it was no mask.

'Know that I am made of death from head to foot! There is no escape from me now, Christine Daaé! As long as you thought me handsome, I know you would have come back... but now you have seen my hideousness you will run away for good. So you will stay here forever!'

He said all this with tears streaming down his cheeks. He let go of my wrists and we both fell to the floor, he holding his hand over his face to hide the deformity.

'You can learn to love me, Christine,' he whispered. *'You can learn to see the man and not just the monster. I may be a loathsome gargoyle forced to live in hell, but I dream of beauty, of heaven... Oh, Christine...'*

He turned away from me, concealing his face, crying... and I pitied him, Meg. I felt such pity. He's so... sad and alone... I've never seen such sadness in anyone's eyes before. I very slowly moved closer to where he knelt on the floor. I knew that no apology would do any good, so I just handed him back his mask. He took it from me and replaced it, and then he stood up and looked down at me as if nothing had happened. He took my hand, helped me gracefully to my feet, and said:

'*Come, I must take you back. Madame Giry will be expecting you.*'

We left the drawing room through the door behind the bookcase, via a route that did not involve going in the boat, and the whole time I was expecting him to turn, to change his mind, to drag me back down there and lock me in a cage like a songbird... but he didn't, as you know. He bought me back to you." She heaved a great sigh. "So, there is my story, Meg. You know it all."

I watched her as she wiped her eyes and bit my lip.

"Almost all," I said softly. "Christine, I have to ask you this... The Ph... Erik told me that you were staying with him because you love him." She blushed and looked down. "Do you, Christine? Are you in love with him?"

"I don't know," she whispered, tears flooding her eyes again. "I don't know! He said that I was, he said that he was in love with me, but I don't know what to believe! God, Meg!"

Her strength seemed to have left her again and she grasped my hand in both of hers, bowing her head over it and trembling with sobs. I stroked her hair with my free hand, wishing I knew how to comfort her, and just able to make ineffectual shushing noises.

"How can I?! Tell me, Meg, how can I?! His music, his voice, he makes me feel... but that *face*! God, he was right, I am a demon! How can I judge someone like that? He told me not to remove his mask and I did, I betrayed him in the most terrible way!"

"Christine... *min kära* ..." I knew my Swedish accent was terrible, but I wanted so much to comfort her as I stroked her hair slowly. "You don't *have* to do this. You don't have to return to him this evening if you don't want to."

She looked up, her eyes red and still streaming.

"Then what do you suggest, Meg? That I run away?"

"Well, I—"

"And where would I run to? I am an *orphan*, I have no other home than here! And besides... I respect Erik too much for that. He didn't mean to hurt me, he can't help his face... And the *music*... but what of Raoul? I..."

She shook her head, looking so helpless. I took a deep breath and gently hugged her.

"Whatever happens, you will always have me by your side, Christine. You know that, don't you?"

"Of course I do," she sniffed. "And you know I will be with you. We're family, Meg. Maybe not by blood, but family all the same."

I gave her another squeeze, then passed her the handkerchief that our sandwiches had been wrapped in. She wiped her eyes with it, blew her nose

THE ANGEL'S SHADOW

and then tucked it up her sleeve.

"We should be getting back before someone realises we're missing. We don't want to worry anyone, do we?"

I watched Christine carefully over the next few days. At first she quivered like a mouse at every small sound, every unexpected movement, but she did attend her singing lesson with the Phantom as requested, and returned looking thoughtful, but no worse for the experience.

"He... behaved like it didn't happen," she said as she struggled to undo the laces of my corset. "Honestly, Meg, how do you get these into such knots? It was just... like before. I sang, he offered criticism and encouragement... well, mostly criticism, but it was constructive."

"And how did he react when you told him that the managers were putting Carlotta in the role of Donna Bianca?" I asked, as this reaction was what I had been fearing the most.

"He already knew," she replied and I breathed a sigh of relief. "He said not to worry."

"So did you rehearse something else?"

"No, we rehearsed *Il Muto*."

"But... if he knows you're going to be playing Serafimo and not Bianca..."

My relief was rapidly disappearing. What was he up to?

Rehearsals began for *Il Muto* with Carlotta in the leading role. Christine did not seem at all perturbed by the casting choice and accepted her role as the mute Serafimo with her usual grace. I was giddy at the prospect of my first principle role, although I did worry about my ability, because it felt so different. I was a ballerina, not an actress, and the only time I felt truly relaxed was when we were rehearsing the ballet.

Monsieur Reyer was kind and patient with me, helping when I found myself struggling during the four-part harmony, and Christine was immensely supportive. While Reyer went through solo lines with Carlotta and Piangi, Christine sat by my side and embraced me.

"You're doing so well, Meg." She told me. "It sounded really strong that time. Before you know it, I'll be playing the piano while *you* sing."

"Christine," I giggled. "You can't play the piano."

"True," she replied cheerfully. "But if I could, I would play for you."

"Girls, please!" Mother cried. "Less noise!"

"Sorry, Madame Giry." We said in unison.

Mother was on the verge of losing her temper and I couldn't blame her. A bout of colds had swept through the ballet school, and Mother was reluctantly succumbing. I was surprised and pleased that, despite my almost drowning in a lake and Christine's week underground, we were both healthy.

We ran the first few scenes, and after Carlotta and Piangi had left the stage, began work on the ballet that traditionally opened Act Three. Christine opted to stay, perching on a chair out of the way of the dancers as we went through our warm up exercises. This was another reason for me to be excited about *Il Muto*; for this production, at least, Mother had promoted me to prima ballerina. Pride flickered like a candle flame in my chest.

We had only been practicing the routine for a few minutes when we were interrupted. A stagehand came onto the boards with a note which he passed to Mother. I saw Christine give a start, but it wasn't in a black-edged envelope. Mother read it, then expelled her breath in a frustrated sigh.

"Ladies and gentlemen, I'm sorry. Our managers have requested a brief meeting with Monsieur Reyer and myself. Clearly these *imbeciles* have no respect for other people's—"

She cut herself off, pinching the bridge of her nose. Reyer patted her on the shoulder and looked over the note.

"Talk amongst yourselves, ladies and gentlemen," he said. "We will return shortly."

They left together, and a murmur of conversation started to run through those of us onstage.

"What do you think all that is about?"

"Money, probably."

I sank down onto the boards, legs out in front of me, and leant forward into a hamstring stretch. I went through a routine of stretches, keeping my muscles warm, the conversation buzzing around me.

"Get off me, you son of a bitch!"

I looked up to see Joseph Buquet clutching at Francine, a dancer a few months older than me with red hair. She twisted out of his grip, her furious green gaze burning into him.

"Do you really think any of us would consider even a one-night stand with *you*?" She demanded. "You're nothing! You're beneath us!"

He leered around the stage at the rest of us.

"I would *love* to be *beneath* any of you!" His hand went to his crotch and he aimed a wink in Christine's direction. She blushed a furious scarlet and Buquet laughed as Francine marched away from him.

I thought I caught a movement in the shadows and looked around, expecting to see Mother returning, but there was no-one there. I frowned a little and went back to my stretching, letting the talk fade into background noise.

"Probably something to do with the Opera Ghost," Lycette's voice sounded confident. "Meg would be the person to ask."

THE ANGEL'S SHADOW

"What?" I looked up at the sound of my name.

"I was just saying you are the fount of all knowledge when it comes to the Opera Ghost."

"It's just stories," I protested. "And you've bled me dry. I haven't got anything new."

"I've seen him." Buquet boasted.

Christine went tense beside me and I felt my own muscles clench. In this case, Buquet was telling the truth; he had seen the Phantom by the dressing rooms, returning me home after we had shared a meal.

"I've seen him *without* his mask."

Ah. So he was going to spout a lot of rubbish.

"What does he look like?" Lycette asked.

"Like *death*," came the gleeful reply. "His skin is yellow, like old parchment, and half his nose isn't even there."

My gaze returned to Christine, and her expression was as horrified as mine; even if he was boasting, he was coming too close to the truth for comfort.

"Stay on your guard, ladies," he continued. "Or you'll find yourselves caught in his magical lasso."

He mimed a noose around his throat, and there was a titter from the girls.

"Where was this? Where did you see the Opera Ghost?"

"In the cellars," he replied. "Down past—"

"Joseph Buquet!" Mother's voice cracked across the stage like a whip, and everyone looked at her as she stormed across to him. "Hold your tongue! If you continue speaking like this you'll learn sooner rather than later than you should have stayed silent!" She slapped him hard across the face and we all gasped. "Do not mock the Opera Ghost! Now get off my stage and stop letching after my girls! Enough of my time has been wasted today!"

Buquet gave her a look of pure loathing, made an obscene gesture at her, and left the stage. Mother was breathing hard, her face white and nose red.

"From the beginning of the ballet!" She snapped at us. "Opening positions immediately!" We scurried to obey and Mother turned her glare on Christine. "Leave the stage, please, Mademoiselle Daaé."

Christine nodded her ascent and gave me a smile. We all knew that Mother's attitude could be taken personally by any of us. She took a seat in the stalls, watching us as Monsieur Reyer sat at the piano and the ballet began. *Il Muto* was an opera that had been written many years ago, and remained popular despite being full of asides where the characters told the audience what they already knew, and a ridiculous storyline. It was a farce about a noblewoman who had an affair with her mute pageboy, and the

115

audience loved it. It was funny, the ideal light summertime entertainment.

As we rehearsed, I saw the de Chagny brothers enter the auditorium, and Christine's face lit up when she saw the Vicomte. Both men greeted her, and then sat a respectful distance until the rehearsal ended, and she beckoned me over.

"Philippe and Raoul have invited us to lunch." She beamed.

"Comte de Chagny. Vicomte." I smiled. Philippe kissed the back of my hand.

"Mademoiselle Giry."

"Meg." I corrected.

"Meg." He repeated. "My brother is insisted on taking Mademoiselle Daaé out to lunch and I will be accompanying them as an… escort. We would very much appreciate it if you would join us."

"Do, Meg," Christine pleaded. "I do so want you to be introduced properly."

I hesitated, tempted.

"I would enjoy that, Monsieur, but my mother needs my help. I apologise."

"Another time, perhaps?" He said softly.

"I hope so," I replied. "Excuse me, Messieurs. Christine."

I expected to find Mother in her room preparing lunch, but I eventually located her in her office. She was banging drawers closed and slamming things onto the surface of the desk in a manner horribly familiar to me. I entered with caution.

"Mother?" I asked. "What's wrong?"

She looked up, her red-rimmed eyes not the result of the cold she was suffering. There were tear-tracks lining her cheeks and I went to her at once. I had expected temper, not tears.

"Mother?"

"I've lost my job, Meg." She said, her voice quiet, broken. "Messieurs Firman and André are replacing me as concierge."

CHAPTER SEVENTEEN

I stared at Mother, my mouth going dry. If she had truly lost her job, God knew what would become of us. When Mother had married Claude Giry, pianist at the Opera Populairé, her family had disowned her because of their disapproval of the match. She had chosen to follow her heart and moved into the Opera House with her husband; I had been born here. Her parents had died when I was a toddler, and since Papa had also been an orphan, his death had left us with no one but each other. At the time, we hadn't even been able to afford the funeral, and if it hadn't been for Monsieur Lafevre loaning us the money, then Papa would have been buried in a mass grave. Although I technically got a wage for being in the chorus, it went back to the Opera House in the form of board and lodging with very little to spare. Mother's wage was far larger for her dual roles as concierge and ballet mistress, but if we were thrown out, I didn't know if it would be enough to afford a new home.

"They're replacing you?" I repeated, my voice coming out croakily. "What are they thinking?! They don't know how to run this place, we've only got a season of shows planned because Monsieur Lafevre organised it all before he left. *Why* are you losing your job? They can't keep the Opera House running without you; no-one knows it like you do!"

She sank into a chair behind her cleared desk, coughing into a handkerchief.

"They seem to think," she growled. "That *I* am the Opera Ghost."

"What?" I blinked. "That's ridiculous."

"Or," she sighed. "That I am in league with him."

"Oh." I didn't know what to say to that, as it seemed true to me. She certainly knew more about the Opera Ghost than anyone else and did not share what she knew.

"They say I will stay in the position until after *Il Muto*, while they interview women to replace me." She wiped her eyes.

"What about your role as ballet mistress?" I worried, and she shook her head.

"I don't know, Meg." She said, and started to cry again. I put my arms around her helplessly, rubbing her back and with no idea how to comfort her as she sobbed into my shoulder.

When she had calmed down, she coughed again into the hankie.

"I have to… carry on as usual…" She swallowed hard. "I have to go to the market this evening, for a start."

"Oh no," I said firmly. "You are not going anywhere this evening except to bed. In fact, you should go there now. I'll get the shopping for you."

"Meg, you know how I feel about you going into Paris alone; surely you've not forgotten what happened last time?"

"Last time, I was looking for trouble. I'll be back before nightfall, I promise."

Mother gave me a weak smile. "You're a good girl, Meg."

She wrote a list for me and I studied it. Some basic necessities, fruit, brioche, coffee, wine, rhubarb, rosehip, shaving soap… *shaving soap?* I frowned at the list in my hand, wondering if it were possible for the common cold to relieve a person of their senses.

"Mother? Why is there…" And then I realised. "This list isn't just for us, is it?"

"Is that a problem, Meg?" She looked at me sharply, and I sighed.

"No, Mother… but you're not paying for his shopping yourself?"

"No, he has provided the funds to pay for his supplies."

I nodded, trying to see it from the Ghost's point of view. As a masked man who lived in hiding, I supposed it would be difficult for him to do his own shopping. I couldn't quite imagine him walking through the market in his opera cloak and white half-mask, paying over money for food and other supplies like any other man. Mother coughed again and I added a trip to the pharmacist to the end of the list.

"When you get back, take his supplies to the dressing room at eight o'clock."

"You mean… the one that La Carlotta has reclaimed?"

"Carlotta has already left for the day, she won't be back until tomorrow. Christine doesn't have a rehearsal with him tonight because today is always when I do his shopping so he will be expecting me. You'll have to tell him I'm unwell and be *polite*."

"Yes, Mother."

Be polite. It was easier said than done for me, especially around the Phantom, but I had to try for Mother's sake. She had enough to worry about at the moment.

The market was crowded, but I was able to pick up the items on my list with ease. I knew many of the stall holders, since I had come here often with Mother in the past, and I was surprised and pleased to learn that she had arrangements with a lot of them which lowered the price of the shopping considerably. It also took me to shops that I hadn't been into for many years, such as the music shop where I purchased score sheets and ink. The man behind the counter looked at me for a moment as I carried up the items I wanted to buy before he said:

"It's Marguerite Giry, isn't it?"

"Yes," I said, surprised.

"Well, well," he said. "I haven't seen you for… oh, must be coming on seven years now. Not since…" He trailed off and I realised the last time I had been in here must have been with my father. "Madame Giry is not coming in this week?"

"She's ill," I said. "She has a cold."

"A shame," he replied. "Summer colds can be troublesome. Give her my regards, won't you?"

"Yes, Monsieur." I replied and paid for the paper and ink—no discount to be had here, unfortunately.

I returned to the Opera House well before dark. The May sunshine lingered in the Paris streets until almost nine o'clock in the evening, but true to my word to Mother, I was outside La Carlotta's dressing room just before eight with the Phantom's supplies in a box. I couldn't think what to do once I was at the dressing room door. Should I knock or just go right in? Mother had given me her ring of keys and I decided that knocking would be pointless, unlocked the door and entered. The room was dark, windowless as all the dressing rooms were, and my first action was to fumble in the box for the matches and light the candles that stood on a candelabrum by the door.

There was no-one in there besides myself, and I gave a relieved sigh. Perhaps I could just leave the box and go? But no, it didn't seem right somehow, so I sat at the vanity table, box in front of me, and studied the reflection of the room in its three mirrors. I moved a tiny pot of dried petals to one side and lit another candle on the vanity, its flame coming back to life threefold in the reflections. The huge, gold-framed looking glass at the far end of the room seemed blank and cold, and even if I had not known there was a hidden passageway behind it, I would not have thought it's size odd. This was a dressing room of the prima donna, a diva, who must be appeased. The few things Christine had brought in here on the Gala night were gone, someone had changed the flowers, the air smelled of perfume, and against one wall was a portrait almost as large as the mirror. It showed La Carlotta in an outfit not dissimilar to the one she wore in *Hannibal*, carrying a man's severed head on a platter.

I gave a shudder and looked away. I couldn't imagine Christine having such an image of herself created and kept in her dressing room; she was neither savage nor vain enough.

My eyes met those of my reflected image. It was true that I greatly resembled my father, but the more I looked the more I saw Mother in me, and I hoped I could inherit her poise and calm attitude rather than just Papa's temperament.

What would happen if Mother and I were forced out of the Opera Populairé? Where could we go? We had no friends, no family, no life outside of the Opera House. But, perhaps I was wrong; it was clear from my experience in the market today that Mother was a valued customer of the stall holders there, perhaps one of them would help us? Perhaps her banishment would not be mine as well, and I could continue to live and work here? But would I want that? Could anything be the same without her?

The questions buzzed in my head and I felt the tears start. It was petty and selfish, but I had to be strong in front of Mother and so the only time I could let out these tangled emotions was when I was alone. I put my elbows on the table, covered my face with my hands, and sobbed.

"I was expecting your mother."

The golden voice came out of the darkness so suddenly and made me jump so violently, that I struck my arm on the candle and knocked it sideways. A black-gloved hand caught it before it could fall into the bowl of petals and set them alight. I looked into the vanity mirrors to see the Phantom standing behind my left shoulder, leaning over me to put the candle back in place. His masked face was frowning.

"She's not well," I said, wiping my nose with the back of my hand. "She has a cold and sends her apologies, Monsieur."

"And yet she was well enough to go shopping?"

"No. I did it. She wrote out a list and I bought everything that was on it."

I couldn't help imagining the face Christine and Buquet had described behind that mask; yellowed, parchment-like skin, veins and tissues visible, no nose…He was studying me intensely and it made me squirm.

"I haven't even raised my voice yet and you are already in tears," he observed. "I made my position on you turning up in places I don't want you to be very clear, but there are exceptions. Illness is one. Am I such a brute that the very idea of missing something off my shopping list distresses you?"

"No," I snapped, wiping away more tears. "Not everything distressing in our lives is because of you. Although…" I turned on the stool to glare at him. "This time, *yes*, it is entirely your fault!"

"*My* fault?" He repeated as I felt another sob rise through me. "Oh, for goodness sake, stop snivelling, girl!" He pushed a plain white handkerchief into my hand and then sat down on the chaise longue opposite me. "Now,

THE ANGEL'S SHADOW

compose yourself and tell me why you are in such a state."

"Why do you care?" I shot back, blowing my nose.

"Because I am interested to see what I am being accused of," he replied. "So, speak. Surely Buquet's leering hasn't caused this sudden outpouring? You put up with that every day."

"You know about that? About what he said today?"

"Yes, and you need not concern yourself about him for much longer. When I saw how he looked at Christine…"

His gaze was fixed on a point over my head, his expression so dark that I shivered.

"It's Mother." I explained. "The managers have given her notice."

He looked genuinely shocked at that.

"What?"

Not omnipresent after all then. I wanted to say it, but didn't quite dare, somehow sure that as he treated me like a naughty puppy, he might very well punish me like one if I were that openly disrespectful.

"They say they're replacing her as soon as *Il Muto* is over, because they believe that *she* is the Opera Ghost."

He rolled his eyes heavenward, his lips moving in what might have been a swear word, and then focused his attention on me again.

"Don't look at me like that," he growled. "Did you purchase paper and ink?"

"Yes," I said, surprised by the question. "Why—"

"Out of the way." He instructed, standing and waving his hand at me as if shooing a cat. I got up from the stool and he sat in my place, rummaging in the box until he found the bottle of ink and one of the plain sheets of paper. He folded it, tore it in half, and then took a quill pen from the inside of his cloak. I looked over his shoulder as he dipped the pen into the ink and began to write:

My dear managers:

So, it is to be war between us? I see you continue to ignore my commands, but if you still wish for peace then here is my ultimatum, consisting of the following conditions.

1: You must give me back my private Box, which I am aware that you have sold, and it will be at my free disposal from henceforward.

2: You will cease to hide Mademoiselle Daaé in the chorus and give her the roles she deserves; this can only be in your best interests as La Carlotta sings like a toad.

3: I absolutely insist upon the good and loyal services of Madame Giry, my Box-Keeper, whom you will reinstate in her functions at once.

4: You will terminate the employment of Joseph Buquet, whose harassment of the females in the Opera House is beyond toleration.

Let me know you accept these terms by handing a letter to Madame Giry, who will see that it reaches me. If you refuse, next week's performance of Il Muto *will have a*

curse upon it. Take my advice and be warned in advance.
   O.G.

"I thought your last note to them was their 'one last chance'?" I queried.

"Do you make a habit of reading other people's private letters, Meg Giry?" He demanded and I withdrew.

"No, Monsieur."

He drew a border around the note in black ink, and set it aside to dry as he went through the box, checking the other items.

"Monsieur?" I took a step forward.

"What?" He looked up at me briefly in the vanity table's mirrors.

"Do you think this note will work? They'll give Mother her job back? Obey your orders?"

"I have no doubt about it." He gave me a cruel smile. "They will curse the day they did not."

I shifted uncomfortably on my feet and his hand slammed down on the edge of the box.

"What is it now?!"

"Rosehips," I said slowly, swallowing hard as he turned to look me directly in the eye. He was so *tall*. "Rosehips have seeds inside… and the seeds are surrounded by little hairs…" He didn't say anything, nor did he move his eyes from mine. "If those hairs are ingested, they irritate the throat and the digestive system… the leaves of the rhubarb are also poisonous…"

"You need to stop reading the works of Edgar Allan Poe," he said. "Quite the little Dupin, aren't you? Do I need to threaten you for your silence?"

I shook my head.

"Then you are learning at last." He picked up the dried note, folded it in two, wrote the names on the outside and handed it to me. "Deliver this to Messieurs Firman and André, and watch the tide turn."

"Are you so sure it will?"

"Trust me." His dangerous smile was back. "Goodnight, little dancer."

I turned and left the dressing room without another word, the note clutched in one hand, turning the key in the lock behind me. The line of candlelight coming from under the door went out and I moved slowly along the corridor. I couldn't really interpret the way I was feeling; for whatever reason he was invested in Mother's future and welfare. I tucked his handkerchief into the sash around my waist, and allowed myself to wonder. What if this note worked? What if it did not? And what was he intending to do with rosehips and rhubarb leaves, both of which could harm and even kill?

CHAPTER EIGHTEEN

I walked through the Opera House, carrying the Phantom's latest note, full of unspecified threats. It made me feel apprehensive, knowing what was contained in those few brief lines, and I allowed myself to imagine what delivering it personally might be like. Firman would open it, read it to André, and then they would both glower at me. They would demand to know how I came to be delivering it, what I thought I was trying to accomplish. Was *I* the Opera Ghost? Well, if I was as unwilling as my mother to reveal the Ghost's secrets, then I would be thrown out along with her, onto the streets and into the poverty that awaited us.

Thankfully, the manager's office was dark, the door locked. I opened it with Mother's ring of keys, leaving the note prominently on the manager's desk.

Mother's cold worsened overnight, and by the day after, she was confined to her bed. I worried for her, not so much because of the cold, but because of the additional stress it was causing her. Falling ill was one thing—falling ill when your job was on the line was another.

As prima ballerina for this production, I took over the dance rehearsals for *Il Muto*, and found myself taking on Mother's other duties as well. Wrapped up in my own selfishness, I hadn't realised just how hard Mother worked, how much she contributed to the day-to-day running of the Opera House. Firman and André couldn't replace her, they just couldn't. That day, I found myself wondering how Mother found time to eat and sleep, let alone raise a child, bury a husband and run around after the resident ghost.

I ended the day in Mother's apartment in the Opera House, sitting by her bedside and making sure she finished the bowl of soup I had provided, while I sewed the adjustments needed for my *Il Muto* costume. The opera was notorious for its fast costume changes and needed some inventive work to ensure they could come off and on quickly. Christine, as Serafimo, wore a shirt and breeches, with a maid's skirt over the top that could be whipped off in a second. My role as Nicciola also required a maid's costume, but a full one that could fit over the shepherdess costume I wore during the ballet, since I had just the space of a scene change in which to transform from one to the other.

"Have the managers said anything?" Mother's voice was no more than a whisper.

"Not a word," I replied. "I know they got the Ghost's note, but so far there has been no response."

She sniffed. "What a time to fall ill..."

"You're getting better," I told her comfortingly. "And I've been keeping up with things... just about." I smiled. "I don't know how you manage it."

"Experience, my love." She returned my smile tiredly.

I thought about telling her of the woman I had seen in the posh coat and vulgar hat, being shown around the Opera House by Firman and André earlier in the day. I didn't know if she was an interviewee or had been officially chosen as the new concierge, but Mother had enough to worry about. It felt strange to be sitting at her bedside, soothing her through illness rather than the other way around. Inwardly, I was terrified. Christine had told me that the illness resulting in her father's death seemed to have begun as nothing more than a cold. She had been too young to understand the details at the time, but it seemed that he had developed pneumonia. Could Mother's condition worsen in the same way? Was that how pneumonia worked? I didn't know.

I stayed by her side that night, falling asleep in the armchair next to her bed with my costume draped over my knees. When I woke with a crick in my neck, the fire was dying and I could just make out the clock on the mantelpiece above it—ten past two in the morning. I turned my head to look at my mother, and felt myself go cold inside. Her skin looked waxy and there was a sheen of sweat across her brow. Her cheeks were flushed, but all the colour had gone from her lips. I reached out to touch her, and felt the fever burning under her skin. Panic seized me, freezing my brain and my common sense. Fever. Doctor. My mother needed a doctor. I didn't know one, there wasn't one in the employ of the Opera House. The only reason Christine had been tended to by Dr. Forrester when she collapsed was that he was already in the building, seeing to La Carlotta. Who did I know with medical experience? Mother, of course, but she was in no state to help solve her own illness. The idea was so laughable I actually heard a giggle escape my lips. There must be someone else, anyone, my mind whirled, and then settled on a name.

I got up and ran from the room, hurrying to my dormitory and banging the door open. Christine opened her eyes, startled from sleep, gazing at me confusedly as I lurched to her side.

"Meg? What's wrong?" She sat up, the moonlight coming through the

THE ANGEL'S SHADOW

gap in the curtains catching on the white of her nightdress and the lace ribbon braided through her hair.

"It's Mother!" I gasped, clutching at the stitch in my side. "She's developed a fever! Her temperature feels... so high and I don't know what to do! Christine! You have to find your Erik and tell him! He helped me when I was hurt and he has some... sort of connection with her! He has to help, he has to!"

"Meg, Meg, slow down!" Christine put both hands on my shoulders, but I wouldn't be calmed.

"Please, Christine!" I was almost begging her. "You have to go and find him for me, please!"

"All right," she said gently. "I'll go and tell Erik, but... Meg, you go back to Madame Giry. I'll tell him."

I ran from the room without even thanking her, desperate to return to Mother, fear giving me wings, and reached her bedside to find her condition unchanged. Had I expected otherwise?

A voice in my head told me to stop, to be calm, to think. Moths of panic fluttered around the flame of my intelligence, I had to push them away so I could use my brain. That voice in my head... Papa's voice. I took a deep breath. I had to get her temperature down, and that required the jug of water on the nightstand. I found Mother's facecloth, dipped it into the water and began sponging her forehead. I didn't know if this was the right thing to do, but it couldn't harm, and it felt good to be doing something. The drumbeat of my pulse began to slow as I calmed, the moths of panic dispersing. I was sixteen years old, a ballet dancer; illness and injury were part of my everyday life, I knew better than to fall to pieces at the onset of a high temperature.

I made a sound like a startled puppy when the door of the wardrobe behind me opened and Christine came into the room, followed by the Phantom. She was wearing a wrap over her nightdress, her green cloak and white slip-on shoes. The Phantom was wearing black trousers and a white frothy shirt, partially open almost to the waist. How was he not cold? Christine must have woken him from sleep, but his mask was firmly in place and his hair was immaculate. He disregarded my surprised yelp and came at once to the bed, putting a canvas bag on the blanket and reaching to place his hand on Mother's forehead.

"How long has she been like this?" He asked.

"I don't know," I admitted. "I woke and found her..."

His palm left her forehead and he touched her cheek with the back of his hand.

"Antoinette?" He shook her shoulder. "Annie?"

Annie? I felt my heart jump. Only one person, as far as I knew, had ever called her Annie.

125

The Phantom beckoned at me with his fingers.

"Light the candle and pass it to me." He snapped his fingers in his impatience. "Quickly, Meg!"

With fumbling hands I did as I was told, and he leant over Mother, lifting each of her eyelids and shining the light into her eyes. Christine was by my side, her arm around my shoulders. The Phantom pulled a pocket watch from the bag and held Mother's wrist, frowning.

"Her pulse is too fast," he said. "And her hands are freezing."

He placed her hand down gently, then moved to the end of the bed and folded back the blanket, touching her feet. It seemed inappropriate somehow, and I moved to stop him, but Christine held me firmly in place.

"Meg, you have to trust Erik."

His eyes flicked to mine for a second.

"I trust him." I whispered, and at that moment it was the truth, anything if he could help my mother.

"You've done well, Meg," he told me, his voice unusually gentle. "You've been doing the right thing. Keep bathing her forehead; try to prevent her temperature from going any higher. I have something I can make, a medicine I learned long ago, which should help."

"Did you learn it from gypsies?" I asked, and he paused before answering:

"Yes."

A herbal remedy, medicine from the earth, knowledge passed orally through the generations, tried, tested, proven. Erik took his bag over to Mother's vanity table and, to my astonishment, pulled out a small pair of scales and a pestle and mortar.

"I need light," he commanded, and Christine lit the oil lamp on the chest of drawers and brought it over to him. I heard him murmur a word of thanks, and then he pulled more small glass containers from the bag and started measuring out their contents. I half watched him, the rest of my attention focused on Mother, her pale skin and fevered brow. It broke my heart. His voice moved around me as he spoke to Christine, something about boiling water, and she left the room. There were small scraping sounds as Erik crushed ingredients together. I sat on the edge of the bed, bathing Mother's forehead, my other hand closing around her icy fingers. She felt so cold...

Christine returned and Erik stoked up the fire, his position in front of it casting a shadow over Mother's face. Their voices, mingling in quiet conversation, were like music, drowning out the ticking of the clock. I started when Erik's cold fingers touched me on the shoulder.

"Excuse me," he bid, and I moved around the bed while he pushed up the sleeve of Mother's nightdress and fastened a leather strap around her upper arm, pulling it tight, before returning to the vanity table. I flinched

THE ANGEL'S SHADOW

when he came back holding a syringe containing a golden liquid, and Christine shushed into my hair, rubbing my shoulder. He slid the needle into her arm, at the crook of her elbow, and slowly pushed the plunger home. I bit my lip as he drew back, then stood and began packing his things away.

"Christine," he said quietly. "Take Meg back to the dormitory. I will stay with Madame Giry tonight."

"No." I said, surprising myself, and he looked up.

"You need to rest, Meg. There is nothing more you can do. Either the medicine will work and her fever will break, or..."

"I'm staying here." I replied firmly. "She's *my* mother."

He gave a sigh, then nodded.

"Very well. Christine, you had better go back to bed. I don't need to worry about both of you suffering from exhaustion in the morning."

"Yes, Angel." Christine squeezed my shoulder, and left the room. Erik put everything back into the canvas bag as I sat on the edge of the bed, moving a tendril of hair from Mother's burning forehead.

"The recipe may have been gypsy," I said quietly. "But the delivery was not. Why do you have a syringe?"

"For the administration of medicine," he replied. "I have several. What of it? It is the most effective way of getting it into your mother's bloodstream and starting to work." He returned to the bed, gently taking my chin in his hand and turning my face to his. "Go and sit by the fire. Try to get some sleep. I will be here, I assure you, and I will wake you if there is any change." He shook his head as I opened my mouth to speak. "Just... obey me, Meg. For once."

I swallowed, then whispered: "Thank you."

He nodded, his eyes following me as I settled into the armchair next to the fireplace. He sat in the chair I had been sleeping in, taking Mother's hand and I leaned back. Minutes passed, the clock ticked, and at last I broke the silence.

"If I ask you something, will you answer me truthfully?"

He looked up, the firelight glancing off his mask, reflecting in his eyes and making them appear to glow.

"That would depend on the question."

"You care for her," I said. "You called her 'Annie'. Only Papa *ever* called her Annie, no one else. She denies it, but I must know the truth... were you lovers? Are you now?"

He was silent for a second, his head tilting like an inquisitive bird's.

"Meg Giry, you have quite an imagination."

"You're laughing at me!" I accused.

"Not at all," he replied. "You've not been lied to, little dancer. Antoinette Giry and I have never, *ever* been lovers. Truly."

127

"Then what *is* going on between you two?!" I demanded, my tone exasperated. "You're not a long-lost relative or something, are you?"

"For Christ's sake…" He heaved a sigh. "Once upon another time, Meg, your mother saved my life. Indeed, she saved me from a fate worse than death."

"You're laughing at me again." I scowled.

"A little," he admitted. "But in this case, it is the truth. Your mother rescued me from captivity and I owe her my life."

"Where were you—"

"No more questions." He snapped, and I sighed.

"My apologies, Monsieur."

He nodded, then turned his head back to my mother. I watched them both, considering what he had told me, and realised that I believed what he said. She had saved him, and the circumstances of that rescue were still unknown to me, but whatever they were it had formed a bond between them. It was personal, private, and I wanted to know the story behind it.

"Meg?"

I jerked awake, guilt flooding me. When had I fallen asleep? I had wanted to stay awake through the night, by my mother's side, awake for when she awoke, for her to know that I hadn't left her.

Erik was crouched before my chair and he held up a hand in reaction to my startled movement.

"Calm down, Meg…"

"What time is it?"

"Dawn."

I could tell that for myself. Sunlight was creeping in through the bedroom window. Erik looked pale, a dark circle under the one eye I could see.

"The fever has broken."

I stood up fast enough to knock my chair backwards, pushing past him to the bed, reaching for Mother's fingers, touching her forehead with my other hand. Her eyelids flickered as I felt her temperature, normal under my palm.

"Meg…" She whispered, her eyes opening.

"Shh…" I kissed her forehead. "I'm here, you're all right… Go back to sleep…"

Her eyes closed again, her breathing even. I looked around to see Erik standing in front of the fireplace, hands folded behind his back. I stood on trembling legs.

"Thank you…"

I threw myself at him, wrapping my arms around him and pressing my face against his chest. I could feel the soft tickle of sparse chest hair against my cheek, and he went rigid in my grip.

THE ANGEL'S SHADOW

"Child!"

"Sorry!" I let go of him and stepped away, wiping my eyes. How many times had we encountered each other now? And how many of those times had he seen me in tears? "I didn't think... I'm just... thank you, Erik."

He was standing tensed, arms by his sides, and I realised suddenly that it was the first time I had addressed him by his name. I flushed and lowered my eyes.

"Monsieur. Thank you for what you did tonight."

"You're welcome." His hands relaxed. "I will return to check on Antoinette after dark, but I think she is out of any danger."

I nodded, wanting to thank him again and unable to find the words. I honestly believed that he had saved Mother's life. He returned my nod, picked up his bag, and walked into the wardrobe, closing the door behind him. Did the man have access to every room in the Opera House? I fervently hoped that Mother knew about this particular secret entrance.

I took the seat beside the bed, watching Mother's peaceful sleep, and began to think. I could have called Madame Veret or Madame Soirelli, Monsieur Fabier or Toby Marchelaine... there were any number of people I could have called when I found that Mother's temperature had gone so high. I had panicked, the child in me had taken over, wanting my father, who would care for her and watch over me... and I had chosen Erik. I had scarcely hesitated before rushing to Christine, demanding that she fetch him for me.

I hardly knew the man, barely trusted him, respected him, was afraid of him... and had chosen him in my moment of need. What did that say about me? What did it say that when I needed help the most, I had called upon the Phantom of the Opera?

CHAPTER NINETEEN

By sunset, Mother was doing much better. I had wanted to stay by her side all day, but I had rehearsals to attend and duties to see to, and when she woke to find me still in her room, Mother insisted that I leave her. Christine spent time with her while I was at ballet rehearsal, and the three of us had lunch together. Mother was out of bed and dressed, although in no condition to resume her duties, and was swearing that come hell or high fever, she would be attending the opening night of *Il Muto*. As we ate, she asked how the production was coming along, and Christine replied with a giggle that it was the easiest opera she had ever had to prepare for, as she had no lines to learn or routines to memorise. Mother's reaction shocked us both.

"Never let me hear you say such a thing again!" She snapped. "You *are* keeping up with your singing lessons, aren't you?"

"Yes…" she replied hesitantly. "Erik coaches me every day."

Mother was glaring at her.

"And you are being attentive, Christine? You are following the instructions of your master?"

"Of course," Christine was looking worried now. "Madame, I just don't see how La Carlotta—"

"Never you mind how," she replied angrily. "If Erik says you will sing, then you will sing.

"Yes, Madame Giry," Christine said quietly. "I did not mean to be rude or ungrateful."

Mother sighed. "Then choose your words more carefully, Christine. You wouldn't want to disappoint him."

"No, Madame Giry."

The rest of the meal was passed in uncomfortable silence, and Christine and I were both glad when the time came to resume rehearsals. Monsieur Reyer worked us through the body of scenes along with Amand Charmaine, who was directing *Il Muto*, then they dismissed Christine, Carlotta and

Piangi, worked with the chorus, and finally with myself and the three other singers who performed a quartet piece in the first act.

"Very good," Charmaine told us as we finished the rehearsal, gathered around Reyer's piano. "I think we've got a good show, ladies and gentlemen. Just keep the pace up, and all you need is an audience. Dress rehearsal tomorrow. Any notes, Lucius?"

"I agree there are some pacing issues," Monsieur Reyer replied with a small smile. "Remember, you're going to be singing with a full orchestra, not just my piano and I, so *project*..." This comment was directed at Gérard, who seemed to have developed a habit of singing down into the orchestra pit instead of out into the auditorium. "... And do please listen to the timing. You'll have to keep up with the orchestra, not the other way around. And I want absolutely everyone to know all the lyrics tomorrow." He raised an eyebrow at me. "If anyone so much as glances at a libretto in my presence then they will be singing scales for an hour. I think that's it."

"Well done, everyone, good work." Charmaine spread his arms. "Dismissed."

Everyone began to exit the stage, but I stayed where I was, leaning against the back of the piano. Reyer looked up at me.

"Something wrong, Meg? You can ask if you want some extra coaching, you know, I'm not as terrifying as some of the orchestra make me out to be."

I smiled back at him; Reyer was one of the most gentle men I knew and I could never imagine him being terrifying. When my father had been alive, Reyer had been the lead violinist and had always been kind to me. It was quite a boon for him to become the Opera Populairé's director of music, but he had remained himself, not letting it go to his head.

"Thank you, Monsieur, but I'm all right. And I promise I'll know my lines. I won't even write them on my hand or anything. I just thought I'd run through my ballet steps, if that's no trouble?"

"None at all. Did you want me to play for you?"

"No, thank you. The music is all in here." I tapped my temple and he smiled.

"Music of the mind," he said, gathering up his score, tucking it under his arm and closing the lid of the piano. "*'If music be the food of love, play on'.*"

"*Twelfth Night?*" I guessed and he nodded; Reyer loved Shakespeare and seemed to have a quote from the playwright ready for every topic under the sun.

"Act one, scene one." He started into the wings. "Good day to you, Meg."

"Good day, Monsieur."

I watched him go, then closed my eyes, breathing deeply, listening for the sound of the closing door. Hearing it, I tilted my head back to the ceiling far above me.

"I imagine the view would be better from your preferred Box, Monsieur Phantom." I said, and opened my eyes, turning to watch him climb down the ladder from the flies over the stage. He even managed to make that look graceful, goodness knew how. "Reyer knew you were here."

"The old man is no threat to me," he replied, reaching the stage. He was in evening dress again, a three-piece suit and dark red cravat, hands gloved. He approached me and walked around the piano, lifting the lid with care.

"I thought you would be with Christine," I said, suddenly alarmed. "Where is she?"

"Mademoiselle Daaé is testing the length of her leash," he replied, and I did not like his tone at all.

"What do you mean, 'testing the length of her leash'?"

He pulled a folded piece of paper from his pocket, a slip torn from a larger sheet, bearing Christine's hurried scrawl:

Meg,
Out to tea with Raoul. Back before 7.
Christine.

"I take it," he said in silken tones. "That this 'Raoul' is one of the men who have been loitering around my theatre recently?"

I swallowed hard.

Christine, Christine, how could you not know better than this?

"You know who he is," I replied quietly. "The man who came to Christine's dressing room on the night of the Gala, the night you took her away. The man who spent that entire week here, trying to find out what had happened to her."

He looked puzzled.

"Blonde," I clarified. "About… five foot ten… shoulder length hair, blue eyes… the Vicomte de Chagny."

"*Him?!*" He stared at me with anger and incredulity in his face. "*That* selfish, unappreciative, worthless fop is Raoul?"

I wanted to point out that I found this a bit harsh, but didn't dare.

"But of course, how could I have been so blind? The *Vicomte,*" he spat the last word like a curse.

He took a deep breath, closing the piano lid, leant on the instrument and stared at a spot just above my head. I didn't know what to do, knowing that I couldn't just leave. Suddenly, he was looking at me directly again, and I blinked in surprise.

"Monsieur Reyer probably has a Shakespearean quote for this… '*All the world's a stage and all men and women are but players.*'"

"Um… *Much Ado About Nothing?*" I hazarded.

THE ANGEL'S SHADOW

"*'They have their exits and their entrances, and one man in his time plays many parts.'* Many parts…" he repeated.

I stared at him, brow furrowed, feeling my pulse start to increase. He was looking at me in a way I couldn't fathom, thoughtful, calculating almost.

"Meg," he said suddenly. "Would you like a singing lesson?"

"Um…" I hadn't expected that at all. "Uh… yes. I mean, yes, please, Monsieur, that would be very helpful."

"I can't use this instrument," he scowled at the piano. "We'll go to my home." He looked up at me. "I'll need to blindfold you."

"Why?" I asked, almost whined.

"I thought you trusted me, Meg." He snapped. "Or did you lie to me last night?"

"I didn't lie…"

"Then trust me now."

He held out his hand and I took it, curious, uncertain where this urge to give me vocal coaching had come from. To my surprise, he took me to the dressing room first; not Carlotta's one with the mirror, but the ensemble one Christine and I were sharing with the other ballerinas. Christine's Serafimo costume was draped over the back of a chair; the Phantom's eyes fixed on it, then wandered around the room.

"Ah," he said, and picked up a black wool scarf belonging to Lycette. I sighed and clenched my teeth as he fastened it tightly over my eyes.

I trust him, I reminded myself, but I still did not like having my sight taken. His gloved hands left me and I heard a strange scratching noise, the sound of a pen against paper, then he was back, hands on my shoulders.

"Walk forward," he instructed, and guided me the same way he had done weeks earlier, through the hidden corridors and catacombs, until at last I heard a door opening and the air changed from cold to warm.

"No boat trip this time," I noted. "I take it we've arrived?"

"Yes," he sounded annoyed as he undid the scarf and I found myself standing before his grand piano. I could hear the clinking of glasses behind me. "Now, I did notice while I was listening that you have been taking my advice with regards to your breathing, which is good."

I scowled. "I was following Monsieur Reyer's advice, actually. When you gave it, you were intending to knock me unconscious."

"But was it or was it not the same advice?"

"It was," I sighed.

"As I said." He circled me to sit on the piano stool, placing a tumbler containing a finger's breadth of an opaque liquid on top of it. "And your posture is excellent, but then I would expect nothing less of a prima ballerina."

I allowed myself a smile. Was that *pride* in his voice? I hoped so.

"I take it you do wish to shine in *Il Muto*?" He asked, removing his back gloves. A noticed with interest that he was wearing a gold band on the ring finger of his right hand, and wondered where I had seen him wearing it before. He certainly hadn't been wearing it last night. It held a rectangular black stone and looked strangely fitting against his pale skin.

"Very much," I replied, adding hastily. "Although I could never outshine Christine."

He smirked, back straight, fingers splayed over the piano keys.

"Perhaps not, Meg, but your voice is not unpleasant and can improve with coaching. I expect you've seen Carlotta prepare to sing by using a throat spray?"

"You mean that stuff she has her maid spray into her mouth?" I hadn't really considered what it was for, but had somehow got it into my head that it freshened her breath.

"Yes." He indicated the tumbler. "This is something similar, a concoction of my own that will remove mucous from the throat, soothe, hydrate and lubricate the vocal chords so that you can produce a better sound. Unfortunately, it tastes disgusting, but I am sure you have heard before that one must suffer for one's art."

"I have heard something of the sort," I replied, a little sarcastically. The man had clearly never been *en pointe*. "Have you *seen* a ballerina's feet? Mother's are practically deformed."

As soon as I had said the word, I wished I could take it back. How could I talk about deformity when I knew what was hiding behind that mask? A muscle in his cheek twitched, but he simply pushed the tumbler across the piano towards me.

"Gargle it," he told me. "And then swallow."

"Gargle?" I repeated, lifting the tumbler uncertainly. He nodded and I raised the glass in a mock toast. "Your very good health, Monsieur."

I gargled, then swallowed, shuddering from head to toe at the bitter taste.

"Now breathe, as I told you." He commanded. "From the diaphragm." He struck a chord on the piano. "*Sing.*"

His tone had altered, the golden threads in his voice winding around me, that seemed to make me *want* to obey… I knew that I wanted to please him, to impress him, to earn his praise. What was I doing? He was Christine's teacher not mine, and yet I found myself trying harder, putting effort into the vocalisation exercises where before they had been a chore.

"You have a better range than you give yourself credit for," he mused, watching me intensely with those blue-green eyes. "Now, onto your first lines."

He didn't even need the score in front of him, he just played from memory and I sang, feeling the desire for his admiration fill me. The whole time, his eyes were on me, almost frightening me with the power of that stare.

"Relax your shoulders!" He ordered after only a few bars. "Chin up, or you lose the power of the notes!"

I tried, but something was wrong. There was a lightness in my head, a slight tightening to my chest. He was still watching me, the notes stopping as my right hand instinctively reached out to grip the edge of the piano for support.

"Meg?" He was on his feet.

I could feel myself trembling. God, what was happening to me? Was I ill, had I caught Mother's cold? If so it was no wonder she had taken to her bed. My other hand went to my forehead, feeling for the fever. If it was the same condition, then I was in the safest place; the Phantom, Erik, would save me as he had saved her. Indeed, his arms were around me right now as I lost control of my legs altogether and started to collapse.

"There we are, little dancer," he crooned as he lifted me in his arms like a baby. "Nothing to be afraid of. You must forgive me, it will all be over soon."

"N-Nothing?" I stuttered, even my lips were trembling, my fingers twitching.

He carried me the few steps to his throne-like chair in front of the fireplace and looked at the clock on the mantelpiece.

"Eight minutes," he said. "It usually takes a little longer, but I suppose you are lighter than most." He snapped his fingers in my face. "Are you still awake, pet? Keep your eyes open, it wasn't that much."

"W-what w-wasn't?"

His movements were blurred around the edges and all the shapes around me looked wrong, as if they were being distorted by glass. He was suddenly holding handkerchiefs, and I giggled as if it were a magician's trick. Perhaps it was, for I hadn't seen where they came from. He folded them, then wrapped one around each of my wrists.

"W-what are y-you d-doing?"

He was holding a rope, winding around my left wrist and the arm of the chair, over the handkerchief so that it would not burn my skin, but nonetheless firmly tying it down to the arm. He took my right wrist and moved it forward so that my hand was free of the armrest, and again tied the rope so that I was bound securely. The fingers of my right hand twitched in the air uncontrollably, like the legs of a dying spider.

"You see, Meg," he said in that soft golden voice. "Christine seems to have the idea that I am going to excuse her every transgression. True, I did promise not to harm her, indeed I do not think I could ever hurt someone I loved so, but she has placed me in the role of hero in her little tale, which I actively fulfilled last night by taking care of your mother." He looked up from the knots. "Not that I regret that, you understand, Antoinette Giry is very dear to me. But as Shakespeare said, *'one man in his time plays many parts'*, and it is time for me to take on my role as villain." He stood up, reaching out to touch my chin where the trembling was making my teeth chatter. "Do try not to bite into your tongue, my dear. It will not aid your singing. It was *As You Like It*, by the way. The Shakespeare play that quotation comes from, not *Much Ado About Nothing*. Act two, scene seven."

"W-why are you t-tying me?" I whimpered. "W-what are you g-going t-t-to do?"

"I am going to punish Christine, Meg." He replied serenely. "She has to learn what obedience is. I told her, *ordered* her to stay away from that boy, and she has deliberately disobeyed me. I cannot tolerate such defiance. And what does this Vicomte want of her? To bed her, and then cast her aside like any whore on the streets of Paris, and she *willingly* goes to him?"

He sighed and touched my hair. I closed my eyes, even though the darkness increased the spinning sensation in my head. Where was Erik, the man who had *cared* last night, had sat with Mother through the dark hours, whom I had sought out for help and then embraced? Quite gone. It was the Opera Ghost here now, dark, cruel, insane…

"*Open your eyes!*" He roared and my lids obeyed of their own accord. "It pains me to be so cruel, little dancer, but I have no other choice."

"You… d-did this to me," I stammered. "You p-poisoned me?"

Gargle and swallow… I knew something had been wrong the moment he said it. You didn't gargle and swallow, you gargled and spat.

"It is a very mild dose of sedative, Meg, it will do you no harm." He leaned down, his masked face close to mine. "Do you remember what I told you would happen if I caught you near my lake again?" I nodded, a tear sliding down my right cheek. "Yes, of course you do. I told you I would hurt your Mother to punish you, harm someone you love. Christine has no mother, but she loves *you*, and so it is you who will have to suffer for her sins." He was stroking my hair as if he were my father, comforting me. "We won't have long to wait now, and then it will all be over."

"P-please d-don't do this…"

He gave me a sorrowful look as he settled into an armchair by the fire.

"Believe me, my dear, I wish I didn't have to."

CHAPTER TWENTY

I couldn't comprehend what was happening to me. Trembling from head to foot, bound to the chair by the wrists, my mind whirling, in the power of the Opera Ghost. I tasted blood as my chattering teeth caught on my lower lip, and the Phantom sighed.

"Now look what you've done," he murmured, getting to his feet. "You've…"

He stopped speaking, standing in front of me and staring as a bead of blood welled up from my bitten lip, as if it fascinated him. Then, without a word, he walked out of my line of sight and I heard his footsteps leaving the drawing room entirely. I concentrated hard, trying to halt the spinning sensation in my head, to think of some way of getting free from the restraints, but it was hopeless. I had no control over my own body; I couldn't lift my hand, couldn't even move my legs, and they weren't tied. Every part of me was shaking, but I could move nothing of my own free will.

The Phantom returned, and to my astonishment I saw he was carrying stage make-up. Whatever he had tricked me into drinking it was powerful, and that had been a mild dose—what would a strong dose have done to me?

He was humming *The Resurrection of Lazarus* as he applied make-up to my face, using dark colours around my left eye. My spinning mind couldn't fathom what he was doing, but at least he wasn't hitting me. When he was satisfied, he put the make-up back wherever he had found it, turned off the gas lights and lit the candles instead.

He took up the same tune on the violin at double tempo, standing in front of the fire with his back to me, his whole body moving with the energy of the music. In my head I was shrieking the vilest insults I knew at him and promising that once I had control of myself, I would kick him in the groin as hard as I could. For all his claims, the Opera Ghost was a man of flesh and blood.

The clock on the mantelpiece read six fifty when he abruptly stopped playing and I heard a door open, footsteps, Christine's voice.

"Erik?"

"Ah," he spun around to face her, violin in one hand, bow in the other. "The Swedish Songbird has decided to grace me with her presence."

His words dripped with sarcasm, and I heard hesitation and slight trepidation in her reply.

"You said we weren't having a singing lesson today…"

"And therefore you decided that none of my rules apply? Come here, Christine."

I saw her step forward into my line of vision, and knew she saw me at the same moment.

"Meg!" She gasped and took a step towards me, but the Phantom swung the bow towards her like a cane.

"You will stay exactly where you are!"

Christine flinched back, although he had not actually struck her.

"What have you done?!" She cried, her eyes brimming with tears. "Her eye! And her lip is bleeding! You must have punched her! You said you wouldn't harm Meg, Erik, you gave me your word!"

"And what is the word of a liar worth, Christine?!" He suddenly bellowed. "You gave me *your* word that you would stay away from the amorous attentions of the Vicomte, and yet you still go and socialise with him!"

"We're just friends, Erik," she began.

"Don't you dare lie to me! How can you be so naïve?! You deliberately disobeyed me, Christine! And disobedience must be punished."

"Punished?" Christine stuttered. "You're not my father, you can't punish—"

"Hold your tongue!" He snapped, eyes blazing with rage. "Were I your father I would have bent you over for a sound whipping long before this!"

Christine was trembling, terrified, her eyes flicking between him and me. The Phantom crossed away from the fire and out of my sight, and I heard him place the violin and bow down on the piano.

"Let me tell you something about me, Christine," he growled. "Not about the Opera Ghost, or the Angel of Music, but about Erik the man. Are you listening?"

"Yes, master." Came her quiet reply.

"Master?" He barked a laugh. "Don't think flattery from your poisoned tongue can help you now, girl. I spent a number of years in Persia, where I learned many unsavoury skills. Including torture, Christine. I learned that the best way to punish a person was to punish their loved ones."

He moved back into my line of vision, gesturing towards me, and Christine let out a horrified gasp.

THE ANGEL'S SHADOW

"Erik, you can't!"

"Can't?" He echoed. "I assure you I can. And indeed already have. Meg has quite an unpleasant night ahead of her."

I could feel my pulse racing, my mind trapped in my own trembling body as he stood by the chair.

"What have you done to her?" Christine asked, a tear running down her cheek.

"Drugged her." He said, matter-of-factly. "She cannot move, she cannot protest. She can only take what I give her. So, Christine, what punishment do you think your misdemeanours deserve?"

Christine raised both hands, showing her palms in a placating gesture.

"Forgiveness," she said. "Please, Angel. Meg doesn't deserve this, untie her."

"No." He said it simply, and picked up one of the lit candles, kneeling by the chair. Keeping his eyes on Christine, he moved the candle under my right hand, that I realised he had secured purposely free from the armrest and the protection it would have provided. The flame wasn't touching my palm or my shaking fingers, but the point of heat that was being focused on the small area of skin was starting to become uncomfortable.

"Erik..."

"Listen to me, Christine," he said quietly. "And listen carefully. Your angel knows, sees and hears everything. You cannot deceive me, and it is extremely unwise to try."

The heat against my palm was burning, becoming painful. A whimper past my lips and Christine looked desperate.

"Erik, stop!"

"You deserve this, Christine!" He hissed. "You *lied* to me, you *disrespected* me and *disobeyed me*!"

My whimper became a cry as the pain intensified.

"I'm sorry!" She cried. "Stop hurting her!"

"Have you let him kiss you, Christine? Has he tried to bed you yet?"

"Erik, Raoul de Chagny and I are just friends, and he's a noble man—"

"*Noble?* He wants you between his sheets, nothing more! I gave you *my music*, Christine! If it weren't for me, you would still be a *mediocre* chorus girl instead of the star that is rising in your future! One week, Christine, and your name will be in the headlines of every newspaper in Paris!"

The pain in my hand was deep, harsh, damaging, I had started to cry...

"You will cease all contact with the Vicomte de Chagny?"

"Yes! Stop, Erik!"

"You will obey the orders I give you? Whether or not they fall upon a day on which I teach you?"

"I promise!"

He blew out the flame that was causing my hand so much agony. The relief was instant and welcome.

"I hold you to your promise, Christine," he said quietly, standing before her. "Now, my angel... get out of my sight!"

"Erik—"

"Get *out!*"

I saw his hand go back, and Christine flinched, turned, fled from him, from me... I heard her footsteps, running, the concealed door closed behind her, and the Phantom's eyes were back on me.

"It's a farce, Meg," he said softly. "It's all a farce."

He waited for a moment, listening to sounds I could not hear, then undid the ropes binding me to the chair, lent down and hauled me upright before lifting me in his arms again and carrying me over to the sofa. I was limp in his hold, like a ragdoll, unable to focus on anything but the pain in my hand. For a long time I had been afraid of the Opera Ghost, afraid of his strength, power and intentions. I hadn't realised the man was completely off his head. I wanted to fight, to scream and kick and bite. I wanted to faint, slip away into unconsciousness and not be aware of what this madman was going to do to me next. He left my side for a few moments and I listened to the ticking of the clock, the crackling of the fire. He came back with a jar of cream, then took my hand and began applying it to my palm. It felt like ice, and I heard my breath hiss in through my teeth at the sensation.

"Shh..." he murmured. "I know, Meg, I know it hurts..."

I tried to clench my trembling fingers and pull away from him, but it was hopeless.

"B-bas..." I forced the syllable past my lips and the Phantom went completely rigid. "...t-tard!"

It felt so *good* to say it, to enact that tiny bit of rebellion. He took a deep breath.

"As you have just been through a rather traumatic experience at my hands, I will pretend I did not hear that vulgarity *this once.*"

He put the lid on the jar and placed his cool hand on my forehead, glancing at the clock again. If I could have done, I would have shuddered. He drew his hand back over my hair, again and again as if he was petting a cat, and I realised that he was trying to comfort me.

"How are you feeling? Is the dizziness subsiding yet?"

To my amazement, I realised that it was. The spinning had slowed, and instead my stomach had begun churning.

"I... I feel..."

"Nauseous?"

"Y-yes..." I swallowed hard, again and again.

"It's a side effect of the drug I gave you, it will pass." He sounded completely calm, as if drugging women was a normal, everyday occurrence

THE ANGEL'S SHADOW

for him. Maybe it was; this was the second time he had done it to me. "Take deep, slow breaths."

"Y-you're... you're... a...a..." I stuttered. "B-beast!"

He gave a long-suffering sigh.

"Meg, I drugged you. Mostly, the pain you were experiencing was all in your mind."

He lifted my right hand to show me my palm. There was a small red mark which simply did not correspond to the amount of pain I had been suffering. When I was about six, I had knocked a hot pan off a stove and it had momentarily made contact with my arm as it fell. The candle flame not even touching my skin had felt worse than that, out of proportion to what was happening. My eyes travelled from my hand up to meet the Phantom's blue-green gaze.

"You... you tricked me..." I struggled to stop the trembling caused by the drug, to keep breathing and not vomit. "You... tricked me... drugged me... manipulated me... You *burned* me! And w-why?"

"Because Christine needed to be taught a lesson," he said coldly. "I cannot allow her to throw away the gift I have given her! I cannot allow her to be so disobedient, so disrespectful! To be taken advantage of by—"

"Taken advantage of?!" I repeated, my voice rising, words coming more freely now. "It's *you* who took advantage of her! You made her believe you were a messenger from her *dead father*! You've used her shamefully, Phantom!"

"Used her?!" He shouted back and straddled me on the sofa, gripping the material of my bodice. "I *love* her!"

I stared at him.

"You call it love, what you do to her? That's not love. It's selfishness."

"And you would know?" His masked face was inches from mine, his voice calm again, cold. "You're such an expert, are you, little girl? You, who have never so much as seen a man's—"

The chime of a bell somewhere stopped his words. He was still leaning over me, frozen, head turned to the side.

"Do not move if you value your life," he whispered, his body sliding off mine. He crossed the drawing room in silence, stealthy as a cat. I saw him crouch beside the grand piano and pull a Punjab lasso from the shadows underneath it. As I heard hurrying footsteps approaching the drawing room, his entire stance changed, weight balanced on the balls of his feet, readying himself to throw. A door opened, but the back of the sofa prevented me from seeing the person who entered.

"Antoinette."

The Phantom's entire frame relaxed. Antoinette, my mother? I struggled to sit up on the sofa, but before I could manage it, the lady herself had marched across the room and landed him a slap on his unmasked cheek.

141

The look of shock and anger that crossed his face was quickly rearranged into an expression of calm serenity.

"I see you're feeling better." He said with a raise of the eyebrow.

Mother grabbed him by the lapels of his jacket and shoved him against the piano.

"Where is she?!" She snarled.

The Phantom still dwarfed her; nevertheless Mother seemed to dominate the taller man as she shook him by the jacket.

"What have you done to my daughter?!"

"Madame, control yourself!" He slithered out of her grasp so quickly I didn't see how he did it. "Meg is on the sofa directly behind you."

He straightened his jacket, his expression annoyed, as Mother rushed to my side and put her arm around me while I tried to sit upright. The dizziness and nausea were passing, the feeling and control returning to my body. Mother's other hand went to my face.

"Meg, love..." Her fingers hovered over my left eye and she turned back to him. "What have you *done*?! How did she get this black eye?!"

Black eye? When did I get a black eye? The Phantom was standing in front of the piano, his hands behind his back. He appeared to be relaxed, but I was almost certain he was holding his Punjab lasso.

"It is just make-up, Madame," he said in that quiet, dangerous voice. "I have not hit her. The bruise is not real. A little soap and water and it will be gone."

"And her hands?" Mother took them and turned them to look at my palms. "You burned her..."

"A little," he replied. "But it is minor, insignificant. The mark will be healed in only a few days. It was a farce, Madame. The whole thing was a farce."

Mother licked her thumb, then drew it under my eye, pulling it back and I saw the bruise-like colours transferred to it. She cupped my cheek in her hand.

"Are you injured, apart from the burn? Has Erik harmed you?"

I shook my head.

"He just frightened me... drugged me..."

She sighed and stood, turning to face the Phantom.

"Erik," her voice was low and serious. "Christine told me what you've done."

"I had surmised that much myself," he replied evenly.

"She told me that you had beaten, drugged and tortured my daughter! The black eye may have been faked, one of your clever tricks, but you have still *abused* my child!"

"Christine had to be punished," he growled. "What would you have had me do? Thrash her with a belt the way Claude did Meg? I was trying—"

THE ANGEL'S SHADOW

"I know what you were trying," she interrupted. "You were trying to terrify Christine into obeying you, the way you did Meg when you killed that cat! I have put up with a hell of a lot from you, Erik, I've tried to care for you like a son, made allowances for you because of your past, tried to provide you with a future, never interfered with your part in Christine's life... but this has gone too far. You've betrayed me in the worst way by harming Meg. Mark me now, boy... if you ever so much as lay a finger on my Meg again, I will end you."

They were only a few feet apart now, his mismatched eyes locked with her dark ones. He said nothing in reply to her angry words, and made no move to stop us as Mother helped me stand, and we walked through the bookcase-concealed doorway into the passageway beyond. With every step I expected to feel his Punjab lasso around my neck, to feel my life ending beneath the wrath of the Opera Ghost. But we made it through the catacombs unscathed, emerging into Carlotta's dressing room through the mirror.

As soon as we had left the dressing room, with the door locked behind us, Mother pulled me into her arms.

"I'm sorry, Meg," she whispered and I felt her tears drip into my hair. "I'm so, so sorry..."

"Mother," I swallowed hard. "Have we just made an enemy of the Opera Ghost?"

CHAPTER TWENTY ONE

"No, Meg," Mother replied grimly to my frightened question. "We have not made an enemy of the Opera Ghost. The Opera Ghost has made an enemy of me."

For all her violent outburst at the Phantom, she still looked pale, and I remembered that it was only last night that she was burning with a fever so high that I had thought she might die. Christine was completely devastated by what her mentor had done to me, even after the make-up had been washed off. She pressed her lips to my injured palm, tears streaming down her cheeks.

"Meg, I'm so sorry," she told me. "I had no idea he would treat you like that."

We were sitting in Mother's rooms again, the three of us huddled around the fireplace, sipping tea. I had stopped shaking, although I still felt a bit... odd. Everything and everyone around me seemed to have a phantasmagorical feel, as if I were dreaming. Maybe this is what it felt like to be drunk.

"What are you going to do about it, Christine?" Mother asked, her voice a little bitter.

"Me?" Christine blinked in surprise. "What *can* I do? I'm working as hard as I can..."

"You can break off your relationship with the Vicomte de Chagny, for the present."

Christine looked as if Mother had just slapped her.

"But... we're friends..."

"Christine!" Mother began, then sighed and softened her tone. "Erik is a... jealous man. Whether or not your relationship with the Vicomte is platonic, he will see it as a threat, don't you see?"

"Mama..." I stood up, trying not to give into the wave of head rush, and put down my cup, then moved behind her and began rubbing her shoulders. She gave a sigh and let her head drop back, eyes closed as my fingers worked on the knots of tension in her shoulders.

"You're a good girl, Meg." She murmured.

"No," I sighed, "I'm not. But I do try."

I dropped a kiss on the top of her dark hair. Christine was watching us, sipping her tea, and I felt a sudden unexpected flicker of shame. Our lives had been difficult, especially after the death of my father, but throughout everything, Mother and I had each other. Christine didn't have anyone, so it was no wonder that she valued the attentions of Raoul de Chagny and the Phantom of the Opera.

Before we left, I saw Mother put a chair in front of the wardrobe door to prevent it from being opened from the other side. I swallowed hard, remembering how the Phantom had entered the room through it the previous night. Only a few hours ago, he had been coming to her as a carer, as the man who could save her life. Now, he was a threat to all of us.

I woke with a dry mouth and pounding headache, the sunlight streaming across the dormitory too bright for my eyes. Christine was lying on top of my bed beside me, both hands clasped around one of mine. Her eyes were closed, her breathing slow and even. I was under the sheets, and dripping with sweat; my nightdress was sticking to me, my hair stiff with it. My throat was sore.

I pulled back my sheets, wriggling my hand from Christine's grasp. She stirred and opened her eyes as I sat up.

"Meg? Are you all right?"

"I'm not sure..." I replied. "I feel... disgusting."

"You were screaming all night."

I stared at Christine. She looked exhausted, dark circles under her eyes.

"I'm... sorry..." I said. "I must have kept you awake. What... what was I saying?"

Christine hesitated. "You were talking about... Erik..." she admitted. "And about your father. Your mother says it was the drug Erik gave you, that it made you have the nightmares."

"She was here?" I felt a wave of panic.

"Not for long," she said softly. "Meg... I didn't tell her what you were dreaming about. But I think you should."

I shook my head; I never wanted Mother to know that I had nightmares about my father. It wasn't surprising, I supposed, given the circumstances in which he had died, and I had witnessed, but I wanted her to believe that I remembered him in happier times; not as a spectre who terrorised my dreams.

The dress rehearsal of *Il Muto* was today and I was determined that yesterday's events would not have a negative effect on it. We ran the opera from start to finish without incident, but at least once I *thought* I saw the flash of a white half-mask in the shadows of Box Five. Reyer nodded to me, and assembled the entire cast when the rehearsal was over.

"Well done, ladies and gentlemen," he told us. "We've got a good show."

Mother, watching from the wings, held out her arms to me and wrapped me in a tight hug.

"I'm so proud of you, Meg," she whispered. "So proud."

That evening, when I returned to my dormitory, I found a vase containing a dozen white roses on my nightstand. I scowled at it, knowing the Phantom had sent them. An apology for what he had done to me, for the burn on my palm? Perhaps, but it was not good enough for me. I knelt, pulling the box that contained my books from under the bed, as the room was too small for a bookcase. It didn't take me long to realise that every book I owned by Edgar Allan Poe had disappeared from my collection. Everything else remained; from *Notre Dame de Paris* and *Les Misérables* by Victor Hugo in French, to *Jane Eyre* and *Wuthering Heights* by the Brontë sisters in English, a number of Penny Dreadfuls and other magazines in both languages… but all of my Poe was missing. At the bottom of the box was a book with a blue cover, devoid of title, author or decoration. It was tied closed with a piece of twine, and beneath the twine was a black-edged envelope with my name written in neat handwriting.

I opened the envelope, and read the note inside:

Meg,
I trust you will find this more useful than Dupin and the Masque of the Red Death.
O.G.

I opened the blue book to find it was full of medical advice, remedies and life-saving techniques. Some of it was printed, as in any book, but other pages held hand-written instructions in that familiar handwriting. Some of it was information I already knew, but a lot of it was new to me, and not something that a girl of my class was permitted to learn.

I stood in the wings, waiting for curtain up on the opening night of *Il Muto*, the nerves fluttering in my stomach, for several reasons. It was my first principle role, however small, in a production, and the word running around the cast and crew was that every seat in the house had been sold. Every seat, including Box Five.

As the overture ended and the curtain rose, I saw that the rumour was true; Box Five was sold, and the two men seated in it were Philippe and Raoul de Chagny. We were less than five minutes into the performance, and

THE ANGEL'S SHADOW

I had only just sung my first lines, when the Phantom's voice echoed throughout the auditorium.

"Was I not clear when I demanded my Box remain unsold?!"

My eyes scanned the auditorium as a murmur went through the audience and the orchestra. Heads turned, focus turned upwards towards the mighty chandelier. Even Monsieur Reyer turned his attention from the orchestra, distracted by those angry, golden tones that seemed to fill the huge space. I could see my Mother in the wings, leaning out to discover where the voice had come from. I caught the sight of a dark shape in the gallery surrounding the chandelier, hidden behind the dangling tears, and my eyes met Christine's.

"He's here," I murmured. "The Phantom of the Opera."

"It's him…" Christine's voice was barely more than a whisper.

Carlotta seized her by the arm, her performance interrupted, needing to take her anger out on someone.

"You have the *silent* role!"

"Indeed, madam?" The Phantom's voice seethed, and then quieted. "Perhaps you are the one who should be silenced."

Carlotta took a deep breath and called her maid. The woman rushed on as Carlotta swept to the edge of the stage, carrying a spray bottle full of a rose-coloured liquid. I remembered what the Phantom had said to me in the drawing room; this was Carlotta's throat spray, used to improve the quality of her voice.

"Why do you always spray on my chin?" She asked, before testing her voice with a couple of vocalisations. She moved back to centre-stage, and leaned out to address Monsieur Reyer in Italian. He nodded, and the orchestra struck up again. Carlotta beamed out into the audience. She managed perhaps a dozen words before the remainder were cut off in a strange, strangled croak. A titter ran through the audience as Carlotta's eyes bulged in shock. I was staring at her, as was Christine, the young soprano reaching out to touch the older woman's arm. I felt a lurch of pity as Carlotta attempted to sing again and let out another croak. More laughter was filling the theatre, high, cold, maniacal laughter.

I had heard the Phantom laugh before; chuckle when I had described Arabic text as 'squiggly', give a whole-hearted laugh of surprise when I had asked it he were my biological father. This was something utterly different, he sounded… *insane.*

Carlotta rushed offstage in floods of tears, into Piangi's arms, and the curtains swept back across the stage. I backed into the wings as Christine turned to speak to Gérard, her expression wrought with concern. The two managers had scrambled down from Box Eight, where they had been watching the performance, and onto the stage in front of the curtains. I could see Carlotta's maid trying to comfort her, still clutching the bottle of throat spray, and felt a cold sinking feeling in my stomach. Ever since the cast list had been announced, the Phantom had insisted that Christine sing in the role of Donna Bianca. He had threatened a disaster, and now it had happened; he had used his cunning and knowledge of herbs and poisons to steal Carlotta's voice. I was almost certain that the rhubarb and rosehips *I* had bought for him had found their way into the throat spray, and the guilt turned from cold to hot in my belly.

"Ladies and Gentlemen," Firman was booming to the audience. "Our sincerest apologies! We shall be continuing *Il Muto* in ten minutes time, when the role of Donna Bianca—" he reached through the gap between the curtains and grabbed Christine by the arm, dragging her forward "—*will* be sung by Mademoiselle Christine Daaé!"

Christine freed herself and ducked back onto the stage, gave me an almost terrified look, then turned to my Mother, who was beckoning her from the opposite wings. I knew that Mother would have no trouble getting Christine into the Donna Bianca costume within the ten-minute time frame.

"While we wait for Mademoiselle Daaé to prepare," André said with a slight quaver to his voice. "We would like to show you the ballet from the third act of this opera!"

The ballet... Act Three... the Shepherdess's dance! I scuttled deeper into the darkest area of the wings, tearing at the clasps of my costume. Thank God the costumes were layered, that I was wearing the Shepherdess costume under the maid's outfit. I wriggled out of the maid costume and snatched the floppy hat from my head. An arm snaked around my waist, pulling me against a hard body, alcohol-laden breath brushing against my cheek as groping hands squeezed my breasts.

"What the—" I gasped in shock.

"Do you need anything else taken off?" Buquet murmured in my ear, his lecherous grasp so tight it hurt.

"Get *off* of me!"

Buquet's hands were roaming and I heard a sudden gasp as he let me go. I spun, ready to slap him, and saw the Phantom holding the stagehand by the throat. I stared at them; I was sure I had seen him standing on the gallery surrounding the chandelier, how had he appeared in the deep shadows of the backstage area so quickly? Buquet elbowed the taller man in the stomach, escaping his hold and darting to the nearest ladder as the Phantom doubled over. Despite myself, I found my hand reaching out to the masked man as the music to the ballet began.

"Get on stage!" He hissed at me. "Go!"

He reached out, giving me a shove towards the light. I stepped onto the stage just in time for my cue. This was my moment, earlier than I had anticipated, perhaps, but my chance to shine as prima ballerina of the Opera Populairé. The music, initially scatty as the orchestra struggled to find their places, began to flow again and I tried to let the tune surround me. I knew it so well, had practiced hour after hour, knew every step, every lift of the arm, every tilt of the head… there were shadows moving above me. I glanced up to where a game of cat-and-mouse was being played; Buquet and the Phantom were on the planks overhead, chasing like children.

I launched into the triple pirouette, and something dropped directly in front of me. It was a second before the dizziness passed enough for me to recognise the red face of Joseph Buquet, his wide-staring eyes just above mine. I had started screaming before I had fully registered what was going on. Buquet was hanging in the air in front of me, a noose, a Punjab lasso around his neck. Just as suddenly, he dropped again, the end of the lasso striking him across the cheek as he landed on the stage. I looked up from the grizzly display at my feet to see a white masked face looking back down at me, a smirk on his lips, and then with a melodramatic swish of the cloak, he was gone.

The audience were just as shocked as the rest of us, and someone—Firman, I think—was yelling that there was no need to panic, that what had happened was nothing but a terrible accident.

We all rushed off the stage and it was only a few moments before I found Mother and flung myself at her, sobbing.

"What is it?" She asked in alarm. "What's happened?"

Christine was patting me on the back, looking just as confused as Mother, as chaos descended on everyone.

"He killed Buquet!" I sobbed. "He killed him! Right in the middle of the ballet!"

"My God…" Mother whispered, stroking my hair.

"Christine!" A familiar, aristocratic voice drew my attention, and I looked up to see the Vicomte de Chagny reaching out to my friend. "Christine, are you all right?"

"Raoul," she took his hands. "We can't talk here!"

She drew him away as I clung to my mother, unable to stop shaking.

I don't know what Monsieur Lafevre would have done had he still been manager of the Opera Populairé, but I would have expected the House to be emptied of patrons and the police summoned. Instead, Messieurs Firman and André plied the audience with complimentary drinks and snacks, while the mortal remains of Joseph Buquet were removed from the public eye. The former chief of the flies was covered in a sheet and laid out on the floor of the chapel.

I felt sick every time I thought of Buquet plunging towards the dancers with the rope around his neck. The talk backstage was that Buquet had

149

been strangled before being displayed to the opera-viewing public like meat hanging in a butcher's window. One thing everyone was agreed upon: this was no accident.

It took a little while before I had calmed down enough to notice that Christine and Raoul were still absent. Mother was occupied comforting distraught ballerinas, and I was starting to panic when I caught sight of the pair, emerging from one of the staircases that led up to the rooftop. Something was different; Christine's hair was dishevelled, her lips slightly swollen. Raoul pressed a kiss to the back of her hand before leaving her.

"Christine?" I asked. "What's going on?"

"I'll tell you later," she replied. She was wearing the Donna Bianca costume under her pale green cloak. Monsieur Reyer pushed his way through the throng of actors, singers and dancers.

"Our managers," he began, and I could tell he was trying to maintain his composure. "Are demanding that we restart the opera with you in the lead role, Mademoiselle Daaé. Do you feel up to it?"

"Yes," Christine replied. "If Signor Piangi is willing."

"I take it," I asked, "that the idea of refunding the audience and telling them to go home is out of the question?"

"They won't hear of it," Reyer sighed.

Forty five minutes after Carlotta had lost her voice, *Il Muto* began again. The de Chagny brothers had vacated Box Five and moved to Box Eight, with the managers standing behind them. This time, there were no menacing voices, no polluted throat spray, no bodies dropping out of the flies. The audience loved Christine in the role of Donna Bianca, and Giselle was pulled out of her spot in the ballet to play Serafimo. I played my role without incident, established my part as prima ballerina, got through the ballet without missing a single step.

It was as we were taking our bows that the light in the auditorium changed. The chandelier was juddering, the crystal tears crashing into each other, tinkling like glass bells. Plaster rained down onto the aristocrats below, and then the supporting chain ripped through the ceiling completely. The confused murmurs of the crowd that had been largely lost in the applause became screams of terror. I stared in disbelief as the chandelier dropped straight down and then swung directly at us, and the Phantom's maniacal laughter filled my ears. I felt someone seize me around the waist and drag me out of the way, as it crashed in a cacophony of crystal and wax and fire, onto the stage.

CHAPTER TWENTY TWO

The chandelier was a wreck. Two point two tonnes of metal rings and Austrian crystal was lodged partly on the edge of the stage and partly over the orchestra pit, as if a huge sea creature had beached itself. The ceiling of the Opera House, painted with clouds and cherubs, had a long tear in it, like a rip in fabric, where the weight of the chandelier had pulled the supporting chain through. After the initial terror had passed, I realised that it could have been far worse. Whoever had designed the support system for the chandelier had made it so that it swung towards the stage rather than dropping directly down onto the crowds below, thereby injuring less people.

A flash of genius from one of the stagehands had possibly saved lives. The moment the chandelier had settled on the stage, he had used a pocket knife to cut open one of the sandbags that held the scenery in place, dumping the sand onto the flames that had shot up the stage left curtain when the chandelier's candles made contact with it. Together with his colleagues, they had cut and ripped the curtain down, stamping on it to extinguish the fire. Monsieur Reyer had a broken wrist, the bone fractured when he had hauled himself over the edge of the orchestra pit. The chandelier had come perilously close to crushing him. There were various scrapes and bruises, and a couple of people had broken ribs. The one fatality was a woman named Mademoiselle Jeanette de Bonneville, who had been trampled in the panic of the patrons to leave the auditorium. It wasn't until later that I learned Jeanette de Bonneville was the woman I had seen in the vulgar hat, the woman Firman and André had chosen to replace Mother as concierge.

Gérard had been the one to save us. Taking his bow between myself and Christine, he had wrapped his right arm around Christine's waist and his left around mine, and dragged us out of danger. While the question on the lips of the general public was how this had occurred, the question from the occupants of the Opera Populairé was *why*. We knew who was responsible for the chandelier's crash, but his reasons were a mystery to us. Box Five had been empty, Christine had sung the lead role, the Phantom had even been paid. Everything he had asked for had been adhered to.

I passed a hand over my tired eyes. I was standing outside the Opera House in my day dress, wrapped in my cloak and gazing at the hustle of people in the street beyond its gates, illuminated by the lit street lamps. The police had finally been summoned, had asked about Joseph Buquet's demise, and I had felt the sudden overwhelming need for a breath of fresh air. Had Buquet been killed because of me? For some strange reason I hoped the fact that the drunken stagehand had been groping my breasts only minutes before he had been strangled, was mere co-incidence. I didn't want to be responsible for another man's death. My mind flashed back over the words the Phantom had said to me before:

"I will not have another man sully what is mine.*"*

I closed my eyes and swallowed. If the Phantom had killed Buquet because he had been touching me, then it was an act of protection. I remembered the note he had written after I had told him that Mother was being dismissed; he had stipulated that Buquet be removed from the Opera House because of his attitude towards the women. I couldn't understand him; murder and maiming seemed to be perfectly acceptable in his line of morals, but the assault of a woman was beyond the pail. Maybe it was the sexual situation, maybe he would also come to the defence of a man who was being sexually assaulted, or—God forbid—a child.

The rattle of carriage wheels on the cobblestones made me open my eyes. The carriage was large, black and had the de Chagny coat of arms on the doors. The moment it stopped, one of the doors opened and Raoul stepped out, followed by his brother.

"We'll not be long, Philippe," he said. "Christine said she would pack a bag while I got the carriage."

"Your young lady doesn't waste time, does she?" The Comte responded with a twinkle of amusement.

"What do you expect, after what happened tonight?" Raoul responded. "Mademoiselle Giry," he acknowledged me briefly as he mounted the steps and passed me into the Opera House.

Philippe de Chagny looked at me properly as he approached, lighting a cigarette. He paused, and then held it out to me.

"You look like you could use this," he said softly.

I hesitated. I had smoked, but it was infrequent and not my particular vice. If Mother caught me or smelled the smoke on my clothes or hair, it would mean a beating. I took the cigarette between my fingers and inhaled, then exhaled, my mind calming, a flood of pleasure racing through me. The Comte had lit a cigarette of his own and I dropped my own cigarette and stepped on it. He raised an eyebrow at the waste, but said nothing. We

THE ANGEL'S SHADOW

stood in silence for a few moments, him smoking, me breathing in the smell, before he spoke in a quiet voice.

"You haven't been injured?"

"No, thank you. I'm fine."

"Hardly fine," he contradicted, his tone gentle. "A dead man fell in front of you in the middle of an opera and then you were nearly killed by an enormous lighting fixture. That's more than enough to let anyone admit that they are not 'fine'."

I felt a grin flash across my face at the chandelier being described as 'an enormous lighting fixture', and clamped down on it. The feeling in my stomach and mind was deeply troubling, familiar in a horrible way, the urge to laugh at a situation that just wasn't funny. Like after my father's funeral. I shook my head slowly.

"It's been quite a night," I sighed. "Not to mention an expensive one. The chandelier alone is—was—worth about sixty thousand francs, I think."

"Three months of your Phantom's pocket money," Philippe said.

"Don't mock him," I responded sharply. "Didn't you understand what happened tonight? The Opera Ghost isn't just a fable, he's a real person and he did this."

I pulled my cloak tighter around myself, shivering in the night air.

"I beg your pardon," he said sincerely. "I want you to know that Raoul and I do take this man seriously. That's why Christine is coming to our château tonight, it's not safe for her to stay here. Would you like another cigarette?"

"No, thank you."

I heard footsteps behind me and saw Raoul and Christine leaving the Opera House, him carrying a suitcase. Philippe bowed to my friend.

"Mademoiselle Daaé," he greeted her.

"Philippe. Thank you so much for letting me stay..."

He waved her thanks away, and Christine turned to me.

"Meg... I'll not be gone long... but I just can't stay here tonight. I'm... I'm too scared." She sounded ashamed.

"Oh, Christine," I reached out to hug her. "I know, I understand. The de Chagnys are family friends, you said... you'll be careful, won't you?"

"Of course." She kissed my cheek, and sighed. "I'm sorry, Meg. It wasn't how I'd imagined tonight ending, even if somehow I did get to sing Donna Bianca..."

The image of the chandelier, its glittering shards reflecting rainbows throughout the room, filled my mind. The audience had been on their feet, applauding Christine, and then the great vessel of light and crystal and fire had come towards the stage with the force of a battering ram. They had been on their feet for her, and then it had all descended into madness. I heard the giggle escape my lips before I realised that I had a made it.

153

"You brought the house down, Christine," I told her jovially. "All he ever wanted for you and you did it. You're a star."

"Don't, Meg." She glowered at me, her skin pale in the streetlamps. "That isn't funny."

"But it is!" I couldn't stop the laughter from welling up in my throat. "You brought the house down! Don't you understand? Down!"

And I howled with laughter like the lunatic I was, doubling over as it caused my stomach to ache, my eyes to water.

"Meg?" Her voice was worried now and she took me by the shoulders and gave me a little shake. "Meg, calm down."

I clutched her arm, shaking my head, roaring with laughter as the tears streamed down my cheeks. I couldn't stop myself, even as I tried, sobbing and laughing in front of my dearest friend, in front of the de Chagnys. These were men of power and wealth who could easily have me committed... Like father like daughter. He could have killed us tonight, on that stage. He could have killed us all.

"Meg, please, stop!" Christine was sounding desperate now.

"Mademoiselle," someone else was in front of me, the Comte, gripping my shoulders, staring into my eyes. "Mademoiselle, I am truly sorry about this..."

The next thing I felt was a sharp blow across my cheek and Christine shrieked.

"Philippe! What are you doing?!"

"Two ways to deal with a hysterical woman," he replied. "Did you expect me to kiss her?"

I had stumbled back from the force of his slap, clutching my cheek, and raised my eyes to his. At that moment, I hated him for daring to lay a hand on me, and in my madness, I flew at him, striking out with my hand. My fingernails scraped his cheek and he yelled, jerking back.

"Meg!" Christine screamed my name, and as I lunged towards Philippe again for a second attack, laughing and crying in a mixed screech, Raoul grabbed me around the waist, pinning my arms down to my sides.

"Mademoiselle Giry! Calm yourself, woman! Calm down!" He was shouting and all I could feel was terror and rage and grief, all boiling up in my head like a stew in a pot.

"I'll get her mother!"

Christine's footsteps sounded clearly across the stone steps of the Opera House, as I kicked and hissed and spat like an angry cat. Raoul kept a grim hold on me.

"Get her in the carriage!"

"Let go of me!" I screamed.

Raoul lifted me off my feet, while I kicked at his shins, the pounding in my head demanding violence, my breast heaving with the sobs. He dragged me into the carriage, and Philippe's hands were around both of mine, clamping them together like cuffs. I couldn't see what was going on around me, my head and vision were now full of black clouds, forked with lightening, Joseph Buquet's face leered at me, then hung dead before my eyes and I could not stop screaming.

"Meg…" I could feel the Vicomte's tight grip holding me still, a hand stroking my wild hair, and smelled something familiar, safe. "Meg… it's Mother, Meg… let it go and then hush, darling… it's all right… it's all right…"

I knew the room I was standing in; I had been here many times over the past seven years, perhaps longer. It was long, with beds lined against either wall, each surrounded by white curtains, and each had huge belts attached to hold the occupant down.

I swallowed hard and squeezed my Papa's hand.

"It's for your own good, Meg," His voice was hoarse from years of tobacco smoke. "They say they can make us well again. Do you believe me?"

"Yes, Papa," I whispered.

Three men in white coats were standing by one of the beds, waiting for me, and he began marching me towards them. His cologne was strong, his suit pristine, the white mask across the right half of his face. I cried out as the three doctors grabbed hold of me and began to strap me down. He watched, his hands folded behind his back.

"It's for your own good, Meg," the Phantom said in his golden, musical voice. "Do you believe your Erik?"

I did not have time to reply before a huge needle was plunged into my arm. The images flashed before my eyes, doctors, my father, a pool filled with iced water, chains, home…

Papa was sitting on the edge of the double bed he shared with my mother, half dressed. He had his breeches and shirt on, but the belt was on the nightstand and his waistcoat and jacket on the bed beside him.

"Papa?" I asked, shaking his shoulder, but he ignored me. "Papa?"

It went on for minutes, everything I tried failed to get his attention. Finally, I lost my temper, and repeated what I had heard one of the German stagehands screaming to a man outside the stage door.

"Scheißkerl!" I shrieked. "Für nichts gut Haufen Scheiße!"

His head snapped towards me, eyes blazing, one blue, one green.

"What did you say to me?!" He roared. "How dare you!" He stood up, seizing the belt from the nightstand and flying at me, grabbing me and pulling me to the bed. "You disrespectful little bitch!"

The belt came down across my back, again and again, and all I could hear were my own screams.

Papa was sitting on the end of his bed, staring at his reflection in the mirror, tears streaming down his face as he held the gun against his temple. He caught my reflection and smiled.

"Look after Mama," he said, and then the gunshot filled my senses.

I woke in a room I had never seen before, and for one terrified moment I thought that I had been admitted to a hospital where I would be restrained and prodded and probed and treated like an animal. But as the nightmare passed, the images that were a combination of truth and fiction leaving my mind, I realised that this was no hospital room, but a residential bedroom, a woman's bedroom, judging by the knickknacks. I was lying in a canopy bed in a frankly luxurious room, and Mother was by my side, holding my hand. The nightgown I was wearing was pure silk by the feel of it, with lots of ruffles, and more expensive than anything I had owned. I remembered Christine telling me that the de Chagny brothers also had two sisters and I wriggled, uncomfortable in the knowledge that I was wearing something that belonged to a stranger.

"Meg?" Mother said softly, stroking my hair, which was loose across the pillows. "Darling?"

"Where are we?" I whispered. A whisper was all I could manage. My throat was sore and my eyelashes stiff with old tears.

"We're in the de Chagny mansion," she explained. "They brought us here with Christine yesterday night after your... incident."

Incident. It was a delicate way of putting it. I went hot with embarrassment, ashamed by my complete breakdown on the steps of the Opera Populairé.

"I... I don't know what happened to me,"

"The doctor says it was shock,"

"Doctor?!" I went tense immediately. "No!"

"Meg, Meg, calm down..." She stroked my hair again, shushing me. "The de Chagnys called a doctor to look at you because you were... completely hysterical, love. You were screaming and thrashing like..."

"Like after Papa's funeral?"

"Yes. But he didn't take you anywhere, and I never left your side. He said it was brought on by shock, by seeing Buquet's body and then almost being hit by the chandelier."

"Is Christine all right?"

"Yes, love, she's fine. She's here as well."

"Did she suffer from shock as well?"

A pause, then: "No."

"You said yesterday night?"

"The doctor gave you a sedative to calm you and make you sleep. You've been out for almost twenty four hours."

I sighed deeply, then thought of something else, confusion wrinkling my

THE ANGEL'S SHADOW

brow.

"Did I... hit someone?"

"Yes," she told me quietly. "The Comte de Chagny."

My hand flew to my mouth. I had hit a noblemen? A patron? Shock or no shock, there was no excuse for physical assault on a man like him.

"He understands, Meg, he doesn't blame you."

"I have to apologise to him," I started sitting up. "If what I did means he withdraws his funds from the Opera House—"

"No," Mother pressed me gently but firmly back against the pillows. "Meg, no. It's the middle of the night. By all means apologise, but apologise tomorrow." She stroked my hair once more. "And I don't think he or the Vicomte will withdraw their funds from the Opera Populairé."

I lay quietly for a moment, sifting thoughts and feelings through my mind.

"Is there any news from the Opera Populairé?" I asked after awhile.

"Joseph Buquet's body has been removed, but the police will still be there for a couple of days longer. The Comte has suggested that we remain here for the time being, until the police investigation is over with."

"And..." I dropped my whisper even lower; walls have ears, they say. "The Phantom?"

"No sign," she replied, as quietly as I. "It is likely, Meg, that the coroner's report will deem Buquet's death an accident, that he lost his footing in the flies due to being drunk, and became caught in the ropes, hanging himself in the fall."

"But... we all saw the noose—the Punjab lasso..."

"We saw a rope caught around his neck. A rope that has not been found."

I swallowed hard. "And... the chandelier?"

"The maintenance on the cable had not been carried out for sometime; it was old and worn. An accident waiting to happen."

"Mother..."

"Hush, Meg..." She told me. "Let it pass. He hasn't been seen since, he hasn't even sent any notes as far as I know. You must rest, love. Get some more sleep."

I turned onto my side, away from her, and faced the huge balcony window. The curtains were partially open, showing the darkness of the night outside. After awhile, Mother turned off the light of the oil lamp on the nightstand, and awhile later, I heard her deep, regular breathing as she fell asleep beside me.

I stared, clear-eyed at the patterned darkness of the balcony windows, and the night beyond it. I didn't want to go back to sleep, to return to my nightmare. Had the Phantom been a part of my nightmare? I tried to remember. The dream was horribly familiar, but the Phantom had never had a part in it before.

Mother had stayed with me, kept me safe, prevented me from being taken away by a doctor. I was humiliated by my undignified collapse outside the Opera House, and frightened by the whole series of events. And what of the Phantom? Why had he crashed the chandelier? He had ordered Christine to stay away from Raoul, tortured me to earn her compliance, so how would he react when he learned, as he surely would, that she was staying in the de Chagny mansion?

At that very thought, I saw a movement outside the balcony window, a darker shape against the darkness. Through the glass, glowing like a cat's, a mismatched pair of eyes was staring at me, one blue and one green.

CHAPTER TWENTY THREE

I stared back at the eyes gazing through the French windows. What were my options? Crying, "He's here, the Phantom of the Opera!" or bursting into tears seemed to be automatic reactions, and I bit down on them. He had seen enough of my tears and it would make me look weak. I could scream and alert the household, and then what? Would he run? He was taken as a serious threat, and even if he weren't, this was trespassing.

Suddenly fed up with my own inner musing, I slipped from the bed silently, careful not to wake Mother. I glanced around the room, but couldn't see a wrap, so just walked over to the window in my silk nightgown and bare feet. After the hysteria that had gripped me and the terror of my nightmare, I now felt numb. I wasn't happy to see him, but nor did I feel distressed or afraid; there was just a void. I lifted the latch and pushed the full-length window open, stepping outside.

The Phantom was leaning against the balcony railing, hands clasped in front of him, mismatched eyes never leaving me. I closed the window behind me, keeping my back to it and my gaze on his. There was furniture out here, an ironwork table and two chairs. Despite the June being hot, the night wind brought a chill wind with it, and I felt my body react, goose bumps rippling over my flesh, nipples hardening against the silk.

"Are you here to abduct me again?" I asked expressionlessly. His visible eyebrow rose.

"No," he replied. "A peculiar question."

"On the last occasion Christine spent time with the Vicomte de Chagny, you abducted me and tortured me." I reminded him.

"I am not here to abduct anyone," he said. "Who hit you?"

I blinked at him.

"I beg your pardon?"

"Your cheek is bruised," he said, reaching out and turning my head so that the moonlight illuminated the left side of my face. "Who hit you?"

"I…" I swallowed, feeling the humiliation making my face flush for a moment. "I had a… breakdown, outside the Opera House. I couldn't stop screaming, so the Comte de Chagny slapped me to try and bring me to my senses. He didn't mean to hurt me."

"You look tired."

"I've been having nightmares about my father. Remembering the day he died."

No point mentioning that my companion on this balcony was suddenly a part of them. I wrapped my arms around my chest with a shiver, and after a moment, the Phantom unclasped his cloak and wrapped it around my shoulders.

"Your mother would have my head if you caught a chill."

"She'll kill you if she sees us out here together," I said, my tone bland; I really didn't care. I sat down on one of the chairs and he took the other, putting his elbows on the table between us and forming a steeple of his fingers.

"Then I am not forgiven."

"For torturing me? Hardly."

"Show me your palm," he ordered, and I held out my right hand, the one he had burned with the heat of a candle flame. The mark was pink and a little sensitive, but no longer painful. I gazed at him while he studied my palm as if he could read my future in it.

"Why are you here, Monsieur?"

He lifted his eyes to mine, and I saw a brief flash of anger, but again the rush of alarm I should have felt was non-existent.

"Have you come to abduct Christine?" I pushed. "You swung a chandelier at her, so is it any wonder she wants to spend a little time away from the Opera House?"

Away from you, I added silently. He let go of my hand.

"The chandelier? That wasn't me. The supporting chain was old and worn. It was an accident."

Liar.

Of course I didn't dare say it aloud; my numbed state hadn't quite done away with my survival instinct altogether.

"Was Joseph Buquet's death an accident too?" I asked. "Did he get drunk, fall from the flies and get a rope caught around his neck?"

"No," the Phantom replied quietly. "I killed him."

"Why?"

"He'd seen too much, said too much and done too much."

I swallowed, wanting to look away, but keeping my eyes on his.

"Did you kill him because of what he was doing to me?"

He regarded me, the visible side of his face as impassive as the masked side. Should I take his silence to mean yes or no?

"It is my turn to ask a question," he said, after a few moments of letting the still air hang between us. I leant back in the chair, drawing the cloak tighter around me, and nodded.

"Why didn't you scream when you saw me out here?"

I shrugged.

"Curiosity is about the only feeling left in me right now," I admitted. "I wanted to know why you're here, but since you won't tell me, I have wasted my time."

"You could scream now," he pointed out. "Wake the entire household."

"I could," I agreed. "But I'm not going to."

As I fidgeted, I could feel pockets inside the cloak, several holding something heavy.

"Why not?"

"Because," I said, "for all you're... 'a villain', to use your own description, you have done me... a good turn. I do owe you my life, definitely my virtue, and Mother's life. I think Buquet would have tried to..." I swallowed hard. "Well... sooner or later. And I feel I owe you for that." I raised an eyebrow. "But you knew I wouldn't give you away, or you would have fled when you knew I'd seen you." I shifted again, feeling something rectangular press into my leg. "What *is* that?"

I found the blue book he had left in my dormitory, the one full of medical advice.

"I thought you might enjoy some reading material," he said, somewhat cryptically. "The next time someone close to you contracts a fever, you need not send Mademoiselle Daaé to disturb me."

I put the book on the table.

"If you wanted to borrow my Edgar Allan Poe books, you could have just asked. I will be expecting them back."

"Possessive little thing, aren't you?"

"I don't own much," I told him stonily. "I never have. That is why I value the belongings I do have." I heaved a sigh, tiredness suddenly seeming to seep into my bones. "You are here to check on Christine. I've been asleep for the last twenty four hours, I'm told. How is she?"

"Unharmed," he said after a moment. "Worried about you. Once she sees you conscious and alert, I have no doubt she will begin enjoying the surroundings of this château and the charm of its occupants." His tone was a little bitter, but that was only to be expected.

"And you?" I asked. "When the police came, I have no doubt that your name was mentioned. From maybe one or two people, they would write it off as theatre superstition... but if they get the same version of events from enough people, they will come looking for you. Can you be sure your lair is well-concealed enough to keep them out?"

"My 'lair'?" He gave a short bark of laugh. "Am I a vampire now, Meg?"

I scowled.

"Your hands are cold and I've never seen you in direct sunlight. Don't mock me."

"My apologies," he said, not sounding apologetic at all. "I assure you, little dancer, even if the police do believe in the existence of the Opera Ghost, it is highly unlikely they will find their way into the hidden entrances, let alone through the catacombs. However, I thank you for your concern. I will make sure all my traps are in good working order."

I didn't know what I had expected. I didn't know what I wanted him to say. But I did not want him to be caught and punished for the death of Buquet. Whether or not I had played a part in the Phantom's decision to kill the stagehand, the man's death came as a... relief, if I allowed myself to think on it selfishly. It was like having a protector, a guardian angel.

"The de Chagnys could be powerful enemies, Monsieur, now the 'Angel of Music' illusion is shattered. Much like the chandelier."

I sighed again, and pinched the bridge of my nose, then rested my hand on the book I had placed on the table, drumming out a rhythm with my fingertips. He watched me as if memorising the pattern for a long moment, then reached across, resting his hand on mine and stopping the movement of my fingers.

"You weren't hurt by the chandelier? You or Christine?"

"Not physically," I gave him a cold look.

"You need to rest." He told me, and I sighed.

"You'll be... safe, where you are, Monsieur? You have everything you need?"

"Everything," he inclined his head, then his ran eyes over the walls of the château. "And you will be enjoying a taste of luxury, it seems."

I rose to my feet, and he stood too, as I shrugged his cloak off my shoulders. I passed it to him, and he handed me the blue book, like an exchange. I looked down at it, then back at him.

"Goodnight, Monsieur."

"Goodnight, Meg," he replied. "Sleep well."

I turned, resting my hand on the window latch.

"Monsieur Erik?"

"Meg?"

"You knew my father... do you, truthfully, believe that he was mad?"

He hesitated.

"*I* believe... he was, yes."

I swallowed.

"Do you think I am too?"

He gave me a dazzling, unnerving smile.

"You, my dear Meg," he said. "Are as sane as I am. Goodnight, little dancer."

The remark was not a comfort to me. I entered the bedroom through the balcony window, closing it behind me. I got back into bed, careful not

THE ANGEL'S SHADOW

to disturb Mother, sliding the book under my pillow, and settled down under the sheets. By the time I had become comfortable and was lying facing the window again, I saw that the Phantom had vanished.

I had just dozed off when a loud bang ripped through the quiet night. I sat up at the same time as my mother, and I knew then that the noise had not been in my head, part of a dream, but part of the real world. It had been a gunshot. We stared at each other without a word, and then scrambled from the bed and to the door. We practically fell into the corridor beyond, and I noticed that it was papered in a beautiful periwinkle blue.

The Comte de Chagny, Philippe, was standing outside a door further down the corridor in a red quilted dressing gown. I saw with a shock that he had three parallel marks on his cheek; marks made, I realised, when I had struck out at him with my fingernails. He was knocking hard.

"Raoul? What's going on in there?!"

The door opposite ours opened, and Christine emerged, tying the cord of her own dressing gown. She looked worried and slightly muddled by sleep.

"Raoul! Open up, man!"

We edged along to stand with Philippe as he banged on the door again. Raoul opened the door in his nightshirt, looking rather shaken, and holding a revolver in a trembling hand. Philippe snatched it from his younger brother.

"Raoul, what is going on?!"

Servants had joined us in the corridor, bearing lights. I felt a bit strange, remembering that the de Chagnys had servants; had I not lived and worked at the Opera House, I could have been one of them.

"I thought I was dreaming, but I wasn't," Raoul said, and the light caught the sheen of sweat on his brow. "I fired at two stars that kept me from sleeping."

"Stars?" Philippe repeated. "You're raving! Are you ill?" He seized the younger man by the shoulder. "For God's sake, Raoul, tell me what happened!"

"I'm not ill," Raoul was visibly trying to pull himself together. "And I'm not raving... I saw Erik, his eyes glowing in the dark."

I heard Christine gasp and saw the colour draining from her face.

"My God," her cry was hardly more than a whisper. "I can't escape from him!"

"Erik?" Philippe looked between Christine and Raoul. "Who is Erik?"

"Erik is the true name of the Phantom of the Opera," Mother explained, her arms around a trembling Christine.

"He was here," Raoul repeated. "I saw him. Come, I'll show you!"

He took a light from one of the servants and turned back into the bedroom. Philippe followed, and I saw no reason to remain excluded, that old dangerous flame of curiosity ignited again, and entered the room as well. It was almost a mirror image of the room I was sleeping in, but distinctly more masculine. The most immediate feature was the bullet hole in the French window, the glass cracked around it.

"You were aiming at eyes?" I murmured.

"Yes," Raoul replied, not looking at me, although Philippe gave me a sharp look and I knew it was not my place to ask the question. However, he did not ask me to leave, instead going over to the window to examine the hole in the glass for himself. If Raoul had been aiming at the eyes of a man standing on the balcony outside the window, then that man must stand at least six feet tall.

Raoul unlocked the window and opened it, stepping out onto his balcony and shining the light on the flooring.

"Here!" He cried. "Blood! And here! And more here!" He grinned, almost laughed. "A ghost who bleeds is not so much of a ghost, hmm?"

There were spots of blood on the floor, along the balcony railing, trailing to the drainpipe and then continuing up it. The Comte looked at it thoughtfully.

"You fired at a creature with glowing eyes that could climb the drainpipe," he stated. "My dear brother, you fired at a cat."

"Perhaps," Raoul admitted. "Although, a fit man could easily climb it. Any sailor or naval officer could, including me. The misfortune is that it's quite possible that it was a cat. With Erik, you never know. Is it Erik? It is a cat? Is it the ghost? No, with Erik, you can't tell."

He sighed, and then looked at me as if he had just noticed I was there. Mother and Christine were further back in the room, but I had come forward to the French windows in order to see the blood for myself.

"Mademoiselle Giry," his tone reflected surprise. "You are feeling better?"

"Yes, thank you, Vicomte," I replied, and looked to his brother. "And I owe you both an apology, especially you, Comte de Chagny, for my behaviour. You must think me little more than a savage."

"Not at all, Mademoiselle," Philippe said. "You were suffering from shock." He looked back at the blood on the drainpipe. "There is nothing to be seen tonight, further investigation will have to wait until the morning."

I got the distinct impression we were being dismissed, confirmed when Mother beckoned to me.

"Goodnight, Messieurs," I murmured as I past them.

"More expense, Raoul," Philippe said as we left the room. "It will cost a small fortune to repair that window."

I wondered if the de Chagny's finances were not as healthy as I thought, or whether it was simply a brotherly reprimand. We walked back down the corridor to our respective bedrooms, stopping outside the doors, where Christine embraced me.

"Meg, don't you ever frighten me like that again," she said fondly.

"Sorry, Christine," I hugged her back. "It frightened me too, if I'm honest."

She stroked my cheek with the backs of her fingers.

"You'll be all right now," she promised. "I'll see you in the morning, hmm?"

I nodded, and Mother and I went back into the bedroom. She told me that, with the abundance of guestrooms in the château, she had a bedroom to herself, but had wanted to remain with me until I had returned to my senses. We settled back into the bed, side by side.

"Do you think the Phantom was here?" I asked in a whisper, although of course I already knew he had been.

"I don't know…"

"Do you think he was hurt?"

"Why should I care?" Her tone was cold. "I am through with him. God knows how long it will be before the Opera House will be open to the public again. And he caused you yet more suffering, Meg."

"So… are you going to tell the police what you know of him?"

"No," she said after a pause. "But I am sorely tempted to sever my ties with him."

We said no more on the subject that night, but I thought it all over before dropping into sleep. I was still uncertain why the Phantom had followed us to the de Chagny mansion, although the likelihood was that he was stalking Christine. In that case, why come to my window and indulge in our little conversation? If it had been the Phantom that Raoul had fired at, then the man was wounded, and I didn't know how badly. I wondered why I even cared. And what would happen if Mother did decide to sever her ties with the Opera Ghost? I had the strong suspicion that her 'ghostly' duties of shopping for him, delivering his notes and keeping his Box unoccupied, might well fall to me. Would Christine remain safe? Would Raoul?

"You, my dear Meg, are as sane as I am."

I shuddered and turned over, burying my face in the pillow. Let there be no more disturbances tonight, and no dreams to trouble me. Let me get my grip back on my world and my own mind. Ever since my father had been admitted into that hospital, in an act that I believed led to his suicide, I had sworn to myself that I would never enter one. But with recent events causing me such a public loss of control, I feared that my nightmares might very soon become a reality.

CHAPTER TWENTY FOUR

After the events of that night, I slept deeply and completely, and if I dreamed I did not remember it in the morning.

On waking, I felt fairly rested and refreshed, and I put that down to my twenty four hour sedation. I do not like doctors, true enough, but their sedatives were another matter altogether.

My first act was to open the French windows and have a daylight look at the splashes of blood that went up the drainpipe between Raoul's balcony and mine. I was relieved to see that there wasn't much; maybe it really was a cat that had sustained an injury. The question of where the animal had gone was one I could avoid. The Phantom would have presumably returned to the Opera Populairé.

There was a bathroom adjacent to the bedroom and I was delighted to find that there was a full-sized tub plumbed in, like the one the Phantom had in his own subterranean home. We also had some of them in the communal bathrooms that the ballerinas used, otherwise we had to bathe standing at the sink or use a portable tub, to be filled with hot water bucket by bucket. It was truly what I needed that morning.

When I emerged, wrapped in a towel with my blonde hair hanging in wet lines to my tailbone, the curls straightened out by the water, I found that Mother was back in the room, fully dressed and carrying my own clothes. While I had been asleep, my clothes had been cleaned and pressed by the de Chagny's servants, and I accepted them gratefully. It was every stitch I had been wearing on the night of the chandelier crash; dress, petticoats, chemise, corset, pantalets.

I held onto the bedpost while Mother laced me into the corset, and as it tightened I reflected that I really did need a new one. It would have been more comfortable to go without, in all honesty, but as I have been 'blessed' in the bust department, given my profession, not wearing one would have been indecent.

"I don't suppose I need to remind you to be on your best behaviour,

THE ANGEL'S SHADOW

Meg?" Mother said as she tugged the laces tight.

"Of course not," I responded crossly. "I'm not a child."

"No, but neither one of us is used to these surroundings. We're both going to have to mind our manners."

"I embarrassed you," I sighed. She tied the laces in a double bow behind my back.

"Meg, you worried me," she gently took me by the shoulders and turned me to her. "I am *worried* about you. You collapsed in complete hysterics, and it's not for the first time in the last few months, is it? When the cat was killed, your reaction was quite similar."

"I was in shock!" I protested.

"Meg," she spoke quietly, steadily. "There were a lot of people on that stage the other night, who also saw Buquet's body and had the chandelier swung at them. None of them fell to pieces."

Her words felt like a knife in my chest. My throat constricted and tears stung my eyes. It took me several attempts to speak.

"I haven't hurt anyone," I tried hard to keep my voice steady. "And I haven't harmed myself. I'm not going to either." It *was* steady, my voice, but cold. "Maybe I am like Papa. But I am not insane. Even if I were, I will *not* submit to the hospital 'treatment' as he did. Know that now, Mother. I know you care about me... I know you're afraid for me... but he didn't survive that treatment, did he? It didn't make him well again."

She swallowed hard.

"Meg... darling..."

"Don't." I've never heard myself sound so hard. "Just... don't. Let's not discuss the option again. I can't bear it, Mother, I can't. Let's just... do what we can for each other and get back to the Opera House."

We didn't speak for the rest of the morning, the tension humming in the silence between us. It was the silence we needed, for each of us to understand the other. I knew that Mother wanted what was best for me, that she truly was worried about me, and that she had been right. No one else had reacted in the manner I had done, and that made me feel ashamed.

We breakfasted in a dining room with Christine, Raoul and Philippe on fruit, croissants and coffee. I apologised again for causing the scratch marks on the Comte's cheek, and again he waved the apology. I could tell, however, that no matter how polite he was to me, he had been unnerved by my behaviour, and did not like me. Nevertheless, he informed Christine, Mother and I that we were all welcome to stay in his home for as long as we needed. We all thanked him profusely.

The closure of the Opera House left the three of us with an unexpected—albeit unpaid—holiday. I was determined that, given the darkness weighing down my shoulders for the last few days, I would do my best to shake it off and enjoy myself. It was June in France, and

167

summertime was glorious, the sun blazing and the temperatures high.

The de Chagny mansion was a magnificent building, beautifully decorated and full of expensive knickknacks and ornaments, opulence was everywhere. Christine fitted in so well with these surroundings, that for the first time in years, I remembered the class difference between us. Had Gustave Daaé lived, his fame as a violinist would surely have spread and his position in society risen. Christine had chosen to train as a ballerina and then continue in that career instead of using her father's reputation to her advantage. People knew and respect the name of Daaé, and I had the impression that the esteemed violinist had left his daughter some money, although I didn't know if there were conditions attached to her accessing it. Christine and I had never discussed the subject, it had simply never come up in conversation between us. I was lower class, Christine was middle class and the de Chagnys… the de Chagnys were members of the aristocracy.

I walked through the de Chagny home, looking up at the oil portraits of the noblemen and their wives. Christine would blend in well here; she had the beauty, the grace and the intelligence. She also had a maternal instinct that would make her a wonderful mother. I would not envy her if this was the life she chose for herself; I just hoped that her career as a soprano would not be ended by becoming a bride. Her voice was so incredible that it would almost be a crime for her not to continue singing.

The two of us spent time together in the magnificent gardens, walking the gravel paths and admiring the neat hedges, beautiful flowers and green trees. There were four gardeners, a father and his three sons, who skilfully kept them maintained. There was even a lake on the property, with a small jetty thrusting out into it, and I learned that it was there purposefully for swimming. Given my near-death experience—and there had been far too many of those in the last few months—by drowning, I made a promise to myself that this year I would learn to swim. It had been more than thirty years since a woman from Stockholm had become the first female swimming instructor, effectively opening up the activity to both genders, but it was still frowned upon for a girl like me.

On our fourth day in the de Chagny mansion, Christine and I sat on one of the ornamental benches, drinking in the sunshine.

"How could anyone give this up?" Christine said, out of the blue. I blinked at her, basking in the light and the floral perfumes of the garden, and realised that her thoughts had been underground, with the Phantom. I considered her questions carefully, both the spoken and the unspoken.

"I suppose…" I began. "Giving up things like this, daylight and fresh air… could be done if it meant that doing so ensured safety from something else. Something more terrible than living in the dark."

"Cold, unfeeling light," she murmured. "Meg… there is magic and beauty in darkness… but I am a woman of the light. I can't survive without

THE ANGEL'S SHADOW

it. The night of *Il Muto*... before we began the second performance, Raoul and I went up to the rooftop."

I nodded, to show I remembered, although at the time I had only caught a glimpse of them as I buried my face in Mother's shoulder, having just witnessed the dead body of Joseph Buquet falling from the flies.

"It was the only place I could think of where Erik wouldn't follow us." Christine allowed herself a small smile, reaching to take my hand. "Raoul proposed to me, Meg. He asked me to marry him."

I stared at her, excitement bubbling through my veins.

"And?" I prompted.

"And I said yes."

"Christine!" I flung my arms around her, giddy with delight on her behalf as I hugged her tightly. "Oh, congratulations! Have you set a date yet? Show me the ring!"

I felt ridiculously happy at her engagement, which came as a surprise. I had expected that, if this news came, I would feel worried and jealous. Instead, I was elated. Maybe my time away from the Opera House was doing me a power of good.

Christine laughed, returning my embrace.

"You go too fast," she told me gently. "We're in the very early stages of our engagement, there's still a lot to decide. I don't have a ring yet, let alone a date for the wedding."

"Oh." I felt vaguely disappointed, then brightened. "Will you need help choosing the wedding dress?"

"Of course," she smiled. "I hoped, Meg, that you would be my chief bridesmaid."

I squealed like a seven-year-old.

"Yes!"

"But," she said, taking my hands. "The engagement is to be kept secret, for the time being at least."

"Why?" I asked in bewilderment. "Secret from whom?"

"From the managers and the people at the Opera Populairé."

The light dawned on me and I raised my eyebrows at her.

"Christine... you know Erik will find out."

She nodded, looking suddenly miserable.

"Do you think he will ever forgive me?"

"Maybe," I murmured. "He says he loves you, but I don't think he truly knows what love is." And then, suddenly, what she had told me slammed into place. "Raoul proposed to you on the roof of the Opera House?"

"Yes..."

"And did you accept straight away?"

"I did."

So the chandelier crash, that seemingly senseless act of violence, must have been in reaction to that. The Phantom had been granted everything else he had asked for, everything he wanted... except Christine. If he had overheard Christine not only speaking with Raoul, when he had specifically forbidden her to, but promising to be his legally wedded wife, it must have sent his jealousy into a rage. She had denied him by rejecting his romantic advances, and he must have seen her acceptance of Raoul's proposal as an act of ultimate betrayal. The Vicomte had so much that Erik lacked; influence, wealth, beauty. In comparison, he must see himself as a hideous monster lurking in the darkness. I felt a sudden, overwhelming rush of pity for Erik; how lonely he must be. On the other hand, a tiny voice in my head interrupted, the chandelier crash could have killed Christine, and me, could have caused the deaths of many people. It was an act of God—or blind luck—that there had only been one fatality.

My mind went back over the conversation he and I had had, on the balcony.

"You weren't hurt by the chandelier? You or Christine?"

His words indicated that he had not intended either of us any physical harm.

"Meg?" Christine prompted, and I realised I had not heard a word she had just said.

"Sorry?"

"I was saying, I know I can't keep it from Erik, and I know he'll be.... upset when he finds out."

'Livid' was the word I would have chosen.

"But I want him to know about the engagement from me, rather than from someone else." She swallowed hard. "I also just don't feel *safe* anymore. For that reason, when the Opera House reopens... I won't be going back to live there with you."

I stared at her, the breath knocked from my lungs as if she had punched me in the stomach.

"Not going back?" I repeated, sounding utterly slow-witted, and Christine squeezed my hands gently.

"Not to *live*. I'll still be part of the company, I'll still sing... but I can't live in the Opera House anymore. I can't live so close to a man who haunts my every breath, someone who murders those around me without a thought."

She was afraid, even terrified of her mentor.

"Will you... continue with your lessons?" I asked, since Erik was foremost in my mind.

"I may find another tutor," she said, after a short hesitation.

"So... where are you going to live?" I looked around the gardens. "Here, with the Vicomte?"

"No," Christine shook her head. "It wouldn't be appropriate for us to live together until after we're married. It is one thing to stay while you and Madame Giry are here to act as chaperones, but that can't last forever. I'll need to find somewhere in the city where I can stay."

"How are you going to manage it?" I asked worriedly. "I mean… financially? And for a woman living alone, Paris can be dangerous."

She smiled.

"You sound like your mother. Father left me some money—quite a lot of money—and Raoul is going to help me look for an apartment somewhere safe. I hoped you might join us?"

"I'd be glad to," I was inwardly relieved by her request, as I would want to know for myself where Christine was, that she was safe. It was a strange feeling, knowing that she would be leaving the Opera House and the dormitory we had shared for the last six years. It was like my twin was leaving home. She would be safe and happy, but she would be taking a tiny piece of my heart with her. Impulsively, I hugged her again.

"I'm so pleased for you," I told her.

"Thank you," she whispered against my cheek. "I know this will sound silly, we'll be seeing each other on a daily basis…. But I'll miss you."

I laughed weakly.

"I'll miss you too." I was still smiling as we broke apart. "You must have had some thoughts about when you want the wedding."

"I think Raoul is keen to get married tomorrow," she replied with a smile. "But I'd rather wait until spring. A summer wedding would be too short notice and I don't like the idea of wedding in winter. I think March or April would be good. There are a lot of things to consider."

March or April. It seemed so soon, even though it was nine or ten months away. By next August, I would probably still be living in the Opera Populairé with my mother, and Christine would be a wife.

A few days later, Christine, Raoul and I were walking through the streets of Paris. We had been to look at an apartment in the city that Christine was considering moving into once we all had word that the Opera Populairé would be opening for business again. The newspapers had been full of the chandelier crash; in a way Erik had been right when he told Christine that her name would appear in every newspaper in Paris, for they all held details of *Il Muto*'s quick recasting and the disaster that followed. The more sensationalist newspapers were printing stories about *Il Muto* being cursed, and the other mishaps that had occurred to companies who had put on that particular opera. Of course, such newspapers and their readers loved the involvement of an Opera Ghost.

Someone—or several persons—had told stories about the Phantom of the Opera. Many were wildly exaggerated, but on two things they were all agreed: the Ghost had half the face of a demon, and he hid that demonic half behind a mask.

The fact that the papers had got hold of these details surprised me. Ever since I was tiny, I had been told stories of the Opera Ghost, *long* before I had discovered he was a man of flesh and blood. His defining characteristic had been the white half-mask. It wasn't until Christine had told me, and the information had been repeated during an *Il Muto* rehearsal by Joseph Buquet, that I knew the mask concealed a deformity. It is possible of course, that one of the people who had heard Buquet's description of the Ghost had repeated that information to the press.

Since the route to the apartment Christine was considering went past the Opera House, I requested a brief pause after we had viewed the property.

"I just want to collect any post that came for us," I told Christine and Raoul. "I won't be more than fifteen minutes. You could go for coffee."

I nodded to the coffee house situated just over the road from the Opera Populairé.

"I have no objection," Raoul told me. "And any news you can pick up about the state of affairs would be welcome. I think Philippe is quite keen to find out how far your managers will want to stretch our pocketbooks."

I smiled, a little surprised by the remark, but given that the de Chagnys were patrons of the Opera House, I should have expected that they would be asked to 'donate' some money for the repairs.

I went to Mother's rooms and collected the two or three letters that had been shoved under her door, then grabbed a sheet of paper and scribbled a few lines in pencil:

O.G.
I heard that you were shot. Are you well?
Meg

I allowed myself a small smile at the thought of the role-reversal; the Phantom of the Opera receiving notes rather than sending them. I knew there was a passageway to his home through my mother's wardrobe, but given that he had talked about ensuring his traps were in working order the last time we spoke, I did not want to venture down an unknown path. Entering the prima donna's dressing room would look odd to the few people in the Opera House, so I decided to leave the note by his secret doorway near the dressing rooms.

I slid the folded sheet of paper under the vase on top of the pillar that rested in the alcove, concealing the door, and wondered how I might receive a reply.

CHAPTER TWENTY FIVE

Since I was in the Opera House and the area of the dressing rooms, I cut through the corridor and into the backstage area. I opened the door and stepped into the wings. The stage and auditorium were as brightly illuminated as they could be, given the absence of the chandelier. There were lamps lit everywhere, and I considered how many of the rooms within the Opera House did not have external windows. The destroyed chandelier had been removed and the shattered crystals cleaned away, and the curtain that it had set fire to had been taken down entirely. There was scaffolding around the Boxes, leading up to the ceiling, which looked oddly naked without the chandelier. The ugly gash in it looked like a wound in the building's flesh, but it was evident from all the scaffolding that surrounded it that repairs were well underway.

There was a table and a couple of chairs on the stage, where Monsieur André was talking to a man who seemed to be some sort of construction engineer, and was definitely involved in the repair work. As he left André's side, the manager turned his head and saw me in the wings.

"Mademoiselle Giry," he smiled at me. "Come here, child."

I stepped towards the table, noticing it was covered in plans and designs; a new chandelier was in the works, it seemed.

"Good afternoon, Monsieur André," I said, returning his smile and trying not to look surprised that he knew my name. I was used to being a little overlooked, but I supposed that given my recent promotion to prima ballerina and connection to the former concierge, he must have made an effort to remember me. "How are... the repairs?"

"Expensive," his smile was less strained than I had anticipated. "Still, the disaster provided a good excuse for some much-needed work to be done. We're having electricity laid on, certainly in the auditorium and the upper storeys." I lifted my eyebrows, surprised. "You're well, Mademoiselle? You and your mother?"

"Yes, thank you, Monsieur. Mother and I are staying at the château owned by the de Chagnys."

"I'm glad to hear it."

"Where is Monsieur Firman?" I asked, realising that this was the first time since Lafevre left the Opera House that I had seen the managers apart.

"Richard is in Carcassonne," he sighed. "He made arrangements to visit family members months ago that could not be postponed, even after this." He waved a hand towards the auditorium to indicate the missing chandelier. "Unfortunately, I've lost my office key and he has of course taken his with him, so I'm locked out. I could do with knowing the route our resident Ghost uses to get around."

"You've not had any trouble from... him?" I asked cautiously.

"Not a peep."

I exhaled, hoping my relief was not obvious.

"I think Mother has her set of keys with her," I kept my tone casual. "She was definitely keeping them until you officially employed another concierge."

"Yes, well, we must talk about that..." He reached into the inside pocket of his jacket and withdrew an envelope, passing it to me. It was addressed to Madame Giry. "Will you see that your mother gets this, please?"

"Certainly," I added it to the couple of letters I had already collected. "The de Chagnys asked me to find out what the... state of affairs is."

André looked tired.

"Firman and I will be writing to all the patrons, but it will be months before we can open again. We will let everyone know by letter, Mademoiselle."

I left the stage the same way I had entered it, and went back past the Phantom's secret doorway. The note I had slid under the vase was missing; that was quick work on his part, but then, he had eyes everywhere. He had probably been observing André and I during our conversation. I left the Opera Populairé entirely, and walked across the road to the café.

Christine and Raoul were seated at one of the round tables with coffee and a slice of cake each. Christine raised a hand in greeting and the Vicomte smiled as I joined them. I was pleasantly surprised to learn that there was a third cup, enough coffee in the pot for me, and declined the offer of cake. I told the two of them the little information I had garnered.

"I'm not sure we can trespass on your hospitality for months," I worried.

"Meg," Raoul smiled. "We have talked about this. You are all welcome to stay as long as you need to."

"You're very kind," I told him, and Christine gave him a dazzling smile.

When we returned to the château, I told Mother about Monsieur

THE ANGEL'S SHADOW

André's request for a key to the manager's office, which made her laugh, and gave her the envelopes. We sat in the drawing room while Mother read the letters, her eyebrows rising so high when she read the one from the Opera House, that I thought they might vanish into her hair.

"What is it?" I asked.

"The managers are reinstating me as concierge," she said. "At double the salary."

"Double?" I repeated, astonished but delighted.

"As of this week," she looked up from the letter, as surprised and pleased as I was.

"How can they afford it?" I wondered. "Along with the repairs to the Opera House and the new electricity and paying the Phantom's fees…"

Mother waved her hand dismissively.

"If they want to buy my loyalty, then so be it," she said. "I shall write and accept."

I shrugged; I knew nothing about the Opera House's financial affairs but if André and Firman thought they could pay Mother twice her wages, then neither she nor I was going to reject it. She opened the other envelopes, and I saw a couple of sheets in one of them. One letter was in writing I didn't know, but the other, smaller sheet, had a black border and I saw the Phantom's handwriting. I opened my mouth to ask what he had to say, but Mother crumpled the paper in her palm, her lips pressed into a thin line.

Dear Meg,

I am pleased to report that the Vicomte is a poor shot. Although I did sustain some small injuries, it was as a result of the broken French window, rather than a bullet. See page 86 of your book.

O. G.

The note was on the nightstand beside my bed the following morning, propped against the silver candlestick. It made me shiver to realise that the Phantom must have entered the room through the window while I slept. Had he also been in Christine's room? I pushed the disturbing thought from my mind and reached under the bed for the blue book Erik was referring to. Page eighty six covered the treatment of lacerations caused by glass. Such wounds could be serious. Any glass remaining in them should be removed with extreme care, the cut cleaned with alcohol, and stitched if necessary. There was a diagram of how to sew a wound closed and I was surprised to see how simple the stitches were; I had been using the same ones all my life when altering clothing.

LOUISE ANNE BATEMAN

* * *

Summer blazed itself through cloudless days, and nights of crashing thunderstorms, into the blues and browns and golds of Autumn. Mother ensured that Christine and I did not 'neglect' our vocations by taking it upon herself to tutor us in singing and dance. Meanwhile, notes fluttered between the Phantom and I like pigeons, silent and secret.

Official letters announced that the Opera Populairé would be reopening in early January 1894, with a performance of *Faust*. Mother smiled at me when we got that news.

"We haven't done that opera for almost seventeen years."

"I know," I smiled back.

Faust was the opera that the company had been performing when I was born, and I had been named Marguerite after the leading lady. This production would not have an audition process; the managers had decided that Marguerite would be played by La Carlotta and Christine would play the role of Siébel. There was no named part for me. I found myself slightly anxious by the casting decision, worrying about the Phantom's reaction. It had uncomfortable echoes of *Il Muto*, and the last thing I wanted was another chandelier crash.

It was the second week in September when I overheard the de Chagny brothers arguing. I was in the garden, for the days were still warm, sitting on a bench underneath one of the château's windows. As it turned out, this window, slightly open to admit the fresh morning air, belonged to the study of the Comte Philippe de Chagny. I heard him greet Raoul in a somewhat cold manner, then the rustle of a newspaper.

"Read that!" Philippe ordered.

Raoul sighed and began to read aloud.

"'*The news in the* Faubourg *is that there is a promise of marriage between Mademoiselle Christine Daaé, the opera singer, and Monsieur le Vicomte Raoul de Chagny.*' Well, brother? Our engagement is not a secret, what of it?"

"Keep reading."

"'*If the gossips are to be credited, Comte Philippe has sworn that, for the first time on record, the de Chagnys shall not keep their promise. But, as love is as all-powerful at the Opera as—and even more than—elsewhere, we wonder how Comte Philippe intends to prevent the Vicomte, his brother, from leading Mademoiselle Daaé to the altar.*' Yes, Philippe, I should be interested to know that as well. Ah, but this little piece of tattle-tale is not finished! *The two brothers are said to adore each other; but the Comte is curiously mistaken if he imagines that brotherly love will triumph over love pure and simple.*'" The paper rustled again as Raoul put it down. "I do not know what you want me to say, Philippe. The reporting style of the *Epoque* is certainly not improving, given that they turn to the *Faubourg* for their gossip."

THE ANGEL'S SHADOW

I kept my eyes on a bush covered in white roses ahead of me, their leaves and petals trembling in a light breeze. I was tempted to stand and turn so that I could see into the window, but I supposed that all I would end up looking at would be my own reflection, and I had no wish for the men to know that I was eaves-dropping.

"Raoul, you are making us look ridiculous. There should be *no* gossip for the *Faubourg* to be reporting. And all the papers are having an immense laugh at our expense due to all this talk about the Opera Ghost."

"What are you saying?"

"Raoul... Christine is a... a very pleasant, well-spoken girl who has turned your head. But she is an opera singer."

"Oh, I see," I could hear the fury rising in the Vicomte's tone. "And therefore not good enough for the de Chagny family, is that it?"

"Raoul that's not—"

"That's exactly what you mean! My God, Philippe, I thought better of you! Christine is more than just an opera singer! Her talent surpasses everyone else on that stage!"

I swallowed hard, feeling a tingling in the back of my throat.

"And even if she weren't, I *love* her, Philippe! I *love* Christine Daaé and I *am* going to marry her! You shall not prevent me!"

Overhearing that conversation made me think carefully about different concepts of love. Raoul's love for Christine was as close to that which I had seen in the operas and read in my books as I thought it could be. It was true love. I thought back to the Phantom, Erik, and his idea of love. He wanted Christine, *desired* her, but not in the same way as Raoul. Perhaps, with her remarkable voice, he intended Christine to sing his own compositions; but he wanted to *possess* her, body and soul. Was that love? He thought so.

Dear Meg,

Your assistance is required at my home in the Opera House this Friday at seven o'clock. Enter through the mirror by pressing the switch behind the flower design on the left hand side of the frame. Follow the corridor down the staircase and take the second right. Go down the next staircase and then the one on the right. Turn left at the bottom, follow the corridor and take the third right. Go down the final staircase and use the lever to open the door into my home. Memorise these instructions and then BURN THIS LETTER. If I am absent when you arrive, wait for me.

O.G.

P.S. If you are forced to wait, try to confine your curiosity to just the one room.
E.

I blinked at the note, intrigued not just by the demand for my presence and the list of instructions, but the final sign-off. E for Erik. Were we on a first-name basis now, in written correspondence at least?

Rehearsals had begun for the production of *Faust*, so I had no difficulty in telling Mother I wanted to stay at the Opera Populairé a little longer after she and Christine returned to the château.

As requested, I burned the note, unsurprised by that instruction; the Phantom was showing a huge amount of trust in me by giving away details of his secret passageways. He wouldn't want those details lying around where anyone could get at them. I entered the dressing room and walked over to the mirror. It was, of course, flat against the wall, but my questing fingers found the left-hand side of the frame slightly raised. I slid my fingers behind it and fumbled for the switch that would release the catch of the looking-glass. Something gave way under my fingertips and I heard a click. Placing my other hand on the glass, I pushed it gently so that the mirror slid into the right-hand frame. I stepped into the passageway beyond and closed the mirror behind me, taking a moment to look through the transparent glass to the dressing room beyond. I was reminded of the chill I had felt when I first learned that the Phantom had windows into my world.

A few feet from me, a lantern sat on the floor, a box of matches beside it; that was thoughtful. I lit the lantern and pocketed the box of matches, then carefully made my way along the passageway. The light picked up eyes glowing in the dark, rats skittering on horrid little claws across my path. I *hate* rats, but was determined not to be frightened off by them. Ever since Figaro had been killed, the rat population had flourished, although now I thought about it, I didn't recall seeing any trace of rats in Erik's home. Surely they were drawn there by the food in his kitchen? Perhaps the mighty Opera Ghost used poison, or a miniature version of his Punjab lasso. I tried to imagine him practicing his technique on rats, then remembered seeing the lasso around Joseph Buquet's throat and felt quite sick.

I descended the staircase and took the second turning on the right, which led to a second staircase. This led to yet another set of stairs that branched off in three directions. I took the right-hand set, turning left at the bottom and following the corridor along. This place truly was a maze and I wondered how the builders had gotten their heads around the original designs. Perhaps several sets of builders had been involved in the construction, unconnected with one another, so that the secret passageways remained secret. How could it be that just one man had the run of the place via all these hidden routes?

I took the second right and continued along, looking for the final staircase that would lead me to the Phantom's home. Perhaps I was now above his lake; I tried to remember what the ceiling looked like when I had been flat on my back after the Phantom had saved me from drowning, but I had been too busy breathing to take much notice.

"Keep your hand at the level of your eyes."

The words jumped suddenly into my memory as if they had been spoken into the lantern light ahead of me. The thought which leapt into my mind was that perhaps I was being lured here simply to be used as target practice for the Phantom and his Punjab lasso, as I had just imagined him doing with rats. No. It couldn't be true.

"Keep your hand at the level of your eyes."

Slowly, I lifted my free hand beside my face. If a noose were thrown around my neck, I would be able to use my hand to prevent it from tightening and crushing my throat. The Phantom might be stalking my steps even now, preparing for an attack on a moving target.

I was holding the lantern in my left hand, my right reached up, and it was for that reason alone that when the ground suddenly vanished from beneath my feet, I was able to cling with the very tips of my fingers, onto the edge of the hole that tried to swallow me.

CHAPTER TWENTY SIX

The lantern fell from my left hand and clattered away into the darkness beneath my feet as I gripped the edge of the hole. Adrenaline coursed through my veins and my sweating fingers struggled to maintain a hold. Struggled in vain, as it turned out; I lost my grip and dropped helplessly into the darkness. I came into contact with at least two mercilessly hard objects as I fell, landing on a smooth, cold floor with all the breath knocked from my body. The lantern had been extinguished during the fall and was probably shattered. It took me several moments to get my breath back and evaluate what had happened to me. The fall had been substantial, and whatever I had crashed into had badly bruised my back on the right-hand side, maybe cracked a rib. I lay on my back, breathing gently, allowing myself to feel the aches and pains; my ribs hurt terribly and the likelihood that one of them was broken seemed high. I was waiting for my eyes to adjust to the darkness, but when that didn't happen I worried that the fall might have damaged my sight. Ridiculous. I forced myself to breath calmly; the room I was in was simply… black as pitch.

Very cautiously, I sat up and felt in my dress for the box of matches, congratulating myself for thinking to put them in my pocket. I opened the box, extracted a match and felt along the edge for the right place to strike. I struck it and saw the small flame jump to life all around me. My hand was trembling as I held up the match, and saw the light multiplied in the walls surrounding me.

Keep calm. Just keep calm.

The lantern was lying on the floor, surrounded by shards of glass, but the candle was in it and seemed to be undamaged by the fall. I lit it and swept the glass into a pile with my foot. I raised the remains of the lantern above my head to take a clear look at my surroundings. The light leapt back at me from every direction, multiplied against the walls and floor. I couldn't tell how large the room was. The floor was made of a silver-coloured metal, but the walls… the walls were mirrors. Dozens of them, of many different

THE ANGEL'S SHADOW

shapes and sizes, fitted together like a mosaic, undisturbed by a door or even a handle. I could see my own frightened eyes staring back at me, again and again.

In the centre of the room was a tree, sculpted in life-like detail from the same material as the floor. It glittered and shone as my lantern light caught a leaf or branch. It reached up to the ceiling over my head, where the stone panel I had fallen through must have tipped back into place, the hole concealed and the trap ready for its next victim. The trap... I had *known* that the Phantom had traps guarding his domain, that some of them were lethal; he had even spoken to me of making sure they were in good working order. Was that why he had summoned me here? As bait for his experiments, a pawn in his game?

I swallowed hard, trying to keep my breathing steady, pressing my free hand over my sore ribs. I must have crashed into the tree's branches or trunk as I fell. In a way, that was a blessing; it had broken my fall. The ceiling with its concealed trap door was at least ten foot over my head and I could have easily broken a leg. Or my neck. The mirrors turned the one tree into a wood full of them, surrounding me with no escape.

This room *must* have an exit, some way for the Phantom himself to get in and out. I circled my prison, pressing my hands to the mirrors, trying to find some secret panel or concealed switch. There was nothing. The room was hexagonal, with six walls and that huge tree spreading its branches. As a work of art, it was remarkable. When I was on the other side of the trunk, I saw that there was something among the leaves, hanging down. It was a rope, one end affixed to the metal branch, the other tied into the unmistakable shape of a noose. The sickening sight repeated itself again and again in the mirrors, stretching into infinity so that I wondered how I had not noticed it before. With an angry shriek—anger was better than horror, in my opinion—I thumped my fist against one of the mirrors. It cracked, splintering out like the threads of a spider's web, but the glass did not shatter or fall.

Keep calm. Keeping breathing. Think.

The Phantom's note had instructed the meeting to be at seven o'clock, and it must be that time now. If I shouted, perhaps he would hear me. He seemed to have systems in place that let him know when someone was getting close. I took a deep breath, and—thanking Monsieur Reyer's advice on voice projection—shouted at the top of my lungs.

"Monsieur Erik! It's Meg!"

Silence.

"I am trapped in the mirrored room!"

Still nothing. I could feel panic starting to tighten in my chest and throat.

"Phantom! Let me out! For God's sake, let me out!"

So much for keeping calm. I took another deep breath, which made my ribs hurt, and sat down where I was on the floor, closing my eyes to block out the infinitive reflections. Beating the walls would do me no good and could cause me more harm if I cut myself on broken glass. The only way out that I knew of was the way I had come in, the trap door I had fallen through. If it did work on a tipping mechanism, perhaps I could push it from the underside and then climb through. Provided I could reach it at all. I opened my eyes and looked up with a smile; I had always been good at climbing trees.

The tree was constructed of iron by the feel of it, strong and unbending. Even with my injury, I found it surprisingly easy to ascend—at least as far as the branch that had the noose hanging from it. I edged around it, feeling a lurch of nausea in my stomach, and climbed higher. The flickering illumination of the lantern I had left on the ground danced through the branches, throwing my shadow into the mirrors which bounced it back to me.

I was just reaching out towards the stone in the ceiling that I thought I had fallen through, when the room suddenly blazed with light. Compared to the candle it was as if someone had turned on the sun. The light was coming from above me and all around me, and for one wild moment I thought the Second Coming might be upon me. What was this magic? I tried to seek out the sources, but they were simply too bright. Were there five? Six? Seven? I was dazzled, dazed, and in danger of falling. I clutched onto the branch and focused on the pain of my ribs, the tangible, real feeling. This light could not have just appeared without reason, and it could not be sorcery or a spiritual epiphany; St. Paul on the Road to Damascus I was not. Something, or someone, had caused this light to be turned on. *The Phantom.*

I scrambled back down the iron tree, noticing that it seemed warmer under my hands somehow, but paying no attention, even when one of the metal leaves caught at my dress and ripped the fabric. My *new* dress, I thought once I had reached ground level again, paid for with money from Mother's salary increase. The undergarments were new too, beautifully fitted to support and mould my growing body. It was getting hot in here.

I ran towards one of the walls, hands raised to strike the mirrors again.

"Monsieur Erik! Monsieur! Mon—"

I leapt back with a startled cry. I had barely made contact with the glass, but it was already hot enough to burn. What was happening? The heat, which was growing more intense by the second, seemed to be coming from the walls themselves, amplified by the dozens of looking glasses. The air was becoming stifling, clawing at my parched throat as I felt sweat streaming down my body. It was like being in some tropical jungle; the iron tree in the centre of the room, repeated in the mirrors, became a forest

THE ANGEL'S SHADOW

scorching under an African sun.

"Erik! Monsieur Erik!"

I called his name over and over.

I lost track of time. I was collapsed on my knees on the burning floor, struggling to inhale the choking air, roasting in this oven. I was dying. This was Hell.

There was music. I could hear music somewhere close, someone was playing a piano... no, an organ.

"Help me..." My voice came out as nothing more than a whisper.

In a sudden burst of inspiration, I put two fingers into my mouth and blew as hard as I could. Mother did not approve of whistling, considering it unladylike, and it was extremely bad luck in a theatre, but that hadn't stopped me from learning how. There was a hesitation in the music, and I whistled again as loudly as I could manage. A third time, a fourth, and I heard a door open behind me. I barely had the strength to remain on my knees, could not turn to look at him, but I heard his voice.

"Good God!"

Hurried footsteps, then his arms were around me, pain jolting through my ribs as he half carried, half dragged me from that deadly room. It was blissfully cool in this new room, and I felt myself set down on something soft. The next thing I was aware of was a glass of cold water at my lips, and I gulped at it.

"Careful!" The voice sounded annoyed, almost angry. "You'll choke yourself, take it slowly!"

I obediently sipped the water more slowly, and he withdrew it after a few seconds and I felt him sponging my forehead with a wet, cold cloth. I opened my eyes to see Erik, the Phantom, leaning over me. He was wearing a white ruffled shirt and black trousers, with a strange foreign-looking robe over the top. It took me a moment to recognise the room as Erik's bedroom, that I was lying on Erik's bed, and I was surprised to see that it was lit with an *electric* light bulb. Monsieur André had told me that the Opera House was being partially wired for the new electric lights, but *surely* not down here, five floors below the level of the street? From this side, in a space between a desk and a small organ, I could see the outline of a door, which presumably concealed that horrific furnace.

I drew in a sharp breath.

"You tried to kill me!" I accused, but he was speaking at the same time, his words overlapping mine.

"Your curiosity will get you killed!"

We stared at each other.

"What?" I said. "You sent me a note, you *told* me to come here!"

"Yes, and I also told you that if I was late for our appointment, you were to wait in the drawing room for me and not go poking around!"

"The drawing room?!" I barked a laugh that made a shock of pain jolt up my ribcage. "I never got as far as the bloody drawing room!"

"How dare you use such language to—"

"I was following *your* instructions and I fell through the *floor* into that horrendous oven of yours!" It was my turn to speak over his words, and he paused mid-scold. He looked at me, and then asked slowly:

"When you came down here... well, to the level above this one... did you take the second right turning or the third?"

"I..." I frowned, trying to remember. "The... second? The second right after the last staircase I went down, I'm sure."

He sighed. "For a well-read, dare I even say *intelligent* girl, you are remarkably stupid."

"Stupid?!" I repeated.

"I gave you *clear* instructions, which I told you to memorise—"

"And then *burn*!"

"And told you to take the *third* right turn, not the second." He sighed again, and passed a hand over his eyes. "I thought, Meg, that your memory for dance routines would extend to my written directions as well."

I pressed my lips together, unwilling to apologise for my mistake and uncertain whether or not the fault was my own. I had known he had traps, and I had failed to follow the directions he had given me... I sat up, and gritted my teeth with a groan as the pain shuddered through my back.

"You are injured?" He asked.

"I fell through a ceiling," I growled. "Of course I'm injured!"

I pressed my hand over the area of my back where the ribs were causing me pain, and very carefully began to stand, but his hand was on my shoulder, preventing me from rising.

"Let me see."

"What?" I blinked at him.

"You are applying pressure to your back; do you think you have hurt your spine? Or your ribs?"

"My ribs hurt... Back right-hand side."

"Undress. Take off your gown and corset and let me see your back. I'll be able to tell if you have a broken bone."

"No!" I cried. "I'm not undressing in front of you!"

"You still don't trust me?"

I hesitated, swallowed, uncertain.

"I... I do trust you," I admitted reluctantly. "I know you have no... interest in me."

Not like the interest he had in Christine.

"Then do as I tell you."

Like the gentleman he pretended to be, he turned his back as I undid the clasps of my gown, worrying again over the rip in the fabric; maybe I could repair it. The corset was more of a struggle, the movements caused me pain, the lacings too tight for my fingers, and after a few minutes I had to admit defeat.

"Monsieur, I... I need help."

I kept my back to him, my cheeks scarlet. I heard his footsteps, and then his fingers began to work at the laces of my corset. They *fumbled*.

"You should invest in a front-lacing corset," he said, sounding almost frustrated.

"I'll bear it in mind," I replied, resisting the urge to comment on his inefficiency. The corset came free and he laid it on the bed beside me, sitting just behind where I perched on the edge of his mattress.

"Lift the chemise," he ordered, and I raised the waist-length chemise, flinching when his fingers gently pressed my back.

"Your hands are cold," I said.

"Eternally," was the answer. "Does this hurt?"

"No."

"This?"

"Yes."

"Mmm." His fingers explored the area of my ribcage with more tenderness than I had anticipated. "I don't think any of your ribs are broken, but there will be substantial bruising."

I sighed.

"I would suggest you visit a doctor."

"There's no need." I let the chemise drop as he withdrew his fingers from my back. "I'm sure your diagnosis is accurate."

I reached down to pick up my corset, but he reached it first.

"Why?"

"Why what?" I turned carefully, holding out my hand for the garment.

"Why won't you consult a doctor?" His eyes held genuine curiosity, and in this new electric light, it was more difficult to see that they were different colours. "You can afford it, I know about your mother's salary increase, so why not go?"

"I don't trust doctors," I told him coldly. "They killed my father."

He stared at me, lips parted, but then he thought better of whatever he was going to say.

"The corset, please."

He left the room as I struggled back into my clothes, lacing the corset loosely around my body as well as I could manage. I could explain away my bruising and the state of my dress by claiming to have fallen down the stairs, but returning to the châteaux without my corset on would give rise to more questions than I could lie my way out of. God, I was turning into a devious woman. I took one last look at the doorway to the room I had fallen into, then walked into the drawing room to find Erik boiling a kettle over the fire. I stood in the doorway, clenching and unclenching my hands by my sides, wanting to ask but uncertain that I wanted to know. He looked up and saw me.

"Meg?"

"That room I fell into… the room with the iron tree… what is it?"

His reply chilled me to my bruised bones.

"It is my torture chamber."

CHAPTER TWENTY SEVEN

Torture chamber.

Coming from someone else, I might have thought it a joke, something said to tease me. But not from him; he was serious and he was truthful. I swallowed hard and sank down into the armchair by the fire. I heard the crack in my voice as I said:

"If I asked, would you tell me?"

"You girls are so curious," he muttered. "It is one of the many traps that guard my home. I first designed and built one in Persia, and it is a remarkably varied way of disposing of an enemy."

"Varied?" I croaked.

"Oh, yes." He wrapped his hand in a cloth and lifted the whistling kettle from over the fire, pouring the boiling water into a coffee pot. "I can use fire, water, or heat, as you experienced."

"Sweet Jesus," I muttered.

"It is a copy of the one I built for the Shah," he continued, either not hearing or choosing to ignore my remark. "Although, of course, on a much smaller scale. The iron tree is a work of art, is it not?"

Do not cry, I ordered myself. *He has seen too many of your tears, do not cry.*

"It is," I swallowed hard, pressing my nails into my palm. "And worthy of better surroundings. Although I did not have much mind for its admiration while I was being roasted alive."

"That is regretful, I admit it. Milk and sugar?"

"I beg your pardon?"

"In your coffee, do you take milk and sugar?"

"Neither, thank you."

Lunatic.

I watched him warily as he poured the scalding liquid into two cups, and noticed that he did not add milk or sugar to his own cup either. The small clock on the mantelpiece began to chime the half hour as he brought the cup over to me, and I hesitated.

"What is it?" He demanded.

"The last beverage you gave me was drugged." I said.

He heaved a sigh, and I anticipated another comment about my inability to trust him. Instead, he raised the coffee cup to his own lips and blew gently. I watched his lips, the top one slightly hidden by the mask, fascinated, as he took a sip.

"Satisfied?" He held the cup out and I accepted it with a nod, hoping he did not notice that my hands were trembling.

"Electricity is something I am not yet fully educated in, and the new wiring in the Opera House is more complex than I had anticipated. Currently, turning on the light in my bedroom also turns on the lights and heat of the torture chamber."

That seemed to be the closest thing to an apology I was going to get from him.

"It was unbearable," I fixed my eyes on his. "If I hadn't managed to get your attention, I would have died, and you would not have known until Mother came to your door."

"That is quite enough." His tone was utterly calm as he sat in his throne-like chair, sipping his coffee. "The fault was yours, my dear, not mine. Perhaps it will teach you to follow my instructions to the letter in future."

We held each other's gaze for a moment longer, before I lowered my eyes to my cup. He shifted in the chair and I could feel his attention still upon me.

"Life at the de Chagny mansion is treating you well," he said. "You've gained three and a half pounds since June."

I looked up, my cheeks flaming scarlet.

"Three."

"A touch more, I think." His mouth quirked in a smile.

"You... have no idea how to speak to a woman, do you?"

"On the contrary," his tone slipped into a seductive purr. "You need not be embarrassed, little dancer. It suits you. Your mother, she is well?"

"Thriving," I replied. "She seems very much at home there. I think the break from... a number of her duties here, is doing her the world of good. Of course she is as... disciplined as ever with regards to my dancing and Christine's singing."

"I am glad to hear that Christine's talent is not being allowed to rust."

"Of course not," I said, surprised. "You must have overheard her during the rehearsals of *Faust*."

"She still has much to learn," he said, and I took a swallow of my coffee to hide the discomfort his words made me feel. He was as observant as ever. "Something I've said has troubled you."

"I have been paying attention to events within the Opera House over the summer," I said slowly. "And there has been no sight or sound from you. The Opera Ghost has been, if you'll pardon the expression, as silent as the grave."

"Meg!" He tutted at me. "I cannot pardon such a dreadful play on words! More coffee, child? Help yourself."

I stood up and walked over to where he had placed the pot on the small table midway between us, and refilled my coffee cup.

"Do you intend to sabotage the performance of *Faust* in January?"

He stretched his long legs towards the fire, crossing them at the ankle and lifted the cup to his lips.

"There will be no performance of *Faust* in January."

"What?" I stared at him.

"I said there will be no performance of *Faust*."

"Why not?"

"Because Meg, the company will be performing another opera. One by an as yet unknown composer, which will take Paris by storm."

"Are you making fun of me?" I queried. "Or are you serious?"

"I am utterly serious," he responded. "I have completed my magnum opus, Meg. Can you imagine what it is to have had a mighty composition in one's mind for a lifetime? Do dancers experience such a thing? Surely all artists must! For me, since infancy, there had been music in my head, which has accompanied me during every waking moment, travelled with me across two continents. But it was not until I settled here, in this... *temple* to performance, that I was finally able to start writing it all down! Seventeen years, Meg! Seventeen years of torment and toil. I had intended, when my opera was complete, to go to my grave with it, but then..."

I watched him gaze into the fire with glittering eyes.

"But then you met Christine," I completed the sentence for him.

"A voice worthy of my composition," he agreed. "*My* Angel of Music."

His fingers drummed on the arm of the chair, and I didn't know what to feel. The silence lengthened between us, and I cleared my throat.

"Monsieur Erik?"

"Mmm?" He turned his masked face to me, still apparently lost in thought.

"Why am I here? Surely you did not summon me simply to share in your achievement?"

He gave me a brief, unnerving smile.

"I have, as you said, remained absent from the events of the Opera Populairé for the last few months, but just because I have not been observed does not mean I have not been *observing*. The preparations for the re-opening of the Opera House are to be quite extravagant. There is even to be a ball on New Year's Eve."

"There is always a ball on New Year's Eve," I said, wondering where this was going.

"But is that ball always a masquerade?" He asked triumphantly.

"No," I was surprised by the information.

"No indeed. It seems our managers are getting ideas above themselves." He was still smiling and I wondered if he had put something in the coffee after all. I put my cup down at my feet. "All accounts of the Opera Ghost agree upon the fact that he wears a mask. It is ironic then, is it not, that they should choose to hold a celebratory dance peopled with paper faces."

"Um... yes." I agreed uncertainly.

"And that is where you come in, my dear. The Opera Ghost shall reinstate his position on that night, and you will be assisting me."

"Me?" I repeated in alarm. "Oh, no. Whatever it is that you intend to do, please leave me out of it."

"You owe me a good turn, little dancer," he reminded me. "You said as much during our last meeting."

"I won't do anything to cause anyone harm," I said, gripping the arms of my chair.

"You seem determined to think the worst of me, Meg," he sighed. "I require your sewing skills, nothing more."

"Sewing skills?" I echoed. "I'm not a seamstress or a tailor..."

"I do not require a seamstress or a tailor, I require someone who can embroider. I assume you can, Meg? It is surely on the list of attributes a young lady should possess?"

"Yes... I can do embroidery..." I admitted, furrowing my brow.

"Excellent." He stood up in a sudden, graceful movement. "Stay here."

He patted me on the shoulder as he passed me, moving back towards his bedroom. As he did so, I inhaled the familiar smell of his cologne, the same one my father had worn, and a chunk of ice hit me in the stomach. Aside from that dream in June, thoughts of my father and nightmares featuring him had been absent. I had enjoyed my summer so much, basked in the sunlight, and now here I was, back down in the dark. The shadows were beginning to creep in again; I could feel them...

I looked around the drawing room, focusing on the details, trying to distract myself. It was beginning to become nastily familiar. The Persian rug, the chair on the other side of the room that I had been tied in, the crossed violin bows over the fireplace, the piano. I could feel my pulse increasing.

Erik returned, carrying a bundle of red fabric, and laid it in my lap.

"I need some lettering embroidered onto this cloak. I have already written it in chalk for you, it merely needs going over in thread by someone with more needlework ability than I possess."

"Surely the Opera Ghost is not admitting a weakness?"

I took hold of the fabric and shook it out to its full length. It was over six foot long and the colour of freshly-spilled blood. In white chalk along

THE ANGEL'S SHADOW

the length of what would be the back of the cloak, were the words:

Je suis la Mort Rouge qui passé.

"I am the Red Death that passes," I read aloud. "Monsieur... what *is* this?"

"The ball will not only be a masque, but a costumed masque, and this is the finishing piece of my costume." He said.

"The Red Death?" I frowned. "As in *The Masque of the Red Death?*"

"Exactly," he replied. "Picture it, Meg! All those unimaginative fools in their dull costumes, and then—" The red cloak fell to the floor as he caught hold of both my hands and pulled me up into a ballroom hold. "—The Red Death walks abroad!"

He swept me across the room in an almost manic version of a waltz. One hand held mine, the other around my waist, digging into my side, his long musician's fingers pressing against my ribs.

"Erik!" I broke away from him, applying pressure to my bruised bones with a shudder of pain. He stood looking at me, breathing hard.

"My apologies," he said, and I glared at him.

"You hurt me!" I growled. His masked eyebrow rose.

"And I apologised," he said coldly.

"Apologised?!" I laughed bitterly. "I think your idea of an apology and mine are two different things. You *hurt* me! I came here at *your* request and get yet another set of bruises for my trouble! And you have a torture chamber! *A torture chamber!* With varied methods of torture! God only knows how many other people you have hurt in there! Or killed! I could have been killed today and you *don't care!* Is *gas* a method of torture? When I struck my match in there I could have made the whole Opera House explode!"

I broke off, breathless. He was standing staring at me with tension edged in every angle of his face and body, his hands clenched into fists by his sides. I put a trembling hand to my mouth, as if I thought I could push my angry words back inside.

"Have you finished?" He asked silkily.

I nodded, eyes fixed on his clenched fist. He raised one hand and pointed to his throne-like chair.

"*Sit.*"

I sat, gripping my hands together in my lap so hard that my knuckles went white.

"I'm... I'm sorry... I... my mouth ran away with me. Please don't strike me..."

The last words came out in a cringe. He continued to stare at me, his gaze boring into me like diamonds-tipped needles.

"*Don't* strike you? You seem to be practically *asking* for a beating. Let me state this for you quite plainly: I need to protect myself, or any blundering fool could come down here and into my home. You know this. I don't need to apologise to you, insolent child! I had no intention of trapping you, *you* ignored my instructions. Be thankful that I got you out of that chamber! Meg Giry, for someone in a profession that requires grace and poise, you are a walking accident. You would get yourself into enough trouble without any interference from me." He folded his hands behind his back. "You are an interesting study, young lady. I have been observing people for a long time, but you... there is something strange about you... Do you fear me, Meg Giry?"

"Yes," I replied without hesitation.

"Do you trust me?"

"Yes," I said again just as quickly.

He leant down, putting his hands on the arms of the chair, his face inches from mine, studying me minutely.

Do not cry...

I was reminded of him backing me against my dormitory door, one hand either side of me so that I could not escape. Could that have only been a matter of months ago? Ever since I had met this man, when he had sprung from fiction into fact, my world seemed to have turned upside-down. I kept my eyes away from his, focusing on the contours of his mask, my breathing coming shallowly.

"Falling into my chamber shocked you more than I realised," his voice was soft. He moved away and I stared into the fire.

Do not cry...

He returned and knelt in front of me after a few seconds, holding the coffee pot in one hand a decanter of brandy in the other. Another brief absence from my line of sight, and he came back with my coffee cup—well, I could only assume it was mine. He poured the coffee into the cup, then added a small amount of brandy.

"Drink," he ordered and I took the cup in trembling hands, sipping the cooling beverage. "All of it."

"I had such a good summer," I blurted as he took the empty cup from me. "And then I came back here. Why did I do that? I don't *want* trust you, Erik, you *frighten* me and I am truly terrified of whatever intentions you have for Christine... I want to run from you. And yet, you call, and I come to you. Why?"

"There is darkness in you, Meg," he said quietly. "It's a part of you, and has been from the time of your childhood. Since your father died, it has taken root and grown." His fingers touched my cheek, forcing me to make eye-contact. "You consider yourself to be a creature of light... but you long for the darkness. It's where you belong. It's who you are."

"Why are you saying this?" I whispered. A single tear rolled down my cheek and he wiped it away with his thumb.

THE ANGEL'S SHADOW

"Do you not think I recognise the parts of a soul that mirror my own?"

"I think I'm going mad," I told him. "Just like my father. I think that, one day, I will find a pistol pressed against my own temple. Just like him."

He shook his head. "That's not going to happen to you, Meg. You and I may be creatures of darkness, but everyone has light inside of them. I found mine through Christine. You will find yours too, one day."

He stood, and I found myself once again gazing into the fire. Could he be right about me? I looked up when he laid a neatly folded wad of cloth in my lap; the red cloak he wanted me to embroider for him, and a small pile of books. All of them by the same author, the top one *The Masque of the Red Death and Other Stories*. My Edgar Allan Poe collection.

"I thank you for the loan of your books."

I blinked. "Well, I didn't exactly *loan* them, you sto—"

"There is still quite some time before the New Year," he said as if there had been no break in the conversation. "And I have every confidence in your handiwork. You can return the finished article to me... shall we say Christmas Eve?" I nodded numbly. "Good. Allow me to fetch my cloak and I will row you across the lake and escort you back into your world. I don't want you walking these catacombs alone."

"You called me a child," I said, standing up and holding the red cloth under one arm. "You always refer to me as a child. But I'm not anymore. By the time we meet again I will have turned seventeen. I am a woman."

He gave me a long, searching look, but did not reply, instead turning and unhooking his black cloak from behind the drawing room door. We did not speak again as he rowed me across the vast lake that shone like glass, and held up another lantern to guide me through the passageways to the hidden door by the stage. I bid him farewell and moved away through the deserted corridor, but he called my name.

"Meg?"

"Erik?" I turned back to him.

"Another outburst like the one you threw at me today and, woman or not, I will take you over my knee and ensure that you won't be able to sit comfortably for a fortnight. No matter what the circumstances your insolence is quite unacceptable. Behave like a child and I will punish you like a child. Do you understand?"

"Yes, Monsieur. Good evening to you."

I turned and walked away before he could see my smile. I knew he was utterly serious and capable of carrying out his threat; his sheer strength and size in comparison to mine proved that. He also believed he had the authority to discipline me if he saw fit. But somehow, with a weight lifted from my heart that I hadn't even known I had been carrying, the notion of being put over the knee of the Phantom of the Opera struck me as immensely funny.

CHAPTER TWENTY EIGHT

I went to my dormitory and found a canvas bag to hold Erik's red cloak and my books, taking a moment to look around the room. For the last few months Christine and I had been living in the de Changy mansion, and I had found myself missing this small, cramped room. In January, I would be returning here alone. Christine had found herself an apartment only five minutes' walk from the Opera House, run by a stern landlady who allowed only female residents. I couldn't help feeling a little sorry about that, a little nostalgic; Christine was moving on with her life, would shortly be married, and I was staying in the same place I had always been.

I went down the stairs to the foyer, cloak over my arm, plucking at the rip in my dress with two fingers, trying to assess, now I was in good light, how bad the damage was. Not as bad as I had thought, I decided, and certainly repairable.

"Mademoiselle Giry?"

I looked around to see Raoul regarding me from the bottom of the staircase.

"Vicomte? What are you doing here?"

He raised an elegant eyebrow. "I had a meeting with your managers. You?"

"Extra rehearsals for *Faust*," I replied, flustered at seeing him here.

"What happened to your dress?" He gestured to the rip in the fabric.

"I... fell down the stairs."

"Are you hurt?" His tone was alarmed.

"Just some bruising," I found myself quite flattered by his concern, and he smiled.

"You know... for a ballet dancer, you do seem to be somewhat accident-prone."

I swallowed. "You're... not the first to have said so."

"I have a carriage waiting," Raoul told me kindly. "Would you like to accompany me back to the château?"

THE ANGEL'S SHADOW

"Yes please," I smiled.

I did up my cloak as Raoul pulled on his gloves and donned a top hat, before we both went out into the darkened street. The new electric lights that surrounded the Opera House were blotting out the stars overhead, and it made me think about how much my own circumstances had changed over the last twelve months. Had the Vicomte not been here, I would have walked the fifteen minutes to the de Chagny mansion alone, something that would have been unthinkable this time last year. Perhaps Mother thought that, since Erik seemed to have taken it upon himself to be my unofficial guardian, he would guard me from all the dangers of Paris. Angel of Music to Christine, guardian angel to me.

Raoul opened the door of his carriage for me and I stepped inside, seating myself as he took the seat opposite and knocked on the roof to tell the driver he was ready to depart. As the carriage rattled off, he reached into the pocket of his cloak.

"I need your opinion on something," he confessed, pulling out a ring box. I smiled at the sight of it.

"Christine's engagement ring?"

Although they had been engaged since June, he had yet to present his intended with a ring, telling her that he was having one custom-made for her.

"Indeed," he replied and opened the box. "Do you think she'll like it?"

I couldn't speak. The ring, nestling in blue velvet, was a huge diamond, surrounded by smaller diamonds like the head of a very expensive flower. Every facet that caught even the smallest glimpse of light, reflected and bounced it back; the perfect setting of those diamonds meant they could not help but sparkle. Raoul was watching me, his expression anxious, and I realised he was waiting for my response.

"She'll love it," I told him truthfully. The ring *was* Christine, beautiful and elegant.

"You don't think it's too... garish?" He pushed, and I shook my head.

"It's beautiful, Vicomte. It is truly worthy of Christine."

He grinned and closed the box, putting it back in his pocket. I watched him, his delight at my approval, the way the light bounced off his golden hair, the features of his handsome face, and my mind flashed back over the conversation I had overheard him having with his brother in September. Philippe had been reading the newspapers and was concerned over the gossip generated by news of Raoul's engagement to an opera singer.

As the carriage drew up to the château, I bit my lip and decided to stop dancing around my curiosity.

"Vicomte... Raoul... I need to talk to you."

He paused in the act of opening the carriage door, his eyes scanning my face and body-language, and then he said:

195

"Very well… Go change your dress and we can talk in the library, would that be all right? If you give it to Sophia, she can repair the rip in the fabric for you. Mother always said she was the best needlewoman in France."

We sat in front of the fire in the library. I had been delighted by this room when I had first seen it, my inner bibliophile doing pirouettes at the sight of so many books. As it turned out, these books were disappointing, mostly non-fiction, largely history and politics. It was warm in here, though, and relaxing. Raoul ordered tea from one of his servants, and we drank as I tried to phrase my question.

"Vicomte, what do you and Christine intend to do after the wedding?"

His raised his eyebrows and I blushed, realising that it sounded like I was referring to their martial relations.

"I mean, will you go on honeymoon?"

"Yes…" he replied cautiously. "We intend to tour Europe, and especially to spend some time in Sweden. Christine wants to visit her homeland."

"When you return, will you live in Paris?"

"Yes. Indeed, we will be living *here*, in this château. Philippe is giving it to us as a wedding gift."

Wedding gift. I would have to get Christine and Raoul a wedding gift; I hadn't even thought about it. I took a deep breath and prepared to ask the question that bothered me the most.

"And… the opera?" I held his blue gaze steadily. "Do you intend to keep Christine from the stage?"

He blinked in surprise, and then laughed.

"Oh, my dear Meg, is that what you've been worrying about?" He leaned forward, his eyes amused but gentle. "Christine is an absolutely exquisite singer and a beautiful woman. I would consider it *selfish* to keep her from her public as if she were a songbird in a cage. Her music is a part of her, a part of what I love. I have no intention in making her give up her career." He tilted his head. "What else is troubling you, Meg?"

"Your family," I admitted quietly. "Raoul… they might not like Christine, simply *because* she is an opera singer."

I tried to make it sound like this was an idea I had come up with on my own, rather than overhearing Comte Philippe saying more or less the same back in September.

"Meg… I have to admit I find it strange that you are worrying like this. My family might be unhappy at first because I'm not marrying some rich heiress, but I know they will adore Christine once they get to know her." He patted my knee. "You'll see for yourself soon. My sisters are joining us for three days over Christmas, along with their husbands and children." He looked at me for a long moment. "You're a kind young woman, Meg. Try not to worry so much. Things will work out, I promise you, and no matter

THE ANGEL'S SHADOW

what anyone says, I am going to marry Christine."

Days and weeks passed without any sign from Erik. The de Chagny family were getting ready for Christmas celebrations, which would involve visits from the two sisters, Hélène and Sylvie, their husbands and children. Members of the Opera Populairé were preparing for the grand reopening of the House in January, and the performance of *Faust*, and I was astonished to learn that I had been invited to the masquerade.

Mother had attended the New Year's ball both before and after Papa's death, her role as the concierge enabling her to mingle with the great and the good. I had joined in the 'below stairs' party thrown by the staff, a far more informal affair, which more often than not involved stealing alcohol from the official ball taking place. This year, I would be mingling with the great and the good myself, and that required a costume and a mask.

It was a surprising perk of living with the de Chagny family, even temporarily, to learn that Mother and I could use the services of their tailor, meaning that we would not have to make the costumes ourselves, but get them custom-made for us. I worried that it would be too expensive, but Mother brushed my concerns aside; she had received some money from an apparently anonymous source. I had a feeling that Erik was attempting an apology for swinging a chandelier at her only child.

My birthday was marked quietly at my request, and I got some lovely gifts from Mother, Christine and—to my surprise—the de Chagny brothers, including new clothing and books. It was just before I went to bed that Mother took me aside, and pressed a small velvet-wrapped package into the palm of my hand.

"This is from me… and your father."

"My father?" I repeated. "What are you talking about?"

"Open it." She smiled.

I unwrapped the black velvet to find a piece of jewellery among its folds. It was a cross, maybe an inch and a half long, made of solid silver, quite plain and unadorned, on a silver chain. I felt a lump rise in my throat and my eyes began to sting. I knew this cross; it had belonged to my father, and he had worn it until the day he died. I couldn't raise my eyes from the gleaming, unblemished metal as Mother spoke:

"Claude's father gave this to him on his seventeenth birthday. He told me when I found out I was pregnant that he wanted it to be passed on to his firstborn on his or her seventeenth birthday." She reached out, gently stroking my hair, teasing a strand out straight and then letting it spring back into a spiral. "I'm sure he intended to be here to give it to you himself…" Her voice wobbled. "I know you don't attend church anymore, but he wanted you to have this, Meg. Will you wear it?"

197

I swallowed hard and looked up at her, blinking quickly.
"Of course."

Saint Louise church had been undergoing restoration for as long as I could remember. When we had held my Father's funeral here, seven years ago, the hymns, sung in full voice by the mourners, had disturbed a family of bats who had started hibernating in the bell-tower. When your colleagues are opera professionals, you can expect the singing at your funeral to be spectacular.

On this Christmas Eve, the iron railings surrounding its small graveyard were rusty and bent, the gate warped out of shape, making the presence of the Gatekeeper almost meaningless. He was an elderly man, sitting in a tiny wooden hut beside the gate, smoking an enormous smelly clay pipe. I gave him a coin—not an entrance fee, you understand, just a tip—and he nodded me in. I wondered whether, wearing my grey cloak, I blended in with the poorly-maintained gravestones. The Gatekeeper's job, it seemed, was merely to prevent grave-robbers and vandalism. The ground crunched under my feet, spiky with frost. We hadn't had any snow yet, having enjoyed a remarkably mild November, but the clouds over my head were dense and white, and I wouldn't be surprised if it turned snowy overnight.

Father's grave was the newest of the ill-kept inhabitants in St. Louise's grounds. It was made of granite, all we could afford, and was about eighteen inches tall. He deserved better than this pauper's resting place, but given the manner of his death it had been a struggle to have him interred in holy ground at all.

I knelt on the freezing ground that covered my father's mortal remains, and ran my fingertips over the equally cold stone; even through my gloves I could feel the icy temperature.

"I miss you, Papa," I whispered as my fingers traced the letters carved into the stone.

Claude Maurice Jules Giry
2nd February 1853 – 16th November 1886
Beloved Husband and Father
Leave the Hurt Behind

I prayed that he had; that he had found the peace that had been ripped from him in life. Seven years on and the hurt he had impaled my heart upon was still white hot. I had read of people who were able to repress traumatic memories, but no matter how hard I tried, I could not forget Father's last words, the gunshot, the blood and brain matter splattered over my face and the rest of the room.

"I wish I could have stopped you," I confessed to the tombstone. "I wish my presence had been enough."

What sort of man sees his ten-year-old daughter watching him, and pulls the trigger anyway? Memory can play the very devil with you sometimes. I remembered my father, in bad times and in good. I remembered his talent, his smile, the sound of his voice and his laugh. I remembered the touch of his hand upon my hair and the smell of his cologne. I heard his footsteps on the frosted ground behind me, the smell growing stronger, before his hand came down on my shoulder. I closed my eyes, tears running hot down my cheeks, before I lifted my head and demanded:

"Can I get no peace from you, Monsieur Erik?"

Before he could withdraw, I placed my hand on his, turned my head and wept into his sleeve. Erik gently squeezed my shoulder.

"Poor, grieving child," his golden voice murmured, frosting in the air. "Every time we meet, it seems, you cry."

"Not a child," I protested. "And you always seem to be with me in my weakest moments." I swallowed hard and wiped my eyes. "Where were you when we needed you?"

He sighed. "Meg…"

"No."

I stood up and turned to him. He was wearing a long black coat with discreet beading at the shoulders, and a black fedora, the wide brim shielding his face, and his mask, from the view of others. Not that there was anyone else to see.

"The sixteenth of November 1886," I said. "The day my father killed himself in front of me. Where were you, Erik?"

He looked at me for a long moment, then replied: "Rome."

"Rome?" I repeated, surprised. I had thought he must have been away from the Opera House, but never imagined that he had been out of the country. "What were you doing in Rome?"

"I was attending a funeral."

His tone was dark and I knew I was touching on a subject he did not want to discuss. I could not blame him for being at a funeral, but there was one more question I needed answered.

"If you had been here… could you have stopped him?"

"You ask the unanswerable," he told me. "We can never know."

I sighed, sniffed, and wiped my eyes on my sleeve. He made a slight noise of distaste and held out a handkerchief in his leather-gloved hand.

"Thank you." I took it and blew my nose. "I thought we were meeting at the Opera Populairé?"

"I saw you out here alone," he said.

"The Angel sees all, the Angel knows everything."

Erik bowed, and I saw the first few snowflakes fluttering from the sky.

To my left, the dome of the Opera House was dark against the white clouds; he must have been watching from the rooftop, viewing the streets of Paris with a bird's eye. He offered me his arm.

"Mademoiselle?"

I picked up the bag I had set beside my father's gravestone, put it over my shoulder and took his arm. The snowfall was thick and fast, and I pulled my hood up as we walked out of the graveyard. The Gatekeeper was asleep in his hut, the extinguished pipe clenched between his teeth. I wondered if Erik had drugged him, and cast him a sideways glance. The brim of his hat was low, the collar of his cloak turned up, and I could not see his face. He moderated his stride to match mine as we walked arm-in-arm through the Paris streets, heads bowed against the weather. The few people we passed paid us little attention, and I wondered what they thought of us; father and daughter, perhaps.

I automatically turned towards the Opera Populairé's main entrance, but Erik steered me onwards and around into the Rue Scribe at the side of the building.

"Lend me your scarf," he ordered, and I was about to ask why when the answer presented itself.

"I thought we were supposed to trust each other," I said. "But you still insist on blindfolding me when you invite me into your home."

"I wouldn't repeat that," he sounded amused. "It might be misinterpreted."

I glared at him, but he held out his hand and snapped his gloved fingers, and I gave a growl and unwound the scarf from my neck. He took it from me and used it to cover my eyes. I heard the rustle of leaves, the scrape of a key in the lock, and then Erik took both my hands in his.

"Four steps forward, Meg," he told me. "Eight steps down. Do not move further."

I counted the steps, assuming that he was backing down the staircase ahead of me.

"One moment," he dropped my hands and I heard his footsteps on the stairs again. When I heard him returning, I reached up to remove the scarf.

"So, you have a secret entrance from the Rue Scribe," I began to say, but stopped when I realised that I was just as blind without the scarf as I had been with it. Somehow, I had imagined that these eight steps would take me directly into Erik's drawing room, even though I knew that it was five storeys below the ground.

"Very observant, little dancer," he said, making me jump. His hands closed around mine again.

"Can you see where you're going?" I asked nervously.

"I can," he replied, and led me down in near silence.

"You must have excellent vision," I said.

THE ANGEL'S SHADOW

"I would have thought that was self-evident," the amused tone was back.

"Do you miss it?"

"Miss what?"

"Daylight. Living above ground."

He was silent for so long, maintaining our downward pace, that I worried I had angered him. I opened my mouth to apologise, but he said:

"Sometimes. I never thought I would... until Christine..."

CHAPTER TWENTY NINE

I held my tongue until Erik opened a door, the light of a single candle piercing through the darkness, showing me a narrow room, lined with floor to ceiling shelves that held jars, packets and bottles.

"Your pantry?"

I caught his nod as he lit a second candle with the first.

"Who designed this place?" I asked as he handed me the second candle, and he gave me a disapproving look.

"Meg Giry, are you telling me that you live in one of the most architecturally interesting buildings in France, and you've never troubled to find out the identity of that architect?"

I shrugged. "Sorry."

"His name was Charles Garnier," he said as he opened the door from the pantry to the kitchen, then led me through into the drawing room. "Look him up."

I gave a sarcastic salute as he switched on the electric lights, lowering my hand just as he turned back to me, the bright illumination filling the room.

"Put a match to the fire, would you?" He requested. "And we will try to forget for awhile the cold, if seasonal, weather."

I did as he asked, and over the next few minutes we removed our outdoor clothing, gloves and shoes, and settled into chairs. Erik even offered soup, which I declined politely.

"I'm sorry, but I mustn't stay too long. There are guests at the de Chagny château and my absence won't go unnoticed for long, even with three small children running around and causing a distraction."

The drawing room seemed bigger somehow, and as I looked around I realised that things were missing. The number of books on the bookcase had been halved, artwork was gone from the walls and one of Erik's chairs had been removed. The violins that hung by the fireplace, and their bows crossed like swords above it—personally, my favourite feature of the room—had also disappeared.

"Are you having a clear out?" I asked, puzzled. He looked at me for a moment, then nodded.

"In a manner of speaking, yes. How did you get on with your commission?"

"If you are referring to the cloak," I said with a roll of my eyes. "It's finished, as you requested."

I opened my bag and passed over the red cloak; he unfolded it to look at the embroidery I had added to the back.

"Very nicely done," he murmured. "This is very good work, Meg. You may have missed your calling."

"It was boring work," I told him. "Nevertheless, I thank you for the compliment. Will you put it on for me? I want to check the hemline."

He looked surprised but nodded, putting the cloak on over his day clothes.

"Well, the colour clashes with your cravat," I smiled and circled him. Erik shifted on his feet, uncomfortable. "Will you stay still?"

He stood to attention, like a soldier, but I got the impression that he did not enjoy my scrutiny.

"Yes, just in the middle at the back here, the hem goes all wobbly. I can even if out for you, where do you keep needles and thread?"

"I'll fetch them."

"Don't take the cloak off!" I called after him as he swept from the drawing room. I frowned at his back, aware of the tension that had filled the space and unable to imagine what I had said or done to cause it. He returned a few minutes later with a spool of red thread, a needle stuck through it, and I flinched slightly as he reached out, brushing my throat.

"What's this?" His fingers traced the chain around my neck and he lifted the silver cross from my skin. I had the sudden, wild notion that the cross should be burning him like it would a vampire.

"It's a gift for my birthday," I said. "It belonged to my father; he wanted me to have it." I cleared my throat, my pulse unaccountably fast. "If you turn around, I'll fix the hemline for you…"

He stood with his back to me while I sat cross-legged on the Persian rug, sewing and humming to myself.

Don't think about the graveyard, don't think about Papa. Leave the hurt behind…

"There," I announced. "All done. I'm sure you'll be the best-dressed man at the ball."

He turned, reaching down a hand to help me to my feet.

"Thank you for your contribution."

I gazed at him, his mismatched eyes reflecting the fire, his white mask glowing under the new electric lights.

"Can I see your face?"

I heard myself say the words before my brain had even started warning against them. Erik's response was immediate, and unexpected.

"Can I see your genitals?"

"No!" I shrieked, backing away from him, totally and utterly shocked. "How dare you?! Ask me that again and I'll—I'll—"

"*You'll—you'll—*" he mimicked my stuttering and stunned rage. "Understand now, Meg Giry, what it means when you ask me to expose my face to you. I am not an attraction in a cage to be gawked at for my hideousness. I will never be so again." His own anger was leashed as he attempted to explain. "My face is... shameful. I hate what God did to me. I hate what it has turned me into."

"I understand," I told him, coming forward again. "I'm sorry. Please forgive me. I won't ask again."

He held my gaze for a long moment, and then nodded.

"I... I must go," I said. "They'll wonder where I am."

Erik rowed me across the lake, gesturing towards the exit that opened by the stage as he passed me a lantern.

"There is a switch concealed on the right-hand wall, about halfway down."

"Thank you." I paused, half in and half out of the boat, uncertain whether to add what I want to say to him, not wishing to remind him of his solitude. "Merry Christmas, Erik."

He bowed his head to me.

"Merry Christmas, Meg." He replied. "See you in the New Year."

I had always thought that Christine Daaé could be dressed in rags and still look beautiful. Tonight, she looked stunning. Her masquerade costume was that of a Star Queen. It was an off-the-shoulder ball gown that started as a deep blue, fading to violet and then pink through the bodice and multi-layered skirt. Silver stars decorated her skirt, she had silver high-heeled boots, a tiara featuring a star and crescent moon, and her hand-held silver mask displayed a spray like a starburst.

If Christine was a Queen tonight, then I was a Princess. My dress had a neckline that swooped low over my generous cleavage; the bodice flitted tight and the full skirt flared out around my hips. The entire gown was pure white, ruffled and gathered to give the impression of feathers, real ones decorating the off-the-shoulder straps. My mask was also white, and there were more feathers in my hair, the ringlets scooped up and pinned into place with faux pearls woven through the style. I wore faux pearl earrings too, but my only other piece of jewellery was my father's silver cross.

I watched my reflection in the bedroom mirror as I adjusted my elbow-length gloves, still unable to believe what I looked like. The de Chagny's tailor had done a wonderful job, the finished garment lovelier than I could

THE ANGEL'S SHADOW

have imagined when I shyly put forward the idea of Odette, the enchanted princess of *Swan Lake* as my costume. He had captured the swan, the magic and the beauty of the ballet I loved, but there was something else too. It seemed to haunt me as I wore that dress. I looked... ethereal. Almost... angelic.

Raoul and Philippe bowed to us when we met them in the mansion's hallway, where they were talking to my mother, resplendent as a Spanish noblewoman. Philippe had chosen the costume of an English Georgian Highwayman, his black silk mask tied around his eyes. It made him look quite dashing. Raoul was not in costume, instead wearing the full dress uniform of his naval office; I did not know how to decipher his rank from it and was too embarrassed to ask. It was customary, it seemed, for aristocratic members of the armed forces to attend occasions such as tonight in uniform. Philippe, being the eldest son, had inherited the de Chagny estate, and second son Raoul had been told to join one of the country's military services. Had there been a third son, he would have joined the Church. The lives of the upper classes, it seemed, were not as unrestricted as I had imagined.

Raoul sighed, lifting the diamond engagement ring from its place around Christine's throat, where it was threaded on a fine silver chain.

"When I pictured you wearing this," he said. "It was on your finger."

Christine blushed. "Yes, look... your future bride. Just think of it."

"Our engagement was announced in the newspapers," he reminded her gently. "We've got nothing to hide from your colleagues. Christine, you promised me..."

"Let's not argue," Christine pleaded, putting her arm through his, and Raoul acquiesced.

The short carriage ride to the Opera Populairé was full of our excitement at attending such a grand event, which Philippe told me he found 'charming'.

"The first of many," Raoul murmured to Christine, and she smiled.

The scene that greeted me was spectacular; faces made of paper, leather, silk and beads surrounded us, their owners beaming in triumph. Some seemed to believe that they would remain undiscovered and unidentified if they hid their faces, that the world would never recognise them. On the contrary, the brightly-adorned costumes singled people out quite well. Monsieur Firman was costumed as a ram, with golden horns curving from his headdress; I hoped it was not a comment upon his sexual prowess. Monsieur André was dressed as a skeleton.

I had a wonderful time. I laughed, I talked, I ate sumptuous food, indulged in expensive wine, and danced with many handsome—and eligible—men. At around eleven p.m., we were escorted into the Opera House's auditorium to admire the new chandelier, as beautiful as its predecessor and wired for the new electric light. There were jokes made about its ability to frighten away the Opera Ghost with its illumination. It had, after all, been six months since the Phantom had been seen, since he had even sent a note. Oh, the relief, the delight, the heavenly peace, the room to breathe! I saw Christine and Raoul dancing with each other, relaxed and happy, and the Vicomte kissed his bride full on the mouth, soft and sweet, as the dance ended. From where I stood, I saw his lips form the words 'I love you'. It made me smile.

I was aware of Erik's presence the moment he joined us. It happened almost simultaneously, the chatter dying, the steps of the dancers faltering as the musicians ground to a halt. He stood at the top of the staircase that led into the ballroom, and as one we turned to watch him start his descent. He was resplendent in bright, hellfire red, from his hat with the extravagant feather in it, down the length of the seventeenth century costume, to the boots. The cloak I had embroidered for him was slung over his shoulders, and there was a sword at his hip. The hilt was a silver skull and I somehow knew from the shine of the blade that this was not a stage prop, but a real, deadly weapon. He carried a bundle of papers, bound in black leather, under his arm. The familiar half-mask concealing the right side of his face was replaced with a full-face skull, as white as bone.

"Do you have nothing to say to me, Messieurs?" He asked as he came down the steps. The jaw of the mask moved as his mouth opened and closed with the words, and I could hear the smile in that golden voice. "Did you think that I had departed?"

He had our undivided attention, the ballroom held its collective breath. Even though I had been expecting him to appear at some point during the evening, his entrance still took me by surprise. I could feel the fear humming through the room.

"Allow me to contradict you, Messieurs! You have not heard from me for months, but that is because I have been completing the score of my new opera, *Don Juan Triumphant!*"

He threw the leather folder to André, who fumbled to catch it and prevent the contents from scattering across the floor. As Erik drew level with me, I saw that he had outlined his mismatched eyes with kohl, which highlighted the difference between the blue and the green. They met mine for only a second as his gaze swept the ballroom.

"You will cancel the performance of *Faust* and perform this instead," he ordered. "Full instructions are included and they should be fully comprehensive, so I advise you to follow them to the letter. I would hate to have to put you out of business for another six months while you repair a second chandelier. Or worse."

He had reached the dance floor now, and with a single crook of his finger, beckoned Christine. I saw with a start that she was alone, without

THE ANGEL'S SHADOW

the Vicomte beside her, but I was certain I had seen Raoul at her side only moments before.

"Christine!" I hissed at her, but she moved towards her Angel of Music as if in a trance. "Christine!"

Mother reached out to prevent me from stepping between Christine and Erik. I could feel my heart racing, afraid that he would hurt her here, in front of everyone. They stood face-to-face, gazing at each other, both breathing hard, and I had the distinct impression that the hypnotic power he held over her seemed to work both ways. He was captivated by Christine. His kohl-rimmed eyes studied her face, then went lower, and fixed on the diamond ring at her throat.

"You are still mine!" He reached forward, breaking the silver necklace with a single sharp tug. "You belong to me!"

He retreated a few steps up the staircase, ring clenched in his fist, swirling the scarlet cloak around him and throwing something to the floor with the other hand. Christine flinched as flames and smoke shot up, surrounding the area where Erik had been standing, and he appeared to vanish into the floor like a devil into Hell. Raoul appeared from somewhere behind me, sword drawn, and dropped through the floor at the same spot, just as I saw the ingeniously designed trapdoor close again.

"Christine!" Philippe rushed forward just in time to catch Christine as she fainted, and my eyes went to Mother.

"He'll kill him!" I tried to scream it, but the words came out as a whisper.

"Stay with Christine!" She ordered, hitched up her skirts and ran from the ballroom. The noise in the ballroom was a panic-stricken staccato, terror radiating from every person there. Philippe was kneeling with Christine draped across his body, surrounded by onlookers, and Monsieur Firman was offering smelling salts. Her eyes opened as I knelt beside her, and she looked at me with horror in her face.

"Raoul?" She croaked.

"He's... gone after Erik," I told her, and Christine began to struggle to get up.

"No! No! He'll kill Raoul! Meg, you have to stop them!"

"Christine!" I put my arms around her as she broke down, sobbing against my shoulder. "Shh... it's all right... Mother has gone after them. Raoul will be safe... shh..."

It was a few minutes before Christine had calmed down enough to be helped to her feet, leaning on Philippe's arm and looking as though she had aged years in this single evening.

"I think you should take her back to the château, Comte," I said to Philippe. "She shouldn't be alone tonight."

"I have to wait for Raoul," Christine protested, but with gentle words,

Philippe escorted her away. I watched the ballroom empty, the departing guests distressed and terrified, and a clock began to strike midnight.

"Happy New Year," I muttered to the deserted space.

I took off my shoes, gathering my skirts up in my other hand, and walked to Mother's chambers. I built up and lit the fire, brewed coffee, and sat in the armchair beside the hearth, the dress ballooning around me. A wonderful evening, destroyed in minutes, and as I thought about Erik's entrance, I found myself grinding my teeth.

"He'll kill him!" I had been referring to Raoul killing Erik, not the other way around. The sword may have looked good, strapped against Erik's hip, but I had no idea if he could actually use it. Raoul, on the other hand, was a trained swordsman.

It was almost twenty to one when Mother came into the room, looking exhausted. I stood up, crossing to her without a word and holding out a cup of coffee. She looked down at it, then up at me.

"I'm tired, Meg."

"So am I." I said coldly. "I'm tired of the secrets, the stories, the myth surrounding the 'Opera Ghost'. I'm tired of being lied to, Mother, and I am old enough now to know the truth. So tell me... Tell me about Erik. Tell me how you two met and why he owes you his life."

She sighed, sitting down on the edge of her bed and undoing her boots. I sat down beside her, sipping the coffee myself, watching as she took them off and her hands went to her hair, pulling out the sticks that held the style in place.

"He told me that you saved him from a fate worse than death," I said quietly. "And he wasn't joking. He's being watching over me since I was born, and yet he didn't stop me from witnessing Father's suicide. He says he was attending a funeral in Rome. Was that true? What happened, Mother? What is Erik's story?"

CHAPTER THIRTY

Mother watched me with exhausted eyes.

"Is your curiosity so insatiable, girl? You haven't even asked where that trapdoor in the ballroom led, whether the Vicomte or the Opera Ghost survived their encounter."

I felt my cheeks flame scarlet, embarrassed and ashamed.

"You would have told me if there had been bloodshed." I rallied.

"I was able to reach the Vicomte just before he tripped a switch that would have left him knee deep in rats," Mother said, her eyebrows raised. "I was able to lead him back to the foyer and see him safely into a carriage that would take him home."

I nodded, and bit my lower lip.

"I know it's not the right time," I said. "But… there is no right time for this. I need to know about you and Erik. Please."

She heaved a deep sigh, and began her story.

"It was years ago, before you were born, Meg. Claude and I had just returned from a holiday in Normandy, as it was a period between operas. There was a travelling fair in Paris…Gypsies from Italy. There were stalls of crafts, food… and there were performers. Tumblers, jugglers, clowns…"

I nodded, having seen such things myself, at the circus Mother and Father had taken me to on my eighth birthday.

"There were… other things too."

"Lions?" I asked, remembering the exotic animals the circus had exhibited.

"No." She shook her head. "People with… differences. Human oddities."

"And… Erik was a part of this fair? I know he spent time with the gypsies, the remedies he uses are gypsy."

She looked at me, seeming surprised.

"Since when have you and he been on a first-name basis, Meg?"

I hesitated, wondering when the formalities *had* dropped between us.

When he had pulled me from his torture chamber? Before that? I shook my head.

"Go on with the story."

Mother swallowed, stood, and began pacing in front of the fireplace.

"Erik was ... an exhibit. One of many. Except, he wasn't at liberty like the others. They kept him in a cage."

"In a cage?" I echoed, horrified, and she nodded, still pacing, her silk skirts rustling.

"He was nineteen years old... and he'd already suffered so much. What happened before we met, Meg, I can't tell you. I won't tell you. That is for him to divulge, if he ever wants you to know. You understand?"

"I understand." I nodded.

"I couldn't.... I couldn't understand why he was caged. Not then. There were many performers inside cages, you see, supposedly to protect the public from their dangerousness. I think it was more to protect the performers from the public becoming too... over-enthusiastic, or getting too close and spotting how an illusion was achieved. He was performing magic... card tricks, close-up magic. I remember they had him dressed in black; black trousers and poet's shirt. His face was masked with black silk tied over his head that came down to his mouth, with holes cut for his eyes. He looked not unlike Comte Philippe did tonight in that Highwayman costume. That sort of mask. I could see there was something wrong with his upper lip, but nothing more, except that his eyes were different colours. Claude and I watched his magic, and he noticed us. He beckoned to us, and when we came forward, he pulled a red rose out of the air. I still don't know how he did that." There was a smile on her lips. "He passed it to me through the bars of his cage, and spoke to me for the first time.

'For the most beautiful woman in Paris,' he bowed to me, and looked to Claude. *'I hope your husband knows what a jewel he has, Madame.'*

'She is my diamond,' Claude said, taking my hand. *'No one knows that better than I... Monsieur.'*"

Mother paused in her pacing and looked at me.

"That fair was rife with pick-pockets, and Claude had already narrowly avoided having his purse snatched three times. It wasn't surprising, I suppose, that when we noticed the child behind us, holding up his hand, Claude assumed this was another attempt to rob him. He seized the boy by the hair, shouting:

'That is it, do you hear me?! I've had enough of you brats and your wandering fingers!'

The boy shouted in German and another man approached, grabbing him from Claude's grasp. He was a gypsy with several inches and at least a hundred pounds on your father.

'You... attack my son?!' He demanded in his heavily accented voice.

THE ANGEL'S SHADOW

'*You... handle my boy?!*'

And he grabbed Claude by the lapels of his coat. I gave a scream and saw Erik look around, although I knew he could do nothing in the cage.

'*Ladies and gentlemen!*' He cried. '*I have nothing up my sleeves! I have nothing but this simple pack of playing cards! I select the Queen of Diamonds, my favourite card in the pack, ladies and gentlemen, and I throw it!*'

He threw the card through the bars of his cage, and... I swear to you, Meg... it transformed into a *dove* and flew out and between Claude and his attacker, who let him go. The man laughed and gestured to Erik.

'*Thank you for your intervention,*' I said to the caged man. '*And for the rose. Are you an escapologist as well as a magician?*'

'*Hardly that,*' he replied gravely. '*Perhaps if you return after nightfall you will discover the reason for my imprisonment.*'

He turned from us and began a new set of tricks with his cards for the people clustered at the other side of the cage. The cards were filthy, I noticed."

"And you returned?"

"We did. As the sky grew darker, so did the... nature of the acts. They became more... explicit, more sexual. As we'd been round the fair during the day, I had seen other women carrying red roses, and after the sun set, one of the gypsies began shouting, with a strong Italian accent.

'*Ladies and gentlemen! The darkness awaits! Come see what hides in the shadows! Come and see what the devil can produce!* Signore e signori!*'

And he began the whole speech again in Italian.

Claude and I were never... sadistic people, Meg. For all the gypsy's talk of darkness and shadows and devils, we had no idea what was coming. The other sideshows had closed gradually, funnelling the spectators towards the large tent that held Erik's cage. They had taken him from the cage, and he was on his knees in front of it. He was tied at the wrists, his arms spread out like the mockery of a crucifixion, with two men holding onto the ropes to keep them taut. They had strung a banner on the outside of the cage. It said *Figlio del Diavolo.*"

"Son of the Devil," I translated in a whisper, and Mother continued as if I had not spoken.

"One of the gypsies was pacing behind him, holding a whip, and he called to us.

'*Ladies and gentlemen! You have seen our magician! He has astounded you with his tricks, flattered your women! Perhaps some of you have even heard him sing! He has the voice of an angel, does he not? But this being, gentlemen, is no angel, nor is he a man! He is a demon who has used his silken voice and silver tongue to enchant his way through the world! He has even built a palace of mirrors for the Shah of Persia himself! But this demon cannot evade the magic of gypsies, our ancient arts and power! We were able to cage the beast and keep his poisoned hands from your daughters! Shall you see what a monster looks like? What the Son of the Devil really is?!'*

And when the crowd bayed and bellowed, he pulled the silk mask back to Erik's forehead to reveal his face. I'd never seen anything like it, Meg. It's… it was…"

"Christine described it to me," I said quickly as she struggled for words. "And Joseph Buquet told us… the day you slapped him."

She nodded.

"I'm not surprised she told you. But… it was worse than that, love. The gypsies had done things to him, tortured him. The man with the whip told us that they had captured this 'fiend' in Italy, that they had dragged him before His Holiness the Pope himself, who had blessed Erik and poured Holy Water over his head. Did we want to see what that did to him? He took the silk from Erik's head completely. He was balding, the thin dark hair hanging from his scalp greasy.

'I see red roses among the crowd!' The gypsy jeered. It was almost as if he was mocking us. *'Gifts from our magician, no doubt. Did he charm you, ladies? Did he seduce you with that silver voice and make you think he wanted you? All lies, ladies! This man feels nothing! Let me prove it!'*

He took a knife and cut the shirt from Erik's body. He was so thin I could see his ribs through his skin, his lungs working beneath them. The gypsy raised the whip and lashed it across Erik's back. Erik moved involuntarily with the blow, but he didn't make a sound. I looked at Claude, and knew the disgust on his face mirrored my own. His arm tightened around my waist.

'Come on,' he said. *'Let's leave this place.'*

We pushed our way through the crowd, who were cheering at the flogging taking place in front of the cage, but another gypsy blocked our path. He was holding a money box in one hand and a riding crop in the other.

'Contribution for the show.' It wasn't a request.

'I don't think so,' Claude replied grimly. *'Magic tricks performed by a skilled magician are entertainment. This—'* he waved his hand over the crowd, who were shouting for more violence as Erik was whipped. *'—is simply barbaric. Thrashing a man just because his face is…'*

'Demonic?' The gypsy suggested.

'Abnormal.' Claude said. *'No man deserves that. Now let us pass.'*

We tried to move forward, but he snapped the riding crop up to stop us.

'You can give your contribution in francs,' he said in a cold voice. *'Or we can take it out of your flesh. Or that of your pretty wife. If we can make the devil scream…'* and he nodded over our heads to where we could hear Erik now crying out with the pain. *'… imagine what we could do to her.'*

He pushed the leather tip of the riding crop under my chin. Claude was tense beside me and I could feel that he wanted to punch the gypsy in the

THE ANGEL'S SHADOW

face. I squeezed his arm, knowing that if he started a fight here, he would lose. He dropped a few francs into the gypsy's box, who grinned and bowed us out of the fair, dismissing us in Italian with vulgar language. He had no way of knowing we could understand his words.

Claude and I returned to the Opera House and went to bed, but neither of us could sleep. Around two o'clock in the morning, he whispered to me:

'Are you awake, Annie?'

'Yes, Claude, I'm awake.'

'I can't stop thinking about that boy... the magician in the cage. How old do you think he was?'

'I don't know. Anywhere between fifteen and twenty years, it's hard to say.'

I turned onto my side to look at him, his face silver in the moonlight that crept through the curtains.

'Do you think we should tell the police?' I asked.

'I doubt the police would do anything.' Claude replied. *'Gypsies are a law unto themselves, and in my experience, the freaks are not forced to stay. They choose to perform in these fairs and expose their... differences to the public.'*

'Are you telling me you believe that man was in that cage of his own free will?'

'Perhaps. I doubt any of that spiel about him being dragged before the Pope and doused in Holy Water was true. It could all be an act; he probably has a cosy caravan and an expensive bottle of cognac waiting for him when the working day is over.'

I made a noise of disgust.

'You saw what they were doing to him, Claude. That was not an act. They were flogging him, just because his face is deformed, because the spectators enjoyed it. You said it yourself, it's barbaric.'

He was quiet for a long moment, and then said:

'The fair is in town for another week; I'll go back tomorrow, do a bit of poking around, see what I can find out. It might all be an act, Annie, truly, but if not...' he shook his head. *'I never considered myself to be a good Catholic, Annie... but everything in my soul is crying out against seeing another human being treated in such a way.'"*

Mother boiled more water, preparing more coffee as she continued to speak. All these secrets she had held onto for such a long time. Now, it seemed, once she had started to relieve herself of them, she could not stop.

"Claude did go back the following day, using a false beard and moustache to disguise himself, just in case the gypsies recognised him and wouldn't readmit him because of his being... a troublemaker. It was gone midnight when he returned, I remember being unable to sleep for worrying about him, but he was quite unscathed. And he was furious, Meg. He told me that there was no doubt about the magician's willingness to be caged and beaten for public entertainment. The freaks *were* in the cages of their own will, and were released at the end of the working day... All except for Erik. He truly was their prisoner." She swallowed hard. "If... if enough

213

money hadn't been made by sundown, they took him from the cage and whipped him, as we saw. Claude heard that sometimes *that* could earn more money in a night than the rest of the acts combined."

"It's… horrible…" I said, as she refilled my coffee cup, unable to find a word strong enough to describe how I felt about what I was being told.

"Erik was kept in that cage all day, every day. At night-time they chained him to the bars. When the fair moved, they would lift the cage onto wheels with him still inside. We both knew it was foolish, but something had galvanised Claude and I. We decided that we were going to rescue Erik from his captivity; we planned it out very carefully. Claude had discovered who held the key to Erik's cage, and would pick his pocket for it. After the public had left, we would unlock the cage and set Erik free. However… it seems that Erik himself had other ideas that night.

We crept into the tent after all the other members of the public had been ushered out, both of us dressed in dark clothes and keeping to the shadows. Erik was shackled to the bars of his cage and the gypsy who had whipped him was kneeling on the floor, collecting the coins that had been thrown. The whip was on the floor beside him. I saw Erik move, fast as snake, and snatch the whip up, then wrap it around the gypsy's throat and pull it tight. He killed that man, Meg, right in front of us… and I watched him do it. I watched his distorted face, teeth bared almost in pain, almost in triumph, and I don't know if *he* knew that we were there." She took a deep breath and paused to sip the coffee. "I remember Claude having to push me to get me moving, telling me that the plan was still unchanged. He took a ring of keys from the gypsy and threw it to me, while he went to the entrance of the tent to keep a lookout. I remember my hands were shaking so much I could hardly get the cage open, and they trembled even more when I approached the skeletally thin creature chained to the bars. I admit, I was afraid of him, Meg. I had seen him murder someone, and appear to take joy in it. Erik didn't speak to me as I tried to find the key that would unlock his shackles and free him. Even when I got them off and pulled him to his feet, he hissed in pain, but said nothing. It was only when Claude came over and threw his coat over Erik's bloodied back that the man spoke:

'My mask!' He gasped.

'What?' Claude was flustered, eager to be gone.

'My mask!' Erik repeated. *'Give me my mask!'*

I found the black silk mask in the straw and filth at the bottom of the cage, and gave it to him. He clutched it as if it was something infinitely precious, and we fled. We had only just left the tent when we heard someone enter it and give a cry at the sight of the body and the empty cage. We both knew that Erik was in terrible pain from the flogging he had received, but we had no time for gentleness. We bundled him into the Opera Populairé and up to our chambers—yes, Meg, these rooms—

THE ANGEL'S SHADOW

without being seen. The moment he was able, Erik put on the mask to cover his face. I tended to his wounds, and Claude gave him wine mixed with some sort of opiate, so that he slept. He slept in this bed, Meg, while Claude and I slept on the sofa in each other's arms. It was not until the following morning, when I woke to see dawn light spilling across Erik's masked face, that I realised that our plan was flawed. Claude and I now had a gypsy runaway and murderer in our care. We had not reported his crime, in fact we had aided his escape from the law, and that made us accessories to it. And now here was a man, deformed, beaten and bloody, but a man, and neither Claude nor I had the slightest idea what to do with him."

CHAPTER THIRTY ONE

Mother had stopped her pacing as she sipped her second cup of coffee. I sat on her bed, my own cup in one hand, my other hand trailing over the sheets. As a young man of nineteen, whipped and bloodied, Erik had slept here, rescued from his unwilling captivity in a travelling fair. Rescued by my parents. I'd had no idea my mother and father had witnessed a murder and rescued the murderer. Maybe it was all the champagne I had been unwisely drinking this evening, but my stomach suddenly felt nauseated with a sharp tug of longing. I wished my father was here to tell me his side of the story himself. How well had I truly known him?

"How did you keep him hidden from everyone else?" I asked. "Surely someone must have noticed him."

She shook her head.

"It's surprising how much can be hidden in plain sight. It's easy enough to provide enough food for a third person without arousing suspicion… especially if that person is malnourished to the point where their stomach has shrunk…."

Mother passed a hand across her brow.

"Erik was… a somewhat difficult patient. He told me how to create potion that would increase his healing, but he was in almost constant pain for more than two weeks. There were occasions when he was almost seen by other people, or they would notice things missing; Erik was an expert thief.

'Antoinette,' he said to me one day two weeks after his rescue. *'Who designed this opera house?'*

His tone was urgent.

'I… think his name was Garnier,' I replied, surprised by the question. *'Among others.'*

'Charles Garnier?' He asked, eyes glittering.

'I believe so, but he was one of many. It took years to build the Opera Populairé. I imagine changes were made along the way.'

THE ANGEL'S SHADOW

He gave an almost wild laugh, eyes flicking around my apartment.

'Which of these walls is interior?' He asked, and I told him. This one."

Mother gently knocked the wall next to her wardrobe. "Erik pressed his hands against the wall and then opened the wardrobe.

'Is this built in?' He demanded, and I nodded. He pushed my clothes aside and began knocking on the back of it. After a few minutes, he gave a laugh under his breath, and I thought I heard him whisper: *'God bless you, Charles.'*

When he stepped clear of the wardrobe, I saw there was an open door, concealed within, and what appeared to be a passageway beyond it. Erik lit a lantern and took my hand, and we explored the passage together... To cut a long story short, Meg, he had been expecting to find it. I don't know how or why, but he discovered the catacombs, chambers and traps concealed within this mighty building. He has never told me so, but I believe that he may have had some connection with Charles Garnier in his earlier life, maybe even some input into the original designs for the Opera Populairé."

I shook my head, struggling to take in all the information I was being told.

"He can't have," I argued. "While this building was being designed, Erik must have been a child."

Her shoulders rose and fell in a shrug.

"Erik doesn't really talk about his past. Can you help me out of this?"

She was struggling with the fastenings of her costume and I rose to assist her.

"But you think he did, and that makes it all right for him to do... what he does." I stated. "You told me that he has a *right* to the Opera House. To all of us as well, I daresay."

I undid the first of the fastenings and pretended not to notice her scowl.

"He did design at least part of this building, Meg. It has become his artistic domain. He knows all its secrets, all its quirks. He's a genius; an architect and designer, a composer and a magician."

And a madman, I added silently and undid the next fastening.

"He designed and constructed the masks he wears; he truly has brought prosperity to the company... Oh, Meg..."

There was little more to be said that night. Mother was distressed by her memories, by the whole evening's events. My questions were by no means all answered, but I was unwilling to force more confessions from her. Questions about Erik's interest in Christine, in me, about his time in Italy, why he had returned there just before my father's death... all would have to wait. I hugged my mother hard, telling her how much I loved her, how I appreciated her trying to protect me. I left her, and returned to my own dormitory in a swoop of white skirts and twisting emotions. As I fought my way out of the ball gown, the caffeine fizzing through my veins, I reflected that sleep would not be easy to come by in the early hours of this New Year's Day.

Three days passed, and the Opera Populairé was buzzing with fear. It ran through the building like the life-blood through my veins. Of course, everyone had heard about Erik's appearance at the New Year's Ball, the demands he had made, and the affair was being discussed under the title 'The Return of the Phantom'. No one could now doubt the existence and malice of the Opera Ghost, his power or his intentions. He truly was lord and master of all he surveyed, and everyone from the youngest ballerina to the prime diva La Carlotta herself, was terrified.

I found myself wishing I could emulate Christine and live outside of the Opera House, to escape its tense atmosphere, but there was no getting away.

I was astonished to learn that I was included in the *Don Juan Triumphant* cast list as someone named Katolina, a side plot involving a girl who turned to prostitution for money and then disguised herself as a boy in order to free herself from an abusive husband. The Phantom had given specific instructions with regards to who should play each role, but I had had no idea that he thought highly enough of my voice to demand I be given a singing part. It made me even more nervous, since I was so aware of his high expectations.

My score was waiting on Christine's vacated bed on the evening of January the third, its pages bound together with a black ribbon, a black-edged envelope on top bearing my name. The top page of the score itself bore the title, and the composer's signature. I could make out the E for Erik, but the rest of the name was just a billowing swirl that I could not decipher.

With a small sigh, I slid my finger beneath the red wax seal that held the envelope shut, its skull grinning up at me, the way Erik had appeared to grin while costumed as the Red Death. I took pleasure in destroying the image as the wax broke and the envelope opened.

Dear Meg,

Review your score carefully. The role of Katolina is not a major part, but is important to the story and still counts you among the principles. I trust you will fulfil the expectations I have of you and put in the amount of work that this will require.

E.

The main story of *Don Juan Triumphant* was about a nobleman who used deception and trickery to lure women of all ages, marital stations and classes into his bed. It reminded me of an opera by Mozart, except told from the villain's point of view, and with whom the audience was supposed to sympathise. Despite his sinful ways including murder, abuse, rape and torture, Don Juan received a divine pardon at the end of the opera and the restoration of Aminta. Aminta was the leading soprano role, initially another victim of Don Juan's sexual escapades, whom he had grown to love, and then killed in a passionate rage.

As I read and interpreted the story, I felt myself blushing with embarrassment, and then turning icy cold with a dread I could not quite place. This new opera and its unknown composer would certainly take Paris by storm, just as Erik had said, but not for the right reasons. It was remarkably explicit, even graphic in places.

The music was nothing like Mozart; it wasn't like anything I had heard in my life. I played it through on the piano, wincing at the cacophony of some pieces, and marvelling at the beauty of others. The song during which Don Juan first seduced Aminta was some of the most stunning scoring I had ever encountered. Mother was right; Erik really was a genius. An antihero in his own life, perhaps, but a genius just the same.

I was in a cage, too small to either stand up or lie down. Someone was holding onto my hair, stopping me from turning my head. I was crouched, filthy, and clutching the bars, staring through them to where a man in a black mask was kneeling on the dirt floor. He was naked above the waist, his arms outstretched like an image of Christ, fair hair on his lightly muscled chest. The gypsy man pacing behind him was shouting to the crowd; a crowd that left a space for me to see clearly what he was doing. He brought the whip in a vicious arc across the masked man's back.

"No!" I shouted as he gave a cry of pain, his body jerking with the impact.

I struggled hard against whoever was holding me, feeling the sobs starting to bubble up from my throat. The whip came down again and again, and my voice mingled with the victim's, as if it was my own skin being cut with the whip.

"Stop!" I cried. "Please! Stop!"

"No, no, little one," it was a male voice in my ear, the voice of whoever was holding me, preventing me from looking away. "See what you have caused."

"Shall you see what the monster looks like?!" The Italian gypsy yelled. "What the Son of the Devil really is?!"

"Don't!" I begged, but the crowd pressed around him were yelling to see the demon's face. Grinning like a gargoyle, the gypsy yanked the black silk mask from the man's head, and the horror twisted my stomach. I knew him, knew every feature of his perfect, unmarred face and voice, and as the gypsy continued to flog him, I screamed his name.

"PAPA!"

The shock of hearing my own voice jolted me into the waking world... almost. I was in my own bed in the Opera House, tangled in my bed sheets and still screaming... and the nightmare was still playing itself out in front of my eyes. It was as if the moving images were being projected onto glass. I could see the dark details of my room thanks to the electric lights surrounding the Opera House, but I could also see the man, kneeling the being viciously whipped. Nightmares like this, occurring when I was half awake and half asleep, came perhaps twice a year, and were always different. It wasn't like the dream of the hospital, always in the same place and with a similar pattern. Something new appeared as this half hallucination, and I struggled between what was real and what was only in my head. Until now, there had always been someone with me, to comfort me and hold me and calm me down. My father, mother, or Christine, using soothing words or songs to help me root myself in reality.

For the first time in my life, I was alone; I had no one to aid me through my distress, and would have to pull myself together on my own. I struggled from the bed sheets, one sleeve of my nightgown dropping off my shoulder as I staggered across the room. It was tiny, no more than twelve steps from the door to the window in the opposite wall, but the nightmare clung to my fevered body and mind, like the sticky threads of a spider's web, impeding me. I climbed onto the windowsill on trembling limbs and forced the window open. An icy blast of wind hit me in the face, snowflakes striking my cheeks like frozen kisses. I gulped in the frigid air and ordered myself to calm down. Here and now, this was what was real. The lashing I was hearing was the wind in the trees, the moans and cries the snowstorm driving through Paris. I would not succumb to this terror; I struggled to push it down, to slow my breathing, picturing a metronome ticking slowly and matching my inhalations to its rhythm. I watched the orange glow of the streetlight below me, flickering in and out of sight as the snow swirled past it.

Slowly, painfully slowly, the nightmare faded, and the trembling in my body was merely a result of the snow being blown against my skin. I sat on the windowsill for awhile longer, analysing without fear. Just hearing of Erik's torment has been enough to give me nightmares, my warped imagination twisting the victim into someone I loved. How must he suffer, having lived it? Did he awaken in the bowels of the Opera House, screaming in the dark as I did?

I closed the window, slipped off the sill and returned to my bed. I lit the candle on the nightstand with steady hands, then opened the drawer to find paper, pen and inkpot. Leaning the paper on the blue book of medical advice, I wrote ERIK across the top. I would list what I knew of him, to organise the facts in my mind.

ERIK

* 'Opera Ghost' 'The Phantom of the Opera' 'Angel of Music'

THE ANGEL'S SHADOW

* French
* Architect (possible input in Opera House? Connection to Charles Garnier? Son?)
* Designer
* Composer
* Magician (cards, close-up magic)
* Artist
* Musician (piano, organ, violin)
* Singing teacher
* Educated, scholar, collects books
* Multi-lingual, reading and writing (French, English, Italian, German? Spanish, Arabic)
* Has knowledge of medicine and healing, especially gypsy
* Lived in Italy and Persia, worked for Shah
* Torture chamber of mirrors
* Murderer (Buquet, gypsy)
* Punjab lasso (Lived in India?)
* Deformed (from birth?) masks deformity
* Captured, displayed and tormented by gypsies

The words he had spoken on Christmas Eve came back to me: *"I am not an attraction in a cage to be gawked at for my hideousness. I will never be so again."*

* Rescued by my parents aged 19
* Current age 36 – 39 years?
* Expects/demands respect
* Blackmailer, 20,000f per month (where does the money go?)
* Violent. Not opposed to using violence/torture against women, animals, innocents
* Does not like rapists
* Does not like swearing
* Cannot embroider
* Genius
* Insane
* Takes coffee black, no sugar
* Cooks
* Watches people, especially me and Christine. Protects me in payment of debt to Mother?
* Knows all of Opera House's secrets
* My godfather? Religious? Does not attend Sunday Mass
* Jealous

At the end of the list, I wrote *In love/obsessed with Christine*, then looked back over it. I had no idea if it could help me to understand the man, indeed if it were possible at all to understand a person I myself labelled insane, but I felt better for having done it. I folded the paper and put it away in the nightstand along with the pen, ink and book, and blew out the candle. I settled down to sleep, lulled by the sound of the storm outside, and if there were more dreams that night, I did not remember them when I awoke.

CHAPTER THIRTY TWO

A production meeting was arranged for January seventh, Mother and I receiving a note about it during a ballet rehearsal. I was finding the lesson soothing in its familiarity, comforted by being back in a routine, but I knew that Mother was very stressed. She had been designated choreographer for *Don Juan Triumphant*, and was struggling with Erik's unusual score. With everyone tense, it was dangerous to interrupt her.

The note—from our managers and on the Opera Populairé's headed notepaper—informed us that the principles and 'creative team' of the new opera, would be gathering in their office at one p.m. to discuss its production. Mother swore under her breath, and instructed me to fetch my score at once and go to the meeting.

"Please tell Messieurs Firman and André that I will join you as soon as I can," she growled. "I cannot simply abandon all my duties at a moment's notice. Off you go. I don't remember telling the rest of you to stop!" She bellowed at the other ballerinas as I headed for the door. "Jammes! Keep that left leg straight!"

When I reached the office, I found La Carlotta and Signor Piangi already there, holding a score between them and muttering in Italian. They both glanced at me as I entered the room, and then ignored me. I went over to the manager's desk and perched on the edge of it, resting my score in my lap. My heart sank when I saw the two black-edged envelopes on top of the other paperwork. Picking up the one addressed to Monsieur Firman, I turned it over to see the red wax seals were unbroken. Oh, what fresh demands and threats did our resident Ghost want to impose upon us now?

I heard voices in the corridor outside and dropped the envelope onto the desk with a guilty start, sliding off it and standing by the wall with my feet together, hands folded around my score, head bowed.

"Have you *seen* this score?" Monsieur Reyer's voice sounded exasperated.

"It's ludicrous!" André said firmly.

"Well... not ludicrous," Reyer said. "But it's just so... different. I'm not sure how well this will go down with our regular audiences."

"This whole thing is complete madness," Monsieur Firman interjected. "Well, you know my opinion on the affair."

"Yes," Reyer agreed and I had the impression he had been hearing Firman's opinions for awhile.

"But how can we turn him down? The man is clearly insane!"

"One more disaster and we're ruined." André said as he entered the office. He sighed and looked around at those of us present as Firman and Reyer came in behind him, closing the door. "Signor Piangi, Signora Gudicelli, Mademoiselle Giry, thank you for joining us. Mademoiselle Daaé is on her way..."

"As is my mother," I replied. "She said she would join us as soon as possible."

"Oh," Firman had spotted the distinctive envelopes on the desk. "Now what?"

He sighed deeply, handed André the one addressed to him, and slit his own envelope open with a paperknife. I felt my curiosity peak, and was surprised when the shorter manager began to read the note aloud:

Dear André,
You must find replacements for the first bassoon player and third trombone player at once. The former over blows every note while the latter is as deaf as a post. It would perhaps be wiser for all concerned if he were to take retirement.
O.G.

He lowered the note and raised his eyebrows at Monsieur Reyer.

"Your opinion?" He prompted.

"Well," Reyer said, a little uncertainly. "He does have a point. I have had words with Mattissier about the... vigorousness of his playing. As for Monsieur Debnar..." He shook his head regretfully. "Well, he *is* losing his hearing. Perhaps it would be better, kinder... I mean... I'd hate for anything to happen to him... to any of us..."

His worry hung in the air and I swallowed hard. We had all seen what the Phantom was capable of. He had stolen or destroyed all the Opera House's violins in his displeasure over a poor performer, what if he did something more drastic to Messieurs Mattissier or Debnar? Firman gave a grunt.

"Something similar here." He cleared his throat.

Dear Firman,
Please find enclose a list of the chorus members who are excluded from performing in

THE ANGEL'S SHADOW

this opera—and if my advice is heeded, all further operas—due to their inability to hold the pitch of the music. I have endeavoured to write parts for all of those with an acceptable quality of talent within the Opera Populairé's current company, including those who are unable to act.

If there was more to this note, it was interrupted by an ejaculation of Italian fury from the back of the room.

"This is *outrageous!*" Carlotta shrieked.

"What is?" Firman looked quite alarmed.

"This whole affair!" She stormed across the office towards him.

"Signora, please…" Firman raised both hands in front of him, still holding the note, as if warding off a tiger.

"Now what's the matter?" André sounded weary.

"Have you seen the size of my role?!" She demanded, thrusting the score at him. "Have you *seen* how *little* this so-called composer has given me to sing?!"

"It's insulting!" Piangi agreed.

"I *demand* an immediate recasting and a larger role this *instant!*" The diva wailed.

In spite of everything, I could feel myself fighting not to show my amusement at her displeasure, as passionate and overdramatic as ever. I kept my head down, wishing my hair was loose and could hide my smile.

The office door opened and Christine entered, followed by both Philippe and Raoul de Chagny. She looked as though she had not had much sleep in the last few days; her skin was deathly pale and there were dark circles beneath her eyes. I was surprised to see that her dress was one of the hand-me-downs from the Opera House. It was the one she had given me to change into after falling into the Phantom's lake, blue with a floral pattern, an old-fashioned bustle and lace ruffles at the elbow-length sleeves. Her hands, clutching the own copy of her score, were trembling slightly.

"Ah, here she is, the star!" Carlotta cried snidely.

"Christine…" I put my score down on the desk, approached her with a smile and kissed her softly on both cheeks. "How are you?"

I was truly alarmed by her appearance, for the only word I could think of to describe it was… haunted. She lifted her eyes to mine and attempted a smile.

"I'm fine, Meg." She replied.

"The lady of the moment," Firman observed. "Thank you for joining us. And you as well, Messieurs." He bowed towards the de Chagny brothers.

"You have been cast in the leading role in this *Don Juan Triumphant,*" André told her.

"Christine Daaé!" Carlotta spat my friend's name as if it were an insult. "She doesn't have the voice!"

225

I glared at the diva.

"Clearly she does, or the Phantom would not have chosen her to be his leading lady," I said. Carlotta glowered back, and I was suddenly aware of Philippe de Chagny's full attention upon me, the prickle of his interest against my skin.

"Then I take it you're agreeing?" Raoul asked.

"It appears we have no alternative," André sighed.

"This is all her doing!" Carlotta burst out, and my stomach gave a horrible lurch as her finger pointed right at me. "Christine Daaé!"

I relaxed as I realised that I was not, after all, under suspicion. Christine, however, had reached the end of her tether.

"How dare you!" She cried, storming across the room. Carlotta tried to say something in retaliation, but Christine was far from finished. "What an *evil* thing to say! This isn't my fault! Who wants their dreams shattered and their every waking moment terrorised?! I don't want anything to do with it!"

"But why?" André did not sound angry, but curious. "I mean… it's your decision, of course."

"Are you saying you're not going to sing it?" Carlotta asked, sounding completely thrown.

"If you do not sing it, this Phantom will only make things worse for us!" Firman reminded her.

"I cannot sing it!" Christine looked as though she was about to burst into tears. "I cannot be a part of this!"

"Christine…" I went to her and put my arm around her shoulders. "You don't *have* to, no one can *make* you. Not even him."

I glared around at Carlotta and the room full of men, feeling my friend trembling under my hands. I wished I knew what to do, how to comfort her. The sound of someone clearing their throat made me look around. Mother was standing in the doorway, and she looked even worse than Christine; unhealthily white, her eyes red from recently shed tears. I crossed to her as Raoul took Christine in his strong embrace, wondering what could have happened in the short time we had been apart.

"Are you all right?" I whispered. "What's happened?"

She shook her head and drew a black-edged envelope from the pocket of her skirt.

"Messieurs, another note."

A groan arose from the assembled company. Mother raised her eyebrows, then opened the envelope herself, unfolded the paper and began to read aloud:

"Fondest greetings,

Don Juan Triumphant *will have its world premiere on the first of March 1894; this gives you eight weeks to prepare. A few instructions just before rehearsals begin:*

THE ANGEL'S SHADOW

I insist that Carlotta be given some lessons in acting before she allowed to set foot upon the stage again. Simply strutting around like a peacock is not good enough for my shows. It is also my wish for Signor Piangi to lose some weight for his role as the Lothario in this production; I am concerned for his health. As for Firman and André, they would do well to keep their noses as far as possible out of things. They have no place within the world of opera."

I swore I could hear Erik's voice, his tones and inflections through the words. Mother's eyes left the page and settled on my friend as she continued.

"As for our star, Mademoiselle Christine Daaé. I have no doubt that she will try her best, and she does have a good voice, but if she wishes to perform to the best of her ability and gain the praise which she so rightly deserves, she should swallow her pride and return to her singing lessons.
Your obedient Friend and Angel."

Silence hung in the air of the crowded office. Christine was staring at the note, her expression a strange mixture of fear and longing. Raoul looked simply furious, but his face suddenly cleared as it someone had struck a match in his head.

"We've all been blind!" He gasped. "The answer is right in front of us. This man has given us the very opportunity we need to capture him!"

"What?" I asked, bewildered, but my voice was drowned out by André and Firman.

"We're listening!"

"Go on!"

"We stage his opera, just as he commands," Raoul continued. "But remember that we have the advantage. If Christine sings, then the Phantom will certainly be in attendance."

"We know where he'll be, so we can lock all the doors once we have confirmation that he's there!" André had caught the drift of Raoul's idea.

"And we can bring in the *gendarmes!*" Firman added.

"Armed *gendarmes*," the Vicomte clarified. "And by the time the curtain falls, his reign of terror will be over!"

"Madness!" Mother cried, and I had to concur.

"This is madness!"

I had a vision of armed police lining the auditorium, weapons ready to fire. How little would it take to cause a shot to be let off, to find an innocent target? The fatality that had occurred as a result of the crashing chandelier had nearly closed the Opera Populairé; a second death among our patrons would be the end of us. Mother slid her arm around my waist as she tried to talk them out of this idea.

LOUISE ANNE BATEMAN

"You could *help us*!" Raoul walked towards us, exasperated.

"Monsieur, I can't!"

"Yes, you could! You know things, Madame Giry, *why* won't you tell us what you know?!"

"I wish I could..."

"Maybe you're on his side?" Philippe de Chagny did not raise his voice, but his accusation cut through the buzz of talk that had begun after Raoul outlined his plan. I swallowed hard, feeling that cold lurch in my stomach as Mother's arm went tense around me, her fingers digging into my ribs. She took a deep, steadying breath.

"Comte, I don't intend any harm," she said. "But, Messieurs, be careful—we have seen him *kill*!"

I shuddered, remembering the two men I had seen murdered by Erik's hand.

"She's his accomplice!" Carlotta shouted, pointing at us. "They both are! Always lurking in corners, probably reporting back to this so-called Ghost!"

"That is absurd!" I protested.

"Is it?" Philippe asked softly, his eyes on mine.

The noise was getting too much for me; I could feel panic starting to clog my throat as voices raised in argument around me, some aimed at us, some at Christine.

"Heed my warning!" Mother insisted. "And do not make him angry!"

No one paid any attention, and under the pressure being piled upon her, Christine snapped. She threw her score across the room.

"Raoul I'm *frightened*!" She screamed. "Don't make me *do* this! It won't work and he will kidnap me! And this time, he won't let me go! He told me once that I would stay with him forever since I had seen his true face, and he may well mean it!"

The room had gone silent in the face of her distress. André brought the chair around his desk and Raoul guided her into the seat as she continued to speak, her voice thick with tears.

"I used to dream about this man, but now I dread him... If he captures me there will be no peace for me. He'll be with me day and night, inside my very soul!"

"She's mad," Carlotta murmured and I gave her a filthy look. Raoul knelt before the chair, taking Christine's hands in his.

"He is no ghost, or angel," he told her gently. "You said so yourself. But while he's alive, we may never be free of him. You will be looking over your shoulder for the rest of your life."

Christine swallowed a sob.

"What am I to answer?" she whispered. "You're asking me to risk my life, Raoul. And what of the Phantom? He *gave* me my voice, taught me to be the singer I am. How can I betray him? Act as bait for your trap? Do I

THE ANGEL'S SHADOW

even have a choice? He *has* killed, we've all seen it, he *is* a murderer… Oh, God!" Her tears fell. "If I agree to this, what horrors await me? This is the Phantom's opera…"

"Christine…" Raoul reached up to wipe away her tears. "I understand that you're afraid. But you are our only hope."

They started in on her again, like wolves attacking a wounded deer as their voices merged into one. Christine bolted from the chair.

"I can't!" She cried, and fled past Mother and I, out into the corridor. Philippe gripped the Vicomte's arm as Raoul rose to follow.

"Let her go, brother," he advised. "Christine is upset, give her time to calm down."

The meeting broke up, Raoul still seething and Carlotta still complaining.

"March the first is our premiere date," Firman said to Mother. "You'd better get on with it."

"Yes, Monsieur," she replied coldly, and we followed Monsieur Reyer out of the door.

It was not surprising that Mother's patience was frayed to breaking point after that meeting. She would not let me go to find Christine, her reasoning the same as Philippe's, that my friend needed time to herself, to think and to pray. We returned to the ballet studio and I went through a routine of stretches to re-warm my muscles. The tension Mother carried on her shoulders was immediately noticed by the other ballerinas and nerves were running high. It was less than an hour later when Mother lost her temper, hurling a wooden-blocked pointe shoe at Sorelli. It missed the girl, colliding with the mirror behind her and causing cracks to splinter out like the intricate designs of a spider's web.

"Out!" Mother stormed. "I've had enough of all of you! Get out!"

The girls fled from her temper in a rustle of rehearsal skirts and twittering concern. I remained, watching Mother as she gazed at the cracks in the glass.

"What happened?" I asked quietly, and she shook her head. "Tell me, Mother, please. Did you run into Erik?"

Her breath came out in a rush and she raised a hand to her throat, nodding. I looked at her distorted reflection and the placement of her hand, alarmed.

"Did he hurt you?" I demanded.

She made a strange sound, halfway between a laugh and a sob, and shook her head.

"No, Meg, he didn't hurt me."

I watched her reflection in the broken mirror.

"Did he threaten you?"
"No… not in so many words."
And then I understood.
"Did he threaten *me?*"

CHAPTER THIRTY THREE

Mother's shoulders sagged and I knew I was right. After all, Erik was a master of mind games, of controlling and deceiving and manipulating, and now he had more power in the Opera House than he had ever had before. It was probably going to his head.

"Erik told me that he has been displeased with my attitude over the last six months," she said. "And that if he did not see an improvement then he would take you from me. Hurt you. Maybe even kill you." She turned to me, her eyes full of pain. "He would do it, Meg, I know he would. He's tortured you before to punish Christine." I shuddered at the memory. "If he were to do so because of me, I couldn't bear it! I couldn't bear it!"

I pulled her into my arms, trying to comfort her and feeling completely helpless.

"He said something similar to me," I reminded her. "The time he warned me to keep away from the lake. He told me he'd kill you if his secrets ceased to be his secrets..."

Mother stroked my hair.

"Never..." she murmured. "Never. I won't let him harm you, Meg, I swear."

We clung to each other, and I could feel her heart beating against my own breast. Anger and despair ran through my veins, the worry that I would not be able to prevent Erik from taking his revenge out on me if he chose to. I wondered if, from behind one of the unbroken mirrors in the ballet room, the Phantom of the Opera was watching.

The snow was still falling in blasts and gusts as I returned to my dormitory, and I realised that I had not seen sunshine all day. The wind was howling around the building, like a pack of wolf cubs baying at the moon, but there would be no moon tonight. The clouds, heavy with more snow, had firmly settled over Paris and showed no sign of dispersing before dawn.

Candlelight shone beneath the doors of the dormitories occupied by the chorus members and ballet girls, and as I reached the top floor, eight whole storeys above Erik's subterranean domain, I saw light coming from under my own door. I thought that Christine must have decided to spend the night in her old bed, so was feeling quite light-hearted when I opened the door.

Christine wasn't in the room, even though four candles were lit. Instead, the Comte Philippe de Chagny was sitting on my bed. He had removed the drawer from my nightstand and the contents were scattered across the blanket. I felt an illogical rush of shame that the room was untidy, the bed unmade and my nightgown strewn across the floor. I picked it up, my eyes still on Philippe as he flicked lazily through the pages of my medical book.

"Comte de Chagny... what are you doing here?"

"I was looking for your diary, Mademoiselle Giry," he replied, not lifting his gaze from the page. "In my experience, most girls your age can be relied upon to confide their secrets to a diary."

"I don't keep a diary," I told him, completely nonplussed.

"So I discovered," his eyes met mine. "But you do have secrets, don't you, Meg?"

I swallowed hard.

"I'm sure everyone has secrets, Monsieur."

My hands were clammy against the white cotton of my nightgown. Philippe gave me a strange smile that was nothing more than a curving of his lips.

"But some secrets are more damning than others."

He held up the list I had written, all the facts I knew about Erik, and I felt nausea coil in my belly.

"Give me that!"

I lunged towards him, dropping my nightgown as I snatched for the paper, but he stood up, raising it high above his head and well out of my reach.

"I don't think so, Mademoiselle," he said in a mocking tone. "This document of yours is very valuable."

"Give that back to me," I snarled, stretching up to try and reach the list. "You have no right to go through my personal possessions, to invade my privacy like this!"

"I think you'll find the law would be on my side," he said coldly. "You've been harbouring a criminal, Little Meg."

I glared at him, knowing my attempts to extract the paper from him were futile, and lowering my heels to the floor.

"Of course I haven't. Where would I harbour someone, under my bed? Maybe in my wardrobe?"

Philippe tutted, shaking his head at me.

THE ANGEL'S SHADOW

"I thought it was your mother who was keeping the Opera Ghost, this *Erik* aware of our movements. But it was you, wasn't it?"

"I don't know what you mean," I countered, even though I was sure I was turning pale.

"Oh come along, Meg!" He snapped. "It's all here, in your own handwriting! You know far more about this man than you've chosen to share with us!"

I shook my head.

"It's not true," I said, my voice coming out croaky. "It's all made up, it's speculation."

"I don't think so," he answered, shaking his head. "You spent six months in my home, Meg, and I have been watching you."

"Why?"

"It's what I do," he replied, matter-of-factly. "I observe people. And you are an interesting study."

Philippe de Chagny was the second person to say that to me in the last few months. The first was, of course, Erik.

"You know about this Phantom," he continued. "And I believe you are in communication with him." He glanced at the list again. "Murderer, deformed genius, blackmailer... all this we knew already. We did not know that this man possibly designed the Opera Populairé, although that would lend some explanation as to how he can appear to move from one place to another with supernatural speed; he clearly knows ways around that are not accessible to the public or the residents. What is a Punjab lasso, by the way? Is that the Ghost's weapon of choice?" I didn't reply and he just shook his head. "Never mind. You can protest all you like, Meg, but it says right here that your own parents rescued this 'Erik' from capture, display and torment by gypsies. Assumedly, this rescue was after he killed one of them, and that, my girl, is a criminal offense."

His movement was sudden and took me by surprise. He backed me against the wardrobe, pocketing the list, and one of the handles pressed into my spine. He reached out for the dormitory door and closed it on the deserted landing outside. I gasped, but as quickly as I could do so, his fingers were around my wrist, pressing my palm flat against the wardrobe, down by my side.

"What are you doing?" I yelped, and he put a finger to my lips.

"I could show this to the police," he said quietly. "To your managers, to your dear Christine. I wonder how she will react when she learns how close you are to her Angel of Music? I expect she would view it as a betrayal."

I was trembling, eyes wide.

"Do you know what happens next, Meg? Your mother is tried for being this Erik's accomplice, aiding and abetting crimes which include blackmail and the murder of that stagehand, Buquet. The official cause of death was

233

an accident, but you have identified it here as murder in black and white. If your mother is lucky, then she'll spend the rest of her days in prison. If not, then it's an appointment with the Widow."

I felt myself stricken, recognising the slang term for the guillotine, horrified by the vision of my mother walking to her execution. Philippe's finger traced the line of my lips and then brushed my cheek.

"And what do you suppose would happen to you then, Little Meg?"

I swallowed hard, trying to find my voice.

"I would be orphaned," I croaked. "And probably thrown onto the streets."

"Only if you were not tried and found guilty along with your mother," Philippe was still stroking my cheek. "You are accomplice as well, you know. But don't worry, my dear. The blade would not await you."

"It wouldn't?" I looked into his blue eyes, so much like those of his brother.

"No. You see, people who are not sound of mind tend to escape the death penalty, although your Opera Ghost may be an exception. It's the lunatic asylum for you."

I felt myself go so cold I thought I would faint. No one, not even Mother had said those words aloud. We had spoken of doctors, hospitals, where my father had been treated. We had never discussed what that hospital had really been. The idea that I myself would be confined to an asylum made me feel breathless and panicky, my reoccurring nightmare come to life. Philippe was studying my reaction as if I was a butterfly partially pinned to a board and he was interested to see how badly I would be willing to damage my wings in order to escape.

"And now you understand," he said softly.

"Please," it came out as a whisper. "You can't show them... you can't tell them what you know."

He grinned.

"Ah, so you do have some intelligence. My silence comes with a price, of course."

"You're blackmailing me..."

"Such an ugly term," he replied. "But it does seem to be the preferred flavour around here and certainly yields results."

"I haven't got any money."

"I know that," he scoffed. "You're worthless in financial terms, Little Meg."

"Then what do you want?"

He smiled again.

"You, Meg Giry," he said. "Just you."

I gaped at him like a fish.

"You're... proposing to me?" I stammered, and he bellowed with

THE ANGEL'S SHADOW

laughter.

"Hardly!" He replied, voice ringing with mirth. "I want your *body*, Meg, not your lifelong commitment. It's been a long while since I've had a virgin."

The words echoed in my head, music in a minor key, the same phrase over and over again. Philippe de Chagny had all the information he needed to have Mother imprisoned or even executed, and myself locked in an asylum for the insane. He could end our lives... but he had given me a choice, a chance to save us. All I had to do was give him my body. To do what with? I was shaking like a leaf in a breeze.

It's been a long while since I've had virgin.

Virgin. A word that meant white, pure, unspoiled. A man or woman who had never had sex; the act where the man pushed some part of his body into the part of mine that bled once a month, that made me a woman. My knowledge was completely theoretical. I had never seen it, only knew that it was something that usually happened between married couples. The music in my head was deafening.

"I'm not—" I began, but Philippe shook his head sternly.

"Don't try that, Meg," he scolded. "It's a wicked thing to tell lies. You, my girl, are as inexperienced as they come... This is my price, Meg. Your virginity in return for my silence."

I stared at him, throat dry, trying to find the strength to speak the words that would bring us salvation. He waited, one hand pressing mine against the wardrobe, the other still touching my cheek.

"Yes," I whispered. "I agree. I'll give you what you want."

The smile he gave me in return was soft, gentlemanly, as though I had accepted an invitation for coffee.

"Excellent," he breathed. "I look forward to being your teacher, Little Meg. Don't look so scared. Be a good girl for me and I will give you pleasure like you've never known. You will be thanking me for keeping your secret and begging me for another lesson."

I could feel my cheeks already burning with shame as he took a step away from me.

"When?" I managed, and he pulled a regretful face.

"Alas," he sighed. "I am called to Germany for several weeks. I leave tomorrow, and do not expect to return much before your *Don Juan* atrocity opens to the public." He studied me thoughtfully. "The night of the debut," he decided. "After your performance and the police are gone. After the curtain comes down and your Opera Ghost is safely incarcerated by the *gendarmes*. I'll take you to supper, Meg."

He nodded, then took the few steps back to my bed, picking up his top hat, gloves and dress cane.

"Until then, my beauty."

235

"Wait!" I cried, and he lifted his eyebrows in a question. "My… my list…"

"I think it would be best if I held onto that, don't you?" His tone held a streak of scorn. "You can have it back once you have consummated our bargain."

He left the room without another word, closing the door behind him. I sat down abruptly on Christine's empty bed, staring at the clutter on my own. How could I have been so stupid as to leave that list lying around in a drawer for anyone to find? Because I had not expected anyone to come looking; at the Opera Populairé we respected each other's personal space and privacy. I had a sudden flash of understanding as to how violated Erik must have felt when I had stumbled upon his secret passages, and why he had taken such extreme measures to keep me out.

Erik. A man whose secrets I had begun to unravel, secrets that I had allowed to fall into the hands of an enemy.

Enemy. Philippe de Chagny was an enemy? I let my head drop into my hands. I had lived in his home for six months, and although I had the impression that he did not like me, there was no indication that I had been under scrutiny. He had never said or done anything that implied he was interested in me as a person either, or even a body. I just couldn't understand what the Comte thought he was gaining by blackmailing me like this. He had never so much as approached me with even the suggestion of a sexual interest, and he clearly thought that Raoul's plan to capture Erik would work. Apart from the one incident outside the Opera Populairé when he had slapped me, in order to shock me out of my attack of hysterics, he had always behaved like the perfect gentleman. It seemed so out of character for him to turn out to be such a snake.

What should I do? Tell Mother about the blackmail and my agreement? She would be devastated and probably disgusted by my submission to Philippe's demands, in addition to adding more stress onto her already over-burdened shoulders. Tell Christine and Raoul? Out of the question. Christine had enough to deal with and Raoul would not believe me. If he did, Philippe would produce the list and my secrets, and Erik's, would be revealed, Mother arrested and myself confined. I took a deep breath. Should I tell Erik? He would be furious, but might be able to do something; retrieve the list or silence the Comte… I shuddered. Erik killed to protect his secrets, and if I sought him out he might well choose to keep me locked up somewhere to ensure Mother's good behaviour. Or would he? He had specifically cast me in *Don Juan Triumphant*, surely he would not want to jeopardise the success of his opera?

I felt like a fly in a spider's web, trapped and threatened from every angle. If I told Erik, he would kill Philippe, and I could not bear the death of another man on my conscience. It was already stained by the murders of

THE ANGEL'S SHADOW

Jacques and Buquet.

I would tell no one. The Comte was out of the country until late February, and when he returned... I would face that fear when the time came, but I *would* do whatever it took to protect Mother.

CHAPTER THIRTY FOUR

Is there a term for delighting in other's people's fear?

I had lived in the Opera Populairé for all of my seventeen years—apart from the six-month spell at the de Changy château—and I had never before felt such a high level of tension concentrated there for so long. Everyone I saw was white-faced and anxious; people spoke in hushed tones or bellowed their terror and frustration at each other. Tempers were short and nerves were shredded, the rehearsals for *Don Juan Triumphant* demanding and not enjoyable. Mother was especially affected, but she was doing her utmost to maintain her usual calm persona, strict but fair, demanding perfection from her dancers, but demonstrating how to achieve it.

The younger girls in the *corps de ballet* had been particularly upset by the uprising of the Opera Ghost; every shadow was him lurking, every moan of the wind was his voice. Erik himself was doing nothing to dispel their fears, instead he appeared to be enjoying it, and was now playing practical jokes.

During a ballet rehearsal, he appeared behind one of the mirrors, clothed in black evening dress and a white bowtie, a fedora hat shadowing his masked face. He held out his cloak like wings, roaring like the angel of death. The dancers broke out into screaming hysterics, two of them fainting, and Erik laughed, vanishing from the glass as he used his left foot to knock the shutter closed on the dark lantern. Mother wouldn't use that room for rehearsals anymore, as the ballerinas refused to enter it.

A few days later, Mother and I were returning from a shopping trip in the city, arms full of groceries, when a scream rang through the corridor. We glanced at each other, and ran to its source without consultation. Madame Imelda Soirelli, the wardrobe mistress, was standing in the doorway to her workroom, one hand clutching onto the doorframe, which was the only reason she was still on her feet. Her other hand was clamped over her mouth in an attempt to muffle her continuing screams. We rushed towards her, abandoning out shopping bags, and Mother seized her by the

THE ANGEL'S SHADOW

shoulders.

"Imelda! What is it, what's happened?!"

She collapsed to her knees, Mother kneeling with her as Madame Soirelli struggled to speak.

"Murder!" She sobbed. "The Ghost has murdered someone in here!"

With a jolt of fear, I stared into the room. It was enormous, filled with rails of costumes, shelves of fabric, boxes of sewing supplies and several workbenches where Madame Soirelli and her staff created the costumes. It was dimly lit, the large windows blackened by the night falling outside and the snow that still hung over Paris like a giant albino crow. The only other light came from a lantern that Madame Soirelli had dropped in her shock, and was now lying on its side next to her, undamaged. I bent down and picked it up, turning it so that the still burning candle illuminated the room, if only partially.

The six free-standing mirrors, usually placed to the sides of the room, had been arranged in a circle, and in the middle of it, a human shape hung by the neck from the ceiling, spinning slowly. It was a man, in a dark jacket and trousers, with shoulder-length black hair, his arms limp by his sides. I felt a thrill of horror as he revolved towards me, and I saw that he had *no face.*

I ignored Mother's order to stay back and stepped around her and the sobbing wardrobe mistress, raising the lantern high in my left hand and walking across the room to the corpse. I poked him with my index finger, and he started to swing like a pendulum.

"Meg!" Mother cried. "Are you mad, girl?! Go and fetch help!"

"It's not real," I said over my shoulder.

"What?!"

"It's not real," I repeated flatly. "It's a tailor's dummy, dressed up and with a wig on.

Mother's eyes closed and I heard her murmur: "Thank God…"

Madame Soirelli was inhaling deep breaths, trying to calm down. A tiny part of me admired this cruel trick; Erik just couldn't resist being dramatic. I turned on the gas lights while Mother helped Madame Soirelli into the room and sat her down in a chair. The illumination dispelled Erik's illusion within a few seconds, and showed a large, thick envelope pinned to the dummy's jacket.

"There's a message, Madame Soirelli…"

"Open it, Meg."

"But it's addressed to you…"

"Just read it!"

I shrugged and removed the pins, opening the envelope to find a sheaf of papers. One was a note in Erik's familiar handwriting, but the other pages were drawings. I thought at first that they were portraits, but then I realised they were costume designs, with the character's name and actor across the head of the page. The top one was *'Don Juan – "No Return" cloak – Ulbaldo Piangi'* and showed a full length black robe with wide sleeves and a huge hood that completely covered the head and face. This was clearly the costume worn when Don Juan first seduced Aminta. I was about to flip through the designs to see what my costumes might look like, but Madame Soirelli was watching me expectantly, so I turned my attention to the note.

Madame Soirelli,
Enclosed are the costume designs for Don Juan Triumphant. *I have no doubt of your ability to bring them to life, and take note that I expect accurate and detailed costumes. I have ensured that all the fabric and equipment you require is available to you.*
My regards to your son.
O.G.

Madame Soirelli stared at me, her brow creased with worry.

"What does he mean, 'regards to your son'?" She asked. "Is that a threat?"

"I don't know…" Mother took the note from me.

"And the… dummy?" She gestured to it, still suspended from the ceiling.

"Just to give you a shock, I think," I said, hoping I was right.

"Well it did that!" She cried bitterly. "Let me see these damned designs!"

I handed them over without saying a word, and she looked through them, nodding to herself, while Mother disentangled the dummy from the noose.

Of course, it wasn't just the ballerinas and wardrobe department that got a taste of Erik's warped sense of humour. Monsieur Reyer had bowed to Erik's demands, sacked the musicians he had singled out, and gone so far as to audition the members of the chorus. This caused a predictable outcry, since the principles hadn't auditioned at all, but Reyer and the managers were more concerned about appeasing the Phantom than dealing with the performer's egos.

We rehearsed on the stage, where rows of chairs had been set up, surrounding Reyer's piano.

The opera's lyrics had assumed a whole new meaning since Philippe had propositioned me in my dormitory ten days before. I had known that they referred to sex, unashamedly, and sometimes graphically, but since I had becoming aware that someone wanted me in such a carnal way, they made me uncomfortable.

Piangi was struggling with the opera for different reasons, unable to

THE ANGEL'S SHADOW

pitch the melody, and I saw Christine's eyes roll heavenward before they closed. I reached across the empty chair between us and squeezed her hand.

"Are you all right?" I whispered, and Christine nodded.

Wearing a black dress with deep red trimming around the neckline, she was looking much better than she had in the manager's office; her skin was back to its usual porcelain perfection and her eyes had regained their sparkle. I had managed to speak to Raoul while Christine was working on a solo, and he had told me that she was finding solace in the Church, her apartment away from the Opera Populairé, and in the music itself. Raoul had been angry when he had admitted that, and I had tried to tell him that music, *any* music, was a comfort to his fiancée, that it was not *this* particular music and its composer that brought her to life, but we both new it was untrue. The Vicomte was now sitting in the auditorium, watching the rehearsal.

"No, no, no!" Monsieur Reyer sounded exasperated by Piangi's mistake. "Chorus, take a seat."

We sat down as Reyer demonstrated the piece on the piano. Piangi tried again and repeated the error, and a frustrated groan arose from the assembled singers. Reyer raised his hand.

"Almost," he admitted. "But still not right."

"I think his way is better," Carlotta said loyally. "At least it sounds like music when he sings it!"

"Signora," Mother said from the right-hand side of the stage. "Would you say things like that if the composer was here?"

"He isn't," Carlotta sneered. "And even if he were, I would—"

"Are you sure he's not here, Signora?" Mother sounded ominous, and I glanced up at Box Five. In the auditorium, Raoul twisted in his seat to follow my look, but if Erik were in the Box, I could not see him.

"Ah, *piu non posso!*" Carlotta cried. "No one will know if it is right or not, they won't even *care!*"

I thought about pointing out that, while our audience would not be familiar with the opera, the Phantom would be watching and most certainly cared about it being accurate to the music in his head. Piangi was repeating the troublesome phrase.

The argument that broke out as Carlotta mocked the music and Reyer defended it was interrupted by the song we had just been rehearsing being played on the piano. At first I thought Monsieur Reyer was playing it, but then I saw that he was standing several feet away, white in the face. No one was touching it, but the keys were moving, the notes resonating across the stage, as if someone invisible were playing. Several of the chorus members crossed themselves or murmured something to keep the Devil away. I felt my own fingers creep up to the silver cross I wore around my throat.

That, I said to myself, *really is a good trick.*

I had no doubt that Erik was responsible, and longed to examine the instrument, to find out what secret made it play by itself. The piano was not positioned over one of the trapdoors, so Erik could not be manipulating it from below, and I wondered if he was somehow using clockwork. Mother gave me a look that told me very clearly to keep my curiosity under control. The piano silenced itself and a very shaken Reyer said:

"Well… from the beginning of the opera, please, ladies and gentlemen…"

He seemed almost afraid to touch the piano, as if it might slam its lid closed on his fingers like a wolf clamping its jaws shut, or maybe burst into flames. It didn't; it just sat there, freed from the spirit that had possessed it, and only made a sound when Reyer pressed the keys. Carlotta too remained silent, except where the score required her vocal input, keeping her opinions of its quality to herself.

By the time we were rehearsed to Monsieur Reyer's satisfaction, Raoul had dozed off in his chair. I stood at the edge of the stage as the company dispersed and called to him in a soft tone.

"Monsieur le Vicomte?"

I felt Christine's hand on my arm as she stood by my side.

"Let him sleep," she said, gazing at him fondly. "The poor man hasn't had any proper rest for days."

"Why not?" I asked, and she gave a sheepish smile.

"He has taken to spending the night times patrolling the street outside my apartment," she explained. "In case Erik should try to… visit me."

I raised my eyebrows. "Do you think he would?"

"No," Christine shook her head. "But Raoul does, and doing that puts him at his ease. It just means he's exhausted himself."

She took her cloak from over the back of her chair and wrapped a red scarf around her neck. It had been a Christmas gift from Raoul, of the finest quality cashmere, a replacement for the lost scarf that he had waded into the sea to retrieve for her all those years before.

"When he wakes," Christine continued as she fastened the cloak. "Tell him I have gone to visit my father's grave."

"You're not going alone?" I asked, alarmed, and Christine gave me a long-suffering look.

"Meg, I know that you—that everyone—cares about me and wants to keep me safe, but I need some time by myself. You like to visit your father privately, don't you? Meg, please… I'll ask Jean-Claude to drive me there and wait for me, then I'll come back here." She took my hands. "You have nothing to fear, I promise."

I sighed, knowing that my attempts to argue her out of her decision were futile. Instead, I wrapped my cream-coloured shawl tighter around my shoulders and walked with her to the Opera House's stable yard. The air was bitterly cold, and a fog was drifting across the ground as if from a marsh in a ghost story.

Jean-Claude, one of the drivers employed by the Opera Populairé, was smoking a cigarette, which he quickly dropped and stamped out when he saw Christine approaching him with her money pouch out.

"Where to, Mademoiselle?"

"The cemetery, please," she replied, handing over the money.

"I'll just have to hitch up the horses, Mademoiselle, only be a couple of minutes."

We retreated into the comparative warmth of the loading bay doors, where the scenery and other supplies were dropped off, and I was glad of it, for the shawl was doing little to protect me against the harsh temperatures.

"Have you arranged for lessons with anyone else?" I asked Christine, and she shook her head.

"No… Raoul talked to some people and gathered some names for me, but… it just doesn't feel right, somehow. Maybe once all this is over…"

She gazed out into the whitened yard, lightly biting her lower lip. I watched her, ached for her, and dreaded the night of *Don Juan Triumphant*, both for her sake and for mine. She would be deprived of her Angel of Music, would at last be free from the grasp of a man who, for all he claimed to love her, might ultimately destroy her. And me… I faced deprivation too. I could feel the goose bumps all along my arms and legs as my cheeks burned with the weight of the question I wanted to ask her.

"Christine, since you and Raoul got engaged," I gabbled before I became too embarrassed to continue. "Has he asked you to… you know?"

She blinked at me. "What?"

"To… be with you. Intimately."

"Oh. Meg!" She was blushing too now. "No, of course not. That is for our wedding night… Why are you asking?"

"Are you scared?" I brushed her question aside with one of my own.

"A little. I don't know what to expect, what to do…" She bit her lip again. "But Raoul is as inexperienced as I am. We'll learn together, teach each other what it means to be intimate."

"He told you he was virgin?" I hadn't meant to say it, nor to sound quite so doubtful, but I had assumed that with his looks, money and title, the Vicomte must have had many lovers. Christine, however, nodded.

"Philippe took him to brothel when he turned eighteen," she said, and I suppressed a shiver at the mention of the elder de Chagny's name. "And told him to… well, take his pick. Raoul refused; he told Philippe he wasn't interested in that sort of meaningless company."

I swallowed hard, feeling a sudden pricking behind my eyes in addition to the burning in my cheeks and the lump rising in my throat. *Meaningless company*. That is all I would be to the Comte de Changy, and how could I be sure, once he had done with me, that he would keep his word and keep what he knew of Erik a secret? Christine touched my arm.

"Meg, what is it? Are you all right?"

The sound of the horse's hooves and carriage wheels ringing against the cobblestones made me look up, forcing back the tears that threatened. Jean-Claude drew the carriage up beside the loading bay doors, bundled up in a long black cloak and hood against the snow that was starting to fall again. There was something odd about his hunched shape, but I couldn't place it.

"You'd better go," I told Christine. "And the sooner you return, the less guilty I shall feel."

"Oh, my dear friend," Christine kissed me on both cheeks in farewell. "I shall be back in less than two hours. Don't feel guilty."

She smiled at me, then turned and climbed into the carriage.

"To my father's grave, please." She told Jean-Claude, and the driver nodded in acknowledgement without speaking. She turned in the seat and lifted her hand as the carriage set off. I returned her wave and then went back into the Opera House proper, grateful for the warmth of the building.

It was less than ten minutes later when Raoul staggered out of the auditorium and saw me. He had taken off his jacket while watching the rehearsal and was now in just his shirtsleeves, his eyes still heavy with sleep.

"Where is Christine?!" He demanded, seizing me by the shoulders. "Meg! Tell me where she went!"

"It's all right, Vicomte," I told him. "Jean-Claude took her to visit her father's grave. They left in the carriage not ten minutes ago."

"Are you sure, girl?" He let me go.

"Quite sure. I watched them leave myself."

He still looked agitated, and hurried to the stable yard. I followed him, unable to stop a dash of anxiety in my own stomach, even though I knew Christine was perfectly safe. We were standing side-by-side when a groan came from the darkness of the stables themselves. Raoul glanced at me, then darted inside. Once my eyes adjusted to the dimness, I saw him kneeling over someone lying in the hay, speaking urgently.

"What happened, Monsieur? Can you speak? Meg, this man requires medical attention!"

I rushed to his side and gasped at the figure lying half-conscious at my feet, blood streaking down his face from a wound at his temple.

"Jean-Claude?"

Raoul looked up at me sharply.

"This is Jean-Claude, the driver?"

I nodded, horrified, and Raoul voiced the question that my own tongue would not utter.

"If this in Jean-Claude, then who drove Christine away in a carriage?!"

CHAPTER THIRTY FIVE

Raoul's question didn't really need a reply; my memory replayed the sight of the carriage drawing up beside the loading bay doors. The driver had been swathed in the cloak and hood, not against the snowfall, but to prevent Christine seeing his masked face. It had been his hunched posture that had given me pause, Erik bending in on himself to disguise his true height.

"The Ghost," Jean-Claude said, his words coming out all slurred together as if he were drunk. "Jumped on me… riding whip… knocked me out with my own bloody riding whip!"

"He's got her!" Raoul leapt to his feet and began undoing the doors of one of the stable's stalls, where a white mare gazed at him, fitted with reigns but no saddle.

"What are you doing?!" I asked in alarm as I struggled to lift the dazed and possibly concussed driver into a sitting position.

"I'm going to rescue Christine from that demon!" He cried.

"Raoul de Chagny!" I shouted, my tone coming out sharp and sounding like my mother. "Before you go charging off, *unarmed*, like a knight in a fairy tale, you will help me get this man inside!"

"There's no time!"

"Vicomte! I can't move Jean-Claude on my own and he'll die if he's left out here!"

It was probably an exaggeration, but it got the required results. Raoul swore and returned to my side, helping get Jean-Claude to his feet and draping an arm around his shoulders. I draped Jean-Claude's other arm over my own shoulders, and together we got him into the Opera House and sitting down. Raoul disappeared into the auditorium and I thought he was going for help, but he re-emerged a moment later, buckling his sword belt around his waist.

"You can't mean to challenge him!" I cried, but he continued past me, still without a jacket. He was out of earshot before I could voice another protest, and through the loading bay doors I saw him riding the white mare, bareback, into the snow and fog.

LOUISE ANNE BATEMAN

* * *

Jean-Claude lay on the couch in the manager's office while I pressed a cloth soaked in cold water against his head wound. It didn't seem to be deep, but was bleeding freely, and I had made him lie down when he complained of feeling dizzy. When he vomited all over the carpet, Monsieur André sent Mother to fetch a doctor.

"Bastard," Jean-Claude slurred. "Bloody ghost bastard…"

Whatever his next words were, they were too garbled for me to make out, and I worried that Erik had hit Jean-Claude so hard that he might die from the injury. Surely that was excessive use of force, as the driver couldn't have been armed.

Worry and guilt lay heavily upon me; perhaps if I had insisted on accompanying Christine to her father's grave, Erik would not have taken the opportunity to abduct her. And what was going through his head? *Don Juan Triumphant* could not be performed without its leading lady. Perhaps he intended to bewitch Christine once again, with his music and his hypnotic voice, to make her return to him. A sudden image of the mannequin I had seen in his bedroom, the double of Christine, bedecked in bridal finery, flashed across my mind. I wondered if I might be sick myself. Was the man so driven by his obsession that nothing would end his attempts to possess her? How many others, aside from Jean-Claude, would become innocent bystanders caught in the crossfire of his passion?

Mother returned with a doctor, who looked Jean-Claude over before stating that his injury should be treated in a hospital.

"But he will be all right?" I asked, and the doctor nodded, hurrying his patient from the office.

"Jean-Claude can't have been a threat to… to the Phantom," I murmured to Mother. "From what I could make out, he just attacked him out of the blue, because he wanted the carriage. If he can hurt a driver with a riding whip so badly that the man has to be hospitalised, what will he do to Raoul when he catches up to him?"

I didn't have to wait long before I got a reply. Less than an hour after his dramatic departure, the Vicomte returned bearing Christine in his arms. At least, he probably thought of it that way. He did have his arms around Christine, gripping the reigns on either side of her as they rode the saddle-less horse together, but he had not come away from the rescue unscathed. His right eye was swollen almost shut, bruised, his shirtsleeve torn and bloodied. There was a gash in his upper arm. Christine slid from the horse as Raoul drew it to a halt and released his hold upon her, and turned to help her fiancé dismount. His teeth bared in a wince as his feet hit the cobbles.

"Good God!" I cried as they entered the Opera House. "What happened?"

THE ANGEL'S SHADOW

My mother joined us as Christine helped Raoul into a chair in the foyer.

"The Phantom," Raoul growled as Mother gently placed her hand against his cheek, turning his face to the light so she could better examine his injured eye. "He attacked us!"

"Meg," Mother said quietly. "This needs a cold compress. Fetch a cloth from the bar and fill it with snow, that will do for now. Fetch another for the arm wound. Quickly, child!"

I did as she instructed, grabbing two clean cloths from under the confused eyes of Marius, the barman, and rushing outside to pack one full of snow. When I returned, Mother was examining the wound on the Vicomte's arm. I handed him the makeshift compress.

"Here," I told him. "Hold this against your eye; it will bring down the swelling."

"Thank you, Mademoiselle Giry." He pressed it to his face. Christine knelt before the chair, watching him worriedly, and I saw with a shock that she also had a cut, on the right side of her forehead.

"He attacked you as well?" I asked, but she shook her head.

"No, Meg, no. I got caught by a branch as we returned here, that's all. Is it bad?"

"No," I said, looking closer. "Just a scratch. It's not even bleeding anymore."

"*This* is more than a scratch," Mother said, looking up from Raoul's arm. "It requires at least one stitch, possibly more. I should fetch your doctor, Monsieur; that appears to be my role for the day. Christine," she took the second cloth from me and handed it to my friend. "Hold this against the wound and keep the pressure just... there. That's it, good girl."

"What did she mean, her role for the day?" Christine asked me as Raoul told Mother his doctor's name and address.

"Erik attacked Jean-Claude to take his place as your carriage driver," I whispered, and Christine looked horrified. "Mother fetched a doctor for him, and he's been taken to hospital with a head wound."

"The poor man..."

"What *happened?*" I asked again, as soon as Mother had gone. "What do you mean, the Phantom attacked you? Was he armed?"

"Demonstratively," Raoul responded with a terse jerk of his head to indicate his wounded arm.

"He abducted you?" I asked Christine.

"Not exactly..." Christine said hesitantly. "He drove me to the cemetery and I got out at the gates. He didn't speak or do anything, he drove the carriage away. I had no idea it wasn't Jean-Claude."

Raoul gave a grunt that sounded almost like a snort.

"He was *singing* to her," he said. "By the time I got there, he was using his damnable music against my Christine!"

"Vicomte, try to remain calm," I said taking the cold compress from him and pressing it to his eye myself. "You may increase the bleeding if your heartbeat goes too fast..."

The bruising was showing a deep purple around his eye now. He sighed, using his freed hand to take hold of Christine's and giving it a gentle squeeze.

"If I did not know better, I would swear this man was the Devil himself," he muttered, and a pained look flashed across Christine's face. "Once again, Christine was his; it was like she was under a spell. She was standing in front of the Daaé mausoleum and his voice was coming from it, coming from all around her... calling her like some... dark seducer. He called her his Angel of Music, said he was hers..." He sighed, letting go of Christine's hand and passing his palm across his brow. "He spoke of watching over her as if he were her father. I couldn't believe how far he was going to manipulate her! I got off the horse and ran to her, screaming at him:

You call yourself the Angel of Music?! You are an Angel of Darkness, stop tormenting her!'

Christine seemed so... strange, so distant somehow. It was as if nothing in the world existed for her but his words, his voice. The doors to the mausoleum were opening unassisted, and I felt sure he was inside, ready to lure her to her doom. I tried calling her name as I raced up to her:

'Christine! Christine, listen to me! He's not your father, nor was he sent by him!'"

I stared at Raoul, unnerved by this new revelation, and my eyes flicked to Christine. Erik had spent the early part of his relationship with her pretending to be the angelic messenger sent to her by her father. Surely she could never believe that he *was* her father, not now? Her face was white...

"I could see that... Phantom standing up on the rooftop of the mausoleum, holding a staff topped with a skull, and I ordered him to let her go, but it wasn't until I actually touched Christine that she seemed to break free from her trance. She spoke to me, but the Phantom was snarling down at us like a wild beast. He thrust the staff out towards me, and a ball of fire burst from the skull's gaping mouth and landed at my feet as I stepped in front of Christine.

He sent another fireball towards me, but I did not flinch; I think I angered him by not showing fear. He dropped the staff and leapt off the roof, crashing into me as he landed and almost making me lose my balance. He whipped his cloak around him and I staggered, unsheathing my sword as I saw, to my horror, that he also had a blade drawn. I lunged at him with my sword, trying to drive him back, away from Christine, my only thought to protect her. I cannot imagine who taught this Phantom to fence, but he is no gentleman. He fights... unfairly, with kicks and fists and teeth. He caught me in the face with the hilt of his sword; hence the black eye. I

THE ANGEL'S SHADOW

retaliated, landing several punches upon him, but he did not seem to feel them. I told him that imprisoning Christine would not make her love him, and he gave a roar and swung his sword, the blade slicing into my arm. Christine cried out to me, but I ordered her to stay back. The Phantom and I continued to fight throughout the graveyard, and at one point I lost him as he darted around a memorial like a rat. Then I heard Christine cry again, and he was behind me, sword raised. He tackled me and we both went down, but I still had a grip on my sword and managed to drive it into his side. He gave a howl like an animal and leapt to his feet, but I regained my stance as well and threw myself at him with fresh vigour, and suddenly he was down. I kicked his sword away through the snow and raised my blade to plunge it into his heart, but Christine begged me not to. I saw the Phantom's eyes flick from me to Christine and back again. I saw him look death in the face, lying on his back in the snow. And I withdrew, at her request. For my Christine. I gathered her into my arms, kissed her, and brought her back here."

Raoul gave a deep sigh, and I let my own held breath escape. Erik was alive; wounded, perhaps, but alive.

"You should have let me destroy him," he said to Christine. "I have every right as your fiancé."

Christine looked him full in the face.

"I would not see the man I love become a murderer," she said quietly. "Your plan will work, Raoul, to seize him on the night of *Don Juan*. The law awaits Erik. If he is to die, let it be in a legal way... after a fair trial, at the hands of an executioner."

She seemed to struggle to get those words out, and I felt the lump rising in my own throat. *Executioner.* It was not just the Phantom of the Opera that needed to fear him, but my own mother if I was not careful. Perhaps myself too. Raoul took her face between his hands.

"Oh, my darling," he murmured. "Would that my soul was as pure as yours." Their foreheads met, resting against one another. "I love you."

"I love you too," she whispered, and they exchanged a soft kiss. I watched them, wondering if I would ever know a love such as that. Would I ever be willing to kill, or die, for the man I loved?

It was only another few minutes before Mother returned with Raoul's doctor, and Raoul repeated his story to André and Firman, who had been alerted to the situation by her. The managers were even more flustered than before, clucking over the Vicomte and Christine like broody hens, and I pulled Mother to one side.

"They fought in a graveyard," I whispered. "Erik is alive, but he's injured. Raoul says he stabbed him in the side. You have to—"

"I'm needed here," she told me in a low voice. "Go to him, Meg."

"But I—"

249

"There are bandages in my apartments. Go to him, and take them with you. You can take the passage that leads from my wardrobe."

"Wardrobe?!"

"Oh, come along Meg, you know the one I mean. You've seen him use it."

It took a moment, but I realised I did remember Erik entering Mother's bedroom through her wardrobe, on the night I begged him to help her through illness.

"Take the passageway behind it, and there is a pattern to the route that leads to the lake; take the first right and the second left each time, do you understand?"

"Yes."

"Repeat it back."

"The first right and the second left each time until I reach the lake."

"Madame Giry!" Firman called impatiently, and she looked to him, but I tugged on her sleeve to make her return her attention to me.

"But he wants me," I whispered. "He wants to take me to hurt you, you said as much."

He had gone after Christine and been thwarted again, his temper must be at boiling point.

"I am not going to let him keep you, love," she kissed my forehead. "I will come for you as soon as I can, I promise. Now you must go, Meg. Go."

She gave me a slight push and I knew that I had no choice but to obey her.

"I love you," I whispered, but she was already walking away from me.

I wondered why I was agreeing to this. Because I didn't want Erik to die. Why not? Because I owed him my life? Because I saw something in him that mirrored my own smudged soul?

Resigned to my fate, I left the foyer and its bewildered occupants, making my way upstairs to Mother's apartments. She always kept a set of bandages in here, which I had no trouble locating. Thinking back to the Vicomte's tale and the slash on his arm, I added several needles of varying sizes and a spool of thread to the bag I picked up to carry everything in. I had never sewn a wound closed before, but the medical book Erik had given me had contained instructions and the stitches looked the same as the ones I used when mending clothing. It could not be that difficult. I tried to think of what else might be needed, but aware that time might vital, decided that I had to do my best with what I had, and opened the wardrobe.

Pushing the garments aside, I inhaled my lost father's scent as I brushed against one of his jackets. If Erik did murder me in revenge for my mother's poor attitude, at least Papa and I would be reunited. And I wouldn't have to keep my promise and submit to the Comte de Chagny. My stomach twisted as I remembered our bargain, my fingers searching the

THE ANGEL'S SHADOW

back of the wardrobe for the concealed switch; all in all, I would happily die a virgin.

I found the switch and the door clicked open. I lit a lantern, gathered up my bag, and entered this new passageway.

First right, second left.

I carefully followed Mother's instructions, zigzagging down staircases and along more passages, with no desire to end up in a trap like last time. It felt like hours before I heard the sound of running water and emerged on the left-hand side of a stone channel, which guided the water towards Erik's home, the main body of the lake behind me. Carved faces, like the theatrical masks of Greek theatre upon the domed roof so far above, grinned and glowered at me from the walls. I could see the portcullis ahead of me, raised to just above the water level, and found that my stone pathway came to an abrupt end. The boat was moored at the jetty beyond the portcullis, and I frowned at the water in front of me. Further back, towards the centre of the lake, it was so deep that I could be several feet below the surface and with no chance of touching the bottom. Maybe here it was shallower…

I placed the bag on the stone walkway and cautiously slid into the water, thankful to find that it came up to my waist, even if it did mean that the white skirt of my rehearsal dress was soaked through. I picked the bag up, holding it above my head as I waded towards the portcullis. I tied the handles to it and then ducked beneath, having to immerse myself fully for a moment and emerging to shake wet tendrils of blonde hair out of my eyes. I untied the bag and waded with it towards the jetty, pulling myself up and already feeling like I had accomplished some huge task. The next time I came down here, I would refuse to be blindfolded; I would find the most direct route into the Phantom's domain, without ending up like a half-drowned rat at the end of the journey.

I opened the door, and almost immediately something shattered above my head, causing me to shriek and cower. It must have been a glass vase or decanter, for I felt small, sharp shards imbed themselves into my exposed skin as I tried to protect my head and face with my arms. The man who had thrown it had obviously been anticipating someone taller than me and aimed higher than my head.

"It's Meg Giry, you insufferable man!" I started to say. "I've come to help you!"

But I had only just reached the end of my own name when the Opera Ghost swooped down on me, his mismatched eyes ablaze, and fastened his fingers in a death-like grip around my throat.

CHAPTER THIRTY SIX

My bag dropped to the floor as Erik shook me by the throat, like a terrier with a rat.

"Are you alone?!" He bellowed.

"Yes!" I managed, and he let me go, backing off warily. I gasped, my right hand clinging onto the doorframe to keep myself upright, my left going to my throat. There would be more bruises.

I had never seen Erik like this before, seeming so bestial, and it frightened me all over again. He was like a wolf with a paw caught in a trap, and everyone knows a wounded animal is dangerous to approach. Erik was naked above the waist, his arms and torso lightly muscled, not unlike some of the male dancers, and blotted with bruises. His jaw was also discoloured and he was clamping a wad of cloth against the lower right-hand side of his back, just above the waistband of his trousers.

"Good God..." I murmured. "The Vicomte really gave you a proper hiding, didn't he?"

Erik snarled.

"The boy is nothing," he replied. "I could have sliced his head clean off his shoulders!"

"Not the way he tells it," I crouched slowly to retrieve my bag, keeping my eyes on his. "Mother sent me to... assist you," I told him, trying to sound neither intimidated nor threatening. "Will you allow it?"

"Do you faint at the sight of blood?" He asked, and his voice came out hoarse with pain.

"No," I lied.

"Then I will allow it. Close and lock the door."

I did as I was told, turning to see Erik walking away from me. His back was a mess of scars, the lines of a whip and other implements glowing against his pale skin in the electric lights he had installed himself. I swallowed hard. I had just one similar scar marring my own back, the result

THE ANGEL'S SHADOW

of my father's belt... what had this poor creature suffered? These surely were not just the marks from his time with the gypsies?

He staggered into the kitchen and sank down into a chair at the table. Where the bruises were not blackening it, the visible side of his face was as white as the mask. As I followed him, I realised that yet more things were missing from his home. Paintings, books, and furniture had vanished from where they once stood. Only his throne-like chair, the sofa, the Persian rug and piano remained in the drawing room. Everything else had gone, the indents in the carpet of where they had once been like ghosts of their presence. I wanted to ask outright what was going on, but Erik had been watching me and spoke first.

"You're wet through."

I rolled my eyes at this stunning observation.

"I had to practically swim the last few feet and ducked under the portcullis."

"You can't swim."

"Last year I couldn't swim. I learned over the summer."

"Where did you come from?"

"Mother's apartments. I used the passageway behind the wardrobe."

"You should have used a route that bypassed the lake."

"*What* route that bypassed the lake?" I exclaimed, exasperated. "Every time you've brought me down here, you blindfolded me! And when Mother took me back through the mirror, I was half out of my mind because you had drugged me!"

"Watch your tongue, girl." He warned, and I gave a small sigh, kneeling by the chair on his right.

"Let me see, please."

He peeled the sodden, red-stained cloth from his side with a grimace and I gasped. The wound was larger than I had anticipated, and deeper, something among the dark redness catching the light. I swallowed hard, fighting back a wave of nausea as I pushed his hand to make him cover it again.

"It's... bad, Erik," I tried not to sound as helpless as I felt. "I think it'll need to be stitched closed, and there's something in there. A... a bit of the blade, or grit, or... something." I let out my breath slowly. "I brought sewing supplies, and I know how to do it... but I didn't bring tweezers and I can't do anything until, whatever it is, it's out of you. Do you have some?"

"Bathroom," he grunted.

"What about painkillers? Laudanum? Morphine?"

"No."

"This... will hurt, Erik."

"It already does!" He snapped. "I don't have anything!"

"What about chloroform?" I asked, brightening suddenly. "You

253

knocked me out with that once."

"*No!*" He repeated, frustrated and pained. "It's gone, girl, understand?"

"I understand…" I said and stood up. "Do you have any alcohol? To clean the tools?"

"No."

I tried not to grind my teeth. Erik's free hand was clenched into a fist on the table, his jaw set, his entire frame tense with the pain of his injury.

"What about for drinking?"

He looked up, snapping furiously: "You intend to drink during this procedure?!"

"It's not for *me*, you fool!" I snapped back. "It's for you! I don't want this to hurt you any more than it must."

I thought he was going to tell me off again, but he just closed his mismatched eyes and said: "End cupboard, top shelf."

I got the bottle of brandy down from the cupboard with difficulty, and placed it on the table in front of him, then rushed to the bathroom and rifled through the cabinet beneath the sink until I found the pair of tweezers. I didn't have time to wonder what he used them for, how he sorted out his own plumbing, where all his possessions were going, or any of the other questions buzzing through my brain; I was just anxious to get that wound sewn as quickly as I could.

I returned to the kitchen and filled a pot with water, dropping in the tweezers, needle and thread, and then setting it to boil over the kitchen fire. Boiling sterilised things, hadn't I read that somewhere? Erik watched me, swigging from the bottle of brandy, and I hoped it would knock him out so I wouldn't cause him too much pain. When the water had boiled, I fished out the tools and sat down, legs crossed, on the floor by Erik's chair.

"Lean forward, over the table."

He did so, still holding the bottle, and lighting a candle and setting it by my side so that the light shone on that ghastly wound, I gently took away the cloth. It was drenched in blood, and I felt my stomach churn as I saw the wound once more. Taking a deep, calming breath, I focused on the tiny point I could see glimmering and aimed the tweezers towards it.

"Ah!" Erik winced and I drew back reflexively.

"Sorry! You have to stay still!"

He took another pull of the brandy and I went back to work. He was so tense I could see the tightness in every muscle of his upper body, knuckles white around the bottle, teeth clenched. It was as I touched the intrusive shining thing again with the tips of the tweezers, that I realised I was no longer shaking. My hand was steady and my nerves calm. I withdrew it and dropped it onto the table; a tiny piece of metal, perhaps the very tip of Raoul's sword.

"There. Take a drink and a breath. Then I must sew the wound."

THE ANGEL'S SHADOW

He drank, still tense and asked:

"Have you done this before?"

"Many times," I assured him. "On dresses."

He might have laughed, but the sound was mixed with his pain. He took another swig of the brandy and then gripped the opposite edge of the table with his right hand. It was the first time I noticed that he, like me, was left-handed. Mother had tried to discourage me from favouring my left hand with the use of a wooden ruler across my palm, but had ultimately failed. Erik was probably ambidextrous.

Taking another deep breath, I threaded the needle, holding it in my left hand, and pinched the edges of the wound closed with the fingers of my right. He winced and I wanted to tell him how sorry I was that I was causing him more pain.

"You must stay still," I told him again, and before I could give myself time for the nerves and doubts to come crowding back into my mind, began to sew.

"*Bitch!*" He cried with the first pass of needle and thread through his flesh.

"Stay *still!*" I repeated, shocked by his language, but unable to chide him for it; the pain must be agonising. He didn't speak again, glugging from the bottle like a man desperate for water on a hot day.

It was an unpleasant sensation, almost like stitching leather, but with the odd, fleshy feeling you sometimes get when you poke a fork into uncooked meat. He kept as still and quiet as he could, and after what felt like twenty minutes, but was probably no more than three, I severed the end of the thread.

"Finished. Now it just needs bandaging."

Erik stood up, unsteady on his feet, but obediently held the end of the bandage against the sewn wound while I wrapped it around his torso like a belt. The scars on his back shone pearly white against his pale skin, the fresh bruising standing out like purple ink splashes. For good measure, I used the needle to sew the end of the bandage to the strip underneath it so that it would not fall away, and at that moment, Erik's knees seemed to give out. Surprised, I took his weight on me, feeling the heat of his body against my shoulder before pushing him back onto the chair. The warmth came as a surprise and a worry; every time Erik had touched me, his hands had been as cold as a corpse's.

"Erik..." I reached out to feel his forehead, but it was concealed by the mask and he batted my hand away.

"Don't touch the mask!" He snarled, his words coming out slurred with drink.

"I promise," I said. "But I think you may be burning up... I don't know what to do, Erik..."

He groaned, his eyes closing.

"Must rest," he whispered, but I knew I couldn't get him into his own bedroom. Instead, I heaved him up, flinging his left arm across my shoulder, as I had done with Jean-Claude, Erik's unlucky victim, only a couple of hours before, and helped him stumble into the drawing room. He flopped face-down onto the sofa with another growl of pain. I looked around for something to cover him, and saw his heavy black cloak hanging on the back of the door. As gently as I could, I draped the material over him.

"Sleep," I said softly. "I'll stay."

"Don't touch the mask…" He said again.

"I promise," I repeated. His eyes closed, and after a few minutes his breathing evened out. All at once, my shaking seemed to return, as if the panic that had been threatening to overwhelm me could only be held at bay for so long.

It came out in tiny gasps as the tears started to run down my cheeks. I wiped at them with bloodied fingertips, trying to cease the flow, but it seemed that all my anxiety had just decided to release itself through my eyeballs. Realising I had no choice but to let the tears pass on their own, I lit the fire in the drawing room, then returned to the kitchen and dropped the tweezers, needle and thread back in the water, and set it boiling once again. When it was done I retrieved the tweezers, and blinking away the tears that were still falling, picked out the tiny bits of glass imbedded in the skin of my arm.

Brute, I told myself. *The man is nothing but a brute, why are you helping him?*

Because he needs my help.

A short break, a swallow of the fiery brandy.

He's hurt you, he's hurt the people you care about, he'll hurt Christine. He's a murderer.

I owe him my life.

Each piece of glass stung like a miniature wasp as I pulled it free.

Why don't you just tell the gendarmes *what you know?*

Because that would be a betrayal.

What has he done to deserve your loyalty, Meg Giry? Why do you even care what becomes of this madman?

I took another swig from the brandy bottle.

Because he's damaged. Like me. Like my father.

I dropped the last fragment of glass onto the table and examined the marks left behind. They weren't deep, or bleeding, there was no need of bandages for me. Erik reminded me of my father. Of myself. What was it that he had said to me?

"Do you not think I recognise the parts of a soul that mirror my own?"

Was that, then, why I felt so drawn to him? Was I so desperate to have a

THE ANGEL'S SHADOW

father-figure back in my life that I would choose this distorted, deformed man who may yet turn out to be a monster?

I went into the bedroom Erik had designed for Christine; relieved to find that here at least, nothing had gone. There was still a hairbrush and comb on the table, clean garments in the draws and wardrobe. I caught sight of my reflection in the mirror as I removed my soiled, damp ballet dress and slipped one of Christine's white nightgowns over my head.

Who are you, Meg Giry? What have you become?

It was a question I could not answer.

Pulling Christine's robe on over the nightgown and tying it at the waist, I returned to the drawing room to find Erik still sleeping on the sofa. I stood over him, examining him. He looked so... normal lying there. It was as if the Opera Ghost was a persona he wore like a cloak, that could be dismissed at will. And yet, I had seen him in manic joy and in anger and in pain... it wasn't a garment that he could just put on or take off whenever he wanted. The Opera Ghost was a part of him, like that mask, some dark spirit that he allowed to swallow his soul when he wanted to feel power. No matter how innocent, how vulnerable he looked now, knocked out by the pain and the drink, there was something demonic there.

My fingers itched to take off his mask and see for myself what Christine and Mother and Buquet had described. Could it really be so terrible? Could it truly have caused a lifetime of suffering and humiliation? I reached out, but Erik moved suddenly, just a slight twitch in his sleep, and I snatched my hand away. Temptation may be the work of the devil, but what form of devil would awaken if he knew I had broken my promise?

I curled up in the throne-like chair in front of the fire, trying not to remember the time he had tied me here as a punishment for Christine. Surely Mother would be here soon; she had promised she would not let him keep me. The fire crackled and sparked, and the sounds became almost musical in my head, a percussive beat to a tune that I would never be able to commit to paper the way a composer like Erik could. Gradually, my eyes closed.

I found myself walking through the backstreets of Paris, the arm of a man around my waist. Was this man a stranger? He was kissing me, pressing me back against the stone wall, and I could smell the alcohol on his breath. But you cannot dream a smell... was it a memory? The man had pushed me down onto the cobblestones, his mouth on mine, and I gave a whimper of protest as I heard my bodice rip. Why wasn't I wearing a corset? Why was my breast now exposed to rough, wanting hands?

"What are you doing?"

"Shh..." He kissed me again, a kiss that was not a kiss, brutal and demanding.

"Don't..." I managed. "Please, don't..."

But Philippe de Chagny paid no attention to my words, pressing one hand over my mouth and he used the other to push my skirts over my knees and around my waist,

257

forcing my legs apart with his own.

"Please!"

My muffled cry had no impact, and there was no movement behind the Comte, no one coming to my rescue. Erik had warned me, the very night he had rescued me from Jacques, that my Opera Ghost might not be there to save me next time.

"We made a bargain, Little Meg," he breathed as he positioned himself above me, moved forward, and I screamed as I felt a stabbing pain at the base of my abdomen. "It is time for you to fulfil it!"

"Meg!" Erik's deep, musical voice filled my mind, but there was pain and I was sobbing. "Meg, wake up! You're dreaming! Meg!"

CHAPTER THIRTY SEVEN

I opened my eyes. I was squashed in a tight ball in Erik's chair and he was leaning against its left hand side, one arm across its back to steady himself. He still looked dreadful, and the firelight caught the sheen of perspiration across his cheek. The black cloak I had draped over him was hanging from his shoulders, and he was looking at me with an odd, penetrating expression.

"What?" I said, as if in response to a question I had not heard. "Erik... you shouldn't be on your feet."

"You were shouting," he said, and his voice sounded a little raw.

"I'm sorry. I must have been dreaming, I didn't mean to disturb you. Erik... I think you have a fever..."

It worried me, the brightness of his eyes.

"You're shivering, child," he said, and took hold of my wrist in his icy grip, pulling me gently onto the Persian rug before the fire. I caught sight of the clock on the mantelpiece and saw that I had been asleep for less than an hour, only just long enough to have begun dreaming. Where was my mother?

"Sit."

I sat, and he shrugged off the cloak and draped it around my own shoulders.

"I'm not a child!" I cried suddenly, ungrateful for the unexpectedly kind gesture. "God in Heaven, if you only knew..."

"Tell me then." He challenged, and sat down beside me. I swallowed hard.

"How is your pain?"

"Irrelevant," he responded coldly. "What causes you to disturb the sleep of a wounded man with such cries?"

I groaned and dropped my face into my hands, but his long, thin fingers gripped my shoulder and gave me a little shake.

"Tell me, Meg."

He'll kill me for what I've done, I thought. But then I wouldn't have to go through with the bargain. I took a deep, shaking breath, and looked up.

"I've done something… terrible." I admitted.

"You have murdered someone?" His head tilted to one side and I saw a bead of sweat roll down his cheek, like a tear.

"No," I said, surprised.

"Then your crimes are nowhere near as terrible as mine. What then? What is it you have done, little dancer, that is so dreadful?"

"I wrote a list," I said and looked into the fire, unable to meet that blue-green gaze. "I wrote a list about you. What I knew, what I suspected, the things I had discovered. And… Philippe de Chagny found it…"

The pressure of Erik's fingers increased on my shoulder and I gave a little squeak of protest.

"And so you fear my wrath, girl, as you should." His voice was quiet, and dangerous, like the hiss of a snake.

"No," I shook my head, still unable to look at him. "Please, let me explain, try to understand. The Comte de Chagny was in my room, he was looking for evidence about you. He suspected that Mother and I know more about you than we've said, you see. I came into my bedroom, and he'd been through all my drawers, all my possessions. He said he was looking for my diary, but he found the list instead."

I forced myself to meet his eyes and tried not to tremble; I do not think I have ever seen him so angry. His lips parted, but I continued in a rush before he could speak.

"He threatened me, he said he would take what he knew to the police and have Mother and me arrested, unless I agreed to… to…"

"To what?" His eyes widened slightly.

"To give him my virginity," I said, feeling myself burning with the shame of it and unable to look at him for any longer. His breath hissed in through his teeth and he shook my shoulder again.

"And did you?" He demanded.

"I gave my consent," I told him in a rush. "He's in Germany until the opening of *Don Juan Triumphant*, he's going to have me on the night they arrest you! That's my nightmare! I dreamt that he was holding me down, that he was…" I clutched at my own stomach, unable to get out the words that would complete the sentence. "And it will happen, Erik, because there's nothing I can do to prevent it!"

The childish part of me wanted to burst into hysterical sobs, but doing so would completely undermine my claims of adulthood, and I seemed to have run out of tears. Erik was watching me, the pressure of his gaze as substantial to me as the grip of his fingers on my shoulder.

"Are you angry with me?" I asked, when I could not tolerate his silence any longer.

"Angry?" He repeated, his golden voice dripping with venom. "I don't think there is a word strong enough to convey the power of my emotions, you *stupid little chit!*"

I flinched, bowing my head to my chest and drawing my legs in close to my body.

"Don't do that!" He snapped. "What happened to the woman who was sewing my wounds closed not two hours ago? One bad dream and I am left with a quivering, cowering kitten?!" He ripped the cloak from my shoulders. "Get up! Fetch the brandy bottle."

I did as he ordered, if only to escape the atmosphere of the room. Erik's fury was like a cloud all around him, a mist pulsing through his home, and yet I wasn't entirely sure where it was directed. He was angered by my stupidity, certainly, but whether it was because I had written the list in the first place, or made the bargain with Philippe to keep the information from the *gendarmes*, I could not tell.

I returned to Erik with the bottle of brandy and he snatched it from me.

"You should have asked my permission before putting on Christine's night things," he frowned and took a swallow of the alcohol.

"Christine wouldn't mind," I argued. "You said yourself my dress was wet through, and filthy. I could have caught my death if I hadn't changed into something warm and dry."

"Oh, so the kitten does have one claw left," Erik's tone was mocking, and I blushed, clenching the material of the dressing gown in clammy hands. He had wrapped the cloak around himself again and I could see him trembling despite the heat of the fire. I crouched slowly.

"You're feverish," I told him.

"I am well aware of that." His over-bright eyes met mine. "Let me ask you something: after you have made this sacrifice and submitted to the lustful attentions of the Comte de Chagny, what exactly would prevent him from going ahead anyway and telling all he knows to the courts?"

I stared at Erik, shocked.

"He wouldn't do that," I said. "He gave me his word."

"Did he indeed? And is the word of a de Chagny to be trusted?"

I clenched my hands together, breathing quickly, wondering how I had not thought about this myself.

"He's a gentleman," I mumbled.

"A 'gentleman' who will resort to blackmail just to deflower a seventeen-year-old ballerina," Erik sneered. "Are you really so naïve? He doesn't care about Christine; I hear he had been doing his utmost to prevent the Vicomte from marrying her, so he clearly has no concern for her welfare. He will take you, girl, willing or not, and then spill all your secrets into the ears of the police."

I felt sick, and wondered if my face looked as green as I felt. Erik was right, of course. There was nothing to stop Philippe going to the police whenever he chose, my list in hand, the connections between myself and my parents to the Opera Ghost plain for all to see.

"What should I do?" I whimpered. "Should I try to get the list back?"

"What good would that do?" Erik asked. "It would still be your word against his. He is Comte and you are a ballet rat, little better than a whore in the eyes of the aristocracy." I flinched, but he did not notice, his gaze on the fire. "I am afraid that in order for your secrets to be kept, the Comte de Chagny will have to die."

I stared at him, my breath catching in my throat. *Die.* And yet, hadn't I known that all along? Hadn't that dark part of my soul that Erik claimed mirrored his own, already decided to ask this fallen angel for aid? But could I have another man's blood on my hands, another death to weigh down my frantically beating heart? I swallowed the bile creeping into my mouth and closed my eyes.

"There must be another option," I croaked.

"Do tell me when you find it."

"Could you do it?" I opened my eyes to see Erik turn his head to me sharply.

"I no longer work as a hired assassin," he spat. "And if I did, you could not afford my prices."

"Is that supposed to sound moral?" Through my rising hysteria I wanted to laugh. "I've seen you kill to protect me! You killed Jacques when he tried to rape me in the street!"

"Then your debt to me is already high."

He wasn't a guardian angel after all. Not for me.

"With a name like Marguerite," he went on. "Directly named after a character from *Faust*, I would have thought that you, of all people, would know not to make deals with devils."

"So is Philippe de Chagny in the role of Méphistophélès?" I asked bitterly. "Or are you?"

"I will not have another man sully what is mine," he muttered.

"You're drunk!" I snapped, and he just gave the fireplace a rather nasty grin and raised the brandy bottle to his lips again. "What does that even mean?! I'm not your daughter or your student! You can have no authority over me!"

"On the contrary," his eyes flicked to mine and away again. "You were born here, you belong to me."

I made a disgusted, dismissive gesture and he looked back at me.

"I brought you into the world," he told me, his voice calm, serious. "I gave you *life*. Were it not for me, you would not have lived seventeen minutes, let alone seventeen years."

"What are you talking about?" I asked, suddenly wary.

THE ANGEL'S SHADOW

"The night of your birth, Meg. Surely you knew you were born midway through a performance of *Faust*?"

"Of course I knew," I snapped. "It's why my Papa wasn't there, it's how I got my name. What's it got to do with you?"

"I was there," he said. "I was watching that performance of *Faust*. I was there when Antoinette Giry went into labour. It was I who delivered her child. You."

I stared at him, mouth open. Why had no one ever told me? I must have asked about the circumstances of my birth, or I would not have known that it had taken place during *Faust* and that my father had been trapped by his role as pianist, unable to attend to his labouring wife while the opera was underway. I even remembered hearing that there had been some sort of staff shortage, which meant no one else was available to play the piano.

I sat down on the Persian rug beside Erik with a bump.

"I don't believe you," I stuttered.

"It is the truth," he said. "Do you want a blow by blow description? It is not a night I am going to forget."

"How would *you* know how to deliver a baby?" I asked scornfully. "Are you going to tell me you learned that from books?"

"I have lived much of my life away from medical aid," he replied, unconcerned by my tone. "Yours was not the first birth I had seen. I had even assisted them, animals and humans. I will admit, however, it was the first and last time I had to deliver a baby alone."

"Tell me," I demanded, unwilling to believe him but my old curiosity getting the better of me again. Erik took another sip from the brandy bottle, his gaze on the fire.

"*Faust* was not a popular opera at the time," he began. "It was unfashionable, and ticket sales had been poor. That night, only the stalls, circle and Boxes had been sold. They hadn't even bothered offering seats in the gods, so the whole area was closed. Antoinette slipped me into a chair in the gods just after curtain-up, so that she and I were concealed by the shadows; the chandelier was not lit that night."

It felt so strange to hear someone talking about my mother by her Christian name.

"The performance was mediocre at best. The soprano in the role of Marguerite was…" he appeared to wince. "All wrong for the part. Too old and past her prime. I had seen that your mother was uncomfortable. At eight months pregnant, she should not have been continuing in her duties as concierge, and I told her so several times. It was in the middle of the third act when she suddenly gripped my arm. I asked her what was wrong, and she told me that it was the baby. We left the auditorium and used a secret passageway to get to her chambers as quickly as possible. Her waters broke just as we arrived, and I realised that we did not have much time. It is my opinion, Meg, that your mother had begun to experience the pains of labour long before she told me that you were coming. Perhaps she hoped that if she ignored them then she could delay the birth until the opera was over, and her husband could be by her side."

I thought that was unlikely. Mother had always been a down-to-earth woman who never believed that ignoring a problem would make it go away.

"She must have been frightened," I murmured. "I would be."

"She was," he nodded. "It was all I could do to keep her near to calm. At least we were in a bed chamber, where she could lie back and be somewhat comfortable. I do not envy women the pain of labour, truly I do not. The birth itself was not slow, but it was difficult for Antoinette. To this day I cannot understand how no-one heard her cries and came to her aid. You were the wrong way round, you see, feet first instead of head. It makes the delivery of a child that much more dangerous; mother and baby rarely survive it, even today. But I got you out, Meg, cut the umbilical cord and held you in my hands. You were such a small baby that both my hands could hold you easily. I remember Antoinette gasping, begging to know why you weren't crying. It was more than that. You weren't breathing at all and your skin was turning blue. I felt... afraid. I admit that I was afraid. Antoinette was growing hysterical, begging me to save her baby, and I did not know if I could. I tapped your back and chest, but to no avail. When I thought hope was lost, I pulled off my mask and pressed my hideous mouth to your tiny one..."

He turned his face from the fire, and twitched the mask. For a moment, I thought he was going to take it off, despite all his insistences that I was never to see his face. Instead, he twisted it ever so slightly so that a misshapen, bloated upper lip, previously always hidden from my sight, was revealed. I felt myself recoil, not intending to, but something deep and primal within me reacted to the sight and made me shudder. He snapped the mask back into place.

"Yes. These deformed lips were the first to touch yours. I drew breath into my lungs and then breathed into yours, three times, and then you gave a tiny cough, and started to wail. Your eyes opened, you looked directly at me and began to cry great, hearty sobs. Only when I was sure that you were breathing freely, did I place you in your mother's arms. I had to leave you two alone and skulk through the darkness, in order to find your father and inform him that he had a daughter." His smile was a little bitter. "He was not pleased to learn that it was I who had delivered his child."

"Why not?" I whispered.

"Claude Giry never trusted me," he mused. "I think he believed I had romantic feelings towards his wife."

He leant forward suddenly, seizing my wrist and pulling me close to him across the rug, his other hand sliding into my hair so that I could neither

THE ANGEL'S SHADOW

pull back nor look away, his voice lowering to a hiss.

"So don't you ever, *ever* try to tell me that I have no right to exert authority over you, little miss! Your very existence is because of *me*, monster that I am! You are *mine* as much as you are your mother's. If you have ever looked up at the sky and thanked God that you are alive, remember that it is because of me that you are. My claim on you runs as deep as the breath in your lungs and you *will* respect that."

I tried to struggle with a little whimper of protest, but he held onto me, his eyes searching my face.

"I have been your shadow, little dancer. As for de Chagny... well, you are foolish, stupid and downright naïve... but you leave him to me. You are worth more than selling your body to some philandering aristocrat to save your own skin, no matter how noble your intentions are. I will see that something is done about the Comte. And then we must discuss how you are to repay me."

CHAPTER THIRTY EIGHT

"You're hurting me," I told Erik quietly, and he made a sort of scoffing sound.

"You girls are so fragile," he let go of my wrist, but did not relinquish his hold on my hair. Instead, he let the gold curls slide through his fingers, watching in apparent fascination. I leant across his lap with care and picked up the bottle of brandy, suddenly very aware that he was half naked and I was in Christine's nightclothes. Heat radiated from his body.

"I think you've had enough of this for now," I began.

"I am in pain."

His grip tightened on my hair and I froze.

"Mother will be here soon," I said, trying to keep my voice steady. "She will bring you medicine."

I prayed that it was true. He lowered his masked face to my hair, inhaling deeply through a nose which, if the rumours were true, was hardly even there. I wondered how much, in his alcohol-laden imagination, I resembled Christine. I could feel his erection against my leg and swallowed hard. Surely he would not demand I paid my so-called debt now? Surely he would not want *that* sort of payment?

"Please let go of me, Erik." I said, my voice sounding much stronger than I felt. He sighed and released me, and I stood up on trembling legs that threatened to betray me, brandy in hand. I heard him get to his feet behind me with a grimace.

"Go to the piano," he ordered. "Entertain me."

I was delighted to put the distance between us, crossing to the piano as he returned to the sofa.

"I'm glad to see it's still here," I remarked, taking my seat. "So much else seems to be missing."

He grunted, wrapping himself in the cloak as he sat, so it thankfully covered his condition.

"Where has it all gone, Erik? Furniture, paintings, books. Even medicines. Why have you gotten rid of it?"

"A Ghost has no need of such things," he replied.

"But you are no ghost," I reminded him. "Nor are you an angel. You are Erik."

He gave me a dangerous smile.

"*Play.*"

I did not argue, shuffling through the sheets of music on top of the piano until I found a Mendelssohn piece I knew. I wanted to quiz him more, about his dwindling possessions and so many other things, but that smile and his tone had made it plain that our conversation was finished.

I had moved from Mendelssohn to Mozart, and Erik had fallen asleep again, sitting upright on the sofa, when the door hidden by the now-empty bookcase opened. Mother stepped into the room, candle in one hand, bag in the other, and I barely waited until she had put the candle down on the bookcase before I flew into her arms. She held me tightly, one hand stroking my hair.

"Are you all right?" She murmured. "Has he hurt you?"

I shook my head, but whether it was in answer to her first question or her second, I did not know. Mother pulled back to look at me properly.

"Darling, your throat…" Her fingers touched my neck where Erik's fingers must have bruised; I would likely have the same marks on my shoulder. She caught hold of my hands and turned them over. "Your wrist, too."

"He didn't mean to hurt me," I began. "At least, I don't think he did. He can't judge his own strength. He says I'm fragile."

"People who don't know their own strength, are generally referred to as bullies," she frowned. "Was he badly injured by the Vicomte?"

I nodded.

"There's a wound in his side, I had to sew it and he doesn't have any painkillers or anything. He only had brandy." I sighed deeply. "He… drank himself to sleep."

She moved around the sofa, shaking Erik's shoulder and speaking his name softly. After a moment he opened his eyes, and Mother felt his temperature and told him she had brought him medicine.

It took both of us to get Erik to his feet and help him into his bedroom. He collapsed onto the bird-framed bed and my eyes flicked nervously to the curtain-covered alcove, where a life-sized mannequin of Christine stood bedecked in bridal finery.

"Meg, fetch two glasses of water, please."

Mother's voice made me jump, but I hurried to obey, returning with the water to find she had broken the stitch I had made to keep the bandages together, and unwrapped them so that she could examine the wound. I found myself absurdly wishing that I had used a different colour thread for his stitches, the black seemed ugly against his pale skin, but at least he was no longer bleeding. Mother had indeed brought medicine; she helped him swallow a few tablets with some of the water, and bound the wound again with fresh bandages. I was just about to move away when his bony hand shot out and gripped me by the sleeve.

"Meg..." he seemed to be struggling to focus on me. "Thank you..."

"You're welcome, Erik." I gently disengaged his fingers and squeezed his hand. "Get some rest."

Mother and I left him drifting into sleep again, collected our belongings, and she showed me how to open the bookcase door from both sides. I concentrated hard as she led me back through the catacombs, mapping the route in my mind so that I could find my way in the future if I needed to. I was trying to ignore the questions buzzing like trapped wasps in my head, had to force myself to wait until we were in the main body of the Opera House, and then in Mother's chambers, where I hung my still-damp rehearsal dress over the fireguard.

"Where's Christine?" I asked, reaching for the kettle over the fire to make tea.

"I sent her home. The Vicomte's injury only needed two stitches from his doctor and he will have no trouble recovering." She frowned, and I knew she was thinking of Erik. "You did well with Erik, Meg. I'm proud of you. The fever is worrying, but I hope he will recover quickly."

"Quickly enough to be arrested," I murmured, and she sighed and began looking through a drawer of soaps and medicines. "He knows."

"Of course he knows," she agreed. "Do you think anything happens around here that he isn't aware of? The secret passages of this building that you and I have seen, Meg, are only a tiny part of the whole. I don't know if there is any room that he is not able to observe." She glanced towards her wardrobe, as if the wounded Phantom might even now be lurking behind her clothes. "If he wasn't overhearing the very meeting in which Raoul de Chagny laid that plan to capture him, then he learned of it soon afterwards. And no, not from me," she added, as I raised my eyebrows at her.

"He might be planning to run," I said, voicing for the first time a theory that had been growing since I noticed his possessions diminishing. "There are things missing from his home, all sorts of things... Maybe the Opera Ghost is going to cease his haunting and go elsewhere."

Even as I said it, I felt the frown between my eyebrows as I remembered asking Erik if he were having a clear out, the day I fell into his torture chamber. That had been long before the announcement of *Don Juan Triumphant*, and Raoul's plan to lure him into a trap using Christine as bait. There was something else going on that I was not aware of, another secret which I was not privy to.

268

THE ANGEL'S SHADOW

"It's a possibility," she agreed. "He has been getting twenty thousand francs a month for awhile now; he must be doing something with it."

Mother set a bottle down on the small table where we ate our meals, and I recognised its golden contents as I poured the tea; Erik's gypsy potion.

"Did he give you that?"

"He taught me the recipe; the herbs it contains are not difficult to obtain. Sit down."

I sat, and she pulled her chair around the table to me and began bathing the marks on my neck and wrist with the liquid, anointing the tiny cuts left by the broken glass. I watched the fire while she worked, wondering, thinking, worrying.

"Meg?" Mother gently took my chin in her hand and turned my head so that I was looking at her. "What's wrong? *Did* Erik do anything to you?"

"No." I shook my head. "When I came in, he threw a decanter or something at the wall above me… that's how I got these little cuts on my arm. He grabbed me by the throat and demanded to know if I was with anyone else. I think he was expecting the *gendarmes*. Later, he grabbed me by the wrist. He… talked to me, Mother. He told me about my birth."

She gave a huge, sad sigh.

"Why keep it such a secret?" I asked. "Especially after I found out about… who he was and his connections with you."

"I don't know," she admitted. "It had to be a secret, Meg, for so long that I almost convinced myself that I had given birth alone, without assistance. I could hardly tell Monsieur Lafevre that the Phantom of the Opera had delivered my baby, could I?"

"You could have told *me*." I insisted. "The way Erik thinks is… peculiar. He thinks that he *owns* me; it's not just that he wants my respect, or that he is interested in my welfare because I am the only child who was born in this building."

And what claim does he have on the building? I wondered. *It was here long before he was.*

"Meg, we have talked about this before," she said firmly. "He deserves your respect, and now you know why."

"But—" I began, but she shook her head.

"Enough. We are not going to discuss it now."

I swallowed, but didn't push the subject. After all, knowing why the Phantom felt that he should have authority over me made no real difference. And so what if Mother had kept it a secret from me? I had secrets from her; there were no circumstances under which I would reveal my bargain with Philippe de Chagny.

I have to admit that it was a shock when Christine burst into tears in the middle of a rehearsal. Carlotta had been making spiteful comments, but they were mostly in Italian, and I hadn't realised that Christine knew enough of the language to be hurt by them. Christine was fairly thick skinned; even on the Gala night, when Paris had been ringing with her name, not all the reviews of her performance had been positive. The young soprano had just taken the criticism in her stride. Today, however, she simply dropped her score, put her face in her hands and began to cry.

"Christine…" I could do nothing pull her into a hug, rocking her. She tried to say something, but the words were unintelligible. Monsieur Reyer cleared his throat.

"I think we'll leave it there for today, ladies and gentlemen," he announced. "We reconvene at the same time tomorrow, please."

He gave me a worried look as I gathered up the scattered music and walked into the wings, my arm around Christine, who was still sobbing.

"I'll look after her," I assured him, and he just nodded, his eyes concerned.

I took Christine back to her dressing room, gave her my handkerchief and found her a glass of water. She was already calmer, sitting on the chaise longue and mopping her eyes with the hankie, her sobs becoming shivery sniffles.

"Thank you, Meg," she sighed as she accepted the water. "Oh, God, I can't do this!"

I sat beside her on the chaise longue and patted her knee.

"I'm sorry," I told her. "I feel like I've abandoned you when you need a friend the most."

She looked at me in surprise.

"No, Meg, of course you haven't. I've been feeling like I was abandoning *you*. When I leave here every evening, I worry for your safety. I can go to my apartment and get away from all this, but you live here. Madame Giry told me Erik had threatened to hurt you if she didn't obey him, and we all know he would, Meg! He's done so because of me!" Fresh tears spilled down her cheeks and I pulled her into another hug.

"Please don't worry about me," I said gently. "Erik isn't going to do me any harm."

It had been a week since anyone had seen or heard anything from the Phantom of the Opera; he hadn't even sent any notes. Mother had visited his underground home and reported that his fever had broken and he was recovering nicely. She had not allowed me to come with her, though.

"And you mustn't let the things that Carlotta says upset you," I went on. "You know she's just jealous."

"Carlotta?" Christine echoed, sounding puzzled. "What was she saying?"

"I thought you knew," I said, confused myself. "She was saying things in Italian, malicious things."

THE ANGEL'S SHADOW

Christine shook her head.

"My Italian is terrible," she said. "Just because I can sing in Italian doesn't mean I can understand it."

"Then what brought all this on, hmm?" I asked, wiping a tear from her cheek with my thumb. Christine swallowed and looked at the scores I had placed beside us on the chaise longue.

"I can't do this," she repeated helplessly.

"Can't... go through with the Vicomte's plan?" I guessed, but Christine shook her head.

"I've gone too far to stop that now." She dragged her wrist across her eyes. "This is Erik's opera, and it's a masterpiece. If Raoul's plan works, it will also be the last opera Erik will ever see performed. It has to be as magnificent as he deserves, and I can't do it justice!"

She began sobbing again. I watched her, frowning a little, trying to make sense of what she was saying.

"You're... worried that you won't impress him?" I summarised. "Christine... Erik worked on this for a long, long time; he has written and rewritten it over and over again. The role of Aminta as it is shown here was written with your voice in mind. He could not be displeased with your performance."

"It's not enough," she insisted. "Nothing seems to work without him to guide my music, nothing I sing feels... whole. I *need* my Angel of Music, Meg... but, God above, how can I ask him to coach me now? When he must know that I am a part of this plot to hand him over to the law?"

I stood up and began walking back and forth in front of the mirror, my eyes on the carpet, my steps the habitual toe-first gait of the ballerina that was so natural to me now that I didn't even know I was doing it.

"He more or less told you to," I said at last. "In that note he sent us all. He said that you should swallow your pride and return to him as your teacher. More or less."

She shook her head, fear flashing across her face.

"He'll lock me up if I go back down there!" She cried, panic elevating her pitch. "He'll keep me with him forever!"

I bit my lip, examining the ties of my slippers.

"What if it could be like it was in the beginning? What if he could go back to being your Angel of Music, just like before?"

"Meg..." Christine smiled through her tears. "Dear Meg... I never thought of you as a romantic, but even you cannot change all that has happened between us. My Angel is gone."

She sounded so heartbroken as she said it, that it made me even more determined to prove her wrong.

"Perhaps not," I insisted. "What if I could convince him to come here as your teacher, to coach you again so that you can give him the

271

performance that you feel he deserves? Would you agree to that?"

"Maybe…" she replied, her eyes on the mirror. "If things went back to the way they were before… But how can they? I can no longer trust him!"

I twisted a strand of hair around my finger that had come loose from my bun.

"What if I were with you, as a sort of chaperone? You could have your lesson here, in this dressing room, for… for old time's sake. I could stay here with you, and he could stay behind the mirror. You wouldn't have to see him, just hear him."

Her gaze moved to me, uncertain, frightened.

"Do you think Erik would agree to that?"

"I don't know," I admitted. "But if you want me to, I will go and ask him."

"Meg, you can't!" She cried, standing and seizing my hands. "He'll hurt you!"

"I don't think he will," I said gently. "I've been into his home before. I know the way. Let me do this, Christine. For both of you."

"But what if he tries to—"

"Give me an hour," I interrupted. "If I haven't returned within an hour, then you can start to panic. Tell my mother before you speak to anyone else. But let me try. If he says no, then you've not lost anything. And if he says yes… well, then it's one last lesson with your Angel of Music."

Christine swallowed hard, her eyes filled with more tears.

"Be careful," she told me, and kissed my cheek.

I took one of the candles from the vanity table, and carefully felt around the edges of the mirror for the switch that would make the glass move. There was a click, and shiver across the surface of the mirror, and I saw the tiny gap appear in the left-hand side of the frame. For a moment I wondered if Erik was standing there, if he had been there the whole time listening to our conversation, but when I slid the glass aside, it revealed the dark passage beyond, echoing with the drip of water and the scuttling of rats. I took a last look back at Christine, inhaled a breath to steel my nerves against both the journey and the Ghost who awaited me at its end, and began to descend, once more, to the Phantom's domain.

CHAPTER THIRTY NINE

I knocked on the reverse side of the bookcase door, even though I knew Erik was aware of my presence. About five minutes previously, I had passed, touched or stepped on something had set a bell ringing and warned him that someone was walking his catacombs. I could hear the piano being played, a quick, passionate tune that I did not recognise, and knocked harder.

"Come in, Meg!" The golden voice commanded, and I opened the door.

"How did you know it was me?" I asked as I entered the drawing room. Erik was indeed sitting at the piano across from me, wearing a ruffled white shirt, partially open and revealing a few inches of pale chest, under a dark green jacket that had lace at the cuffs. His mask was in place, and the bruising that the Vicomte had done to his face was fading, almost healed. His hair looked slightly longer than usual, and I had to remind myself that he was wearing one of a collection of wigs. He flashed me his quick, wicked smile.

"A magician never reveals his secrets, my child," he answered, and I clenched my teeth together at the term he used for me. That smile flashed across his lips again; he knew he had annoyed me. "Why have you come to me?"

I put the candle on the bookcase, and approached until I was leaning against the end of the grand piano, uncertain how to phrase what I wanted to say. His violin and bow sat on top of it, beside an open case. Erik continued to play without looking at the keys, his eyes on my face.

"I need to talk to you about Christine," I said hesitantly. The music didn't falter, although his eyes narrowed. "She's having trouble with the role of Aminta. She would like it if you would coach her."

"Would she indeed?" His unmasked eyebrow rose. "And why should I agree to coach my errant pupil?"

I spread my hands.

"It's your opera, Erik. Don't you want the best performance possible? Isn't that why you've been bullying everyone?"

"The best performance possible, from the woman who chose the youth and beauty of her Vicomte over me?" He stopped playing.

"What do you want to hear?" I tried to keep the exasperation from my tone. "You know what is going to happen on the night of *Don Juan Triumphant*. To put it bluntly, this is your last opportunity to spend time in her company. Christine needs you; she needs her Angel of Music."

He stood up abruptly and turned away from me, gazing into the fire with one hand clutching the mantelpiece. I noticed that there was an embroidered design on the back of the jacket and that it was a little too big for him across the shoulders. Erik was the tallest man I had ever seen, taller than Monsieur Firman, but he did not have the build to match his height.

I moved sideways away from the piano, so that I was standing directly behind him.

"But," I said. "She is afraid of you, especially after what happened in the graveyard. She doesn't want to be abducted and held against her will."

He spun around to face me, but I gabbled onwards before he could start shouting.

"Christine wants to be in the dressing room, with me there with her, and you behind the mirror."

Erik took two strides to cross the distance between us, stopping right in front of me so that I was eye-to-nipple with him. I felt myself blushing, and fought not to back away.

"I am fifteen inches taller than you," he observed. "And several times stronger. What would prevent me from overpowering you and taking Christine?"

"My regard for you?" I suggested. "I can't change what has happened between you, but I trust you to be a gentleman." I raised my eyes from his chest to his mismatched gaze. "Let it be like before, Erik. Teach her what she needs to know, give her your music one last time." I swallowed hard. "If this is to be the last opera you see, then I agree with Christine that *Don Juan Triumphant* should be magnificent, as it deserves to be."

He stayed still and silent for a few seconds, then said:

"I must change." He pointed at the sofa. "Sit down and stay there. I'm in no mood to deal with your snooping tonight."

I raised my hands in a gesture of surrender, sitting down obediently. Erik gave me a glower, and then swept from the room with his customary grace. I watched him go, frowning at his embroidered back; his attitude worried me, but I didn't really know what I had been expecting. I could only hope that he would be the gentleman I trusted him to be.

"That is not sitting down and staying there," Erik said as he returned five minutes later. I had been doing ballet stretches in the middle of the

THE ANGEL'S SHADOW

room and gave him my most insolent scowl as I rose from the floor.

"I did not snoop anywhere, I assure you."

"Come on," he told me with a roll of his eyes, crossed to the piano and placed the violin and bow into its case, snapping it shut.

He was wearing evening dress, the black suit very similar to the one he had been in when he had climbed in through my bedroom window last year and told me off for poking around. The shirt, waistcoat and bowtie were as pristine white as his mask. He wore black gloves and the same fedora hat and beaded cloak he had worn in the graveyard on Christmas Eve. I moved towards the bookcase and collected my candle, but he picked up the case, opened the front door and clicked his tongue at me impatiently.

"We're going across the lake?" I asked, surprised, as I picked up my candle.

"It is quicker," he replied, gesturing me through the door and closing it behind us. "You wouldn't want to worry Christine by being tardy, would you?"

"Were you spying on us?" I glared as I stepped into the boat.

"Hold this," he said in lieu of an answer, passing me the violin case.

We moved in near silence over the lake. Once on the other side, he reclaimed his violin and led me to the staircase that went all the way up to the floor of my dormitory. He took my hand in a grip softened by the leather of his gloves and we started up together, me struggling to see through the darkness, but he as sharp-eyed and sure-footed as a cat. He did not follow the staircase all the way up as I had expected, but took corners and passages that I did not see until they came within the small sphere of light cast by my candle. It may have been intended to muddle me, for that was certainly the effect. In my world, I could walk the corridors of the Opera House in the dark with no difficulty, but the whole time there had been another world just the breadth of a wall away, a secret world of which I knew nothing. It was like living in one of those folk tales where the realm of Faerie ran beside the everyday, with places and days and times weak enough for the Fae people to step between the two worlds, and play tricks on mankind.

"Is your father Charles Garnier?" I asked, voicing a theory that had been with me for some time. Erik stopped and let go of my hand, turning to face me.

"What?" He sounded utterly perplexed by the question, which was not surprising, given that I had asked it out of the blue.

"Charles Garnier," I repeated. "Is he your father?"

He moved his violin case from one hand to the other.

"What is going on in that head of yours, Meg Giry?"

I tried to ignore the way my candle cast shadows on his masked face, making him, even in his puzzlement, look threatening.

275

"Well," I began. "I know that my parents brought you here when you were nineteen, and all these secret tunnels were already in place. And I've said before that your home is just that—a home, designed and built. I wondered how you would know all this was hidden within the Opera House, and thought that maybe you were the son of the architect. You told me to look him up, and I did. He has a wife, Louise, but I couldn't find any mention of children. I just wondered…"

He resituated the violin case again and took my hand, his strides longer now so that I was forced to trot to keep abreast of him.

"My father," Erik said. "Was a stone mason from the North-West of France. He died three months before I was born. I am not the bastard son of Charles Garnier. Satisfied?"

"For now," I replied innocently, and he huffed out a breath that might have been a laugh. It was one more fragment of information to store and to add to the mosaic that was Erik.

When we emerged at last, I was amazed to find myself in the room known as The Organ, a small space completely dominated by the contraption that worked the new electric lights. It was empty now, the technicians having departed when Christine's tears brought an abrupt end to the rehearsal. I'd only been in here a few times before; it was on the opposite side of the auditorium to the dressing rooms. Erik prodded me in the small of the back.

"Go on," he said. "Go and join Christine. I will be there shortly."

"You're not coming with me?" I asked, stupidly.

"I believe the arrangement was that I remained behind the mirror," he reminded me. "Off you go."

I went, baffled by his choice of route. Was I supposed to have memorised all those twists and turns in the near blackness? If so, I had failed.

I walked through the backstage corridors to Christine's dressing room. She was still sitting on the chaise, and jumped as I opened the door, as in fear or guilt. She had lit the gas lamps—electricity had not been wired into the dressing rooms—and the candelabra by the mirror, causing the room to glow, golden and soft.

"He's on his way," I told her, replacing the candle from where I had found it. Christine nodded, inhaling a quick breath.

"He didn't harm you?"

"No," I assured her, taking a seat at her side. "I'm fine."

We sat in silence, both of us tense, wondering what Erik was up to. Three minutes later, the gas lights went out, and I bit down on a curse. Of course, the mains supply for the gas was in The Organ too; the Opera Ghost was back to playing tricks. Neither of us moved, knowing it would be futile to try turning the lights back on. Another couple of minutes

THE ANGEL'S SHADOW

dragged by, and then the candles in the candelabra went out as suddenly as if someone had dowsed them in water. Christine's fingers closed around mine, and I could hear her breathing, fast and soft. The mournful notes of a violin filled the dressing room, and the mirror began to glow.

"Angel..." Christine breathed; she wasn't feeling afraid or guilty, I realised, but excited.

"I am here, Christine," came the golden reply over the music, and I thought grumpily that he could not resist making an entrance. "To guide you once more."

"Thank you," she replied humbly. "When I sing Aminta for you, I want... I want to give you my soul."

"Your soul is beautiful thing," Erik told her, the music ceasing. "But it hardly softens the blow of rejection." I winced at that, and his tone sharpened to an order. "On your feet."

I could see Erik's outline through the glass, looking as ghostly as flesh and blood could, while Christine obeyed the command.

"You too, Marguerite," Erik snapped, and I blinked.

"Me, Monsieur?"

"This is a rehearsal and you are in attendance," he answered. "I will not allow you to idle away the time, child. Now stand."

I rose to my feet, glancing at Christine, absurdly worried that I might make her jealous. What was Erik doing? This was her lesson, not mine. It was as he was giving us a vocal warm up, using his violin to provide pitch, that I worked it out. He was giving me something to do, trying to distract me. No doubt he was going to weave some sort of spell around her with his voice, enchanting her again, as he had in the graveyard.

Well, he won't succeed, I told myself as I reached the top of my range and Christine continued up the scale solo. *I said I would protect Christine and I will.*

They started work on the first duet between Aminta and Don Juan, entitled *The Point of No Return.* I had never heard the phrase before, but its meaning was crystal clear. Erik stopped Christine after only a few lines.

"No, no," he said. "I don't believe you. This song is about desire, about passion. I know you've felt that, my Christine, for my music if for nothing else. Think of how it excites you, makes your skin tingle..." I saw Christine's eyes drift closed, her lips parting. "Now, begin again."

She did, eyes still closed, and this time her voice was stronger and her stance altered. She stood with her feet slightly apart, one hip cocked, a seductive posture more befitting to the role she was portraying. And then, Erik began to sing Don Juan's part as Christine reached the chorus, their joined voices sending shivers racing up my spine. It was powerful, beautiful, erotic. Christine's fingers lightly traced her throat, as though the touch belonged to someone else, and behind the thin sheet of glass that separated them, I heard Erik sigh.

277

"Yes, Christine," he breathed. "Let the song move you. Are you moved?"

"Yes, Angel..." she whispered.

"Tell me how it makes you feel."

"Like... like there is fire in my blood," was her reply, and I bit my lip. This coaching session was making me immensely uncomfortable.

"Fire," Erik repeated, his voice almost fevered. "*Yes*, Christine! Remember how I told you that my *Don Juan* burned? *This* is that burn! Passion, lust, music, taking what your deepest, darkest dreams tell you that you want, but society tells you that you that you cannot have!"

"Um... maybe you should move onto another song?" I suggested. Christine did not respond, and I wondered whether she still wanted me here. Erik ignored me entirely.

"You and I are both outcasts from society, Christine," he continued. "Orphaned, alone in this world, and reaching for some darkness, a beauty in the night that we are told we should not have! I can give you that, Christine! Just let go of all this and join me! I can give you everything you have ever wanted!"

"Erik!" I stepped in front of the mirror, between Christine and her wide-eyed reflection. "Stop this! You promised!"

He gave a soft laugh, and his outline shifted behind the glass.

"I do not recall promising you anything, my dear child." He murmured.

"Erik," I said, trying to get as much warning into my tone as possible. He sighed and made a clicking noise, as if snapping his fingers. Christine drew in a sharp, startled breath behind me and I turned to see her looking hot and flustered. She lifted her hands and slowly ran them through her hair, and I rushed to her in a flood of guilt and sympathy.

"I'm sorry," I whispered, taking hold of her wrists. "I'm sorry... I just can't let him do that to you again. You love Raoul, don't you?"

"Yes." She whispered, her eyes shimmering with tears.

"And you want to marry him?"

"Yes."

"Then don't let Erik manipulate you like this. Christine..."

She nodded, swallowing hard.

"I'm all right, Meg... really..."

I let her go and she took a deep breath. I could hear Erik plucking the strings of the violin as if he needed to keep his fingers busy, and his tone when he spoke, was cool.

"Shall we begin again?"

He did not sing with her this time, he coached her professionally and without any attempt at seduction. Christine sounded perfect to my ears, the emotion she put into the music making it ring around the dressing room. At last, the violin stopped, and Erik said quietly:

THE ANGEL'S SHADOW

"You are magnificent, Christine. You are my Angel of Music and you bring a magic to my opera that I never thought I would hear, in this lifetime or the next."

It broke my heart. I knew, for the first time without a shadow of doubt, that he *did* love Christine. He didn't just want to own her, possess her, keep her like a songbird in a cage. She brought light into his darkness, life into the tomb he had prematurely constructed for himself beneath the Opera House.

"Goodbye, Christine," he murmured, and the light behind the mirror dimmed, and then went out altogether. Christine gasped and went up to the mirror, pressing her hands against it.

"Angel…" She cried.

I wondered if Erik was still standing there, his palms against hers, mere centimetres apart, but worlds away from each other. There was nothing I could do but put my hands on Christine's shoulders as she lowered her forehead against the cold glass, and wept.

CHAPTER FORTY

The rest of January past in broken flurries of snow; Paris was blanketed in it and the chill swept through the corridors and rooms of the Opera Populairé. After his initial bout of practical jokes, Erik was quite reserved, although every shift of a shadow, movement of a curtain or clumsy accident was put down to the Opera Ghost. The younger members of the chorus and ballet moved around the building in packs, bleating at each unexpected noise like frightened sheep, and I found myself roped into shepherding them about with my mother. Mother herself was outstanding; firm but fair, able to soothe or scold, give a hug or a clip around the ear as required. She worked her dancers hard with encouragement and praise, and set me one of the most challenging routines of my career.

"Of course you can manage," she told me when I expressed doubt. "I wouldn't choreograph something that was too difficult for you. You're a born dancer, Meg, and you are more than capable."

I put my doubts aside after that and sent my heart and soul into the dance and the music. It allowed me to lose myself, and forget, for awhile, that I was afraid of what March would bring.

I think Raoul de Chagny spent more time at the Opera House than he did at home. He accompanied Christine everywhere she went, and his constant, albeit silent, presence made me want to swat him like a bluebottle. I wondered if that was what a marriage was about, spending every waking moment with another person and missing them when they weren't there.

Christine didn't seem to mind the Vicomte being there, but Erik certainly did. The entire *Don Juan Triumphant* cast was onstage for a rehearsal, and we were at a scene in which neither Christine nor I was needed. I was sitting at the back of the stage, out of the way, and Christine was working my hair into a French braid, when Carlotta swanned across the stage from right to left. The heel of her shoe had only just moved when a square of stage beneath it disappeared completely. One by one, each of the

THE ANGEL'S SHADOW

trapdoors opened, with a loud thud and the Phantom's laughter resounded throughout the auditorium.

Raoul leapt to his feet from his chair in the stalls, drawing a pistol from the inside pocket of his jacket and I swore.

"You let him come in here with *that*?!" I hissed to Christine.

"He is trying to protect me," her reply was calm, although her grip on my hair was tight.

The laughter bounced around the room, gradually fading away, and all the trapdoors closed with a thud. People were chattering, rushing through the wings to reach the area where the mechanism for the trapdoors was located, but I had no doubt that Erik would already be gone via one of his secret passageways. I noted that absolutely no one had been harmed during this incident, Erik having waited until none of the trapdoors were being stood on before opening them. Carlotta was wailing in Italian and Monsieur Reyer looked shaken, but requested that everyone take five minutes to calm down, and then the rehearsals would continue.

Christine and I did not discuss it as we left the stage when the rehearsal was over; instead we discussed the upcoming wedding, which was to take place in August, a summer wedding after all. These days, we avoided even mentioning the man who might yet bring all these matrimonial plans crashing down.

February brought with it hail and sleet, and the undeniable knowledge that, whatever happened, I was going to lose Christine. Although Raoul had promised me that she would carry on performing at the Opera Populairé, she would be the Vicomtess de Chagny, and a world away from my humble status. I analysed my feelings as I danced until my feet bled, wondering if I was jealous of her, or just sorrowful that the woman I loved like a sister would no longer be as close as one.

I knew all the while, as February waned, the weather warmed and the premiere of *Don Juan Triumphant* came ever closer, that I was using all these thoughts and worries to mask the fact that I was terrified of what March the first would hold for me. For all Erik's low words about leaving the Comte de Chagny to him, there was no doubt in my mind that the Opera Ghost would be imprisoned and Philippe still at liberty before midnight. He would hold me to our bargain, and I would spend the night in his arms, in his bed.

Again and again, I tried to tell my mother, to tell Christine, to tell Raoul, but the shame of what I had done stopped my tongue and I ended up muttering: "Nothing. It doesn't matter." With each of them dealing with their own fears and worries, I did not blame them for not pushing the situation.

By the third week in February, everything was coming together. The opera was rehearsed, the sets constructed, the *gendarmes* informed. I stood in the workroom of Madame Soirelli, the seamstress Erik had played the nasty 'hanged man' joke on, and stared at my reflection. The young woman in the 'Gypsy Girl' costume was barely recognisable as myself; my waist was synched in tight, giving my hips an ample curve. The corseting pushed my bust up as well so that the outfit was completely dominated by my cleavage. All any man saw when he looked at me in this costume would be my breasts, and I hated it.

"What's the matter with you?" Giselle asked as she primped and preened beside me in a similar costume. "You look like you've seen a ghost." Sudden alarm crossed her features. "You haven't, have you?"

"No," I replied hollowly. "It's just... I look like a whore."

Giselle laughed at me.

"That's the whole point! You're one of Don Juan's conquests! Oh, Giry, it's only an opera, don't be such a prude! Most of us would kill to have a figure like yours, that men drool over, so stop feeling sorry for yourself and enjoy it!"

She couldn't know how much her words stung. Men 'drooled over' me like a dog drooled over a piece of meat. That was how I felt, and every male I saw was a potential predator. My bargain with the Comte de Chagny was ruining my life, and it wasn't even consummated yet.

"Meg?"

I gave a shriek at the sound of the male, golden voice and flung up my hands to cover my chest. It was the first of March, the opening night of *Don Juan Triumphant*, and I was in my dormitory applying my make-up for the performance with the help of a small mirror propped against the candlestick on my nightstand.

"Erik!" I hissed. He was standing in the doorway, looking as dashing as ever in full white-tie, immaculately styled hair—wig, I reminded myself— mask, as always, and a black-stoned ring on the little finger of his ungloved right hand. I was wearing my corset, petticoats and nothing else. I had never asked him what the stone was, I realised, but that was not the question which was foremost in my mind.

"What are you doing here?!" I demanded in my most hoity-toity voice. "This is my *bedroom* and I am in my *underwear!*"

"Front-lacing corset," he observed. "Good girl."

"Pig!" I spat back, turning my back and grabbing the shawl from the foot of my bed, wrapping it around me protectively. "You men are all the same, complete pigs."

"Is that so?" His tone was cool. "Well in that case, perhaps you do not wish to know about the surprise I have in store for you."

"Your surprises usually seem to leave me unconscious," I said warily. "What are you up to?" The glitter in his eyes was making me uneasy. "Are

THE ANGEL'S SHADOW

you drunk?"

He sighed.

"No, Meg, I am not drunk, but I am pressed for time. Are you coming or not?"

Erik gestured me to go ahead of him, and I did so, realising that he intended us to use the trapdoor at the end of the corridor. He gave me a sharp swat across the backside and I jumped, yelping like a puppy. Even through the layers of petticoats I felt the sting.

"What was that for?" I demanded, one hand over my buttocks and the other clutching my shawl closed, and he continued past me as though nothing had happened.

"A little attitude adjustment," Erik replied evenly without pausing. "I told you before that if you behave like a child I will punish you like one, remember?"

"I remember," I said, hoping that his hand smarted worse than my bottom. "I'm... I'm sorry." And in that moment I meant it. "Today is... difficult."

"For all of us," he said, and stopped to look at me. "You think you see the future, little dancer, but it cannot be predicted by you, or me, or the de Chagnys, or even my Christine. Now come along, before this surprise of mine slithers away."

He used the picture on the wall to activate the trapdoor and took my hand in his, guiding me swiftly yet carefully down the staircase as the trapdoor closed above us and all light was extinguished. I realised, as I felt the stone steps beneath my thin slippers, that I was not afraid. I trusted him to lead me unharmed wherever it was we were going. He was holding my left hand in his right and I could feel the band of his ring against my own fingers, his cool skin against mine, hear his light footsteps and breathing, while mine were silent entirely.

When we found light again at last, I was astonished. I had given up trying to work out where we were and how long we had been underground, and at first I thought we must have reached some portion of Hell; everything looked so red. It took a few seconds of blinking before I realised I was looking at red velvet curtains trimmed with gold, soft lamplight illuminating everything, our location the auditorium, in the corridor that serviced the Boxes. We had come through a door in the wall that was so carefully concealed by the swoops of plastering that I could still not make out where it was and how it opened, even from this side. Erik gave me a smile and prodded me in the back gently to make me walk forward again. Taking a key from the inside pocket of his jacket, he unlocked the door to Box Five. I shook my head as we entered, my slightly befuddled brain still trying to get my bearings and work out how we had managed to get from my dormitory to the auditorium. It made my head hurt.

"Take a seat," Erik whispered. "And don't make a sound."

I sat in silence, smoothing my petticoats so that they would not rustle against the red velvet chair, and he sat beside me, folding his hands in his lap. The curtains were pulled close together so that from the outside, we would be concealed by the shadows they cast. From within, however, Erik and I had a clear view of the stage, and could observe without being observed. There was someone on the stage, in evening dress with a top hat and walking cane, smoking a cigarette. It wasn't until he looked up to blow the smoke up towards the chandelier, that I recognised him. He had shaven off his moustache and had a haircut, but the arrogant stance of Philippe de Changy was unmistakable.

I caught my breath sharply and Erik's hand landed on mine as I gripped the arm of my chair. He was frowning.

Silence. He mouthed, and I nodded.

I gazed at the Comte, wondering what, if anything, had changed about him. Apart from the shave and the haircut, he looked exactly the same as he had when I had first met him in the foyer of the Opera Populairé, chastising his brother for waking me in order to find out where Christine was. He was the same man who had offered me a cigarette in comfort after the chandelier had crashed, tried to stem my hysterics, given Christine, Mother and I a roof over our heads for six months. He had not seemed a demon then. Perhaps he was not one now, but he had seen my weaknesses and taken advantage of them, and now he might just as well be the devil himself. He paced the stage, swinging the cane around his fingers, and my eyes went to the new chandelier. Surely Erik wouldn't...

There were voices and the doors at ground level opened. I could hear them, although the curtains prevented me from seeing, until the lines of men in blue uniforms and hats began to get closer to the stage. Very carefully, I leaned forward as Erik did the same beside me, his hand still on mine. Together we watched the armed *gendarmes* enter the auditorium, directed by a helmeted man who had walked onto the stage. With him, came Raoul de Chagny, and the Opera Populairé's mangers.

"Are you sure this is going to work, André?" Firman looked white in the face and was wringing his hands like a concerned mother.

"Have you got a better idea?"

Raoul and Philippe were talking too quietly for me to hear, and the man in the helmet, presumably a superior officer, walked over to them.

"Monsieur le Vicomte, am I to give the order?"

Raoul confirmed the request with a nod. The officer nodded in return, then blew a sharp blast on the silver whistle hanging around his neck. His men marched into position throughout the auditorium, presumably guarding every entrance and exit. I could see two in the stage right wings, and could only assume there were two in the stage left wings as well. Every

THE ANGEL'S SHADOW

single one of them held a weapon, either a rifle or a pistol, and I reflected that Raoul and Philippe must be armed as well. A boy, no older than me, was in the orchestra pit, and Raoul addressed him directly.

"You there—do you have a clear view of that Box?"

He pointed directly up to Box Five and I shrank back into the seat, afraid of being seen. Erik did not move, and there was a smile playing about his mouth.

"Yes, Monsieur." The youth replied.

"Remember, if he tries anything you are to shoot him. And do not try to wound him, shoot to kill, do you understand?"

My free hand went over my mouth.

"All ready, Monsieur." The officer reported and Raoul swallowed hard and gave a sharp nod.

"Go ahead."

"Secure the doors!" The officer shouted, and beneath me, I heard a door slam shut.

"Secured!" Came the reply.

It continued all around the auditorium, the doors closing, confirmation that they were guarded by armed men. To my dismay, Erik stood up. I leapt to my feet beside him, my hand on his arm, trying to make him sit down again, but to no avail. He opened his mouth, his words coming out in a mocking sing-song, and from the *other side* of the room.

"*I'm here, the Phantom of the Opera...*"

I stared at him, completely astonished. How on Earth was he doing that? I could see his lips moving, repeating the phrase, but now it sounded like it was coming from the back of the auditorium. I had a sudden memory of months before, standing in the middle of the auditorium. He had played this same trick on me, throwing his voice around the darkened room so that I had no idea of his true location. All the men were as shocked as I was, twisting around to face each new direction as his voice bounced from the walls, and suddenly, Erik moved forward, raising his hands, between the gap in the curtains.

"*I'M HERE!*" He bellowed. I grabbed him by the jacket, pulling him back, and a gunshot rang through the auditorium. We were crouched together in Box Five, below the gilded edge and out of sight, Erik's hand over my mouth to cut off the scream that had left me when the gun had fired. He was unhurt, but grinning like a maniac, his eyes sparkling.

"You fool!" Raoul's voice was angry and afraid.

"But, Monsieur le Vicomte..." Began the boy in the orchestra pit.

"Enough!" Erik raised his voice, seeming to come from everywhere at once. "It's time, gentlemen, to end this game. I have much enjoyed your little display but my patience is running dry. Allow the audience entrance, Messieurs! Let the opera begin!"

285

He gave another, low laugh, and I stared at him as he removed his hand from my mouth.

"Don't do this," I begged him in a whisper. "Don't stay."

"They have the building surrounded, I daresay." He replied. The men were leaving the stage, obeying the Phantom's command, and I was aware of talk and a buzz of fear.

"But you have entrances they don't know about. The Rue Scribe, not even the Comte de Chagny knows about that. You could run. You could get away, right now."

"And why would I want to do that?"

"They'll kill you, Erik!" I cried in near silence, gripping his sleeve. "If you stay, they are going to kill you!"

I could feel the hot tears spilling down my cheeks, blurring my vision. Erik gazed at me, then reached out, and wiped them away with his fingertips.

"What's this?" He asked, softly. "Why are you crying, Meg?"

"I don't want you to die!"

"Why not?"

"Because... I care." I could not explain it, even to myself. "I care about you. I don't *want* to see you shot or executed, I just want..."

I shook my head, unable to continue. What did I want? For him to stay, beneath the Opera House, to continue to be my Guardian Angel; for Christine to marry Raoul and achieve the happiness and fame she so deserved; for the Comte de Chagny to come to a sticky end at the hands of the Opera Ghost.

"Oh, my dear Meg," Erik whispered. "You have a good heart. But this is not a fairytale. The beast does not always get the beauty. Not *always*." He smiled. "Come now, no more tears."

He wiped my cheeks with his fingers, then pressed the two middle fingers of his left hand to his lips, and then held them against my forehead. A kiss. A kiss on the forehead from the Phantom of the Opera, the closest I would ever feel from him.

"The time has come for me to meet my fate, little dancer. Go and get ready for the opera. The night is young. There may be more surprises in store."

CHAPTER FORTY ONE

More surprises.

I let Erik push me, frightened and tearful, from Box Five, his hand on my back guiding me to his secret doorway and into the passages of the Opera House. I knew there was nothing I could do or say that would make him change his mind and leave; he knew the trap that was in place and it was his choice to walk into it. Perhaps he really did have ways out of here that were unknown to me. I wondered why he had let me watch the playing out of this scene with him, with Philippe standing there beside his brother on the stage. Erik hadn't done anything to the Comte as far as I could tell, and there had been no move to cause him harm or even discomfort. That manic glitter in Erik's eyes made me think that perhaps he was so focused on his own plans for tonight, that he had forgotten my jeopardy.

Of course he had. Why wouldn't he? It was Christine he wanted, not me.

We didn't speak as Erik led me by the hand through the blind darkness back to the trapdoor near my dormitory. I squeezed his cool fingers as he opened the door above my head, clearly not intending to go up the last few stairs himself.

"Erik... whatever happens tonight, I just... I want to say... Your *Don Juan*, for all its blatant, sexual overtones... it's beautiful, Erik. I really think it's beautiful."

He studied me in the light that filtered down from the open trapdoor, his expression impassive.

"Thank you, Meg." He replied. "Good luck with the performance."

"Good luck yourself," I nodded. "Try... Try not to get shot."

He laughed, turned, and disappeared into the dark like a bat into the night. I heaved a sigh and returned to my own dormitory to reapply the make-up that had been smudged by my tears. I did not know what tonight would bring, but there was certainly more going on than I was aware of.

When I was made-up properly, I went down to the dressing rooms, still wrapped in my shawl. There were so many of us having to use one space that it had made sense for make-up to be put on separately. There were people everywhere, talking, shouting, getting in each other's way, and with a nasty flip of my stomach, I saw a navy-uniformed *gendarme* with a rifle. They truly were manning everywhere they thought the Phantom might show himself; no doubt there would be men in Box Five by now. I wondered where Erik thought he was going to watch his opera.

I squeezed through the milling backstage crowds and into a room already bustling with dancers getting into costume.

"Help!" Lycette was shouting. "Can someone lace this up for me *please?!*"

For the three of us who were playing prostitutes, our costumes were more-or-less the same; deep red and black gypsy-style skirts with a highly-corseted scarlet bodice, a black scarf decorated with red roses wrapped around the waist. The other dancers were all in black, with red petticoats.

Most of the girls wore black lace underneath their bodices, but mine was white, and much of the corseting at the front of the costume was trickery, the red bodice held together with clasps so that I could effect a fast costume change. I had about six minutes, during *The Point of No Return*, in which to rip the dress off and change into black breeches and a white shirt that my character, Katolina, wore in order to disguise herself as a boy to escape an abusive marriage.

I fixed my blonde hair into a messy chignon, pinning a red fabric rose at the base of it and sliding another into the curls above my left ear.

"That's on the wrong side," Giselle commented, reapplying her lipstick. "Your rose should be on the right, like the rest of us. Only Aminta has hers on the left."

"Oh," I lifted my hand to change it, but Lycette was calling my name from the other side of the dressing room.

"Meg! Someone here to see you!" Her voice was high and giggly, and she was twirling a strand of hair around her finger in a way that annoyed me. She was standing next to the door, and I caught the glimpse of a black suit sleeve. Thinking it must be the Vicomte, I excused my way through the crowded room by tactically using my elbows, and reached the door. I felt my expression change when I realised that the man on the other side was not Raoul de Chagny, but Philippe. His eyes caught mine, then immediately travelled downwards.

"Comte de Chagny," I croaked, and he smiled without looking up.

"Mademoiselle Giry," he said to my breasts. "I trust you have not forgotten our arrangement for tonight?"

"Of course not," I replied, wondering whether my face had turned white with shock or red with embarrassment.

"I am very pleased to hear it." He was leering now. "I have certainly not

THE ANGEL'S SHADOW

forgotten. I have spent the last few weeks in Germany imagining how our evening might play out." He wet his lips, his hand momentarily clenching into a fist and then relaxing again, and I wondered if this was some sort of code that I was not in on. I heard Lycette giggle behind me, then whispering.

"Comte de Chagny," I began. "I'm afraid we cannot speak right now, I have to get ready for—"

"You look quite ready to me, child," he interrupted, and his eyes lifted to mine at last. They were the colour of ice and sharp as flint. "I assume there has been no... *change* in your... *circumstances* since we last spoke?"

I swallowed, this time feeling my face flame with blood.

"No, Monsieur." I mumbled, the shame making me feel sick.

"Good girl." He leaned forward and brushed his lips against my scarlet cheek. I felt so embarrassed I wanted to drop dead on the spot. "I have a gift for you."

"A gift?" I repeated. "Really, Comte, there is no need to—"

"I wanted to." He interrupted, and took a small jewellery box from his trouser pocket. When I glanced down to see what he was reaching for, the effect of my costume on him was plain to see. I had only the vaguest idea of what he would expect from me tonight, but I was suddenly feeling small and afraid and if what I thought would happen did happen... well, he wouldn't fit, surely, he'd tear me open.

Seeing where my attention was, he grinned, and kept the box low as he opened it. Inside was a pair of earrings, gold drop earrings with a red crystal hanging from each one.

"Rubies," he said, before I could speak. "They'll go wonderfully with this costume. Let me put them in for you."

"Really, I don't need—"

"Stand still, girl."

He tilted my head to the side and pushed one of the earrings through the tiny hole in my lobe. Christine and I had gotten our ears pierced together when we were thirteen, bit since I could not afford much jewellery I rarely wore earrings and the holes had started to close. I clenched my teeth as he did the other one, and then stepped back from me with a grin.

"There," he said. "Now you look stunning."

"Thank you, Comte de Chagny." I managed. "You are very kind."

He reached out for my hand and bowed, kissing the back of it.

"The pleasure is all mine," he said, his eyes going to my breasts again as he raised his head. "I will see you after the performance. Wear something that befits you."

He would be happier if I just wore this. I thought bitterly as he nodded to the other giggling girls and Lycette closed the door.

"Well, well, Meg Giry," she exclaimed in mock reproach. "And here we were thinking that you were the *good* one. An evening with a Comte, you are so lucky! And not the first one by the look of you—you're as red as that rose in your hair! It's on the wrong side, by the way, did you know? So have you and he...?" I left the question unanswered and her eyes widened. "Oh my God! You *have*! Why is it that you and Christine end up with the wealthiest men in Paris licking from your very fingertips? Or from elsewhere, eh?"

She giggled and I felt myself blushing yet again. I wished they would just shut up.

"I bet he's *amazing*," Giselle said as I moved back to where my rack of costumes was. "My Thenier, the first time we did it, he didn't even hurt me because he was so *tiny*. I was glad of that, first time, but now..." She pulled a face. "Well... he can't really do *much* with it, if you know what I mean."

Thenier was a dancer, I remembered, a small, slim man who was always polite and shy. He was the only man I had ever met who seemed to be shy. I wondered how he would feel if he knew his... manliness was being discussed like this. How would I feel when the Comte de Chagny boasted with his friends about his conquest of me?

"Hurt?" Aimeé, the youngest of our group, asked. "Does it hurt, the first time?"

"Yes," Giselle said firmly. "It hurts. And the bigger your man, the more it hurts." Aimeé looked completely blank and Giselle giggled. "But after the pain comes the *pleasure* and I think our Mademoiselle Giry has been having quite a lot of that and not telling us, the naughty girl."

She was still giggling when my legs buckled. One moment I was standing upright, red inside and out with shame, and the next I was on the floor, and the girls were twittering around me.

"Meg?"

"She's fainted!"

"Her corset must be too tight, get it off her!"

"I'm fine!" I cried, batting away their concerned hands. "I just... lost my balance for a second, I didn't faint, I'm fine."

"You've gone terribly white," Aimeé told me as I got to my feet shakily. "Do you want some water?"

"I want some air," I said. "I just need to get out of *here* for a bit."

There was another knock on the door just as I reached it and I yanked it open to see a plump stagehand standing outside with a pipe between his teeth and a hand over his eyes.

"Curtain up in ten minutes!" He shouted. "That means beginners on stage in five! If you're not dressed yet then you should be!"

"Thank you, George," I said, slipping past him. "We'll all be ready."

Five minutes. I raced along the crowded corridor and knocked at the dressing room I wanted.

THE ANGEL'S SHADOW

"Christine?"

Christine opened the door, saw me, and pulled me into a tight hug. She was wearing her Aminta costume, a peach-coloured dress that fell to her shins in ruffles and flounces, decorated with black ribbon and lace. She looked so beautiful.

"Dear Meg," she murmured. "Come in. Come in."

"I know we don't have long," I said as she closed the door behind me. I just wanted to wish you… well, luck, I suppose."

Christine walked slowly over to the vanity table, and picked up a red rose with a black silk ribbon tied around the stem.

"I don't think I'm doing the right thing, Meg," she admitted quietly, fingering the ribbon. "But I'm doing the only thing I can do."

"I understand," I told her. "I suppose it's not luck you need tonight, but strength. To do what must be done."

"Oh, Meg…." She bit her lip, and I went to her and put my arms around her again, hoping she would take strength from my embrace, knowing it was all I could give.

"Everything is going to change tonight," she said, her own arms tight around me. "I only pray it will be for the better."

There was brief rap on the door and George called through the wood:

"It's time, Mademoiselle Daaé."

"Oh," we broke apart, and Christine smoothed her curls and gave me a watery smile. "Do I look ready to play the coquette?"

"Just about," I replied. "Don't forget your flower." I took the fabric rose from the vanity table and slid it into her hair near her left ear. "There. Perfect."

We left the dressing room together as George was bellowing down the corridor:

"Act One beginners to the stage, please! Act One beginners to the stage!"

Christine gave my hand a last squeeze.

"I'll see you during the interval," she smiled. "Good luck."

I nodded, and we went our separate ways, she to the stage left wings and I to stage right. I had to excuse my way past three *gendarmes* before I could reach my place beside Piangi, who smiled at me.

"You are looking very pretty, Mademoiselle Giry," he said, and I gave a weak smile in return.

"Thank you, Signor."

The red and black theme of my prostitute costume was continued throughout the set, the backdrop made of red and black stripes. There was a scarlet 'tent' upstage right, meant to be Don Juan's bedchamber, the curtains surrounding it open to show where Piangi and I sat on a bed that was nothing more than wooden crates pushed together and covered in

291

sheets and pillows. A real fire, contained in a round grate, stood centre stage, and to stage left was a long table and benches, set for a feast. The music started, the curtain rose, and the opera began.

From where I sat I could see Box Five was occupied; the two de Chagny brothers sat there, with a *gendarme* behind them holding a rifle. I let my eyes scan along the Boxes, but all had their curtains open and all were occupied. I could see the managers in Box Eight, champagne in hand, also accompanied by an armed man. The faces I saw as my gaze darted across the auditorium did not look impressed by this new opera. I wasn't sure whether the look of outright disgust on one elderly woman's face was caused by the music or the lyrics, but it seemed that Erik had been mistaken when he had claimed *Don Juan Triumphant* would take Paris by storm. Where *was* he?

Piangi ran his hands over my bodice in a display of lust, then let me go as I danced away from him, skirts flying. He threw a bag of 'gold' to me, and I pirouetted with it before racing off into the wings, passing an anxious-looking Christine.

There was no time to offer her further comfort. I had less than six minutes to change my costume and get around to the other side of the stage. I ran in my high heels down the now-deserted corridor, banging into the empty dressing room and rushing over to my costumes. The first thing I did was yank the ruby earrings out. I may have to wear them for my *rendezvous* with the Comte tonight, but after that I would never wear them again. I would sell them, I decided as I ripped the prostitute costume off, they were surely worth a lot of money.

My petticoat came next, then my heels. I slipped on my breeches, reflecting that this was a kind of double bluff on Erik's part and wondering whether it was intentional. Normally, a 'breeches role' was a woman playing the part of a boy. I was a woman playing a woman pretending to be a boy. I pulled on my shirt, shuffled into black, flat shoes and undid the chignon in my hair, removing the roses and tying the blonde tresses away from my face with a black silk ribbon. I picked up the cummerbund that wrapped around my waist, and paused for just a second before picking up my silver cross.

I fastened the chain as I returned to the stage, and stood next to my mother in the stage left wings, tying the cummerbund and looking onto the stage. I had timed my costume change well; Christine and Piangi were still singing *Point of No Return*. Christine was just embarking on the second verse, leaning against the table. Piangi sat at the opposite end, cloaked and hooded by the long black robe, his features completely invisible. All that could be seen of him were his hands, which suddenly gripped my full attention. Those were not the hands that had been around my waist less than ten minutes ago; they were pale, with long musician's fingers. On the little finger of his right hand was a gold ring with a single black stone.

THE ANGEL'S SHADOW

"My God," I whispered, almost to myself. "That's Erik."

Mother nodded, her lips pressed together.

"Where's Piangi?"

"I don't know."

Mother held one hand against her bodice as though she was finding it difficult to breathe, and her other hand took mine in a tight grip. I wondered if Christine knew that she was once again singing to her Angel of Music, that it was an imposter whose hands, which trembled like dry leaves, she now took in her own. She stretched Erik's arms out, then leaned close to him and pressed her left cheek against the hooded face. I saw the very moment she realised that it was Erik under the robe. She gave a start, almost a scream:

"No!"

Christine tried to run into the wings where Mother and I were standing, and my instinct was to rush to her, to protect her, but Mother held me back.

Erik grabbed Christine by the wrist with a growl, pulling her around to face him as he backed towards centre-stage, and remarkably, they both kept singing. As she reached the last note, Christine grabbed the hood of the robe and threw it back to reveal the masked man underneath. All around the auditorium, guns cocked. A *gendarme* tried to shoulder me aside, rifle pointed at Erik, but I did my best to stay in his way. In the opposite wings, I could see more *gendarmes* with their weapons trained on the Phantom, and Raoul pointing a pistol. When had he left Box Five? It must have been while I was getting changed. Erik turned slowly on the spot, looking at all the armed men, weighing up his chances. As he faced my side of the stage, his eyes caught mine.

"Run," I mouthed at him soundlessly. *"Go. Now. Run."*

He made no acknowledgement of my plea, and turned back to Christine.

CHAPTER FORTY TWO

My heart was in my mouth as I stared from the wings at Erik and Christine. I could only see the back of her head, and his blue-green eyes were blazing into her.

"Stay with me," he said suddenly, his voice carrying over the music that Reyer was still conducting. Whatever happened, it seemed, the show went on. "Free me from my solitude, from this lifetime alone. Tell me that you want *me* with you, forever by your side... Wherever you go, allow me to follow!"

He pulled the black-stoned ring from his finger and seized Christine's left hand. She struggled to break free, but he forced the ring onto her left ring-finger, a mockery of an engagement ring... a wedding ring.

"Christine!" The show was over now, he was pouring out his heart, his real, raw emotions, in front of the aristocracy of Paris, the scum of the Opera House, and her fiancé. The word ended in a shriek, a bellow of rage as Christine reached up with both hands and ripped the mask and wig from Erik's head. I couldn't help the scream that tore from my throat as I saw Erik's true face for the first time. Of all the descriptions I had heard, Christine's seemed the most accurate. The right side of his face was discoloured, a yellowish tinge to it like paper that had started to age. It was rough and pitted, part of what looked like brain-tissue exposed. His upper lip was bloated and misshapen, strange, scar-like flesh creeping across his cheek towards his ear.

In all my life, I had never seen anything so *hideous*. It looked as though he had been burned by fire or acid, but this was no accident, this was how God had made him. No wonder Erik was ashamed of his face and wanted to keep it hidden, it must have caused him years of abuse. I was afraid of him. I forgot the man who had saved my virtue, my life, and saw only the *monster* that his face and his rage made him.

I had only a second to take in his extraordinary appearance before he

THE ANGEL'S SHADOW

seized Christine's wrist again, dragging her to the edge of the stage and leaping into the orchestra pit. A gun fired, and I heard the Vicomte's desperate cry:

"Don't shoot! You'll hit Christine, don't shoot!"

We all raced onto the stage, the *gendarmes* aiming their weapons into the pit, where we could hear commotion and scuffling. The audience was staring around, talking, shouting, the auditorium filled with the sounds of complete confusion. They seemed unsure whether what had happened in front of them was a part of the opera or not. Mother and I were among all the others, looking wildly into the pit for clues, and I saw Reyer, dazed, holding a handkerchief against his bleeding nose. I backed up, worried about being knocked right into the pit by the scrum that was forming onstage, and more *gendarmes* rushed past me, shoving me even further back. I found myself funnelled towards the tent where I had started the opera, the scarlet curtains now closed. My legs hit the crates that made up Don Juan's bed and I tripped, getting caught in the red fabric and finding it tumbling down on top of me. I struggled out from under it and found myself staring into a white face, mouth open under a dark beard, eyes bulging. It was Ulbaldo Piangi, a Punjab lasso tight around his neck.

I screamed again, truly horrified, and heard someone else screaming as well. Hands pulled me to my feet and turned me around, and I found myself pressing my face into my mother's shoulder, her arms tight around me. I could hear Carlotta behind me, where she was surely leaning over her husband. I wished I had thought to remove the Punjab lasso from the tenor's throat so that Carlotta didn't have to see him like this, as her words cut like broken glass through me.

"*Ulbaldo! Il mio amore, il mio cuore, la mia vita!*"

Someone grabbed me from behind and wrenched me away from Mother. It was Raoul, still holding the pistol.

"Where has he taken her?!" He demanded, one hand still on my shoulder.

"I can show you, Monsieur," Mother replied. "But you must keep your hand at the level of your eyes!"

"Why?" The Vicomte looked anxious and flustered.

"The Punjab lasso, Monsieur! If that goes around your throat, you're a dead man! Just like poor Piangi!"

"Like this, Vicomte!" I seized his hand and held it up beside his face, where he would be able to use it to escape the lasso if Erik threw it over him. "Look, I'll go with you!"

He had to get to Erik and Christine as quickly as possible; Erik had been baring his very soul to her, and she had committed the ultimate act of betrayal by exposing his deformity to half of Paris. *Why* had she done it? *What* had been going through her head? *What* would he do to punish her?

"No, Meg, no!" Mother looked horrified. "You must stay here! Come with me, Monsieur!"

I could hear the two managers yelling around the auditorium, shouting for the stagehands to bring the curtain in, and the huge red velvet swept across the stage, blocking us from an increasingly hysterical audience. People were pushing past me, trying to follow Mother and Raoul, but I threw out my arms to stop them.

"No!" I cried. "Stop!"

"Why?!" A stagehand snarled. "We all know she's in cohorts with the Phantom!"

"That's not true!" I yelled back, the lie tripping so easily off my tongue that I nearly believed it myself.

Carlotta was still kneeling over the body of her husband, sobbing and apparently ignored by the men and women who were now bent on revenge, but even as I watched, someone wrapped a shawl around her shoulders and someone else covered the corpse. Infected by a sort of unstoppable mob mentality, people were lifting the heavy stage curtain and dropping into the orchestra pit to follow the Phantom's route. I silently wished them bad luck and backed into the wings. I had an advantage, of course. I knew some of the entrances to the Phantom's lair, some ways of reaching it. Could I get there before the mob did? Could I warn Erik of the bloodthirsty crowd barrelling towards him? Did he even *care*?

The backstage corridors of the opera house were still relatively empty, the panic not having spread just yet. I fiddled with the silver cross around my neck, trying to think what the best thing to do would be, and a hand came down heavily on my wrist. I twisted with a gasp, to see the Comte de Chagny standing there, a deep frown furrowing his brow.

"I don't think so, Mademoiselle Giry." He said. "We can't have you skulking off when you're the one with the answers to all the secrets, can we?"

"Comte?" I asked, and he shook his head, his grip tightening.

"Now you listen to me, you little *chit*," he said, giving me a shake. "You might think I'm a rat, and you're right, but I *love* my brother. I'm not about to let any man, Phantom or not, take his life in a squabble over an *opera singer*!" He pushed me against the wall, forcing his leg between mine, pinning me there, but this time there was no sexual intention, he was asserting his dominance. "I *know* that you're aware of what's been going on here. *You* know where his lair is and how to get there, don't you? *Don't you?!*"

He shook me again, and I could do nothing but gasp. He backed off a step and tugged on my wrist to make me move.

"Come with me!"

"Where are you taking me?!" I cried, struggling to free myself from his

THE ANGEL'S SHADOW

grip.

"Where do you think, you idiotic child?!" He snarled, dragging me after him. "Do you have *any* idea how much influence the de Changys have? The chief of the *gendarmes* himself is here tonight, and you are going to tell him everything you know right now!"

"No!" I cried, almost frantic. "You *promised* you wouldn't say anything, Comte! They'll lock us up, they'll kill Mother! You said that if I slept with you, you'd keep our secret! And I will, tonight, I swear!"

"You selfish little brat!" He swung me around to face him without letting go of my wrist and slapped me hard across the cheek with his free hand. "That was before my brother ran headfirst into a trap!"

"I'll take you to the Phantom!" I cried, trying to ignore the red-hot sting that his palm had inflicted. "I'll show you the way! You can stop Raoul from getting hurt if you'll just listen to me!"

Erik had failed me, I realised. I had believed that he would save me from this man, just as he had saved me a year ago on the streets of Paris, but here Philippe de Chagny was, furious and unrelenting. Erik must even now be dragging Christine down to his home, ready to punish her for that ghastly act of betrayal on the stage, and there was nothing I could do to stop him. I could not save Christine, and I could not save Erik from the mob that had already begun the hunt for him. I could only save myself.

"Speak." The Comte said in clipped tones.

"Your pardon, Monsieur," I whispered. "Follow me; I will take you to him."

I led him to Christine's dressing room with my heart pounding in my breast.

"There is a secret passageway behind the mirror," I said.

"Open it," the Comte ordered and pulled a revolver from his pocket. "And no tricks, Giry, or I will put a bullet in your spine. It may not kill you, but it would certainly mean that you would never dance again. Do you understand?"

"I understand," I replied and reached up, feeling around the frame for the switch, and the glass shuddered as the catch released.

"Keep the gun up near your face so that if a lasso gets thrown over your head you can prevent it tightening. It isn't to shoot with, Monsieur; it's to protect your neck."

He nodded, and I almost immediately wished I hadn't given him the information. True, I didn't want the gun pointing in my direction, but warning him against Erik's signature weapon was a mistake. I'd quite like to see this arrogant Comte with his head in a noose.

I pushed the mirror into its frame, turned to Christine's vanity table and picked up a candle in a heavy silver holder before looking to Philippe, who gestured at me with the weapon.

297

"After you, Mademoiselle," he was almost sneering. I went forward into the passageway, listening to the sound of water and the squeak of rats.

"Keep your pistol at the level of your eyes," I repeated, and tried desperately to make my brain stop jabbering away to itself in panic and *think*.

Erik would have taken Christine to his home, and Mother would have shown Raoul the quickest way to get there. I didn't want to see either Raoul or Christine hurt by Erik, but neither did I want to see Erik get arrested. The mob who had followed the Phantom into the orchestra pit were probably tearing the place apart in their search for hidden entrances; I hadn't known there was one there. Could I intercept them once they gained access to the catacombs, maybe head them off? And aside from all that, what in the name of the devil was I going to do about the Comte de Chagny? He would probably try to shoot Erik if he got close.

The candlelight bounced back from the damp walls, green with some kind of fungus, and I saw the tail of a rat as it scuttled away into the receding shadows. Passages branched off to my right and left, and the weeks since I had been here seemed an awfully long time. And then, as I heard de Chagny's footsteps on the damp stone behind me, I knew what I had to do. I went cold all over, goose bumps standing out on my skin, and I felt my heart turn to ice.

"Why have you stopped?" He snapped. "What are you waiting for? Are you going to tell me you've forgotten your way?"

"No, Monsieur," I said tonelessly. "I know the way."

I had only travelled this route once, and yet as soon as that right-hand passageway came into the circle of candlelight, it was as if my feet took over, like remembering the dance steps of a ballet I had seen dozens of times. My mind, begging me to stop and ask forgiveness, to turn back, did not need to be a part of this. My body, wanting to maintain life, liberty and innocence, had taken over.

I ignored both of the passages and went down the flight of stairs to the next level, listening to the footsteps behind me, the slightly hoarse breathing. The Comte de Chagny smoked too much, as my dear father had. Even in the leather shoes, my own steps were silent.

I took the second right turning of this new corridor went down another staircase, onto a third that split into three different directions, down the right-hand set and turned left at the bottom.

"We are almost there, Comte," I said as I approached the second right turning, pausing at its opening. My voice sounded hollow and lifeless, as if I were a doll with the power of human speech. "Keep your hand at the level of your eyes."

I turned into the passage and squeezed my own eyes shut, praying desperately to the God that I no longer knew whether or not to believe in,

THE ANGEL'S SHADOW

that my memory did not play me false.

I heard the Comte enter the passage behind me and blew out the candle, dropping the heavy stick to the ground with a clatter. The man swore vilely as the only source of light in these dark, desperate tunnels was extinguished, and I felt a rush like the high of too much alcohol fizz in my blood. All that money, power and charm, beauty and promises, and he hadn't thought to bring a light of his own!

I opened my eyes, already adjusted to the new darkness, and started to run, my footfalls coming loud as my feet fell heavily.

"Stop!" de Changy bellowed after me. "Come back here, Giry, or I swear to God I'll shoot you!"

I kept going, counting my steps, praying again and again that I had got it right. The gun fired, a brief spark in the darkness, but the bullet did not find its target, another three steps and I jumped, a huge, graceful leap honed from years of ballet practice, carrying myself several feet into the air and three feet forward.

Please! Let me have gotten it right!

"Stop you little bitch!" He howled.

"I'm here, Comte!" I screamed back at him as I landed with as much grace as I could manage. "Here for the catching!"

Please let me be right!

He swore again, the gun fired for a second time, and I heard him running along the corridor towards me, then a scuffle, a gasp, a *scream* as the stone that concealed the entrance to the Phantom's torture chamber opened under the Comte's feet, and he fell through it. I heard a dull thud and my racing heart leapt into my throat.

I had remembered it correctly, jumping over the trapdoor. I had fallen through that very one… but I had survived the fall by managing to grip onto the edge of the hole as the floor vanished from under my feet. Those few seconds, that brief moment that had taken approximately five feet and most of the momentum from my fall, was the only reason I had reached the floor with nothing more than bruised bones. Some part of me had remembered the route I had taken, how many steps it had been before the floor disappeared, presumably so I would not make the same mistake again. De Chagny might well survive the fall, as I had done, but then he was Erik's to deal with, as he had promised me.

I couldn't stop shaking. My whole body was trembling uncontrollably, as if Erik had once again made me swallow the drug that had paralysed me in order to punish Christine. At some point, the black silk ribbon had fallen from my hair and it was trailing around my face like the threads of a spider's web. I didn't want to imagine what the Comte might look like if he was lying dead on the torture chamber floor. I had to get out of here without meeting the same fate. In the dark. Alone.

299

I pressed my right hand against the damp wall, moving step by step, testing my weight before moving. When I felt the stone that rocked beneath me, I took several steps back, ran and jumped over it, pretending that I was back on the stage and going through a routine. Not that I had just murdered a man.

I walked, trying to ignore the terrible buzzing in my head, trying to see through the darkness, forgetting my way and how to find the route back to my own world. I don't know how long it was before I saw flickering light ahead of me and started to hear footsteps and chatter. Men and women, voices I recognised; I increased my pace and found myself looking down the barrel of a rifle.

"Identify yourself!" A man in *gendarmes* uniform ordered.

Did they seriously believe the Phantom of the Opera would come strolling into their midst? These people were fools! God, I had to stop this wretched shaking...

"Don't shoot!" I cried, raising both my hands. "It's Marguerite Giry! Don't shoot!"

CHAPTER FORTY THREE

"What are you doing down here?" The *gendarme* demanded.

"I was with all of you!" I insisted, my eyes scanning the group of people. "I took a wrong turn and lost you! I want to track down this murderer as much as the rest of you!"

The man grunted and the mob began to move again, continuing along the path they had chosen. I didn't know who was leading them, but slipped in towards the front of the group, close behind the armed men, and I felt the trembling in my limbs increase. The Opera Ghost was going to die tonight.

We moved through the catacombs as one, the darkness banished by the lit torches people were carrying. Many of them were armed too, and there were shouts of exacting revenge for the deaths of Piangi and Buquet, to pay the Phantom back for the spiteful tricks he had been playing. I didn't hear anyone expressing concern for Christine. What if Erik had harmed her, what if we were too late?

The *gendarmes* were calm and organised, sending groups with an armed man in each, off to investigate every one of the side tunnels and report back. It was a good thing too, for the catacombs were full of traps, from more trapdoors to places where the ceiling gave way. One man narrowly avoided being crushed by a counterweight falling from above, which looked as though it might have come from the old chandelier. These incidents quashed the cries of the mob to hurry through the passages; care was essential to reach the Phantom alive.

Time had become a meaningless muddle in my head, and I had no way of knowing whether it was minutes or hours before we reached an area I recognised. We had found the part of this underground kingdom that I had gone through when coming to tend Erik's wounds after his fight with the Vicomte. It was where a stone walkway channelled the water towards his home. We could see his 'house' ahead of us, blazing with the light from hundreds of candles, and silhouetted against it, the boat was coming across the water towards us.

"Hold your fire!" One of the *gendarmes* cried. "It's the Vicomte and Mademoiselle Daaé!"

I felt almost dizzy with relief as I realised he was right. Christine was looking dishevelled but unhurt, her dark curls untidy and her cheeks tear-stained. She was wearing the wedding dress I had seen on the mannequin in Erik's room, but I could not see a ring on her finger. Perhaps Raoul had reached her in time after all. Raoul himself was in a far worse condition than Christine. He was wet through, his jacket, waistcoat and cravat gone, and his shirt torn in several places. There was an angry red rope burn around his neck; apparently he had neglected to keep his hand at the level of his eyes...

They were both here, alive and safe... so where was Erik? I dropped off the end of the stone walkway and began to wade towards the portcullis, which was fully open.

A man called for me to stop, and I heard Christine call my name, but I ignored them and kept wading towards the jetty, hauling myself onto the damp wood and weaving my way around the blazing candelabras outside Erik's home.

The front door was wide open and once again light filled the place, both electric and flame. The fire was burning in the hearth but the room looked Spartan. The sofa and chairs were gone, the bookcase entirely stripped of its volumes, the walls bare of pictures. There was no Persian rug on the floor; instead, a wedding veil lay in a heap like a forgotten pile of blossom. Everything was gone, except the grand piano, and Erik's throne. In the throne, a human shape was covered by a black cloak.

"Erik?" I whispered, and reached out trembling hands to the covered figure. Would I find him dead when I pulled it off? Could I stand to see that hideous face again, dead or alive? Screwing up my remaining courage, I tugged the cloak from the chair. Underneath, there was no one. No corpse, no living man, just a white half-mask on the throne's black leather seat. I lifted it as the *gendarmes* came charging in, and held it up for them to see.

"He's not here," I told them, voice steady. "He's gone."

They didn't believe me; of course they didn't, I wouldn't have believed me if our roles had been reversed. The man in charge, who might well be the chief that Philippe de Chagny had threatened me with, split his men into groups again and dispatched them to search the Phantom's home. The pantry and kitchen were as stripped as the drawing room, as was the Louis-Philippe room, which had been designed with Christine in mind. Erik's bedroom was the most disturbing of the lot. Again, books, ornaments and sheet music were gone, and the curtain that had concealed the alcove was pulled away. The waxwork that so resembled Christine was lying on its back on the floor, divested of its clothing, the dark curly wig of hair fanned out

THE ANGEL'S SHADOW

behind its head. On Erik's phoenix-shaped bed, Christine's *Don Juan* costume lay, and I saw that the seams had been ripped. Erik must have torn it directly from her body. The thought made me shiver, and my fingers tightened around the edges of the mask I was still holding as I kept finding my eyes drawn again and again to the organ, and the invisible door beside it, behind which was the torture chamber.

A bell rang somewhere, one of Erik's alarms, startling me so much that I gasped aloud. I had to get out of this room before the torture chamber was discovered; surely my own guilt would give me away if I saw the body of the Comte de Chagny... if he *was* a body.

I returned to the drawing room on shaking legs and perched on the arm of Erik's throne-like chair, gazing around the stripped room. Everything, it seemed, that could have been moved from the underground home, had been. The grand piano must have been too bulky to get out, and the throne... the throne was bolted to the floor. I had never noticed that before. I stared at the leather seat next to me, the wooden frame, my gaze flicking around the base of it.

I knew where Erik was. It was a crazy notion, but he was a master of trapdoors and secret hiding places.

There was noise, shouts and footsteps coming from the passageway behind the bookcase, and after a moment I heard the sounds of people ramming themselves against the concealed door. A few moments more, and the combined weight of the men behind it forced the bookcase door open, and they spilled in, all anger and makeshift weapons and raised voices. More of the *gendarmes* were among them, and there too, was Mother, her face flushed.

"Dearest!" She rushed to me, gathering me into her arms. "Oh, Meg, what are you doing down here?"

I clutched at her, pressing my cheek to hers, and whispered Erik's secret in her ear. She nodded, eyes wide, and sat me down in the throne-like chair, gently taking the mask from me. My heart thudded in my ears, so loud that it deafened me to the voices of the *gendarmes* and other men around me. Mother stood beside the chair, her arm around my shoulders, and there we stayed for as long as we could, while the hive of officers buzzed around us, eventually ushering us out of the underground home and back into the Opera House proper. We had to allow an armed *gendarme* to show us the way, a route that had been marked with string and came out in the orchestra pit. It was far longer than the path we could have taken alone, but the last thing we wanted was people suspecting that we knew more than the official force.

Finding information about what had happened proved immensely difficult, and Mother and I went from rumour to rumour, grasping for the grains of truth which linked them. Christine and Raoul had been shut up in the manager's office and were being interrogated by the *gendarmes*, but details of their story were mixed and unreliable. No-one seemed to know why Christine was wearing a wedding dress, or how Raoul had been wounded. Some claimed he had killed the Opera Ghost, others said the Ghost had simply disappeared, but no one knew for certain.

What would happen when they found Philippe de Chagny?

Mother and I went back to the dressing room, where I pulled on my own clothes and slipped the ruby earrings into the pocket of my skirt, and then went up to her chambers. She heated some soup over the fire and I toyed with the spoon.

"Eat it," Mother ordered. "We can't do anything until the *gendarmes* leave, so we will eat and we will rest."

I swallowed the soup down, not tasting it, my mind full of worry, and searching for a distraction, I found myself asking a completely irrelevant question.

"What does 'chit' mean?"

Mother frowned. "In what context?"

"As a derogatory term. 'You stupid little chit'."

"It's... an English word, it means... I think it means a disrespectful or arrogant young woman... who's been calling you a chit, Meg?"

"Erik," I said. "Mother... what if he *is* captured?"

She leaned across the table between us and ran her thumb over the mark left by Philippe de Chagny's slap on my cheek.

"If that happens," she murmured. "Then no one will be able to say that you were anywhere near him."

I understood that she wanted to protect me, that it was the reason she had told me to stay behind while she told Raoul how to reach the Phantom, but I still could not tell her the real reason I had been in the catacombs.

Time crawled by, and I slept fitfully, fully dressed, in Mother's bed. The small clock on the mantelpiece was chiming three when she lit a lantern, I put Erik's mask in a canvas bag and slung it over my shoulder, and we moved together through the clothes hanging in her wardrobe and into the secret passageway beyond. By the time we reached the lake, we could see the string that the *gendarmes* were using to map the tunnels, as if a giant spider had begun to build a web. Mother swore under her breath, then carefully guided me down a tunnel I had never used before, that went around the lake. It took a painstakingly long time, but eventually we reached Erik's front door. I was afraid that there would still be an officer there guarding the place, but the underground realm was deserted; the only sound the water lapping against the jetty. We went into the house, using only the lantern to penetrate the darkness of the drawing room.

Together, we investigated the throne, and found that it took two actions to release the mechanism, clearly designed to be done by one person seated in the chair, rather than two fumbling around it. I had sat here, even slept in this very spot, and had no idea that the chair had a false back and seat. When the seat moved aside, we found another entrance beneath a square hole in the floor.

"Erik?" Mother called down, but there was no answer, save a slight echo. She lowered the lantern into the hole.

"Is it far?" I asked, and she shook her head.

"Not really... eight, maybe ten feet. But I can't see any rungs or anything; there's no way back up."

"He might not still be down here," I ventured, not relishing the idea of dropping yet another level below ground.

"If he were up here, we would know," Mother raised her eyebrows. "One of us would have a Punjab lasso around her neck."

I swallowed hard.

"All right," I said, nodding. "I'll go first, and then you can lower the lantern and join me."

I climbed onto the framework of the chair, turned onto my stomach and lowered myself until I was holding on with my fingertips. The remaining drop was not far, and I landed with ease. Mother lowered the lantern to me by tying one end of her shawl to the handle, and then dropped down herself, landing with the grace of the prima ballerina she had once been.

The passageway we found ourselves in sloped sharply downwards and was wide enough for the two of us to walk side by side, but we could only walk in one direction; a wall of solid brick stood at our backs. We followed the passage with slow, cautious steps, wary of traps. It was clear by the water dripping from the ceiling and running down the increasingly green and slime-covered walls, that our path had taken us out from under Erik's home, that we were now beneath the lake. I breathed slowly, trying not to imagine the weight of all that water above my head.

The brickwork here seemed older, but maybe that was a result of the damp in the air. It was smelly, cheerless, and the chill bit through my layers of clothing and seemed to sink to my bones. Every sound echoed, and the darkness was so deep that the lantern light could barely penetrate more than a few feet ahead of us.

"Stay where you are!" The golden voice barked through the blackness and something primal made both Mother and I freeze. There was no sound of footsteps, but after a moment, the light reflected in a pair of eyes as it would a cat's, one blue and one green. A moment more, and the tall outline was visible, Mother's lantern light reflecting off the barrel of a revolver. The sight made my heart give a horrible lurch in my chest.

"Erik!" I gasped, instinctively raising both my hands to demonstrate that I was no threat.

"Erik..." Mother's voice was calm and quiet, as if she were a lion tamer

305

facing a beast. "It is just Meg and I, we're alone. The *gendarmes* have left for tonight, the threat is temporarily past. Put down the gun."

She took a step forward, more of the light illuminating him, and Erik's arm moved as he lifted the revolver slightly higher, a sharp click echoing off the damp walls as he thumbed off the safety catch.

"Erik…" Mother sounded alarmed.

"You!" He glared at me. "You have my mask?"

"Y-Yes, Monsieur…" I stammered, aware of the tension in the atmosphere around the three of us.

"Bring it to me," he ordered, and I saw that he was trembling.

"Put down the gun," I returned without thinking, and his monstrous face split into a grin. He looked like a demon, with his deformity exposed and his eyes glowing like stars in the dark. Why had I ever wanted to see this face, with thin, wispy hair floating around it? He was in the same suit I had seen him in earlier that evening, but his white bowtie was undone, shirt collar open, and jacket missing. I couldn't help thinking, in a detached sort of way, that he must be cold down here; the damp air was bleeding through my layers of clothing. His glowing eyes were red-rimmed, and I realised with a shock that he had been crying.

I took the mask from my bag and put the bag on the floor in case Erik might still believe I had a weapon. I approached him slowly, holding the mask out at arm's length, and he snatched it from me as soon as I was close enough. He lowered the gun and put the mask over his face, and the moment he did so, his entire demeanour changed. He took a deep breath, eyes closing, his spine straightened, his trembling stopped, and when he exhaled, opening his eyes again it was as though another man stood there, as if concealing his deformity also hid the ugly, frightened part of his soul.

"Ladies," he said quietly. "I ask your forgiveness for the trick. The gun isn't loaded. Now that the law has found its way into my realm, I cannot be too careful. I have no doubt that there are many who would like to witness my appointment with the guillotine."

I shuddered, and Mother stepped to my side.

"The *gendarmes* are gone for now," she said, and I could tell from her tone that she was angry. "But they will be back tomorrow… well, when it's light. I was going to try and protect you, Erik, but after that display, after threatening my daughter *again*, I have half a mind to turn you over to them!"

Erik's eyes flashed and he looked from her face to mine.

"Not with the Comte de Chagny after all?" He enquired, and I felt my stomach twist. Surely he wouldn't tell Mother of the bargain I had made?

"The Comte went looking for you and his brother after you abducted Christine from the stage," I replied. "I imagine he has more to think about tonight than a supper appointment he was unable to keep."

THE ANGEL'S SHADOW

He raised his eyebrow, but said nothing more, and I blessed Mother for not asking for further information. She just sighed, unwrapped her shawl from around her shoulders, and threw it to Erik.

"Put that on and let's get out of here. Before you catch your death."

He pocketed the empty gun without a word and slung the shawl over his shirtsleeves, somehow making it look like a cape worn by a dark prince.

"Follow me," was all he said before turning on his heel and striding off into the dark, leaving us to hurry after him.

"Welcome to the Communist's Road," he said as we caught up. "Created during the Franco-Prussian war, one of many such passages under Paris, to provide secret routes through the city."

"These tunnels go beneath the whole of Paris?" I asked.

"Not anymore," came his grim reply. "But they are good enough to hide me like a rat while the *gendarmes* conduct their search."

"What happened?" I said bluntly. "What happened between you, and the Vicomte, and Christine?"

He looked down at me, his pace slowing slightly.

"Christine didn't tell you?"

"The *gendarmes* wouldn't let me see her."

"The tale can wait," Mother said. "Until we are away from these dark tunnels, back in my chambers and warm. Erik needs food and sleep."

His head turned from me to her.

"You would offer me hospitality, even now?"

"Claude would call me a fool," she answered. "But yes, I would."

CHAPTER FORTY FOUR

I knew I was dreaming the moment I recognised the room, but the knowledge was not a comfort. It was long, white, and lined with beds. The one meant for me did not have huge leather belts to hold me down, but chains. The three doctors in their white coats stood waiting for me, expressionless, and terror stole the breath from my lungs.

"Don't," I whispered. "Please, I'm sorry, I'll be good!"

There was no answer. Someone seized my upper right arm, someone else my left, and I turned my head desperately to see whether it was my Papa or Erik who was marching me towards my doom. It was neither. Instead, a tall man in gendarmes uniform held me in a grip like iron on either side. They forced me forward to the bed where two of the white-coated doctors proceeded to chain me down.

There was another man watching me from the foot of the bed; the Comte Philippe de Chagny, standing upright in spite of the fact that his neck was broken in two places so that his head lolled sideways onto his right shoulder.

"It's for your own good, Little Meg," he sneered. "You always knew this was going to happen."

I woke, silent and stiff, my body rigid, heart pounding, teeth clenched together. It was a long second before I realised the burning in my lungs was because I was holding my breath, before I remembered where I was and why. I exhaled quietly, anxious not to disturb Mother, in the double bed beside me. We were sharing her bed, as we had done when she watched over me after the chandelier crash. She wanted me close, protected, and I knew she was afraid for all of us. She was lying on her side with her back to me, and her soft, steady breathing confirmed that I had not woken her. Everything had changed; even if Christine was returned, unharmed and in the company of her fiancé, there was no denying the existence of the Opera Ghost now. Ulbaldo Piangi was dead, and it was doubtless who was

THE ANGEL'S SHADOW

responsible. I slipped from the bed and wrapped a huge, pale shawl around my shoulders. It had been given to Mother when she was pregnant with me, and it felt familiar and safe.

The Opera Ghost himself lay under a thick blanket on the chaise longue in the next room. His waistcoat, bowtie and trousers were folded next to chaise along with his boots, but he was still wearing the white shirt. In the faint, pre-dawn light that came through the small window, I could see his face was almost as pale as the mask he still wore, his chest rising and falling rapidly as he breathed. He had found a wig from somewhere, which was dark and a little longer than I was used to seeing on him, but he had not found a change of clothes. I was just wondering whether he was dreaming, when his eyes opened, his gaze focusing on me with the instant alertness of someone used to defending himself.

"Good morning, Meg," he said without expression.

"Why did you kill Piangi?" I asked, pulling the shawl tightly around my shoulders.

"He was in my way," was the reply.

I shook my head, disgusted.

"He was *in your way*?! He had a family, Erik, people who loved him! He was no threat to you, he did nothing wrong, and you *killed* him just to take his place in that *sham* of an opera."

I kept my voice to a whisper, not wishing to wake Mother in the bedroom, but the injustice, the senselessness of Piangi's death enraged me. Anything to avoid thinking about the Comte de Chagny.

"Do I take it, then, that you disagree with your mother's choice?" There was no anger in his tone, just weariness and a mild curiosity.

"You didn't kill Raoul..." I ran a hand through my tangled hair and turned to the fireplace and the basket of kindling beside it.

"I *wanted* to," his words were quiet, and intense. "I had the boy in my power... although I strongly suspect that he did not find his way into my home without assistance..."

I looked back at him to see him tilt his head in a silent question.

"Not from me," I said. "Although I was terrified of what you were going to do with Christine after she... exposed you like that. I thought... you were going to kill her, just as you killed Piangi."

"Never," he replied quietly. "I would never kill Christine Daaé. I love her."

"What happened, Erik?" I was almost begging him to tell me. "What happened after you left the stage?"

He was quiet for such a long time that I thought he was not going to share his story. I turned from him and knelt on the hearth to build the fire, laying the kindling and coal, when at last he spoke.

"I was... so angry." His voice was soft, and I didn't dare look around in

309

case he regretted his decision. "I dragged Christine down into the catacombs, raging at her the entire time. I was almost mad with fury, *how dare* she do that to me, betray me like that! I handed my heart to that selfish child and she—"

He took a deep breath, apparently composing himself, for when he spoke again, his voice was calmer.

"She resisted me with every step—of course she did, my Christine has developed a strong will since the fall of her Angel of Music. She didn't scream or entreat me to stop; she was as good as silent for the entire journey while I unleashed my poisonous words upon her. She lost her footing once, and I gathered her up in my arms with as much care as my anger would permit. I demanded answers from her, to know why my... *abhorrent* face had cursed me, caused me to be hounded and hated by everyone throughout my life. She did not reply. I rowed her across the lake and pulled her from the boat, into my home, into my bedroom. It was only then that I saw fear in her eyes.

'What are you doing?' She asked, as I revealed her wedding gown.

'What do you think, Christine?' I replied tersely. *'I have spent too much of my life in the dark, denied the joys that other men take for granted. I want a wife I can take for walks on Sundays, I want light and love and music. I can give you all that, Christine, and you can give it to me. You will be the happiest of women, and we will sing. Put on the dress. I had it made especially for you, and is it not fine? It is tailored to your measurements, the first of many considerations I have made for you. I offer you everything that any normal, whole human man can give a woman, and so much more. Our music, Christine, that so binds our souls...'*

She shook her head.

'My promise is already given.'

'Then consider it broken,' I snapped. *'You belong to me.'*

She glared at me, and I seized her by the shoulders.

'Must I force you?' I demanded. *'Will you begin our marriage with an act of violence? Will you do as I tell you, or must I do it for you?'*

I turned her and started to tear at the lacing of her costume, so forcefully that the seams began to rip. She clutched at the fabric.

'Stop!' She cried. *'I'll change! But... give me some privacy, Erik. I deserve that until we are married at least; you have always behaved like a gentleman in my presence before.'*

I ground my teeth and snatched the veil from the mannequin.

'You have ten minutes,' I told her, and left the room, slamming the door behind me. I started the drawing room fire, lit every candle I could see, and paced, twisting the veil in my fists in a fever of impatience. At last, she joined me.

'Are you divested of your barbarism now?' She demanded. *'Will you use me to slake your lust?'*

THE ANGEL'S SHADOW

I turned to her, and struggled to speak. She looked more beautiful than I had ever imagined a woman could look, Meg, standing before me in the wedding dress *I* had designed for her... my bride.

'*My face*,' I managed. '*Made me into a killer. There was nothing else that so-called society would let me become, but an assassin and a monster. It also ensured that I have never been able to enjoy those... pleasures of the flesh that all others are free to pursue. Ever since I was born... my mother never kissed me, Christine, never showed me a scrap of affection. She made her hatred and fear of me plain, and forced me to wear a mask, on pain of instant punishment...*'"

I put a match to the built fire, and stared at Erik in the light of the flames that leapt from the logs. He was looking at the fire himself, but suddenly his eyes met mine.

"Do not look at me like that!" He snapped. "She looked at me like that! I do not want *your* pity any more than I wanted hers!"

I looked away, back to the fire, hoping that I had not drawn him from his memories with my attention.

"And... what answer did she give?" I said to the flames. Erik made a soft sound that might have been a laugh.

"I forced the veil onto her head, thrust a bouquet of flowers into her hands, and she told me that she wasn't horrified by my face anymore. That it was my soul that was twisted out of shape. Perhaps she was right."

I could hear his fingers drumming on the chaise's cushion.

"I was ready to make Christine my wife, by God and law, and then the Vicomte came staggering into my home looking like a drowned rat! I have to admit I was delighted! Was there ever a more pathetic image of a white knight coming to save his distressed damsel?!"

He threw back his head and laughed, but there was no humour in it. He sounded more desperate than amused.

"Shh!" I hissed. "Someone will hear you! Tell me what you did to Raoul."

"I invited him in."

"Of course you did," I rolled my eyes. "Silly of me to ask."

"Little Giry. Sarcasm, it does not become you."

"Then I'll leave it to you. Please continue."

He glared at me.

"I invited in the boy, allowing him to see that Christine was quite unharmed before I threw my Punjab lasso around his neck and strung him up from the lighting hook in the wall! Picture it, Meg! There he is, with his hands all over my Christine, forgetting that he is up against one of the finest assassins in Persia! The next thing he knows, he has his back against the wall and a rope practically choking him, while I turned to Christine and made her an ultimatum."

"Ultimatum?" I repeated, my mouth dry.

311

"Oh yes. I told that she had to choose between us, Meg. Become my wife, or watch her Vicomte die at the end of a rope."

I stared at him, mouth hanging open, unable to believe what he was telling me.

"And she…"

"She cursed me, ripped the veil from her head and threw it at me, raged at me with a flaming passion I have never before seen… I had her exactly where I wanted her, in a situation where, whichever choice she made, she could not win. Even de Chagny acknowledged that fact… I watched her heart breaking, seeing her lover struggling to breathe, and my own monstrous heart gloried in it!

'*Do you submit to a life with me?!*' I demanded as I seized her delicate wrists in my powerful hands. "*Or watch your lover perish?!*'

She beseeched me to show mercy, invoked her fallen Angel, while I told her that it was too late for her prayers and pleading."

His mouth twisted in an agonised smile and his eyes shone as they began brimming with tears.

"'*You were my Angel of Music,*' she wept. '*You lied to me! And I gave you everything, without thought, without question, on pure faith!*'

Faith. She had such accusation in her eyes, and my heart was burning, twisting, *hurting*… I am dying, Meg. Dying of love. I… I had to hide it from her, my loneliness, my emptiness. I had found my way into my chair and she was on her knees before me in that *beautiful* gown, and I knew I had to make her mine.

'*You try my patience.*' I told her coldly. '*Make your choice.*'

I stood, dropping her veil in front of her, and turned away. The next moment, I felt her hand on my shoulder, and she made her vow to me… that I was not alone. That I would never be alone again. And then she kissed me, Meg. She took my hideous face in her hands and pressed her lips to mine. In all my years, Meg, I have never felt a kiss and it made me…"

He shook his head, swallowing, and his tears began to fall, trickling over the white mask.

"I was shocked and… felt the greatest joy I had ever known… and… I was devastated. She pressed her perfect lips to mine for a second time and I felt myself come undone, and I sobbed… She did not run from me, Meg… She said:

'*Poor, unhappy Erik…*'

And I knew I could not force her to remain with me… I love her, Meg. Because I love her, I let them go. I released the Vicomte and told them to leave me… to leave and never reveal my secrets… and Christine… she came to me, just long enough to return the ring I had forced upon her. Long enough for me to take her by the hand, and tell her…

'*Christine… I love you…*'

THE ANGEL'S SHADOW

She wept *for me*, Meg. An angel wept for me, and kissed my hands, and I could do nothing but stroke her hair and release my own grief in my tears! It was all I could do to speak:

'*Go to your boy... I know you love him.*'

She went, and I was left to cry alone. I had no time to wallow, however, before you and your mob came *smashing* into my home, and so I had no choice but to hide, and wait for the search to die down."

I swallowed the lump in my throat, and finally remembered to swing the kettle, already filled with water, over the flames.

"And now?" I asked.

"Now?" He repeated. "What is there now, for me? Christine gave me wings; she inspired my music and provided me with a soul... I hide from the *gendarmes*, take advantage of the sympathies of you and your mother, because I have no desire to meet my death, Meg. And yet, I do not know how to live."

CHAPTER FORTY FIVE

The rest of my day was perhaps best described as surreal. Usually, the day after a show began late, as cast and crew slept off the previous night's performance and, where applicable, the after-party. Everyone would then meet on the stage where we would be given notes by the director, musical director or choreographer, and then we would rehearse for that evening's show. Meals and errands would be fitted in around the rehearsal, and before you knew it, it was time to begin applying the heavy stage make-up again.

That second of March found me trying to find clean clothes for a man of six foot four inches in height, without drawing attention to myself. There would be no show tonight, but every cast, crew, and otherwise member of the Opera House, from the youngest stable-hand to prima donna Christine Daaé herself, was ordered to come to the building and remain there until they were interviewed by the *gendarmes*. I tried again and again to speak with Christine, to ask her if she was all right, to ask for her version of events, but she was quickly led away by the officers, who continued to question her. I couldn't imagine they had anything more to say to her that had not been said the previous night, and it seemed to me as though they were treating *her* as a criminal. When I caught sight of her at last, around four o'clock in the afternoon, she looked exhausted and fragile. I had been circling the interior of the Opera House all day, trying to establish how far the *gendarmes* had gotten with mapping out Erik's secret tunnels. I had reached the lobby, and it looked like Christine was preparing to go home at last, but I could not resist the urge to call her.

"Christine!"

She looked up and around, defeat in her eyes as she anticipated another round of interrogation. She relaxed as she saw me coming towards her and held out her arms with a tired smile.

"Dearest Meg," she murmured as we embraced tightly. "I was worried about you."

THE ANGEL'S SHADOW

"I was worried about *you*," I told her. "And about Raoul. How is he?" Her brow furrowed.

"He's bruised and sore. And he's worried. His brother hasn't been seen since last night." She shifted uncomfortably. "I expect Philippe just spent the night with some girl... but we can't be certain."

"And you?" I asked quickly, keen to avoid conversation of the Comte de Chagny. She glanced around the lobby, noting the other people wondering aimlessly.

"Not here," she replied. "Not now. I did try to find you earlier, but I couldn't. Which dormitory are you moving into?"

"What?" I gave her a blank look, unable to comprehend the sudden change in topic. Christine raised her eyebrows, surprised by my surprise.

"When I went up there, all your things had gone... I assumed you were moving into a different room..."

My stomach twisted and my heart started to beat at double its usual rhythm. The *gendarmes* had found me out, discovered my connection to Erik, maybe to Philippe de Chagny. They had gone through my possessions, just as he had done, and uncovered my secrets. Confirmation came in the form of an unfamiliar, male voice speaking my name behind me.

"Marguerite Giry?"

I turned around to face the *gendarme* officer.

"Yes?"

"We're ready for you now." His expression was grim. Christine caught my hand in hers, reading my own expression accurately.

"It'll be all right, Meg," she squeezed gently. "It's just a few questions."

I nodded, tasting bile in my mouth as I turned and allowed the *gendarme* to lead the way to the manager's office. Firman and André had been turned out, and the moustached chief of the *gendarmes* was seated at the desk, an open notebook in front of him. There was a uniformed man to either side of him and in one of the two chairs before the desk, was my mother. I didn't know whether to feel relieved or even more terrified as the *gendarme* gestured me to the empty chair and I sank down into it, clenching my hands together in my lap. Mother looked calm, her clothing neat, and her cane resting across her knee as she sat with legs crossed.

"Madame Giry, Mademoiselle, thank you for your time." The man said in his smooth Parisian accent. "I am Inspector Edgar Barraé, chief of police for Paris, and I am leading the investigation into the events that have been happening here."

"All this has been very upsetting," Mother replied without much inflection in her voice. "My daughter and I are both happy to assist you in any way we can."

I hoped I didn't look as sick as I felt when Barraé turned his attention on me.

"Christine Daaé tells me you are her dearest friend," he said.

"Yes," I replied, wondering if this was a trick question. "Since we were little girls. She has asked me to be the maid of honour at her wedding to the Vicomte de Chagny."

He nodded and looked back to Mother.

"It is clear from everyone we have spoken to that you have the closest relationship with this so-called Opera Ghost, apart from Mademoiselle Daaé herself. You are the one who brings his notes to the managers, and returns their replies to him. You are also the one who told the Vicomte de Chagny where to look for his abducted fiancée." He raised one fair eyebrow. "So perhaps you would like to tell me where we can track him down now?"

"I don't know." She lied without flinching. One of the men beside the chief had his eyes focused on me and I could feel myself blushing under his gaze.

"Madame, people have *died*."

"I am aware of it. I'm telling you, I don't know where you can find this man; I already told your men the route to the house across the lake, the same route I told the Vicomte, and I only found that by accident."

"Please relate the accident in which you discovered where the Ghost lived."

Mother hesitated. "I was foolish. I stumbled across the entrance hidden in the fifth cellar, the one I described to Raoul and your men. I followed it as far as the lake, where the Phantom caught me. He intended to kill me with the lasso, like the one he used to murder Signor Piangi, but I begged for my life… and that of my unborn child."

Her eyes flicked to me, as did those of Barraé.

"The Phantom agreed, on the condition that I become his Box-Keeper, and basically his servant within the Opera House."

The chief wrote in the notebook on the desk.

"You served him well, it seems. Messieurs Firman and André passed on several of the notes 'O.G.' sent to them, and many mention you; most particularly the one in which he ordered your reinstatement. He calls your services 'good and loyal'. Did you tell your late husband about the hold this man had over you?"

"He was the only one I told. No-one else."

"Why not, Madame?"

"Because I was afraid that if I displeased the Phantom, he would take it out on my daughter, Meg. Do you have children, Inspector Barraé?"

"Yes, Madame, I have two sons."

"Then you know the lengths a parent will go to protect their child. I did not want Meg to be endangered, so I held my tongue."

THE ANGEL'S SHADOW

Barraé looked at me again, then back to Mother. "You were in communication with him then, for seventeen years?"

"I received his notes, and left the managers' replies in Box Five, written and otherwise. I heard him speak when he was in the Box and knew I was outside. He would ask me for things."

"What sort of things?"

"A programme, or something to eat or drink. Once a footstool."

"A footstool? A strange sort of demand from a Phantom, don't you think?"

She sighed, and her fingers tightened around the cane.

"He knocked on the door from the inside of the Box, and asked me very politely to bring a footstool. He said it was for his lady."

"His lady? He had a woman with him, then?"

"I never saw a woman enter or leave Box Five, Inspector. But then I never saw the Phantom enter or leave it either."

"Judging by all these passageways we are discovering, I would surmise that he used one of those. Of course, that still doesn't leave us with any information as to where this man is now. Do you have any suggestions to make, Marguerite?"

"Me?" I jumped in my chair. "No, of course, not!"

Mother reached over and took hold of my hand.

"Calm down, love," she said softly. "It's only a few questions."

"I'm sorry, Inspector," I said to Barraé, squeezing Mother's hand gratefully. "After what happened last night... after seeing Signor Piangi like that... you can imagine I didn't get much sleep."

"I understand, Mademoiselle," he replied. "We are speaking to everyone in the Opera Populairé, as you know. What encounters have you had with this Opera Ghost?"

I stared at him, without any idea what to say.

Well, let's see. He was there at my birth, and actually delivered me and ensured that I started breathing. Sixteen years later, he rescued me from a would-be rapist on the streets of Paris and has been a fixture in my life ever since. He knows more about me, my parents and my friends than anyone else, and we have gone so far as to tend to each other's injuries. He is a mad genius with a torture chamber, and is obsessed with Christine Daaé. As of six o'clock this morning, he was in my mother's chambers.

"I'm not sure what you mean." I said at last. "I've heard his voice sometimes, and occasionally I thought I saw him, but it always turned out to be just a shadow, or a trick of the light. I've always been a little... anxious, I suppose, I jump at anything."

"Tell me about his voice, what's it like?"

I felt myself blush. "He's got a lovely voice... deep, musical. I've heard him speak, and I've heard him sing with Christine when she didn't know I was there, but whenever I joined her, she was alone."

317

"Had you ever been down any of these secret passages before? Word is you're a curious little thing."

"No, Inspector."

I spoke firmly, and hoped that I could lie as well as my mother. I did not know whether the story she had told Barraé, of Erik threatening her life and then agreeing to spare it because she was pregnant, had a single grain of truth in it or was fiction from start to finish. The chief of police wrote in his notebook again and then looked up at me.

"The Vicomte de Chagny told us that you volunteered to go with him when Mademoiselle Daaé was abducted. Why did you do that?"

"Because… because I wanted to help…" I knew I had to think very carefully before giving my answer. "I was scared for Christine; I wanted to do anything I could to ensure her safety."

"But if you did not know how to reach her, what help could you have been?"

"I just… couldn't bear to think of my dearest friend in danger."

"And you were found by Monsieur Grenoble in the tunnels. You were the first one to enter the house on the lake."

I could feel my face getting hot.

"I was with the group that went down there, and I got lost," I gabbled. "Separated from them. When I saw Christine in the boat, that she and Raoul were safe, I just—"

The rest of my words were cut off by an almighty explosion. It rolled throughout the building as if a cannon had been fired, causing everything to tremble and plaster dust to fall from the ceiling. I jumped in terror, but so did everyone else in the room.

"What on earth?!"

There was a lot of noise from the corridor outside; shouting, running feet, and a strong, male voice raised in a cry:

"*Fire!*"

Inspector Barraé leapt to his feet.

"Out!" he ordered. "Out of the building, right now!"

We obeyed without hesitation, and the moment the office door was yanked open, we were met with a stream of grey smoke. There wasn't a large amount of it yet, but it was enough to seize me by the throat and set me coughing, my eyes beginning to tear up.

The scene was chaotic, with what seemed like hundreds of people pushing along the corridor towards the grand staircase and the main lobby. I found myself swept up by them like a cork in a river, forced to move whether I wanted to or not, and I seized Mother's hand, desperate not to lose her in the crush of panicked bodies. We made it outside with little grace, and turned back towards the Opera Populairé just as a second explosion rocked the very cobblestones beneath our feet. One of the

THE ANGEL'S SHADOW

decorative windows blew outwards in a spout of flame, as if blasted by an angry dragon, and more people screamed. There was a thin, persistent rain falling from clouds that darkened the Paris afternoon into evening, but it was no match for the fire that was beginning to lick hungrily up the walls of the building. My imagination insisted I could actually hear the sound of the raindrops sizzling away as they came into contact with the flames.

"Girls!" Mother raised her voice over the panic and the crackle of fire, as though she were doing nothing more strenuous than addressing a rowdy dance class. "Come to me!"

Every female who considered Madame Giry her mistress hurried over and surrounded us like a flock of terrified doves. Remarkably, the only injury among them was a small cut, sustained by a girl who had been standing too close when the window blew out. Most were in a state of shock, but there were a few laments over possessions that would never be seen again, from dearly loved dolls to fur coats. I felt a jolt in my own chest as I realised the only thing I had left of my dear, tormented father, was the silver cross that hung around my neck.

To give them their credit, the *gendarmes* were brilliant. They had taken down the names of everyone who had been in the Opera House that day and when they had left, so they knew exactly who was there, and ticked us off to make sure the burning building was empty. They behaved as calmly and efficiently as if they had done the same thing for every day of their careers. I sent up a silent prayer of gratitude that Christine and Raoul had gone, and as I watched the fire consuming the place I had spent my childhood, the home I loved, I didn't know what to feel.

The rain was coming down harder but the fire raged on, and even as I heard the clang of bells that indicated a fire engine was on its way, I knew it was too late. The Opera House could not be saved, and with its destruction came the knowledge that the evidence of my sin might well be destroyed with it. It was likely that the body of Philippe de Chagny would never be discovered. I had wandered a little way from the rest of the girls. The rain plastered my blonde hair to my head and caused my gown to cling to my body, but my heart was completely numb as my future went up in smoke. I had always seen myself as a member of the opera company, rising to prima ballerina, marrying someone within the theatre, having children...

Mother joined me a few moments later and I reached out, intertwining my fingers with hers. Neither of us said a word. We stood side by side, hand in hand, and watched the Opera Populairé burn.

This concludes 'The Angel's Shadow', Book 1 of 'The Angels of Music Saga'.
Meg Giry's story continues in Book 2...
'The Angel's Flight'

ABOUT THE AUTHOR

Louise Anne Bateman lives and works in West Sussex, England, and decided to become a writer somewhere around her fifth birthday (probably). She is a graduate of Roehampton University and her great loves include books and musical theatre. She has written several pantomimes based on popular fairytales and legends, and *The Angel's Shadow* is her début novel.

Printed in Great Britain
by Amazon